MOCKINGJAY

SCHOLASTIC PRESS / NEW YORK

SUZANNE COLLINS

MOCKINGJAY

Published by Scholastic Singapore, operating under Grolier International Inc.,
#05-04, CISCO Centre II, 20 Jalan Afifi, Singapore 409179,
a subsidiary of Scholastic Inc., New York

ISBN 978-981-08-6874-1

Printed in Malaysia
First edition, October 2010

The text type was set in Adobe Garamond Pro.
Book design by Elizabeth B. Parisi

For Cap, Charlie, and Isabel

PART I
"THE ASHES"

I stare down at my shoes, watching as a fine layer of ash settles on the worn leather. This is where the bed I shared with my sister, Prim, stood. Over there was the kitchen table. The bricks of the chimney, which collapsed in a charred heap, provide a point of reference for the rest of the house. How else could I orient myself in this sea of gray?

Almost nothing remains of District 12. A month ago, the Capitol's firebombs obliterated the poor coal miners' houses in the Seam, the shops in the town, even the Justice Building. The only area that escaped incineration was the Victor's Village. I don't know why exactly. Perhaps so anyone forced to come here on Capitol business would have somewhere decent to stay. The odd reporter. A committee assessing the condition of the coal mines. A squad of Peacekeepers checking for returning refugees.

But no one is returning except me. And that's only for a brief visit. The authorities in District 13 were against my coming back. They viewed it as a costly and pointless venture, given that at least a dozen invisible hovercraft are circling overhead for my protection and there's no intelligence to be gained. I had to see it, though. So much so that I made it a condition of my cooperating with any of their plans.

Finally, Plutarch Heavensbee, the Head Gamemaker who had organized the rebels in the Capitol, threw up his hands. "Let her go. Better to waste a day than another month. Maybe a little tour of Twelve is just what she needs to convince her we're on the same side."

The same side. A pain stabs my left temple and I press my hand against it. Right on the spot where Johanna Mason hit me with the coil of wire. The memories swirl as I try to sort out what is true and what is false. What series of events led me to be standing in the ruins of my city? This is hard because the effects of the concussion she gave me haven't completely subsided and my thoughts still have a tendency to jumble together. Also, the drugs they use to control my pain and mood sometimes make me see things. I guess. I'm still not entirely convinced that I was hallucinating the night the floor of my hospital room transformed into a carpet of writhing snakes.

I use a technique one of the doctors suggested. I start with the simplest things I know to be true and work toward the more complicated. The list begins to roll in my head. . . .

My name is Katniss Everdeen. I am seventeen years old. My home is District 12. I was in the Hunger Games. I escaped. The Capitol hates me. Peeta was taken prisoner. He is thought to be dead. Most likely he is dead. It is probably best if he is dead. . . .

"Katniss. Should I come down?" My best friend Gale's voice reaches me through the headset the rebels insisted I wear. He's up in a hovercraft, watching me carefully, ready to swoop in if anything goes amiss. I realize I'm crouched down now, elbows on my thighs, my head braced between

4

my hands. I must look on the verge of some kind of breakdown. This won't do. Not when they're finally weaning me off the medication.

I straighten up and wave his offer away. "No. I'm fine." To reinforce this, I begin to move away from my old house and in toward the town. Gale asked to be dropped off in 12 with me, but he didn't force the issue when I refused his company. He understands I don't want anyone with me today. Not even him. Some walks you have to take alone.

The summer's been scorching hot and dry as a bone. There's been next to no rain to disturb the piles of ash left by the attack. They shift here and there, in reaction to my footsteps. No breeze to scatter them. I keep my eyes on what I remember as the road, because when I first landed in the Meadow, I wasn't careful and I walked right into a rock. Only it wasn't a rock—it was someone's skull. It rolled over and over and landed faceup, and for a long time I couldn't stop looking at the teeth, wondering whose they were, thinking of how mine would probably look the same way under similar circumstances.

I stick to the road out of habit, but it's a bad choice, because it's full of the remains of those who tried to flee. Some were incinerated entirely. But others, probably overcome with smoke, escaped the worst of the flames and now lie reeking in various states of decomposition, carrion for scavengers, blanketed by flies. *I killed you,* I think as I pass a pile. *And you. And you.*

Because I did. It was my arrow, aimed at the chink in the force field surrounding the arena, that brought on this firestorm of retribution. That sent the whole country of Panem into chaos.

In my head I hear President Snow's words, spoken the morning I was to begin the Victory Tour. *"Katniss Everdeen, the girl who was on fire, you have provided a spark that, left unattended, may grow to an inferno that destroys Panem."* It turns out he wasn't exaggerating or simply trying to scare me. He was, perhaps, genuinely attempting to enlist my help. But I had already set something in motion that I had no ability to control.

Burning. Still burning, I think numbly. The fires at the coal mines belch black smoke in the distance. There's no one left to care, though. More than ninety percent of the district's population is dead. The remaining eight hundred or so are refugees in District 13 — which, as far as I'm concerned, is the same thing as being homeless forever.

I know I shouldn't think that; I know I should be grateful for the way we have been welcomed. Sick, wounded, starving, and empty-handed. Still, I can never get around the fact that District 13 was instrumental in 12's destruction. This doesn't absolve me of blame — there's plenty of blame to go around. But without them, I would not have been part of a larger plot to overthrow the Capitol or had the wherewithal to do it.

The citizens of District 12 had no organized resistance movement of their own. No say in any of this. They only had the misfortune to have me. Some survivors think it's good luck, though, to be free of District 12 at last. To have escaped the endless hunger and oppression, the perilous mines, the lash of our final Head Peacekeeper, Romulus Thread. To have a new home at all is seen as a wonder since, up until a short time ago, we hadn't even known that District 13 still existed.

The credit for the survivors' escape has landed squarely on Gale's shoulders, although he's loath to accept it. As soon as the Quarter Quell was over — as soon as I had been lifted from the arena — the electricity in District 12 was cut, the televisions went black, and the Seam became so silent, people could hear one another's heartbeats. No one did anything to protest or celebrate what had happened in the arena. Yet within fifteen minutes, the sky was filled with hoverplanes and the bombs were raining down.

It was Gale who thought of the Meadow, one of the few places not filled with old wooden homes embedded with coal dust. He herded those he could in its direction, including my mother and Prim. He formed the team that pulled down the fence — now just a harmless chain-link barrier, with the electricity off — and led the people into the woods. He took them to the only place he could think of, the lake my father had shown me as a child. And it was from there they watched the distant flames eat up everything they knew in the world.

By dawn the bombers were long gone, the fires dying, the final stragglers rounded up. My mother and Prim had set up a medical area for the injured and were attempting to treat them with whatever they could glean from the woods. Gale had two sets of bows and arrows, one hunting knife, one fishing net, and over eight hundred terrified people to feed. With the help of those who were able-bodied, they managed for three days. And that's when the hovercraft unexpectedly arrived to evacuate them to District 13, where there were more than enough clean, white living compartments, plenty of clothing, and three meals a day. The compartments had the disadvantage of being underground, the clothing was identical, and the food was relatively tasteless, but for the refugees of 12, these were minor considerations. They were safe. They were being cared for. They were alive and eagerly welcomed.

This enthusiasm was interpreted as kindness. But a man named Dalton, a District 10 refugee who'd made it to 13 on foot a few years ago, leaked the real motive to me. "They need you. Me. They need us all. Awhile back, there was some sort of pox epidemic that killed a bunch of them and left a lot more infertile. New breeding stock. That's how they see us." Back in 10, he'd worked on one of the beef ranches, maintaining the genetic diversity of the herd with the implantation of long-frozen cow embryos. He's very likely right about 13, because there don't seem to be nearly enough kids around. But so what? We're not being kept in pens, we're being trained for work, the children are being educated. Those over fourteen have been given entry-level ranks in the military and are addressed respectfully as "Soldier." Every single refugee was granted automatic citizenship by the authorities of 13.

Still, I hate them. But, of course, I hate almost everybody now. Myself more than anyone.

The surface beneath my feet hardens, and under the carpet of ash, I feel the paving stones of the square. Around the perimeter is a shallow border of refuse where the shops stood. A heap of blackened rubble has replaced the Justice Building. I walk to the approximate site of the bakery Peeta's family owned. Nothing much left but the melted lump of the oven. Peeta's parents, his two older brothers—none of them made it to 13. Fewer than a dozen of what passed for District 12's well-to-do escaped the fire. Peeta would have nothing to come home to, anyway. Except me . . .

I back away from the bakery and bump into something, lose my balance, and find myself sitting on a hunk of sun-heated metal. I puzzle over what it might have been, then remember Thread's recent renovations of the square. Stocks, whipping posts, and this, the remains of the gallows. Bad. This is bad. It brings on the flood of images that torments me, awake or asleep. Peeta being tortured—drowned, burned, lacerated, shocked, maimed, beaten—as the Capitol tries to get information about the rebellion that he doesn't know. I squeeze my eyes shut and try to reach for him across the hundreds and hundreds of miles, to send my thoughts into his mind, to let him know he is not alone. But he is. And I can't help him.

Running. Away from the square and to the one place the fire did not destroy. I pass the wreckage of the mayor's house, where my friend Madge lived. No word of her or her family. Were they evacuated to the Capitol because of her father's position, or left to the flames? Ashes billow up around me, and I pull the hem of my shirt up over my mouth. It's not wondering what I breathe in, but who, that threatens to choke me.

The grass has been scorched and the gray snow fell here as well, but the twelve fine houses of the Victor's Village are unscathed. I bolt into the house I lived in for the past year, slam the door closed, and lean back against it. The place seems untouched. Clean. Eerily quiet. Why did I come back to 12? How can this visit help me answer the question I can't escape?

"What am I going to do?" I whisper to the walls. Because I really don't know.

People keep talking at me, talking, talking, talking. Plutarch Heavensbee. His calculating assistant, Fulvia Cardew. A mishmash of district leaders. Military officials. But not Alma Coin, the president of 13, who just watches. She's fifty or so, with gray hair that falls in an unbroken sheet to her shoulders. I'm somewhat fascinated by her hair, since it's so uniform, so without a flaw, a wisp, even a split end. Her eyes are gray, but not like those of people from the Seam. They're very pale, as if almost all the color has been sucked out of them. The color of slush that you wish would melt away.

What they want is for me to truly take on the role they designed for me. The symbol of the revolution. The Mockingjay. It isn't enough, what I've done in the past, defying the Capitol in the Games, providing a rallying point. I must now become the actual leader, the face, the voice, the embodiment of the revolution. The person who the districts—most of which are now openly at war with the Capitol—can count on to blaze the path to victory. I won't have to do it alone. They have a whole team of people to make me over, dress me, write my speeches, orchestrate my appearances — as if *that* doesn't sound horribly familiar — and all I have to do is play my part. Sometimes I listen to them and sometimes I just watch the perfect line of Coin's hair and try to decide if it's a wig. Eventually, I leave the room because my head starts to ache or it's time to eat or if I don't get aboveground I might start screaming. I don't bother to say anything. I simply get up and walk out.

Yesterday afternoon, as the door was closing behind me, I heard Coin say, "I told you we should have rescued the boy first." Meaning Peeta. I couldn't agree more. He would've been an excellent mouthpiece.

And who did they fish out of the arena instead? Me, who won't cooperate. Beetee, an older inventor from 3, who I rarely see because he was pulled into weapons development the minute he could sit upright. Literally, they wheeled his hospital bed into some top secret area and now he only occasionally shows up for meals. He's very smart and very willing to help the cause, but not really firebrand material. Then there's Finnick Odair, the sex symbol from the fishing district, who kept Peeta alive in the arena when I couldn't. They want to transform Finnick into a rebel leader as well, but first they'll have to get him to stay awake for more than five minutes. Even when he is conscious, you have to say everything to him three times to get through to his brain. The doctors say it's from the electrical shock he received in the arena, but I know it's a lot more complicated than that. I know that Finnick can't focus on anything in 13 because he's trying so hard to see what's happening in the Capitol to

Annie, the mad girl from his district who's the only person on earth he loves.

Despite serious reservations, I had to forgive Finnick for his role in the conspiracy that landed me here. He, at least, has some idea of what I'm going through. And it takes too much energy to stay angry with someone who cries so much.

I move through the downstairs on hunter's feet, reluctant to make any sound. I pick up a few remembrances: a photo of my parents on their wedding day, a blue hair ribbon for Prim, the family book of medicinal and edible plants. The book falls open to a page with yellow flowers and I shut it quickly because it was Peeta's brush that painted them.

What am I going to do?

Is there any point in doing anything at all? My mother, my sister, and Gale's family are finally safe. As for the rest of 12, people are either dead, which is irreversible, or protected in 13. That leaves the rebels in the districts. Of course, I hate the Capitol, but I have no confidence that my being the Mockingjay will benefit those who are trying to bring it down. How can I help the districts when every time I make a move, it results in suffering and loss of life? The old man shot in District 11 for whistling. The crackdown in 12 after I intervened in Gale's whipping. My stylist, Cinna, being dragged, bloody and unconscious, from the Launch Room before the Games. Plutarch's sources believe he was killed during interrogation. Brilliant, enigmatic, lovely Cinna is dead because of me. I push the thought away because it's too impossibly painful to dwell on without losing my fragile hold on the situation entirely.

What am I going to do?

To become the Mockingjay . . . could any good I do possibly outweigh the damage? Who can I trust to answer that question? Certainly not that crew in 13. I swear, now that my family and Gale's are out of harm's way, I could run away. Except for one unfinished piece of business. Peeta. If I knew for sure that he was dead, I could just disappear into the woods and never look back. But until I do, I'm stuck.

I spin on my heel at the sound of a hiss. In the kitchen doorway, back arched, ears flattened, stands the ugliest tomcat in the world. "Buttercup," I say. Thousands of people are dead, but he has survived and even looks well fed. On what? He can get in and out of the house through a window we always left ajar in the pantry. He must have been eating field mice. I refuse to consider the alternative.

I squat down and extend a hand. "Come here, boy." Not likely. He's angry at his abandonment. Besides, I'm not offering food, and my ability to provide scraps has always been my main redeeming quality to him. For a while, when we used to meet up at the old house because we both disliked this new one, we seemed to be bonding a little. That's clearly over. He blinks those unpleasant yellow eyes.

"Want to see Prim?" I ask. Her name catches his attention. Besides his own, it's the only word that means anything to him. He gives a rusty meow and approaches me. I pick him up, stroking his fur, then go to the closet and dig out my game bag and unceremoniously stuff him in. There's no other way I'll be able to carry him on the hovercraft, and he means the world to my sister. Her goat, Lady, an animal of actual value, has unfortunately not made an appearance.

In my headset, I hear Gale's voice telling me we must go back. But the game bag has reminded me of one more thing that I want. I sling the strap of the bag over the back of a chair and dash up the steps to my bedroom. Inside the closet hangs my father's hunting jacket. Before the Quell, I brought it here from the old house, thinking its presence might be of comfort to my mother and sister when I was dead. Thank goodness, or it'd be ash now.

The soft leather feels soothing and for a moment I'm calmed by the memories of the hours spent wrapped in it. Then, inexplicably, my palms begin to sweat. A strange sensation creeps up the back of my neck. I whip around to face the room and find it empty. Tidy. Everything in its place. There was no sound to alarm me. What, then?

My nose twitches. It's the smell. Cloying and artificial. A dab of white peeks out of a vase of dried flowers on my dresser. I approach it with cautious steps. There, all but obscured by its preserved cousins, is a fresh white rose. Perfect. Down to the last thorn and silken petal.

And I know immediately who's sent it to me.

President Snow.

When I begin to gag at the stench, I back away and clear out. How long has it been here? A day? An hour? The rebels did a security sweep of the Victor's Village before I was cleared to come here, checking for explosives, bugs, anything unusual. But perhaps the rose didn't seem noteworthy to them. Only to me.

Downstairs, I snag the game bag off the chair, bouncing it along the floor until I remember it's occupied. On the lawn, I frantically signal to the hovercraft while Buttercup thrashes. I jab him with my elbow, but this only infuriates him. A hovercraft materializes and a ladder drops down. I step on and the current freezes me until I'm lifted on board.

Gale helps me from the ladder. "You all right?"

"Yeah," I say, wiping the sweat off my face with my sleeve.

He left me a rose! I want to scream, but it's not information I'm sure I should share with someone like Plutarch looking on. First of all, because it will make me sound crazy. Like I either imagined it, which is quite possible, or I'm overreacting, which will buy me a trip back to the drug-induced dreamland I'm trying so hard to escape. No one will fully understand—how it's not just a flower, not even just President Snow's flower, but a promise of revenge—because no one else sat in the study with him when he threatened me before the Victory Tour.

Positioned on my dresser, that white-as-snow rose is a personal message to me. It speaks of unfinished business. It whispers, *I can find you. I can reach you. Perhaps I am watching you now.*

Are there Capitol hoverplanes speeding in to blow us out of the sky? As we travel over District 12, I watch anxiously for signs of an attack, but nothing pursues us. After several minutes, when I hear an exchange between Plutarch and the pilot confirming that the airspace is clear, I begin to relax a little.

Gale nods at the howls coming from my game bag. "Now I know why you had to go back."

"If there was even a chance of his recovery." I dump the bag onto a seat, where the loathsome creature begins a low, deep-throated growl. "Oh, shut up," I tell the bag as I sink into the cushioned window seat across from it.

Gale sits next to me. "Pretty bad down there?"

"Couldn't be much worse," I answer. I look in his eyes and see my own grief reflected there. Our hands find each other, holding fast to a part of 12 that Snow has somehow failed to destroy. We sit in silence for the rest of the trip to 13, which only takes about forty-five minutes. A mere week's journey on foot. Bonnie and Twill, the District 8 refugees who I encountered in the woods last winter, weren't so far from their destination after all. They apparently didn't make it, though. When I asked about them in 13, no one seemed to know who I was talking about. Died in the woods, I guess.

From the air, 13 looks about as cheerful as 12. The rubble isn't smoking, the way the Capitol shows it on television, but there's next to no life aboveground. In the seventy-five years since the Dark Days—when 13 was said to have been obliterated in the war between the Capitol and the districts—almost all new construction has been beneath the earth's surface. There was already a substantial underground facility here, developed over centuries to be either a clandestine refuge for government leaders in time of war or a last resort for humanity if life above became unlivable. Most important for the people of 13, it was the center of the Capitol's nuclear weapons development program. During the Dark Days, the rebels in 13 wrested control from the government forces, trained their nuclear missiles on the Capitol, and then struck a bargain: They would play dead in exchange for being left alone. The Capitol had another nuclear arsenal out west, but it couldn't attack 13 without certain retaliation. It was forced to accept 13's deal. The Capitol demolished the visible remains of the district and cut off all access from the outside. Perhaps the Capitol's leaders thought that, without help, 13 would die off on its own. It almost did a few times, but it always managed to pull through due to strict sharing of resources, strenuous discipline, and constant vigilance against any further attacks from the Capitol.

Now the citizens live almost exclusively underground. You can go outside for exercise and sunlight but only at very specific times in your schedule. You can't miss your schedule. Every morning, you're supposed to stick your right arm in this contraption in the wall. It tattoos the smooth inside of your forearm with your schedule for the day in a sickly purple ink. *7:00—Breakfast. 7:30—Kitchen Duties. 8:30—Education Center, Room 17.* And so on. The ink is indelible until *22:00—Bathing.* That's when whatever keeps it water resistant breaks down and the whole schedule rinses away. The lights-out at 22:30 signals that everyone not on the night shift should be in bed.

At first, when I was so ill in the hospital, I could forgo being imprinted. But once I moved into Compartment 307 with my mother and sister, I was expected to get with the program. Except for showing up for meals, though, I pretty much ignore the words on my arm. I just go back to our compartment or wander around 13 or fall asleep somewhere hidden. An abandoned air duct. Behind the water pipes in the laundry. There's a closet in the Education Center that's great because no one ever seems to need school supplies. They're so frugal with things here, waste is practically a criminal activity. Fortunately, the people of 12 have never been wasteful. But once I saw Fulvia Cardew crumple up a sheet of paper with just a couple of words written on it and you would've thought she'd murdered someone from the looks she got. Her face turned tomato red, making the silver flowers inlaid in her plump cheeks even more noticeable. The very portrait of excess. One of my few pleasures in 13 is watching the handful of pampered Capitol "rebels" squirming as they try to fit in.

I don't know how long I'll be able to get away with my complete disregard for the clockwork precision of attendance required by my hosts. Right now, they leave me alone because I'm classified as mentally disoriented — it says so right on my plastic medical bracelet — and everyone has to tolerate my ramblings. But that can't last forever. Neither can their patience with the Mockingjay issue.

From the landing pad, Gale and I walk down a series of stairways to Compartment 307. We could take the elevator, only it reminds me too much of the one that lifted me into the arena. I'm having a hard time adjusting to being underground so much. But after the surreal encounter with the rose, for the first time the descent makes me feel safer.

I hesitate at the door marked *307*, anticipating the questions from my family. "What am I going to tell them about Twelve?" I ask Gale.

"I doubt they'll ask for details. They saw it burn. They'll mostly be worried about how you're handling it." Gale touches my cheek. "Like I am."

I press my face against his hand for a moment. "I'll survive."

Then I take a deep breath and open the door. My mother and sister are home for *18:00 — Reflection*, a half hour of downtime before dinner. I see the concern on their faces as they try to gauge my emotional state. Before anyone can ask anything, I empty my game bag and it becomes *18:00 — Cat Adoration*. Prim just sits on the floor weeping and rocking that awful Buttercup, who interrupts his purring only for an occasional hiss at me. He gives me a particularly smug look when she ties the blue ribbon around his neck.

My mother hugs the wedding photo tightly against her chest and then places it, along with the book of plants, on our government-issued chest of drawers. I hang my father's jacket on the back of a chair. For a moment, the place almost seems like home. So I guess the trip to 12 wasn't a complete waste.

We're heading down to the dining hall for *18:30—Dinner* when Gale's communicuff begins to beep. It looks like an oversized watch, but it receives print messages. Being granted a communicuff is a special privilege that's reserved for those important to the cause, a status Gale achieved by his rescue of the citizens of 12. "They need the two of us in Command," he says.

Trailing a few steps behind Gale, I try to collect myself before I'm thrown into what's sure to be another relentless Mockingjay session. I linger in the doorway of Command, the high-tech meeting/war council room complete with computerized talking walls, electronic maps showing the troop movements in various districts, and a giant rectangular table with control panels I'm not supposed to touch. No one notices me, though, because they're all gathered at a television screen at the far end of the room that airs the Capitol broadcast around the clock. I'm thinking I might be able to slip away when Plutarch, whose ample frame has been blocking the television, catches sight of me and waves urgently for me to join them. I reluctantly move forward, trying to imagine how it could be of interest to me. It's always the same. War footage. Propaganda. Replaying the bombings of District 12. An ominous message from President Snow. So it's almost entertaining to see Caesar Flickerman, the eternal host of the Hunger Games, with his painted face and sparkly suit, preparing to give an interview. Until the camera pulls back and I see that his guest is Peeta.

A sound escapes me. The same combination of gasp and groan that comes from being submerged in water, deprived of oxygen to the point of pain. I push people aside until I am right in front of him, my hand resting on the screen. I search his eyes for any sign of hurt, any reflection of the agony of torture. There is nothing. Peeta looks healthy to the point of robustness. His skin is glowing, flawless, in that full-body-polish way. His manner's composed, serious. I can't reconcile this image with the battered, bleeding boy who haunts my dreams.

Caesar settles himself more comfortably in the chair across from Peeta and gives him a long look. "So . . . Peeta . . . welcome back."

Peeta smiles slightly. "I bet you thought you'd done your last interview with me, Caesar."

"I confess, I did," says Caesar. "The night before the Quarter Quell . . . well, who ever thought we'd see you again?"

"It wasn't part of my plan, that's for sure," says Peeta with a frown.

Caesar leans in to him a little. "I think it was clear to all of us what your plan was. To sacrifice yourself in the arena so that Katniss Everdeen and your child could survive."

"That was it. Clear and simple." Peeta's fingers trace the upholstered pattern on the arm of the chair. "But other people had plans as well."

Yes, other people had plans, I think. Has Peeta guessed, then, how the rebels used us as pawns? How my rescue was arranged from the beginning? And finally, how our mentor, Haymitch Abernathy, betrayed us both for a cause he pretended to have no interest in?

In the silence that follows, I notice the lines that have formed between Peeta's eyebrows. He has guessed or he has been told. But the Capitol has not killed or even punished him. For right now, that exceeds my wildest hopes. I drink in his wholeness, the soundness of his body and mind. It runs through me like the morphling they give me in the hospital, dulling the pain of the last weeks.

"Why don't you tell us about that last night in the arena?" suggests Caesar. "Help us sort a few things out."

Peeta nods but takes his time speaking. "That last night . . . to tell you about that last night . . . well, first of all, you have to imagine how it felt in the arena. It was like being an insect trapped under a bowl filled with steaming air. And all around you, jungle . . . green and alive and ticking. That giant clock ticking away your life. Every hour promising some new horror. You have to imagine that in the past two days, sixteen people have died—some of them defending you. At the rate things are going, the last eight will be dead by morning. Save one. The victor. And your plan is that it won't be you."

My body breaks out in a sweat at the memory. My hand slides down the screen and hangs limply at my side. Peeta doesn't need a brush to paint images from the Games. He works just as well in words.

"Once you're in the arena, the rest of the world becomes very distant," he continues. "All the people and things you loved or cared about almost cease to exist. The pink sky and the monsters in the jungle and the tributes who want your blood become your final reality, the only one that ever mattered. As bad as it makes you feel, you're going to have to do some killing, because in the arena, you only get one wish. And it's very costly."

"It costs your life," says Caesar.

"Oh, no. It costs a lot more than your life. To murder innocent people?" says Peeta. "It costs everything you are."

"Everything you are," repeats Caesar quietly.

A hush has fallen over the room, and I can feel it spreading across Panem. A nation leaning in toward its screens. Because no one has ever talked about what it's really like in the arena before.

Peeta goes on. "So you hold on to your wish. And that last night, yes, my wish was to save Katniss. But even without knowing about the rebels, it didn't feel right. Everything was too complicated. I found myself regretting I hadn't run off with her earlier in the day, as she had suggested. But there was no getting out of it at that point."

"You were too caught up in Beetee's plan to electrify the salt lake," says Caesar.

"Too busy playing allies with the others. I should have never let them separate us!" Peeta bursts out. "That's when I lost her."

"When you stayed at the lightning tree, and she and Johanna Mason took the coil of wire down to the water," Caesar clarifies.

"I didn't want to!" Peeta flushes in agitation. "But I

couldn't argue with Beetee without indicating we were about to break away from the alliance. When that wire was cut, everything just went insane. I can only remember bits and pieces. Trying to find her. Watching Brutus kill Chaff. Killing Brutus myself. I know she was calling my name. Then the lightning bolt hit the tree, and the force field around the arena . . . blew out."

"Katniss blew it out, Peeta," says Caesar. "You've seen the footage."

"She didn't know what she was doing. None of us could follow Beetee's plan. You can see her trying to figure out what to do with that wire," Peeta snaps back.

"All right. It just looks suspicious," says Caesar. "As if she was part of the rebels' plan all along."

Peeta's on his feet, leaning in to Caesar's face, hands locked on the arms of his interviewer's chair. "Really? And was it part of her plan for Johanna to nearly kill her? For that electric shock to paralyze her? To trigger the bombing?" He's yelling now. "She didn't know, Caesar! Neither of us knew anything except that we were trying to keep each other alive!"

Caesar places his hand on Peeta's chest in a gesture that's both self-protective and conciliatory. "Okay, Peeta, I believe you."

"Okay." Peeta withdraws from Caesar, pulling back his hands, running them through his hair, mussing his carefully styled blond curls. He slumps back in his chair, distraught.

Caesar waits a moment, studying Peeta. "What about your mentor, Haymitch Abernathy?"

Peeta's face hardens. "I don't know what Haymitch knew."

"Could he have been part of the conspiracy?" asks Caesar.

"He never mentioned it," says Peeta.

Caesar presses on. "What does your heart tell you?"

"That I shouldn't have trusted him," says Peeta. "That's all."

I haven't seen Haymitch since I attacked him on the hovercraft, leaving long claw marks down his face. I know it's been bad for him here. District 13 strictly forbids any production or consumption of intoxicating beverages, and even the rubbing alcohol in the hospital is kept under lock and key. Finally, Haymitch is being forced into sobriety, with no secret stashes or home-brewed concoctions to ease his transition. They've got him in seclusion until he's dried out, as he's not deemed fit for public display. It must be excruciating, but I lost all my sympathy for Haymitch when I realized how he had deceived us. I hope he's watching the Capitol broadcast now, so he can see that Peeta has cast him off as well.

Caesar pats Peeta's shoulder. "We can stop now if you want."

"Was there more to discuss?" says Peeta wryly.

"I was going to ask your thoughts on the war, but if you're too upset . . ." begins Caesar.

"Oh, I'm not too upset to answer that." Peeta takes a deep breath and then looks straight into the camera. "I want everyone watching—whether you're on the Capitol or the rebel side—to stop for just a moment and think about what this war could mean. For human beings. We almost went extinct fighting one another before. Now our numbers are even fewer. Our conditions more tenuous. Is this really what we want to do? Kill ourselves off completely? In the hopes that—what? Some decent species will inherit the smoking remains of the earth?"

"I don't really . . . I'm not sure I'm following . . ." says Caesar.

"We can't fight one another, Caesar," Peeta explains. "There won't be enough of us left to keep going. If everybody doesn't lay down their weapons—and I mean, as in *very soon*—it's all over, anyway."

"So . . . you're calling for a cease-fire?" Caesar asks.

"Yes. I'm calling for a cease-fire," says Peeta tiredly. "Now why don't we ask the guards to take me back to my quarters so I can build another hundred card houses?"

Caesar turns to the camera. "All right. I think that wraps it up. So back to our regularly scheduled programming."

Music plays them out, and then there's a woman reading a list of expected shortages in the Capitol—fresh fruit, solar batteries, soap. I watch her with uncharacteristic absorption, because I know everyone will be waiting for my reaction to the interview. But there's no way I can process it all so quickly—the joy of seeing Peeta alive and unharmed, his defense of my innocence in collaborating with the rebels, and his undeniable complicity with the Capitol now that he's called for a cease-fire. Oh, he made it sound as if he were condemning both sides in the war. But at this point, with only minor victories for the rebels, a cease-fire could only result in a return to our previous status. Or worse.

Behind me, I can hear the accusations against Peeta building. The words *traitor, liar,* and *enemy* bounce off the walls. Since I can neither join in the rebels' outrage nor counter it, I decide the best thing to do is clear out. As I reach the door, Coin's voice rises above the others. "You have not been dismissed, Soldier Everdeen."

One of Coin's men lays a hand on my arm. It's not an aggressive move, really, but after the arena, I react defensively to any unfamiliar touch. I jerk my arm free and take off running down the halls. Behind me, there's the sound of a scuffle, but I don't stop. My mind does a quick inventory of my odd little hiding places, and I wind up in the supply closet, curled up against a crate of chalk.

"You're alive," I whisper, pressing my palms against my cheeks, feeling the smile that's so wide it must look like a grimace. Peeta's alive. And a traitor. But at the moment, I don't care. Not what he says, or who he says it for, only that he is still capable of speech.

After a while, the door opens and someone slips in. Gale slides down beside me, his nose trickling blood.

"What happened?" I ask.

"I got in Boggs's way," he answers with a shrug. I use my sleeve to wipe his nose. "Watch it!"

I try to be gentler. Patting, not wiping. "Which one is he?"

"Oh, you know. Coin's right-hand lackey. The one who tried to stop you." He pushes my hand away. "Quit! You'll bleed me to death."

The trickle has turned to a steady stream. I give up on the first-aid attempts. "You fought with Boggs?"

"No, just blocked the doorway when he tried to follow you. His elbow caught me in the nose," says Gale.

"They'll probably punish you," I say.

"Already have." He holds up his wrist. I stare at it uncomprehendingly. "Coin took back my communicuff."

I bite my lip, trying to remain serious. But it seems so ridiculous. "I'm sorry, Soldier Gale Hawthorne."

"Don't be, Soldier Katniss Everdeen." He grins. "I felt like a jerk walking around with it anyway." We both start laughing. "I think it was quite a demotion."

This is one of the few good things about 13. Getting Gale back. With the pressure of the Capitol's arranged marriage between Peeta and me gone, we've managed to regain our friendship. He doesn't push it any further — try to kiss me or talk about love. Either I've been too sick, or he's willing to give me space, or he knows it's just too cruel with Peeta in the hands of the Capitol. Whatever the case, I've got someone to tell my secrets to again.

"Who are these people?" I say.

"They're us. If we'd had nukes instead of a few lumps of coal," he answers.

"I like to think Twelve wouldn't have abandoned the rest of the rebels back in the Dark Days," I say.

"We might have. If it was that, surrender, or start a nuclear war," says Gale. "In a way, it's remarkable they survived at all."

Maybe it's because I still have the ashes of my own district on my shoes, but for the first time, I give the people of 13 something I have withheld from them: credit. For staying alive against all odds. Their early years must have been terrible, huddled in the chambers beneath the ground after their city was bombed to dust. Population decimated, no possible ally to turn to for aid. Over the past seventy-five years, they've learned to be self-sufficient, turned their citizens into an army, and built a new society with no help from anyone. They would be even more powerful if that pox epidemic hadn't flattened their birthrate and made them so desperate for a new gene pool and breeders. Maybe they are militaristic, overly programmed, and somewhat lacking in a sense of humor. They're here. And willing to take on the Capitol.

"Still, it took them long enough to show up," I say.

"It wasn't simple. They had to build up a rebel base in the Capitol, get some sort of underground organized in the districts," he says. "Then they needed someone to set the whole thing in motion. They needed you."

"They needed Peeta, too, but they seem to have forgotten that," I say.

Gale's expression darkens. "Peeta might have done a lot of damage tonight. Most of the rebels will dismiss what he said immediately, of course. But there are districts where the resistance is shakier. The cease-fire's clearly President Snow's idea. But it seems so reasonable coming out of Peeta's mouth."

I'm afraid of Gale's answer, but I ask anyway. "Why do you think he said it?"

"He might have been tortured. Or persuaded. My guess is he made some kind of deal to protect you. He'd put forth the idea of the cease-fire if Snow let him present you as a confused pregnant girl who had no idea what was going on when she was taken prisoner by the rebels. This way, if the districts lose, there's still a chance of leniency for you. If you play it right." I must still look perplexed because Gale delivers the next line very slowly. "Katniss . . . he's still trying to keep you alive."

To keep me alive? And then I understand. The Games are still on. We have left the arena, but since Peeta and I weren't killed, his last wish to preserve my life still stands. His idea is to have me lie low, remain safe and imprisoned, while the war plays out. Then neither side will really have cause to kill me. And Peeta? If the rebels win, it will be disastrous for him. If the Capitol wins, who knows? Maybe we'll both be allowed to live—if I play it right—to watch the Games go on. . . .

Images flash through my mind: the spear piercing Rue's body in the arena, Gale hanging senseless from the whipping post, the corpse-littered wasteland of my home. And for what? For what? As my blood turns hot, I remember other things. My first glimpse of an uprising in District 8. The victors locked hand in hand the night before the Quarter Quell. And how it was no accident, my shooting that arrow into the force field in the arena. How badly I wanted it to lodge deep in the heart of my enemy.

I spring up, upsetting a box of a hundred pencils, sending them scattering around the floor.

"What is it?" Gale asks.

"There can't be a cease-fire." I lean down, fumbling as I shove the sticks of dark gray graphite back into the box. "We can't go back."

"I know." Gale sweeps up a handful of pencils and taps them on the floor into perfect alignment.

"Whatever reason Peeta had for saying those things, he's wrong." The stupid sticks won't go in the box and I snap several in my frustration.

"I know. Give it here. You're breaking them to bits." He pulls the box from my hands and refills it with swift, concise motions.

"He doesn't know what they did to Twelve. If he could've seen what was on the ground—" I start.

"Katniss, I'm not arguing. If I could hit a button and kill every living soul working for the Capitol, I would do it. Without hesitation." He slides the last pencil into the box and flips the lid closed. "The question is, what are you going to do?"

It turns out the question that's been eating away at me has only ever had one possible answer. But it took Peeta's ploy for me to recognize it.

What am I going to do?

I take a deep breath. My arms rise slightly—as if recalling the black-and-white wings Cinna gave me—then come to rest at my sides.

"I'm going to be the Mockingjay."

Buttercup's eyes reflect the faint glow of the safety light over the door as he lies in the crook of Prim's arm, back on the job, protecting her from the night. She's snuggled close to my mother. Asleep, they look just as they did the morning of the reaping that landed me in my first Games. I have a bed to myself because I'm recuperating and because no one can sleep with me anyway, what with the nightmares and the thrashing around.

After tossing and turning for hours, I finally accept that it will be a wakeful night. Under Buttercup's watchful eye, I tiptoe across the cold tiled floor to the dresser.

The middle drawer contains my government-issued clothes. Everyone wears the same gray pants and shirt, the shirt tucked in at the waist. Underneath the clothes, I keep the few items I had on me when I was lifted from the arena. My mockingjay pin. Peeta's token, the gold locket with photos of my mother and Prim and Gale inside. A silver parachute that holds a spile for tapping trees, and the pearl Peeta gave me a few hours before I blew out the force field. District 13 confiscated my tube of skin ointment for use in the hospital, and my bow and arrows because only guards have clearance to carry weapons. They're in safekeeping in the armory.

I feel around for the parachute and slide my fingers inside until they close around the pearl. I sit back on my bed cross-legged and find myself rubbing the smooth iridescent surface of the pearl back and forth against my lips. For some reason, it's soothing. A cool kiss from the giver himself.

"Katniss?" Prim whispers. She's awake, peering at me through the darkness. "What's wrong?"

"Nothing. Just a bad dream. Go back to sleep." It's automatic. Shutting Prim and my mother out of things to shield them.

Careful not to rouse my mother, Prim eases herself from the bed, scoops up Buttercup, and sits beside me. She touches the hand that has curled around the pearl. "You're cold." Taking a spare blanket from the foot of the bed, she wraps it around all three of us, enveloping me in her warmth and Buttercup's furry heat as well. "You could tell me, you know. I'm good at keeping secrets. Even from Mother."

She's really gone, then. The little girl with the back of her shirt sticking out like a duck tail, the one who needed help reaching the dishes, and who begged to see the frosted cakes in the bakery window. Time and tragedy have forced her to grow too quickly, at least for my taste, into a young woman who stitches bleeding wounds and knows our mother can hear only so much.

"Tomorrow morning, I'm going to agree to be the Mockingjay," I tell her.

"Because you want to or because you feel forced into it?" she asks.

I laugh a little. "Both, I guess. No, I want to. I have to, if it will help the rebels defeat Snow." I squeeze the pearl more tightly in my fist. "It's just . . . Peeta. I'm afraid if we do win, the rebels will execute him as a traitor."

Prim thinks this over. "Katniss, I don't think you understand how important you are to the cause. Important people usually get what they want. If you want to keep Peeta safe from the rebels, you can."

I guess I'm important. They went to a lot of trouble to rescue me. They took me to 12. "You mean . . . I could demand that they give Peeta immunity? And they'd have to agree to it?"

"I think you could demand almost anything and they'd have to agree to it." Prim wrinkles her brow. "Only how do you know they'll keep their word?"

I remember all of the lies Haymitch told Peeta and me to get us to do what he wanted. What's to keep the rebels from reneging on the deal? A verbal promise behind closed doors, even a statement written on paper — these could easily evaporate after the war. Their existence or validity denied. Any witnesses in Command will be worthless. In fact, they'd probably be the ones writing out Peeta's death warrant. I'll need a much larger pool of witnesses. I'll need everyone I can get.

"It will have to be public," I say. Buttercup gives a flick of his tail that I take as agreement. "I'll make Coin announce it in front of the entire population of Thirteen."

Prim smiles. "Oh, that's good. It's not a guarantee, but it will be much harder for them to back out of their promise."

I feel the kind of relief that follows an actual solution. "I should wake you up more often, little duck."

"I wish you would," says Prim. She gives me a kiss. "Try and sleep now, all right?" And I do.

In the morning, I see that *7:00—Breakfast* is directly followed by *7:30—Command*, which is fine since I may as well start the ball rolling. At the dining hall, I flash my schedule, which includes some kind of ID number, in front of a sensor. As I slide my tray along the metal shelf before the vats of food, I see breakfast is its usual dependable self—a bowl of hot grain, a cup of milk, and a small scoop of fruit or vegetables. Today, mashed turnips. All of it comes from 13's underground farms. I sit at the table assigned to the Everdeens and the Hawthornes and some other refugees, and shovel my food down, wishing for seconds, but there are never seconds here. They have nutrition down to a science. You leave with enough calories to take you to the next meal, no more, no less. Serving size is based on your age, height, body type, health, and amount of physical labor required by your schedule. The people from 12 are already getting slightly larger portions than the natives of 13 in an effort to bring us up to weight. I guess bony soldiers tire too quickly. It's working, though. In just a month, we're starting to look healthier, particularly the kids.

Gale sets his tray beside me and I try not to stare at his turnips too pathetically, because I really want more, and he's already too quick to slip me his food. Even though I turn my attention to neatly folding my napkin, a spoonful of turnips slops into my bowl.

"You've got to stop that," I say. But since I'm already scooping up the stuff, it's not too convincing. "Really. It's probably illegal or something." They have very strict rules about food. For instance, if you don't finish something and want to save it for later, you can't take it from the dining hall. Apparently, in the early days, there was some incident of food hoarding. For a couple of people like Gale and me, who've been in charge of our families' food supply for years, it doesn't sit well. We know how to be hungry, but not how to be told how to handle what provisions we have. In some ways, District 13 is even more controlling than the Capitol.

"What can they do? They've already got my communicuff," says Gale.

As I scrape my bowl clean, I have an inspiration. "Hey, maybe I should make that a condition of being the Mockingjay."

"That I can feed you turnips?" he says.

"No, that we can hunt." That gets his attention. "We'd have to give everything to the kitchen. But still, we could . . ." I don't have to finish because he knows. We could be aboveground. Out in the woods. We could be ourselves again.

"Do it," he says. "Now's the time. You could ask for the moon and they'd have to find some way to get it."

He doesn't know that I'm already asking for the moon by demanding they spare Peeta's life. Before I can decide whether or not to tell him, a bell signals the end of our eating shift. The thought of facing Coin alone makes me nervous. "What are you scheduled for?"

Gale checks his arm. "Nuclear History class. Where, by the way, your absence has been noted."

"I have to go to Command. Come with me?" I ask.

"All right. But they might throw me out after yesterday." As we go to drop off our trays, he says, "You know, you better put Buttercup on your list of demands, too. I don't think the concept of useless pets is well known here."

"Oh, they'll find him a job. Tattoo it on his paw every morning," I say. But I make a mental note to include him for Prim's sake.

By the time we get to Command, Coin, Plutarch, and all their people have already assembled. The sight of Gale raises some eyebrows, but no one throws him out. My mental notes have become too jumbled, so I ask for a piece of paper and a pencil right off. My apparent interest in the proceedings — the first I've shown since I've been here — takes them by surprise. Several looks are exchanged. Probably they had some extra-special lecture planned for me. But instead, Coin personally hands me the supplies, and everyone waits in silence while I sit at the table and scrawl out my list. *Buttercup. Hunting. Peeta's immunity. Announced in public.*

This is it. Probably my only chance to bargain. *Think. What else do you want?* I feel him, standing at my shoulder. *Gale,* I add to the list. I don't think I can do this without him.

The headache's coming on and my thoughts begin to tangle. I shut my eyes and start to recite silently.

My name is Katniss Everdeen. I am seventeen years old. My home is District 12. I was in the Hunger Games. I escaped.

The Capitol hates me. Peeta was taken prisoner. He is alive.
He is a traitor but alive. I have to keep him alive. . . .

The list. It still seems too small. I should try to think bigger, beyond our current situation where I am of the utmost importance, to the future where I may be worth nothing. Shouldn't I be asking for more? For my family? For the remainder of my people? My skin itches with the ashes of the dead. I feel the sickening impact of the skull against my shoe. The scent of blood and roses stings my nose.

The pencil moves across the page on its own. I open my eyes and see the wobbly letters. *I KILL SNOW.* If he's captured, I want the privilege.

Plutarch gives a discreet cough. "About done there?" I glance up and notice the clock. I've been sitting here for twenty minutes. Finnick isn't the only one with attention problems.

"Yeah," I say. My voice sounds hoarse, so I clear my throat. "Yeah, so this is the deal. I'll be your Mockingjay."

I wait so they can make their sounds of relief, congratulate, slap one another on the back. Coin stays as impassive as ever, watching me, unimpressed.

"But I have some conditions." I smooth out the list and begin. "My family gets to keep our cat." My tiniest request sets off an argument. The Capitol rebels see this as a nonissue — of course, I can keep my pet — while those from 13 spell out what extreme difficulties this presents. Finally it's worked out that we'll be moved to the top level, which has the luxury of an eight-inch window aboveground. Buttercup may come and go to do his business. He will be expected to feed himself. If he misses curfew, he will be locked out. If he causes any security problems, he'll be shot immediately.

That sounds okay. Not so different from how he's been living since we left. Except for the shooting part. If he looks too thin, I can slip him a few entrails, provided my next request is allowed.

"I want to hunt. With Gale. Out in the woods," I say. This gives everyone pause.

"We won't go far. We'll use our own bows. You can have the meat for the kitchen," adds Gale.

I hurry on before they can say no. "It's just . . . I can't breathe shut up here like a . . . I would get better, faster, if . . . I could hunt."

Plutarch begins to explain the drawbacks here — the dangers, the extra security, the risk of injury — but Coin cuts him off. "No. Let them. Give them two hours a day, deducted from their training time. A quarter-mile radius. With communication units and tracker anklets. What's next?"

I skim my list. "Gale. I'll need him with me to do this."

"With you how? Off camera? By your side at all times? Do you want him presented as your new lover?" Coin asks.

She hasn't said this with any particular malice — quite the contrary, her words are very matter-of-fact. But my mouth still drops open in shock. "What?"

"I think we should continue the current romance. A quick defection from Peeta could cause the audience to lose sympathy for her," says Plutarch. "Especially since they think she's pregnant with his child."

"Agreed. So, on-screen, Gale can simply be portrayed as a fellow rebel. Is that all right?" says Coin. I just stare at her. She repeats herself impatiently. "For Gale. Will that be sufficient?"

"We can always work him in as your cousin," says Fulvia.

"We're not cousins," Gale and I say together.

"Right, but we should probably keep that up for appearances' sake on camera," says Plutarch. "Off camera, he's all yours. Anything else?"

I'm rattled by the turn in the conversation. The implications that I could so readily dispose of Peeta, that I'm in love with Gale, that the whole thing has been an act. My cheeks begin to burn. The very notion that I'm devoting any thought to who I want presented as my lover, given our current circumstances, is demeaning. I let my anger propel me into my greatest demand. "When the war is over, if we've won, Peeta will be pardoned."

Dead silence. I feel Gale's body tense. I guess I should have told him before, but I wasn't sure how he'd respond. Not when it involved Peeta.

"No form of punishment will be inflicted," I continue. A new thought occurs to me. "The same goes for the other captured tributes, Johanna and Enobaria." Frankly, I don't care about Enobaria, the vicious District 2 tribute. In fact, I dislike her, but it seems wrong to leave her out.

"No," says Coin flatly.

"Yes," I shoot back. "It's not their fault you abandoned them in the arena. Who knows what the Capitol's doing to them?"

"They'll be tried with other war criminals and treated as the tribunal sees fit," she says.

"They'll be granted immunity!" I feel myself rising from my chair, my voice full and resonant. "You will personally pledge this in front of the entire population of District Thirteen and the remainder of Twelve. Soon. Today. It will be recorded for future generations. You will hold yourself and your government responsible for their safety, or you'll find yourself another Mockingjay!"

My words hang in the air for a long moment.

"That's her!" I hear Fulvia hiss to Plutarch. "Right there. With the costume, gunfire in the background, just a hint of smoke."

"Yes, that's what we want," says Plutarch under his breath.

I want to glare at them, but I feel it would be a mistake to turn my attention from Coin. I can see her tallying the cost of my ultimatum, weighing it against my possible worth.

"What do you say, President?" asks Plutarch. "You could issue an official pardon, given the circumstances. The boy . . . he's not even of age."

"All right," Coin says finally. "But you'd better perform."

"I'll perform when you've made the announcement," I say.

"Call a national security assembly during Reflection today," she orders. "I'll make the announcement then. Is there anything left on your list, Katniss?"

My paper's crumpled into a ball in my right fist. I flatten the sheet against the table and read the rickety letters. "Just one more thing. I kill Snow."

For the first time ever, I see the hint of a smile on the president's lips. "When the time comes, I'll flip you for it."

Maybe she's right. I certainly don't have the sole claim against Snow's life. And I think I can count on her getting the job done. "Fair enough."

Coin's eyes have flickered to her arm, the clock. She, too, has a schedule to adhere to. "I'll leave her in your hands, then, Plutarch." She exits the room, followed by her team, leaving only Plutarch, Fulvia, Gale, and myself.

"Excellent. Excellent." Plutarch sinks down, elbows on the table, rubbing his eyes. "You know what I miss? More than anything? Coffee. I ask you, would it be so unthinkable to have something to wash down the gruel and turnips?"

"We didn't think it would be quite so rigid here," Fulvia explains to us as she massages Plutarch's shoulders. "Not in the higher ranks."

"Or at least there'd be the option of a little side action," says Plutarch. "I mean, even Twelve had a black market, right?"

"Yeah, the Hob," says Gale. "It's where we traded."

"There, you see? And look how moral you two are! Virtually incorruptible." Plutarch sighs. "Oh, well, wars don't last forever. So, glad to have you on the team." He reaches a hand out to the side, where Fulvia is already extending a large sketchbook bound in black leather. "You know in general what we're asking of you, Katniss. I'm aware you have mixed feelings about participating. I hope this will help."

Plutarch slides the sketchbook across to me. For a moment, I look at it suspiciously. Then curiosity gets the better of me. I open the cover to find a picture of myself, standing straight and strong, in a black uniform. Only one person could have designed the outfit, at first glance utterly utilitarian, at second a work of art. The swoop of the helmet, the curve to the breastplate, the slight fullness of the sleeves that allows the white folds under the arms to show. In his hands, I am again a mockingjay.

"Cinna," I whisper.

"Yes. He made me promise not to show you this book until you'd decided to be the Mockingjay on your own. Believe me, I was very tempted," says Plutarch. "Go on. Flip through."

I turn the pages slowly, seeing each detail of the uniform. The carefully tailored layers of body armor, the hidden weapons in the boots and belt, the special reinforcements over my heart. On the final page, under a sketch of my mockingjay pin, Cinna's written, *I'm still betting on you.*

"When did he . . ." My voice fails me.

"Let's see. Well, after the Quarter Quell announcement. A few weeks before the Games maybe? There are not only the sketches. We have your uniforms. Oh, and Beetee's got something really special waiting for you down in the armory. I won't spoil it by hinting," says Plutarch.

"You're going to be the best-dressed rebel in history," says Gale with a smile. Suddenly, I realize he's been holding out on me. Like Cinna, he's wanted me to make this decision all along.

"Our plan is to launch an Airtime Assault," says Plutarch. "To make a series of what we call propos—which is short for 'propaganda spots'—featuring you, and broadcast them to the entire population of Panem."

"How? The Capitol has sole control of the broadcasts," says Gale.

"But we have Beetee. About ten years ago, he essentially redesigned the underground network that transmits all the programming. He thinks there's a reasonable chance it can be done. Of course, we'll need something to air. So, Katniss, the studio awaits your pleasure." Plutarch turns to his assistant. "Fulvia?"

"Plutarch and I have been talking about how on earth we can pull this off. We think that it might be best to build you, our rebel leader, from the outside . . . *in*. That is to say, let's find the most stunning Mockingjay look possible, and then work your personality up to deserving it!" she says brightly.

"You already have her uniform," says Gale.

"Yes, but is she scarred and bloody? Is she glowing with the fire of rebellion? Just how grimy can we make her without disgusting people? At any rate, she has to be something. I mean, obviously this"—Fulvia moves in on me quickly, framing my face with her hands—"won't cut it." I jerk my head back reflexively but she's already busy gathering her things. "So, with that in mind, we have another little surprise for you. Come, come."

Fulvia gives us a wave, and Gale and I follow her and Plutarch out into the hall.

"So well intended, and yet so insulting," Gale whispers in my ear.

"Welcome to the Capitol," I mouth back. But Fulvia's words have no effect on me. I wrap my arms tightly around the sketchbook and allow myself to feel hopeful. This must be the right decision. If Cinna wanted it.

We board an elevator, and Plutarch checks his notes. "Let's see. It's Compartment Three-Nine-Oh-Eight." He presses a button marked *39*, but nothing happens.

"You must have to key it," says Fulvia.

Plutarch pulls a key attached to a thin chain from under his shirt and inserts it into a slot I hadn't noticed before. The doors slide shut. "Ah, there we are."

The elevator descends ten, twenty, thirty-plus levels, farther down than I even knew District 13 went. It opens on a wide white corridor lined with red doors, which look almost decorative compared to the gray ones on the upper floors. Each is plainly marked with a number. *3901, 3902, 3903 . . .*

As we step out, I glance behind me to watch the elevator close and see a metallic grate slide into place over the regular doors. When I turn, a guard has materialized from one of the rooms at the far end of the corridor. A door swings silently shut behind him as he strides toward us.

Plutarch moves to meet him, raising a hand in greeting, and the rest of us follow behind him. Something feels very wrong down here. It's more than the reinforced elevator, or the claustrophobia of being so far underground, or the caustic smell of antiseptic. One look at Gale's face and I can tell he senses it as well.

"Good morning, we were just looking for—" Plutarch begins.

"You have the wrong floor," says the guard abruptly.

"Really?" Plutarch double-checks his notes. "I've got Three-Nine-Oh-Eight written right here. I wonder if you could just give a call up to—"

"I'm afraid I have to ask you to leave now. Assignment discrepancies can be addressed at the Head Office," says the guard.

It's right ahead of us. Compartment 3908. Just a few steps away. The door—in fact, all the doors—seem incomplete. No knobs. They must swing free on hinges like the one the guard appeared through.

"Where is that again?" asks Fulvia.

"You'll find the Head Office on Level Seven," says the guard, extending his arms to corral us back to the elevator.

From behind door 3908 comes a sound. Just a tiny whimper. Like something a cowed dog might make to avoid being struck, only all too human and familiar. My eyes meet Gale's for just a moment, but it's long enough for two people who operate the way we do. I let Cinna's sketchbook fall at the guard's feet with a loud bang. A second after he leans down to retrieve it, Gale leans down, too, intentionally bumping heads. "Oh, I'm sorry," he says with a light laugh, catching the guard's arms as if to steady himself, turning him slightly away from me.

That's my chance. I dart around the distracted guard, push open the door marked *3908*, and find them. Half-naked, bruised, and shackled to the wall.

My prep team.

The stink of unwashed bodies, stale urine, and infection breaks through the cloud of antiseptic. The three figures are only just recognizable by their most striking fashion choices: Venia's gold facial tattoos. Flavius's orange corkscrew curls. Octavia's light evergreen skin, which now hangs too loosely, as if her body were a slowly deflating balloon.

On seeing me, Flavius and Octavia shrink back against the tiled walls like they're anticipating an attack, even though I have never hurt them. Unkind thoughts were my worst offense against them, and those I kept to myself, so why do they recoil?

The guard's ordering me out, but by the shuffling that follows, I know Gale has somehow detained him. For answers, I cross to Venia, who was always the strongest. I crouch down and take her icy hands, which clutch mine like vises.

"What happened, Venia?" I ask. "What are you doing here?"

"They took us. From the Capitol," she says hoarsely.

Plutarch enters behind me. "What on earth is going on?"

"Who took you?" I press her.

"People," she says vaguely. "The night you broke out."

"We thought it might be comforting for you to have your regular team," Plutarch says behind me. "Cinna requested it."

"Cinna requested *this?*" I snarl at him. Because if there's one thing I know, it's that Cinna would never have approved the abuse of these three, who he managed with gentleness and patience. "Why are they being treated like criminals?"

"I honestly don't know." There's something in his voice that makes me believe him, and the pallor on Fulvia's face confirms it. Plutarch turns to the guard, who's just appeared in the doorway with Gale right behind him. "I was only told they were being confined. Why are they being punished?"

"For stealing food. We had to restrain them after an altercation over some bread," says the guard.

Venia's brows come together as if she's still trying to make sense of it. "No one would tell us anything. We were so hungry. It was just one slice she took."

Octavia begins to sob, muffling the sound in her ragged tunic. I think of how, the first time I survived the arena, Octavia sneaked me a roll under the table because she couldn't bear my hunger. I crawl across to her shaking form. "Octavia?" I touch her and she flinches. "Octavia? It's going to be all right. I'll get you out of here, okay?"

"This seems extreme," says Plutarch.

"It's because they took a slice of bread?" asks Gale.

"There were repeated infractions leading up to that. They were warned. Still they took more bread." The guard pauses a moment, as if puzzled by our density. "You can't take bread."

I can't get Octavia to uncover her face, but she lifts it slightly. The shackles on her wrists shift down a few inches, revealing raw sores beneath them. "I'm bringing you to my mother." I address the guard. "Unchain them."

The guard shakes his head. "It's not authorized."

"Unchain them! Now!" I yell.

This breaks his composure. Average citizens don't address him this way. "I have no release orders. And you have no authority to—"

"Do it on my authority," says Plutarch. "We came to collect these three anyway. They're needed for Special Defense. I'll take full responsibility."

The guard leaves to make a call. He returns with a set of keys. The preps have been forced into cramped body positions for so long that even once the shackles are removed, they have trouble walking. Gale, Plutarch, and I have to help them. Flavius's foot catches on a metal grate over a circular opening in the floor, and my stomach contracts when I think of why a room would need a drain. The stains of human misery that must have been hosed off these white tiles . . .

In the hospital, I find my mother, the only one I trust to care for them. It takes her a minute to place the three, given their current condition, but already she wears a look of consternation. And I know it's not a result of seeing abused bodies, because they were her daily fare in District 12, but the realization that this sort of thing goes on in 13 as well.

My mother was welcomed into the hospital, but she's viewed as more of a nurse than a doctor, despite her lifetime of healing. Still, no one interferes when she guides the trio into an examination room to assess their injuries. I plant myself on a bench in the hall outside the hospital entrance, waiting to hear her verdict. She will be able to read in their bodies the pain inflicted upon them.

Gale sits next to me and puts an arm around my shoulder. "She'll fix them up." I give a nod, wondering if he's thinking about his own brutal flogging back in 12.

Plutarch and Fulvia take the bench across from us but don't offer any comments on the state of my prep team. If they had no knowledge of the mistreatment, then what do they make of this move on President Coin's part? I decide to help them out.

"I guess we've all been put on notice," I say.

"What? No. What do you mean?" asks Fulvia.

"Punishing my prep team's a warning," I tell her. "Not just to me. But to you, too. About who's really in control and what happens if she's not obeyed. If you had any delusions about having power, I'd let them go now. Apparently, a Capitol pedigree is no protection here. Maybe it's even a liability."

"There is no comparison between Plutarch, who masterminded the rebel breakout, and those three beauticians," says Fulvia icily.

I shrug. "If you say so, Fulvia. But what would happen if you got on Coin's bad side? My prep team was kidnapped. They can at least hope to one day return to the Capitol. Gale and I can live in the woods. But you? Where would you two run?"

"Perhaps we're a little more necessary to the war effort than you give us credit for," says Plutarch, unconcerned.

"Of course you are. The tributes were necessary to the Games, too. Until they weren't," I say. "And then we were very disposable — right, Plutarch?"

That ends the conversation. We wait in silence until my mother finds us. "They'll be all right," she reports. "No permanent physical injuries."

"Good. Splendid," says Plutarch. "How soon can they be put to work?"

"Probably tomorrow," she answers. "You'll have to expect some emotional instability, after what they've been through. They were particularly ill prepared, coming from their life in the Capitol."

"Weren't we all?" says Plutarch.

Either because the prep team's incapacitated or I'm too on edge, Plutarch releases me from Mockingjay duties for the rest of the day. Gale and I head down to lunch, where we're served bean and onion stew, a thick slice of bread, and a cup of water. After Venia's story, the bread sticks in my throat, so I slide the rest of it onto Gale's tray. Neither of us speaks much during lunch, but when our bowls are clean, Gale pulls up his sleeve, revealing his schedule. "I've got training next."

I tug up my sleeve and hold my arm next to his. "Me, too." I remember that training equals hunting now.

My eagerness to escape into the woods, if only for two hours, overrides my current concerns. An immersion into greenery and sunlight will surely help me sort out my thoughts. Once off the main corridors, Gale and I race like schoolchildren for the armory, and by the time we arrive, I'm breathless and dizzy. A reminder that I'm not fully recovered. The guards provide our old weapons, as well as knives and a burlap sack that's meant for a game bag. I tolerate having the tracker clamped to my ankle, try to look as if I'm listening when they explain how to use the handheld communicator. The only thing that sticks in my head is that it has a clock, and we must be back inside 13 by the designated hour or our hunting privileges will be revoked. This is one rule I think I will make an effort to abide.

We go outside into the large, fenced-in training area beside the woods. Guards open the well-oiled gates without comment. We would be hard-pressed to get past this fence on our own — thirty feet high and always buzzing with electricity, topped with razor-sharp curls of steel. We move through the woods until the view of the fence has been obscured. In a small clearing, we pause and drop back our heads to bask in the sunlight. I turn in a circle, my arms extended at my sides, revolving slowly so as not to set the world spinning.

The lack of rain I saw in 12 has damaged the plants here as well, leaving some with brittle leaves, building a crunchy carpet under our feet. We take off our shoes. Mine don't fit right anyway, since in the spirit of waste-not-want-not that rules 13, I was issued a pair someone had outgrown. Apparently, one of us walks funny, because they're broken in all wrong.

We hunt, like in the old days. Silent, needing no words to communicate, because here in the woods we move as two parts of one being. Anticipating each other's movements, watching each other's backs. How long has it been? Eight months? Nine? Since we had this freedom? It's not exactly the same, given all that's happened and the trackers on our ankles and the fact that I have to rest so often. But it's about as close to happiness as I think I can currently get.

The animals here are not nearly suspicious enough. That extra moment it takes to place our unfamiliar scent means their death. In an hour and a half, we've got a mixed dozen — rabbits, squirrels, and turkeys — and decide to knock off to spend the remaining time by a pond that must be fed by an underground spring, since the water's cool and sweet.

When Gale offers to clean the game, I don't object. I stick a few mint leaves on my tongue, close my eyes, and lean back against a rock, soaking in the sounds, letting the scorching afternoon sun burn my skin, almost at peace until Gale's voice interrupts me. "Katniss, why do you care so much about your prep team?"

I open my eyes to see if he's joking, but he's frowning down at the rabbit he's skinning. "Why shouldn't I?"

"Hm. Let's see. Because they've spent the last year pretty-ing you up for slaughter?" he suggests.

"It's more complicated than that. I know them. They're not evil or cruel. They're not even smart. Hurting them, it's like hurting children. They don't see . . . I mean, they don't know . . ." I get knotted up in my words.

"They don't know what, Katniss?" he says. "That tributes —who are the actual children involved here, not your trio of freaks—are forced to fight to the death? That you were going into that arena for people's amusement? Was that a big secret in the Capitol?"

"No. But they don't view it the way we do," I say. "They're raised on it and—"

"Are you actually defending them?" He slips the skin from the rabbit in one quick move.

That stings, because, in fact, I am, and it's ridiculous. I struggle to find a logical position. "I guess I'm defending anyone who's treated like that for taking a slice of bread. Maybe it reminds me too much of what happened to you over a turkey!"

Still, he's right. It does seem strange, my level of concern over the prep team. I should hate them and want to see them strung up. But they're so clueless, and they belonged to Cinna, and he was on my side, right?

"I'm not looking for a fight," Gale says. "But I don't think Coin was sending you some big message by punishing them for breaking the rules here. She probably thought you'd see it as a favor." He stuffs the rabbit in the sack and rises. "We better get going if we want to make it back on time."

I ignore his offer of a hand up and get to my feet unsteadily. "Fine." Neither of us talks on the way back, but once we're inside the gate, I think of something else. "During the Quarter Quell, Octavia and Flavius had to quit because they couldn't stop crying over me going back in. And Venia could barely say good-bye."

"I'll try and keep that in mind as they . . . remake you," says Gale.

"Do," I say.

We hand the meat over to Greasy Sae in the kitchen. She likes District 13 well enough, even though she thinks the cooks are somewhat lacking in imagination. But a woman who came up with a palatable wild dog and rhubarb stew is bound to feel as if her hands are tied here.

Exhausted from hunting and my lack of sleep, I go back to my compartment to find it stripped bare, only to remember we've been moved because of Buttercup. I make my way up to the top floor and find Compartment E. It looks exactly like Compartment 307, except for the window — two feet wide, eight inches high — centered at the top of the outside wall. There's a heavy metal plate that fastens over it, but right now it's propped open, and a certain cat is nowhere to be seen. I stretch out on my bed, and a shaft of afternoon sunlight plays on my face. The next thing I know, my sister is waking me for *18:00 — Reflection.*

Prim tells me they've been announcing the assembly since lunch. The entire population, except those needed for essential jobs, is required to attend. We follow directions to the Collective, a huge room that easily holds the thousands who show up. You can tell it was built for a larger gathering, and perhaps it held one before the pox epidemic. Prim quietly points out the widespread fallout from that disaster —

the pox scars on people's bodies, the slightly disfigured children. "They've suffered a lot here," she says.

After this morning, I'm in no mood to feel sorry for 13. "No more than we did in Twelve," I say. I see my mother lead in a group of mobile patients, still wearing their hospital nightgowns and robes. Finnick stands among them, looking dazed but gorgeous. In his hands he holds a piece of thin rope, less than a foot in length, too short for even him to fashion into a usable noose. His fingers move rapidly, automatically tying and unraveling various knots as he gazes about. Probably part of his therapy. I cross to him and say, "Hey, Finnick." He doesn't seem to notice, so I nudge him to get his attention. "Finnick! How are you doing?"

"Katniss," he says, gripping my hand. Relieved to see a familiar face, I think. "Why are we meeting here?"

"I told Coin I'd be her Mockingjay. But I made her promise to give the other tributes immunity if the rebels won," I tell him. "In public, so there are plenty of witnesses."

"Oh. Good. Because I worry about that with Annie. That she'll say something that could be construed as traitorous without knowing it," says Finnick.

Annie. Uh-oh. Totally forgot her. "Don't worry, I took care of it." I give Finnick's hand a squeeze and head straight for the podium at the front of the room. Coin, who is glancing over her statement, raises her eyebrows at me. "I need you to add Annie Cresta to the immunity list," I tell her.

The president frowns slightly. "Who's that?"

"She's Finnick Odair's—" What? I don't really know what to call her. "She's Finnick's friend. From District Four. Another victor. She was arrested and taken to the Capitol when the arena blew up."

"Oh, the mad girl. That's not really necessary," she says. "We don't make a habit of punishing anyone that frail."

I think of the scene I walked in on this morning. Of Octavia huddled against the wall. Of how Coin and I must have vastly different definitions of frailty. But I only say, "No? Then it shouldn't be a problem to add Annie."

"All right," says the president, penciling in Annie's name. "Do you want to be up here with me for the announcement?" I shake my head. "I didn't think so. Better hurry and lose yourself in the crowd. I'm about to begin." I make my way back to Finnick.

Words are another thing not wasted in 13. Coin calls the audience to attention and tells them I have consented to be the Mockingjay, provided the other victors—Peeta, Johanna, Enobaria, and Annie—will be granted full pardon for any damage they do to the rebel cause. In the rumbling of the crowd, I hear the dissent. I suppose no one doubted I would want to be the Mockingjay. So naming a price—one that spares possible enemies—angers them. I stand indifferent to the hostile looks thrown my way.

The president allows a few moments of unrest, and then continues in her brisk fashion. Only now the words coming out of her mouth are news to me. "But in return for this unprecedented request, Soldier Everdeen has promised to devote herself to our cause. It follows that any deviance from her mission, in either motive or deed, will be viewed as a break in this agreement. The immunity would be terminated and the fate of the four victors determined by the law of District Thirteen. As would her own. Thank you."

In other words, I step out of line and we're all dead.

5

Another force to contend with. Another power player who has decided to use me as a piece in her games, although things never seem to go according to plan. First there were the Gamemakers, making me their star and then scrambling to recover from that handful of poisonous berries. Then President Snow, trying to use me to put out the flames of rebellion, only to have my every move become inflammatory. Next, the rebels ensnaring me in the metal claw that lifted me from the arena, designating me to be their Mockingjay, and then having to recover from the shock that I might not want the wings. And now Coin, with her fistful of precious nukes and her well-oiled machine of a district, finding it's even harder to groom a Mockingjay than to catch one. But she has been the quickest to determine that I have an agenda of my own and am therefore not to be trusted. She has been the first to publicly brand me as a threat.

I run my fingers through the thick layer of bubbles in my tub. Cleaning me up is just a preliminary step to determining my new look. With my acid-damaged hair, sunburned skin, and ugly scars, the prep team has to make me pretty and *then* damage, burn, and scar me in a more attractive way.

"Remake her to Beauty Base Zero," Fulvia ordered first thing this morning. "We'll work from there." Beauty Base Zero turns out to be what a person would look like if they stepped out of bed looking flawless but natural. It means my nails are perfectly shaped but not polished. My hair soft and shiny but not styled. My skin smooth and clear but not painted. Wax the body hair and erase the dark circles, but don't make any noticeable enhancements. I suppose Cinna gave the same instructions the first day I arrived as a tribute in the Capitol. Only that was different, since I was a contestant. As a rebel, I thought I'd get to look more like myself. But it seems a televised rebel has her own standards to live up to.

After I rinse the lather from my body, I turn to find Octavia waiting with a towel. She is so altered from the woman I knew in the Capitol, stripped of the gaudy clothing, the heavy makeup, the dyes and jewelry and knick-knacks she adorned her hair with. I remember how one day she showed up with bright pink tresses studded with blinking colored lights shaped like mice. She told me she had several mice at home as pets. The thought repulsed me at the time, since we consider mice vermin, unless cooked. But perhaps Octavia liked them because they were small, soft, and squeaky. Like her. As she pats me dry, I try to become acquainted with the District 13 Octavia. Her real hair turns out to be a nice auburn. Her face is ordinary but has an undeniable sweetness. She's younger than I thought. Maybe early twenties. Devoid of the three-inch decorative nails, her fingers appear almost stubby, and they can't stop trembling. I want to tell her it's okay, that I'll see that Coin never hurts her again. But the multicolored bruises flowering under her green skin only remind me how impotent I am.

Flavius, too, appears washed out without his purple lipstick and bright clothes. He's managed to get his orange ringlets back in some sort of order, though. It's Venia who's the least changed. Her aqua hair lies flat instead of in spikes and you can see the roots growing in gray. However, the tattoos were always her most striking characteristic, and they're as golden and shocking as ever. She comes and takes the towel from Octavia's hands.

"Katniss is not going to hurt us," she says quietly but firmly to Octavia. "Katniss did not even know we were here. Things will be better now." Octavia gives a slight nod but doesn't dare look me in the eye.

It's no simple job getting me back to Beauty Base Zero, even with the elaborate arsenal of products, tools, and gadgets Plutarch had the foresight to bring from the Capitol. My preps do pretty well until they try to address the spot on my arm where Johanna dug out the tracker. None of the medical team was focusing on looks when they patched up the gaping hole. Now I have a lumpy, jagged scar that ripples out over a space the size of an apple. Usually, my sleeve covers it, but the way Cinna's Mockingjay costume is designed, the sleeves stop just above the elbow. It's such a concern that Fulvia and Plutarch are called in to discuss it. I swear, the sight of it triggers Fulvia's gag reflex. For someone who works with a Gamemaker, she's awfully sensitive. But I guess she's used to seeing unpleasant things only on a screen.

"Everyone knows I have a scar here," I say sullenly.

"Knowing it and seeing it are two different things," says Fulvia. "It's positively repulsive. Plutarch and I will think of something during lunch."

"It'll be fine," says Plutarch with a dismissive wave of his hand. "Maybe an armband or something."

Disgusted, I get dressed so I can head to the dining hall. My prep team huddles in a little group by the door. "Are they bringing your food here?" I ask.

"No," says Venia. "We're supposed to go to a dining hall."

I sigh inwardly as I imagine walking into the dining hall, trailed by these three. But people always stare at me anyway. This will be more of the same. "I'll show you where it is," I say. "Come on."

The covert glances and quiet murmurs I usually evoke are nothing compared to the reaction brought on by the sight of my bizarre-looking prep team. The gaping mouths, the finger pointing, the exclamations. "Just ignore them," I tell my prep team. Eyes downcast, with mechanical movements, they follow me through the line, accepting bowls of grayish fish and okra stew and cups of water.

We take seats at my table, beside a group from the Seam. They show a little more restraint than the people from 13 do, although it may just be from embarrassment. Leevy, who was my neighbor back in 12, gives a cautious hello to the preps, and Gale's mother, Hazelle, who must know about their imprisonment, holds up a spoonful of the stew. "Don't worry," she says. "Tastes better than it looks."

But it's Posy, Gale's five-year-old sister, who helps the most. She scoots along the bench to Octavia and touches her skin with a tentative finger. "You're green. Are you sick?"

"It's a fashion thing, Posy. Like wearing lipstick," I say.

"It's meant to be pretty," whispers Octavia, and I can see the tears threatening to spill over her lashes.

Posy considers this and says matter-of-factly, "I think you'd be pretty in any color."

The tiniest of smiles forms on Octavia's lips. "Thank you."

"If you really want to impress Posy, you'll have to dye yourself bright pink," says Gale, thumping his tray down beside me. "That's her favorite color." Posy giggles and slides back down to her mother. Gale nods at Flavius's bowl. "I wouldn't let that get cold. It doesn't improve the consistency."

Everyone gets down to eating. The stew doesn't taste bad, but there's a certain sliminess that's hard to get around. Like you have to swallow every bite three times before it really goes down.

Gale, who's not usually much of a talker during meals, makes an effort to keep the conversation going, asking about the makeover. I know it's his attempt at smoothing things over. We argued last night after he suggested I'd left Coin no choice but to counter my demand for the victors' safety with one of her own. "Katniss, she's running this district. She can't do it if it seems like she's caving in to your will."

"You mean she can't stand any dissent, even if it's fair," I'd countered.

"I mean you put her in a bad position. Making her give Peeta and the others immunity when we don't even know what sort of damage they might cause," Gale had said.

"So I should've just gone with the program and let the other tributes take their chances? Not that it matters, because that's what we're all doing anyway!" That was when I'd slammed the door in his face. I hadn't sat with him at breakfast, and when Plutarch had sent him down to training this morning, I'd let him go without a word. I know he only spoke out of concern for me, but I really need him to be on my side, not Coin's. How can he not know that?

After lunch, Gale and I are scheduled to go down to Special Defense to meet Beetee. As we ride the elevator, Gale finally says, "You're still angry."

"And you're still not sorry," I reply.

"I still stand by what I said. Do you want me to lie about it?" he asks.

"No, I want you to rethink it and come up with the right opinion," I tell him. But this just makes him laugh. I have to let it go. There's no point in trying to dictate what Gale thinks. Which, if I'm honest, is one reason I trust him.

The Special Defense level is situated almost as far down as the dungeons where we found the prep team. It's a beehive of rooms full of computers, labs, research equipment, and testing ranges.

When we ask for Beetee, we're directed through the maze until we reach an enormous plate-glass window. Inside is the first beautiful thing I've seen in the District 13 compound: a replication of a meadow, filled with real trees and flowering plants, and alive with hummingbirds. Beetee sits motionless in a wheelchair at the center of the meadow, watching a spring-green bird hover in midair as it sips nectar from a large orange blossom. His eyes follow the bird as it darts away, and he catches sight of us. He gives a friendly wave for us to join him inside.

The air's cool and breathable, not humid and muggy as I'd expected. From all sides comes the whir of tiny wings, which I used to confuse with the sound of insects in our woods at home. I have to wonder what sort of fluke allowed such a pleasing place to be built here.

Beetee still has the pallor of someone in convalescence, but behind those ill-fitting glasses, his eyes are alight with excitement. "Aren't they magnificent? Thirteen has been studying their aerodynamics here for years. Forward and backward flight, and speeds up to sixty miles per hour. If only I could build you wings like these, Katniss!"

"Doubt I could manage them, Beetee," I laugh.

"Here one second, gone the next. Can you bring a hummingbird down with an arrow?" he asks.

"I've never tried. Not much meat on them," I answer.

"No. And you're not one to kill for sport," he says. "I bet they'd be hard to shoot, though."

"You could snare them maybe," Gale says. His face takes on that distant look it wears when he's working something out. "Take a net with a very fine mesh. Enclose an area and leave a mouth of a couple square feet. Bait the inside with nectar flowers. While they're feeding, snap the mouth shut. They'd fly away from the noise but only encounter the far side of the net."

"Would that work?" asks Beetee.

"I don't know. Just an idea," says Gale. "They might outsmart it."

"They might. But you're playing on their natural instincts to flee danger. Thinking like your prey . . . that's where you find their vulnerabilities," says Beetee.

I remember something I don't like to think about. In preparation for the Quell, I saw a tape where Beetee, who was still a boy, connected two wires that electrocuted a pack of kids who were hunting him. The convulsing bodies, the grotesque expressions. Beetee, in the moments that led up to his victory in those long-ago Hunger Games, watched the others die. Not his fault. Only self-defense. We were all acting only in self-defense. . . .

Suddenly, I want to leave the hummingbird room before somebody starts setting up a snare. "Beetee, Plutarch said you had something for me."

"Right. I do. Your new bow." He presses a hand control on the arm of the chair and wheels out of the room. As we follow him through the twists and turns of Special Defense, he explains about the chair. "I can walk a little now. It's just that I tire so quickly. It's easier for me to get around this way. How's Finnick doing?"

"He's . . . he's having concentration problems," I answer. I don't want to say he had a complete mental meltdown.

"Concentration problems, eh?" Beetee smiles grimly. "If you knew what Finnick's been through the last few years, you'd know how remarkable it is he's still with us at all. Tell him I've been working on a new trident for him, though, will you? Something to distract him a little." Distraction seems to be the last thing Finnick needs, but I promise to pass on the message.

Four soldiers guard the entrance to the hall marked SPECIAL WEAPONRY. Checking the schedules printed on our forearms is just a preliminary step. We also have fingerprint, retinal, and DNA scans, and have to step through special metal detectors. Beetee has to leave his wheelchair outside, although they provide him with another once we're through security. I find the whole thing bizarre because I can't imagine anyone raised in District 13 being a threat the government would have to guard against. Have these precautions been put in place because of the recent influx of immigrants?

At the door of the armory, we encounter a second round of identification checks—as if my DNA might have changed in the time it took to walk twenty yards down the hallway—and are finally allowed to enter the weapons collection. I have to admit the arsenal takes my breath away. Row upon row of firearms, launchers, explosives, armored vehicles. "Of course, the Airborne Division is housed separately," Beetee tells us.

"Of course," I say, as if this would be self-evident. I don't know where a simple bow and arrow could possibly find a place in all this high-tech equipment, but then we come upon a wall of deadly archery weapons. I've played with a lot of the Capitol's weapons in training, but none designed for military combat. I focus my attention on a lethal-looking bow so loaded down with scopes and gadgetry, I'm certain I can't even lift it, let alone shoot it.

"Gale, maybe you'd like to try out a few of these," says Beetee.

"Seriously?" Gale asks.

"You'll be issued a gun eventually for battle, of course. But if you appear as part of Katniss's team in the propos, one of these would look a little showier. I thought you might like to find one that suits you," says Beetee.

"Yeah, I would." Gale's hands close around the very bow that caught my attention a moment ago, and he hefts it onto his shoulder. He points it around the room, peering through the scope.

"That doesn't seem very fair to the deer," I say.

"Wouldn't be using it on deer, would I?" he answers.

"I'll be right back," says Beetee. He presses a code into a panel, and a small doorway opens. I watch until he's disappeared and the door's shut.

"So, it'd be easy for you? Using that on people?" I ask.

"I didn't say that." Gale drops the bow to his side. "But if I'd had a weapon that could've stopped what I saw happen in Twelve . . . if I'd had a weapon that could have kept you out of the arena . . . I'd have used it."

"Me, too," I admit. But I don't know what to tell him about the aftermath of killing a person. About how they never leave you.

Beetee wheels back in with a tall, black rectangular case awkwardly positioned between his footrest and his shoulder. He comes to a halt and tilts it toward me. "For you."

I set the case flat on the floor and undo the latches along one side. The top opens on silent hinges. Inside the case, on a bed of crushed maroon velvet, lies a stunning black bow. "Oh," I whisper in admiration. I lift it carefully into the air to admire the exquisite balance, the elegant design, and the curve of the limbs that somehow suggests the wings of a bird extended in flight. There's something else. I have to hold very still to make sure I'm not imagining it. No, the bow is alive in my hands. I press it against my cheek and feel the slight hum travel through the bones of my face. "What's it doing?" I ask.

"Saying hello," explains Beetee with a grin. "It heard your voice."

"It recognizes my voice?" I ask.

"*Only* your voice," he tells me. "You see, they wanted me to design a bow based purely on looks. As part of your costume, you know? But I kept thinking, *What a waste.* I mean, what if you do need it sometime? As more than a fashion accessory? So I left the outside simple, and left the inside to my imagination. Best explained in practice, though. Want to try those out?"

We do. A target range has already been prepared for us. The arrows that Beetee designed are no less remarkable than the bow. Between the two, I can shoot with accuracy over one hundred yards. The variety of arrows — razor sharp, incendiary, explosive — turn the bow into a multipurpose weapon. Each one is recognizable by a distinctive colored shaft. I have the option of voice override at any time, but have no idea why I would use it. To deactivate the bow's special properties, I need only tell it "Good night." Then it goes to sleep until the sound of my voice wakes it again.

I'm in good spirits by the time I get back to the prep team, leaving Beetee and Gale behind. I sit patiently through the rest of the paint job and don my costume, which now includes a bloody bandage over the scar on my arm to indicate I've been in recent combat. Venia affixes my mockingjay pin over my heart. I take up my bow and the sheath of normal arrows that Beetee made, knowing they would never let me walk around with the loaded ones. Then we're out on the soundstage, where I seem to stand for hours while they adjust makeup and lighting and smoke levels. Eventually, the commands coming via intercom from the invisible people in the mysterious glassed-in booth become fewer and fewer. Fulvia and Plutarch spend more time studying and less time adjusting me. Finally, there's quiet on the set. For a full five minutes I am simply considered. Then Plutarch says, "I think that does it."

I'm beckoned over to a monitor. They play back the last few minutes of taping and I watch the woman on the screen. Her body seems larger in stature, more imposing than mine. Her face smudged but sexy. Her brows black

and drawn in an angle of defiance. Wisps of smoke—
suggesting she has either just been extinguished or is about
to burst into flames—rise from her clothes. I do not know
who this person is.

Finnick, who's been wandering around the set for a few
hours, comes up behind me and says with a hint of his old
humor, "They'll either want to kill you, kiss you, or be you."

Everyone's so excited, so pleased with their work. It's
nearly time to break for dinner, but they insist we continue.
Tomorrow we'll focus on speeches and interviews and have
me pretend to be in rebel battles. Today they want just one
slogan, just one line that they can work into a short propo
to show to Coin.

"People of Panem, we fight, we dare, we end our hunger for justice!" That's the line. I can tell by the way they
present it that they've spent months, maybe years, working
it out and are really proud of it. It seems like a mouthful
to me, though. And stiff. I can't imagine actually saying it
in real life—unless I was using a Capitol accent and making fun of it. Like when Gale and I used to imitate Effie
Trinket's "May the odds be *ever* in your favor!" But Fulvia's
right in my face, describing a battle I've just been in, and
how my comrades-in-arms are all lying dead around me,
and how, to rally the living, I must turn to the camera and
shout out the line!

I'm hustled back to my place, and the smoke machine
kicks in. Someone calls for quiet, the cameras start rolling,
and I hear "Action!" So I hold my bow over my head and

yell with all the anger I can muster, *"People of Panem, we fight, we dare, we end our hunger for justice!"*

There's dead silence on the set. It goes on. And on.

Finally, the intercom crackles and Haymitch's acerbic laugh fills the studio. He contains himself just long enough to say, "And that, my friends, is how a revolution dies."

6

The shock of hearing Haymitch's voice yesterday, of learning that he was not only functional but had some measure of control over my life again, enraged me. I left the studio directly and refused to acknowledge his comments from the booth today. Even so, I knew immediately he was right about my performance.

It took the whole of this morning for him to convince the others of my limitations. That I can't pull it off. I can't stand in a television studio wearing a costume and makeup in a cloud of fake smoke and rally the districts to victory. It's amazing, really, how long I have survived the cameras. The credit for that, of course, goes to Peeta. Alone, I can't be the Mockingjay.

We gather around the huge table in Command. Coin and her people. Plutarch, Fulvia, and my prep team. A group from 12 that includes Haymitch and Gale, but also a few others I can't explain, like Leevy and Greasy Sae. At the last minute, Finnick wheels Beetee in, accompanied by Dalton, the cattle expert from 10. I suppose that Coin has assembled this strange assortment of people as witnesses to my failure.

However, it's Haymitch who welcomes everyone, and by his words I understand that they have come at his personal invitation. This is the first time we've been in a room together since I clawed him. I avoid looking at him directly, but I catch a glimpse of his reflection in one of the shiny control consoles along the wall. He looks slightly yellow and has lost a lot of weight, giving him a shrunken appearance. For a second, I'm afraid he's dying. I have to remind myself that I don't care.

The first thing Haymitch does is to show the footage we've just shot. I seem to have reached some new low under Plutarch and Fulvia's guidance. Both my voice and body have a jerky, disjointed quality, like a puppet being manipulated by unseen forces.

"All right," Haymitch says when it's over. "Would anyone like to argue that this is of use to us in winning the war?" No one does. "That saves time. So, let's all be quiet for a minute. I want everyone to think of one incident where Katniss Everdeen genuinely moved you. Not where you were jealous of her hairstyle, or her dress went up in flames or she made a halfway decent shot with an arrow. Not where Peeta was making you like her. I want to hear one moment where *she* made you feel something real."

Quiet stretches out and I'm beginning to think it will never end, when Leevy speaks up. "When she volunteered to take Prim's place at the reaping. Because I'm sure she thought she was going to die."

"Good. Excellent example," says Haymitch. He takes a purple marker and writes on a notepad. "Volunteered for sister at reaping." Haymitch looks around the table. "Somebody else."

I'm surprised that the next speaker is Boggs, who I think of as a muscular robot that does Coin's bidding. "When she sang the song. While the little girl died." Somewhere in my head an image surfaces of Boggs with a young boy perched up on his hip. In the dining hall, I think. Maybe he's not a robot after all.

"Who didn't get choked up at that, right?" says Haymitch, writing it down.

"I cried when she drugged Peeta so she could go get him medicine and when she kissed him good-bye!" blurts out Octavia. Then she covers her mouth, like she's sure this was a bad mistake.

But Haymitch only nods. "Oh, yeah. Drugs Peeta to save his life. Very nice."

The moments begin to come thick and fast and in no particular order. When I took Rue on as an ally. Extended my hand to Chaff on interview night. Tried to carry Mags. And again and again when I held out those berries that meant different things to different people. Love for Peeta. Refusal to give in under impossible odds. Defiance of the Capitol's inhumanity.

Haymitch holds up the notepad. "So, the question is, what do all of these have in common?"

"They were Katniss's," says Gale quietly. "No one told her what to do or say."

"Unscripted, yes!" says Beetee. He reaches over and pats my hand. "So we should just leave you alone, right?"

People laugh. I even smile a little.

"Well, that's all very nice but not very helpful," says Fulvia peevishly. "Unfortunately, her opportunities for being wonderful are rather limited here in Thirteen. So unless you're suggesting we toss her into the middle of combat—"

"That's *exactly* what I'm suggesting," says Haymitch. "Put her out in the field and just keep the cameras rolling."

"But people think she's pregnant," Gale points out.

"We'll spread the word that she lost the baby from the electrical shock in the arena," Plutarch replies. "Very sad. Very unfortunate."

The idea of sending me into combat is controversial. But Haymitch has a pretty tight case. If I perform well only in real-life circumstances, then into them I should go. "Every time we coach her or give her lines, the best we can hope for is okay. It has to come from her. That's what people are responding to."

"Even if we're careful, we can't guarantee her safety," says Boggs. "She'll be a target for every—"

"I want to go," I break in. "I'm no help to the rebels here."

"And if you're killed?" asks Coin.

"Make sure you get some footage. You can use that, anyway," I answer.

"Fine," says Coin. "But let's take it one step at a time. Find the least dangerous situation that can evoke some spontaneity in you." She walks around Command, studying the illuminated district maps that show the ongoing troop positions in the war. "Take her into Eight this afternoon. There was heavy bombing this morning, but the raid seems to have run its course. I want her armed with a squad of bodyguards. Camera crew on the ground. Haymitch, you'll be airborne and in contact with her. Let's see what happens there. Does anyone have any other comments?"

"Wash her face," says Dalton. Everyone turns to him. "She's still a girl and you made her look thirty-five. Feels wrong. Like something the Capitol would do."

As Coin adjourns the meeting, Haymitch asks her if he can speak to me privately. The others leave except for Gale, who lingers uncertainly by my side. "What are you worried about?" Haymitch asks him. "I'm the one who needs the bodyguard."

"It's okay," I tell Gale, and he goes. Then there's just the hum of the instruments, the purr of the ventilation system.

Haymitch takes the seat across from me. "We're going to have to work together again. So, go ahead. Just say it."

I think of the snarling, cruel exchange back on the hover-craft. The bitterness that followed. But all I say is "I can't believe you didn't rescue Peeta."

"I know," he replies.

There's a sense of incompleteness. And not because he hasn't apologized. But because we were a team. We had a deal to keep Peeta safe. A drunken, unrealistic deal made in the dark of night, but a deal just the same. And in my heart of hearts, I know we both failed.

"Now you say it," I tell him.

"I can't believe you let him out of your sight that night," says Haymitch.

I nod. That's it. "I play it over and over in my head. What I could have done to keep him by my side without breaking the alliance. But nothing comes to me."

77

"You didn't have a choice. And even if I could've made Plutarch stay and rescue him that night, the whole hovercraft would've gone down. We barely got out as it was." I finally meet Haymitch's eyes. Seam eyes. Gray and deep and ringed with the circles of sleepless nights. "He's not dead yet, Katniss."

"We're still in the game." I try to say this with optimism, but my voice cracks.

"Still in. And I'm still your mentor." Haymitch points his marker at me. "When you're on the ground, remember I'm airborne. I'll have the better view, so do what I tell you."

"We'll see," I answer.

I return to the Remake Room and watch the streaks of makeup disappear down the drain as I scrub my face clean. The person in the mirror looks ragged, with her uneven skin and tired eyes, but she looks like me. I rip the armband off, revealing the ugly scar from the tracker. There. That looks like me, too.

Since I'll be in a combat zone, Beetee helps me with armor Cinna designed. A helmet of some interwoven metal that fits close to my head. The material's supple, like fabric, and can be drawn back like a hood in case I don't want it up full-time. A vest to reinforce the protection over my vital organs. A small white earpiece that attaches to my collar by a wire. Beetee secures a mask to my belt that I don't have to wear unless there's a gas attack. "If you see anyone dropping for reasons you can't explain, put it on immediately," he says. Finally, he straps a sheath divided into three cylinders of arrows to my back. "Just remember: Right side, fire. Left side, explosive. Center, regular. You shouldn't need them, but better safe than sorry."

Boggs shows up to escort me down to the Airborne Division. Just as the elevator arrives, Finnick appears in a state of agitation. "Katniss, they won't let me go! I told them I'm fine, but they won't even let me ride in the hovercraft!"

I take in Finnick—his bare legs showing between his hospital gown and slippers, his tangle of hair, the half-knotted rope twisted around his fingers, the wild look in his eyes—and know any plea on my part will be useless. Even I don't think it's a good idea to bring him. So I smack my hand on my forehead and say, "Oh, I forgot. It's this stupid concussion. I was supposed to tell you to report to Beetee in Special Weaponry. He's designed a new trident for you."

At the word *trident*, it's as if the old Finnick surfaces. "Really? What's it do?"

"I don't know. But if it's anything like my bow and arrows, you're going to love it," I say. "You'll need to train with it, though."

"Right. Of course. I guess I better get down there," he says.

"Finnick?" I say. "Maybe some pants?"

He looks down at his legs as if noticing his outfit for the first time. Then he whips off his hospital gown, leaving him in just his underwear. "Why? Do you find this"—he strikes a ridiculously provocative pose—"distracting?"

I can't help laughing because it's funny, and it's extra funny because it makes Boggs look so uncomfortable, and I'm happy because Finnick actually sounds like the guy I met at the Quarter Quell.

"I'm only human, Odair." I get in before the elevator doors close. "Sorry," I say to Boggs.

"Don't be. I thought you . . . handled that well," he says. "Better than my having to arrest him, anyway."

"Yeah," I say. I sneak a sidelong glance at him. He's probably in his mid-forties, with close-cropped gray hair and blue eyes. Incredible posture. He's spoken out twice today in ways that make me think he would rather be friends than enemies. Maybe I should give him a chance. But he just seems so in step with Coin. . . .

There's a series of loud clicks. The elevator comes to a slight pause and then begins to move laterally to the left. "It goes sideways?" I ask.

"Yes. There's a whole network of elevator paths under Thirteen," he answers. "This one lies just above the transport spoke to the fifth airlift platform. It's taking us to the Hangar."

The Hangar. The dungeons. Special Defense. Somewhere food is grown. Power generated. Air and water purified. "Thirteen is even larger than I thought."

"Can't take credit for much of it," says Boggs. "We basically inherited the place. It's been all we can do to keep it running."

The clicks resume. We drop down again briefly — just a couple of levels — and the doors open on the Hangar.

"Oh," I let out involuntarily at the sight of the fleet. Row after row of different kinds of hovercraft. "Did you inherit these, too?"

"Some we manufactured. Some were part of the Capitol's air force. They've been updated, of course," says Boggs.

I feel that twinge of hatred against 13 again. "So, you had all this, and you left the rest of the districts defenseless against the Capitol."

"It's not that simple," he shoots back. "We were in no position to launch a counterattack until recently. We could barely stay alive. After we'd overthrown and executed the Capitol's people, only a handful of us even knew how to pilot. We could've nuked them with missiles, yes. But there's always the larger question: If we engage in that type of war with the Capitol, would there be any human life left?"

"That sounds like what Peeta said. And you all called him a traitor," I counter.

"Because he called for a cease-fire," says Boggs. "You'll notice neither side has launched nuclear weapons. We're working it out the old-fashioned way. Over here, Soldier Everdeen." He indicates one of the smaller hovercraft.

I mount the stairs and find it packed with the television crew and equipment. Everyone else is dressed in 13's dark gray military jumpsuits, even Haymitch, although he seems unhappy about the snugness of his collar.

Fulvia Cardew hustles over and makes a sound of frustration when she sees my clean face. "All that work, down the drain. I'm not blaming you, Katniss. It's just that very few people are born with camera-ready faces. Like him." She snags Gale, who's in a conversation with Plutarch, and spins him toward us. "Isn't he handsome?"

Gale does look striking in the uniform, I guess. But the question just embarrasses us both, given our history. I'm trying to think of a witty comeback, when Boggs says brusquely, "Well, don't expect us to be too impressed. We just saw Finnick Odair in his underwear." I decide to go ahead and like Boggs.

There's a warning of the upcoming takeoff and I strap myself into a seat next to Gale, facing off with Haymitch and Plutarch. We glide through a maze of tunnels that opens out onto a platform. Some sort of elevator device lifts the craft slowly up through the levels. All at once we're outside in a large field surrounded by woods, then we rise off the platform and become wrapped in clouds.

Now that the flurry of activity leading up to this mission is over, I realize I have no idea what I'm facing on this trip to District 8. In fact, I know very little about the actual state of the war. Or what it would take to win it. Or what would happen if we did.

Plutarch tries to lay it out in simple terms for me. First of all, every district is currently at war with the Capitol except 2, which has always had a favored relationship with our enemies despite its participation in the Hunger Games. They get more food and better living conditions. After the Dark Days and the supposed destruction of 13, District 2 became the Capitol's new center of defense, although it's publicly presented as the home of the nation's stone quarries, in the same way that 13 was known for graphite mining. District 2 not only manufactures weaponry, it trains and even supplies Peacekeepers.

"You mean . . . some of the Peacekeepers are born in Two?" I ask. "I thought they all came from the Capitol."

Plutarch nods. "That's what you're supposed to think. And some do come from the Capitol. But its population could never sustain a force that size. Then there's the problem of recruiting Capitol-raised citizens for a dull life of deprivation in the districts. A twenty-year commitment to the Peacekeepers, no marriage, no children allowed. Some buy into it for the honor of the thing, others take it on as an alternative to punishment. For instance, join the Peacekeepers and your debts are forgiven. Many people are swamped in debt in the Capitol, but not all of them are fit for military duty. So District Two is where we turn for additional troops. It's a way for their people to escape poverty and a life in the quarries. They're raised with a warrior mind-set. You've seen how eager their children are to volunteer to be tributes."

Cato and Clove. Brutus and Enobaria. I've seen their eagerness and their bloodlust, too. "But all the other districts are on our side?" I ask.

"Yes. Our goal is to take over the districts one by one, ending with District Two, thus cutting off the Capitol's supply chain. Then, once it's weakened, we invade the Capitol itself," says Plutarch. "That will be a whole other type of challenge. But we'll cross that bridge when we come to it."

"If we win, who would be in charge of the government?" Gale asks.

"Everyone," Plutarch tells him. "We're going to form a republic where the people of each district and the Capitol can elect their own representatives to be their voice in a centralized government. Don't look so suspicious; it's worked before."

"In books," Haymitch mutters.

"In history books," says Plutarch. "And if our ancestors could do it, then we can, too."

Frankly, our ancestors don't seem much to brag about. I mean, look at the state they left us in, with the wars and the broken planet. Clearly, they didn't care about what would happen to the people who came after them. But this republic idea sounds like an improvement over our current government.

"And if we lose?" I ask.

"If we lose?" Plutarch looks out at the clouds, and an ironic smile twists his lips. "Then I would expect next year's Hunger Games to be quite unforgettable. That reminds me." He takes a vial from his vest, shakes a few deep violet pills into his hand, and holds them out to us. "We named them *nightlock* in your honor, Katniss. The rebels can't afford for any of us to be captured now. But I promise, it will be completely painless."

I take hold of a capsule, unsure of where to put it. Plutarch taps a spot on my shoulder at the front of my left sleeve. I examine it and find a tiny pocket that both secures and conceals the pill. Even if my hands were tied, I could lean my head forward and bite it free.

Cinna, it seems, has thought of everything.

The hovercraft makes a quick, spiral descent onto a wide road on the outskirts of 8. Almost immediately, the door opens, the stairs slide into place, and we're spit out onto the asphalt. The moment the last person disembarks, the equipment retracts. Then the craft lifts off and vanishes. I'm left with a bodyguard made up of Gale, Boggs, and two other soldiers. The TV crew consists of a pair of burly Capitol cameramen with heavy mobile cameras encasing their bodies like insect shells, a woman director named Cressida who has a shaved head tattooed with green vines, and her assistant, Messalla, a slim young man with several sets of earrings. On careful observation, I see his tongue has been pierced, too, and he wears a stud with a silver ball the size of a marble.

Boggs hustles us off the road toward a row of warehouses as a second hovercraft comes in for a landing. This one brings crates of medical supplies and a crew of six medics — I can tell by their distinctive white outfits. We all follow Boggs down an alley that runs between two dull gray warehouses. Only the occasional access ladder to the roof interrupts the scarred metal walls. When we emerge onto the street, it's like we've entered another world.

The wounded from this morning's bombing are being brought in. On homemade stretchers, in wheelbarrows, on carts, slung across shoulders, and clenched tight in arms. Bleeding, limbless, unconscious. Propelled by desperate people to a warehouse with a sloppily painted *H* above the doorway. It's a scene from my old kitchen, where my mother treated the dying, multiplied by ten, by fifty, by a hundred. I had expected bombed-out buildings and instead find myself confronted with broken human bodies.

This is where they plan on filming me? I turn to Boggs. "This won't work," I say. "I won't be good here."

He must see the panic in my eyes, because he stops a moment and places his hands on my shoulders. "You will. Just let them see you. That will do more for them than any doctor in the world could."

A woman directing the incoming patients catches sight of us, does a sort of double take, and then strides over. Her dark brown eyes are puffy with fatigue and she smells of metal and sweat. A bandage around her throat needed changing about three days ago. The strap of the automatic weapon slung across her back digs into her neck and she shifts her shoulder to reposition it. With a jerk of her thumb, she orders the medics into the warehouse. They comply without question.

"This is Commander Paylor of Eight," says Boggs. "Commander, Soldier Katniss Everdeen."

She looks young to be a commander. Early thirties. But there's an authoritative tone to her voice that makes you feel her appointment wasn't arbitrary. Beside her, in my spanking-new outfit, scrubbed and shiny, I feel like a recently hatched chick, untested and only just learning how to navigate the world.

"Yeah, I know who she is," says Paylor. "You're alive, then. We weren't sure." Am I wrong or is there a note of accusation in her voice?

"I'm still not sure myself," I answer.

"Been in recovery." Boggs taps his head. "Bad concussion." He lowers his voice a moment. "Miscarriage. But she insisted on coming by to see your wounded."

"Well, we've got plenty of those," says Paylor.

"You think this is a good idea?" says Gale, frowning at the hospital. "Assembling your wounded like this?"

I don't. Any sort of contagious disease would spread through this place like wildfire.

"I think it's slightly better than leaving them to die," says Paylor.

"That's not what I meant," Gale tells her.

"Well, currently that's my other option. But if you come up with a third and get Coin to back it, I'm all ears." Paylor waves me toward the door. "Come on in, Mockingjay. And by all means, bring your friends."

I glance back at the freak show that is my crew, steel myself, and follow her into the hospital. Some sort of heavy, industrial curtain hangs the length of the building, forming a sizable corridor. Corpses lie side by side, curtain brushing their heads, white cloths concealing their faces. "We've got a mass grave started a few blocks west of here, but I can't spare the manpower to move them yet," says Paylor. She finds a slit in the curtain and opens it wide.

My fingers wrap around Gale's wrist. "Do not leave my side," I say under my breath.

"I'm right here," he answers quietly.

I step through the curtain and my senses are assaulted. My first impulse is to cover my nose to block out the stench of soiled linen, putrefying flesh, and vomit, all ripening in the heat of the warehouse. They've propped open skylights that crisscross the high metal roof, but any air that's managing to get in can't make a dent in the fog below. The thin shafts of sunlight provide the only illumination, and as my eyes adjust, I can make out row upon row of wounded, in cots, on pallets, on the floor because there are so many to claim the space. The drone of black flies, the moaning of people in pain, and the sobs of their attending loved ones have combined into a wrenching chorus.

We have no real hospitals in the districts. We die at home, which at the moment seems a far desirable alternative to what lies in front of me. Then I remember that many of these people probably lost their homes in the bombings.

Sweat begins to run down my back, fill my palms. I breathe through my mouth in an attempt to diminish the smell. Black spots swim across my field of vision, and I think there's a really good chance I could faint. But then I catch sight of Paylor, who's watching me so closely, waiting to see what I am made of, and if any of them have been right to think they can count on me. So I let go of Gale and force myself to move deeper into the warehouse, to walk into the narrow strip between two rows of beds.

"Katniss?" a voice croaks out from my left, breaking apart from the general din. "Katniss?" A hand reaches for me out of the haze. I cling to it for support. Attached to the hand is a young woman with an injured leg. Blood has seeped through the heavy bandages, which are crawling with flies. Her face reflects her pain, but something else, too, something that seems completely incongruous with her situation. "Is it really you?"

"Yeah, it's me," I get out.

Joy. That's the expression on her face. At the sound of my voice, it brightens, erases the suffering momentarily.

"You're alive! We didn't know. People said you were, but we didn't know!" she says excitedly.

"I got pretty banged up. But I got better," I say. "Just like you will."

"I've got to tell my brother!" The woman struggles to sit up and calls to someone a few beds down. "Eddy! Eddy! She's here! It's Katniss Everdeen!"

A boy, probably about twelve years old, turns to us. Bandages obscure half of his face. The side of his mouth I can see opens as if to utter an exclamation. I go to him, push his damp brown curls back from his forehead. Murmur a greeting. He can't speak, but his one good eye fixes on me with such intensity, as if he's trying to memorize every detail of my face.

I hear my name rippling through the hot air, spreading out into the hospital. "Katniss! Katniss Everdeen!" The sounds of pain and grief begin to recede, to be replaced by words of anticipation. From all sides, voices beckon me. I begin to move, clasping the hands extended to me, touching the sound parts of those unable to move their limbs, saying hello, how are you, good to meet you. Nothing of importance, no amazing words of inspiration. But it doesn't matter. Boggs is right. It's the sight of me, alive, that is the inspiration.

Hungry fingers devour me, wanting to feel my flesh. As a stricken man clutches my face between his hands, I send a silent thank-you to Dalton for suggesting I wash off the makeup. How ridiculous, how perverse I would feel presenting that painted Capitol mask to these people. The damage, the fatigue, the imperfections. That's how they recognize me, why I belong to them.

Despite his controversial interview with Caesar, many ask about Peeta, assure me that they know he was speaking under duress. I do my best to sound positive about our future, but people are truly devastated when they learn I've lost the baby. I want to come clean and tell one weeping woman that it was all a hoax, a move in the game, but to present Peeta as a liar now would not help his image. Or mine. Or the cause.

I begin to fully understand the lengths to which people have gone to protect me. What I mean to the rebels. My ongoing struggle against the Capitol, which has so often felt like a solitary journey, has not been undertaken alone. I have had thousands upon thousands of people from the districts at my side. I was their Mockingjay long before I accepted the role.

A new sensation begins to germinate inside me. But it takes until I am standing on a table, waving my final good-byes to the hoarse chanting of my name, to define it. Power. I have a kind of power I never knew I possessed. Snow knew it, as soon as I held out those berries. Plutarch knew when he rescued me from the arena. And Coin knows now. So much so that she must publicly remind her people that I am not in control.

When we're outside again, I lean against the warehouse, catching my breath, accepting the canteen of water from Boggs. "You did great," he says.

Well, I didn't faint or throw up or run out screaming. Mostly, I just rode the wave of emotion rolling through the place.

"We got some nice stuff in there," says Cressida. I look at the insect cameramen, perspiration pouring from under their equipment. Messalla scribbling notes. I had forgotten they were even filming me.

"I didn't do much, really," I say.

"You have to give yourself some credit for what you've done in the past," says Boggs.

What I've done in the past? I think of the trail of destruction in my wake—my knees weaken and I slide down to a sitting position. "That's a mixed bag."

"Well, you're not perfect by a long shot. But times being what they are, you'll have to do," says Boggs.

Gale squats down beside me, shaking his head. "I can't believe you let all those people touch you. I kept expecting you to make a break for the door."

"Shut up," I say with a laugh.

"Your mother's going to be very proud when she sees the footage," he says.

"My mother won't even notice me. She'll be too appalled by the conditions in there." I turn to Boggs and ask, "Is it like this in every district?"

"Yes. Most are under attack. We're trying to get in aid wherever we can, but it's not enough." He stops a minute, distracted by something in his earpiece. I realize I haven't heard Haymitch's voice once, and fiddle with mine, wondering if it's broken. "We're to get to the airstrip. Immediately," Boggs says, lifting me to my feet with one hand. "There's a problem."

"What kind of problem?" asks Gale.

"Incoming bombers," says Boggs. He reaches behind my neck and yanks Cinna's helmet up onto my head. "Let's move!"

Unsure of what's going on, I take off running along the front of the warehouse, heading for the alley that leads to the airstrip. But I don't sense any immediate threat. The sky's an empty, cloudless blue. The street's clear except for the people hauling the wounded to the hospital. There's no enemy, no alarm. Then the sirens begin to wail. Within seconds, a low-flying V-shaped formation of Capitol hover-planes appears above us, and the bombs begin to fall. I'm blown off my feet, into the front wall of the warehouse. There's a searing pain just above the back of my right knee. Something has struck my back as well, but doesn't seem to have penetrated my vest. I try to get up, but Boggs pushes me back down, shielding my body with his own. The ground ripples under me as bomb after bomb drops from the planes and detonates.

It's a horrifying sensation being pinned against the wall as the bombs rain down. What was that expression my father used for easy kills? *Like shooting fish in a barrel.* We are the fish, the street the barrel.

"Katniss!" I'm startled by Haymitch's voice in my ear.

"What? Yes, what? I'm here!" I answer.

"Listen to me. We can't land during the bombing, but it's imperative you're not spotted," he says.

"So they don't know I'm here?" I assumed, as usual, it was my presence that brought on punishment.

"Intelligence thinks no. That this raid was already scheduled," says Haymitch.

Now Plutarch's voice comes up, calm but forceful. The voice of a Head Gamemaker used to calling the shots under pressure. "There's a light blue warehouse three down from you. It has a bunker in the far north corner. Can you get there?"

"We'll do our best," says Boggs. Plutarch must be in everyone's ear, because my bodyguards and crew are getting up. My eye instinctively searches for Gale and sees he's on his feet, apparently unharmed.

"You've got maybe forty-five seconds to the next wave," says Plutarch.

I give a grunt of pain as my right leg takes the weight of my body, but I keep moving. No time to examine the injury. Better not to look now, anyway. Fortunately, I have on shoes that Cinna designed. They grip the asphalt on contact and spring free of it on release. I'd be hopeless in that ill-fitting pair that 13 assigned to me. Boggs has the lead, but no one else passes me. Instead they match my pace, protecting my sides, my back. I force myself into a sprint as the seconds tick away. We pass the second gray warehouse and run along a dirt brown building. Up ahead, I see a faded blue facade. Home of the bunker. We have just reached another alley, need only to cross it to arrive at the door, when the next wave of bombs begins. I instinctively dive into the alley and roll toward the blue wall. This time it's Gale who throws himself over me to provide one more layer of protection from the bombing. It seems to go on longer this time, but we are farther away.

I shift onto my side and find myself looking directly into Gale's eyes. For an instant the world recedes and there is just his flushed face, his pulse visible at his temple, his lips slightly parted as he tries to catch his breath.

"You all right?" he asks, his words nearly drowned out by an explosion.

"Yeah. I don't think they've seen me," I answer. "I mean, they're not following us."

"No, they've targeted something else," says Gale.

"I know, but there's nothing back there but —" The realization hits us at the same time.

"The hospital." Instantly, Gale's up and shouting to the others. "They're targeting the hospital!"

"Not your problem," says Plutarch firmly. "Get to the bunker."

"But there's nothing there but the wounded!" I say.

"Katniss." I hear the warning note in Haymitch's voice and know what's coming. "Don't you even think about —!" I yank the earpiece free and let it hang from its wire. With that distraction gone, I hear another sound. Machine gun fire coming from the roof of the dirt brown warehouse across the alley. Someone is returning fire. Before anyone can stop me, I make a dash for an access ladder and begin to scale it. Climbing. One of the things I do best.

"Don't stop!" I hear Gale say behind me. Then there's the sound of his boot on someone's face. If it belongs to Boggs, Gale's going to pay for it dearly later on. I make the roof and drag myself onto the tar. I stop long enough to pull Gale up beside me, and then we take off for the row of machine gun nests on the street side of the warehouse. Each looks to be manned by a few rebels. We skid into a nest with a pair of soldiers, hunching down behind the barrier.

"Boggs know you're up here?" To my left I see Paylor behind one of the guns, looking at us quizzically.

I try to be evasive without flat-out lying. "He knows where we are, all right."

Paylor laughs. "I bet he does. You been trained in these?" She slaps the stock of her gun.

"I have. In Thirteen," says Gale. "But I'd rather use my own weapons."

"Yes, we've got our bows." I hold mine up, then realize how decorative it must seem. "It's more deadly than it looks."

"It would have to be," says Paylor. "All right. We expect at least three more waves. They have to drop their sight shields before they release the bombs. That's our chance. Stay low!" I position myself to shoot from one knee.

"Better start with fire," says Gale.

I nod and pull an arrow from my right sheath. If we miss our targets, these arrows will land somewhere — probably the warehouses across the street. A fire can be put out, but the damage an explosive can do may be irreparable.

Suddenly, they appear in the sky, two blocks down, maybe a hundred yards above us. Seven small bombers in a V formation. "Geese!" I yell at Gale. He'll know exactly what I mean. During migration season, when we hunt fowl, we've developed a system of dividing the birds so we don't both target the same ones. I get the far side of the V, Gale takes the near, and we alternate shots at the front bird. There's no time for further discussion. I estimate the lead time on the hoverplanes and let my arrow fly. I catch the inside wing of one, causing it to burst into flames. Gale just misses the point plane. A fire blooms on an empty warehouse roof across from us. He swears under his breath.

The hoverplane I hit swerves out of formation, but still releases its bombs. It doesn't disappear, though. Neither does one other I assume was hit by gunfire. The damage must prevent the sight shield from reactivating.

"Good shot," says Gale.

"I wasn't even aiming for that one," I mutter. I'd set my sights on the plane in front of it. "They're faster than we think."

"Positions!" Paylor shouts. The next wave of hoverplanes is appearing already.

"Fire's no good," Gale says. I nod and we both load explosive-tipped arrows. Those warehouses across the way look deserted anyway.

As the planes sweep silently in, I make another decision. "I'm standing!" I shout to Gale, and rise to my feet. This is the position I get the best accuracy from. I lead earlier and score a direct hit on the point plane, blasting a hole in its belly. Gale blows the tail off a second. It flips and crashes into the street, setting off a series of explosions as its cargo goes off.

Without warning, a third V formation unveils. This time, Gale squarely hits the point plane. I take the wing off the second bomber, causing it to spin into the one behind it. Together they collide into the roof of the warehouse across from the hospital. A fourth goes down from gunfire.

"All right, that's it," Paylor says.

Flames and heavy black smoke from the wreckage obscure our view. "Did they hit the hospital?"

"Must have," she says grimly.

As I hurry toward the ladders at the far end of the warehouse, the sight of Messalla and one of the insects emerging from behind an air duct surprises me. I thought they'd still be hunkered down in the alley.

"They're growing on me," says Gale.

I scramble down a ladder. When my feet hit the ground, I find a bodyguard, Cressida, and the other insect waiting. I expect resistance, but Cressida just waves me toward the hospital. She's yelling, "I don't care, Plutarch! Just give me five more minutes!" Not one to question a free pass, I take off into the street.

"Oh, no," I whisper as I catch sight of the hospital. What used to be the hospital. I move past the wounded, past the burning plane wrecks, fixated on the disaster ahead of me. People screaming, running about frantically, but unable to help. The bombs have collapsed the hospital roof and set the building on fire, effectively trapping the patients within. A group of rescuers has assembled, trying to clear a path to the inside. But I already know what they will find. If the crushing debris and the flames didn't get them, the smoke did.

Gale's at my shoulder. The fact that he does nothing only confirms my suspicions. Miners don't abandon an accident until it's hopeless.

"Come on, Katniss. Haymitch says they can get a hovercraft in for us now," he tells me. But I can't seem to move.

"Why would they do that? Why would they target people who were already dying?" I ask him.

"Scare others off. Prevent the wounded from seeking help," says Gale. "Those people you met, they were expendable. To Snow, anyway. If the Capitol wins, what will it do with a bunch of damaged slaves?"

I remember all those years in the woods, listening to Gale rant against the Capitol. Me, not paying close attention. Wondering why he even bothered to dissect its motives. Why thinking like our enemy would ever matter. Clearly, it could have mattered today. When Gale questioned the existence of the hospital, he was not thinking of disease, but this. Because he never underestimates the cruelty of those we face.

I slowly turn my back to the hospital and find Cressida, flanked by the insects, standing a couple of yards in front of me. Her manner's unrattled. Cool even. "Katniss," she says, "President Snow just had them air the bombing live. Then he made an appearance to say that this was his way of sending a message to the rebels. What about you? Would you like to tell the rebels anything?"

"Yes," I whisper. The red blinking light on one of the cameras catches my eye. I know I'm being recorded. "Yes," I say more forcefully. Everyone is drawing away from me — Gale, Cressida, the insects — giving me the stage. But I stay focused on the red light. "I want to tell the rebels that I am alive. That I'm right here in District Eight, where the Capitol has just bombed a hospital full of unarmed men, women, and children. There will be no survivors." The shock I've been feeling begins to give way to fury. "I want to tell people that if you think for one second the Capitol will treat us fairly if there's a cease-fire, you're deluding yourself. Because you know who they are and what they do." My hands go out automatically, as if to indicate the whole horror around me. "*This* is what they do! And we must fight back!"

I'm moving in toward the camera now, carried forward by my rage. "President Snow says he's sending us a message? Well, I have one for him. You can torture us and bomb us and burn our districts to the ground, but do you see that?" One of the cameras follows as I point to the planes burning on the roof of the warehouse across from us. The Capitol seal on a wing glows clearly through the flames. "Fire is catching!" I am shouting now, determined that he will not miss a word. "And if we burn, you burn with us!"

My last words hang in the air. I feel suspended in time. Held aloft in a cloud of heat that generates not from my surroundings, but from my own being.

"Cut!" Cressida's voice snaps me back to reality, extinguishes me. She gives me a nod of approval. "That's a wrap."

Boggs appears and gets a firm lock on my arm, but I'm not planning on running now. I look over at the hospital — just in time to see the rest of the structure give way — and the fight goes out of me. All those people, the hundreds of wounded, the relatives, the medics from 13, are no more. I turn back to Boggs, see the swelling on his face left by Gale's boot. I'm no expert, but I'm pretty sure his nose is broken. His voice is more resigned than angry, though. "Back to the landing strip." I obediently take a step forward and wince as I become aware of the pain behind my right knee. The adrenaline rush that overrode the sensation has passed and my body parts join in a chorus of complaints. I'm banged up and bloody and someone seems to be hammering on my left temple from inside my skull. Boggs quickly examines my face, then scoops me up and jogs for the runway. Halfway there, I puke on his bulletproof vest. It's hard to tell because he's short of breath, but I think he sighs.

A small hovercraft, different from the one that transported us here, waits on the runway. The second my team's on board, we take off. No comfy seats and windows this time. We seem to be in some sort of cargo craft. Boggs does emergency first aid on people to hold them until we get back to 13. I want to take off my vest, since I got a fair amount of vomit on it as well, but it's too cold to think about it. I lie on the floor with my head in Gale's lap. The last thing I remember is Boggs spreading a couple of burlap sacks over me.

When I wake up, I'm warm and patched up in my old bed in the hospital. My mother's there, checking my vital signs. "How do you feel?"

"A little beat-up, but all right," I say.

"No one even told us you were going until you were gone," she says.

I feel a pang of guilt. When your family's had to send you off twice to the Hunger Games, this isn't the kind of detail you should overlook. "I'm sorry. They weren't expecting the attack. I was just supposed to be visiting the patients," I explain. "Next time, I'll have them clear it with you."

"Katniss, no one clears anything with me," she says.

It's true. Even I don't. Not since my father died. Why pretend? "Well, I'll have them . . . notify you anyway."

On the bedside table is a piece of shrapnel they removed from my leg. The doctors are more concerned with the damage my brain might have suffered from the explosions, since my concussion hadn't fully healed to begin with. But I don't have double vision or anything and I can think clearly enough. I've slept right through the late afternoon and night, and I'm starving. My breakfast is disappointingly small. Just a few cubes of bread soaking in warm milk. I've been called down to an early morning meeting at Command. I start to get up and then realize they plan to roll my hospital bed directly there. I want to walk, but that's out, so I negotiate my way into a wheelchair. I feel fine, really. Except for my head, and my leg, and the soreness from the bruises, and the nausea that hit a couple minutes after I ate. Maybe the wheelchair's a good idea.

As they wheel me down, I begin to get uneasy about what I will face. Gale and I directly disobeyed orders yesterday, and Boggs has the injury to prove it. Surely, there will be repercussions, but will they go so far as Coin annulling our agreement for the victors' immunity? Have I stripped Peeta of what little protection I could give him?

When I get to Command, the only ones who've arrived are Cressida, Messalla, and the insects. Messalla beams and says, "There's our little star!" and the others are smiling so genuinely that I can't help but smile in return. They impressed me in 8, following me onto the roof during the bombing, making Plutarch back off so they could get the footage they wanted. They more than do their work, they take pride in it. Like Cinna.

I have a strange thought that if we were in the arena together, I would pick them as allies. Cressida, Messalla, and — and — "I have to stop calling you 'the insects,'" I blurt out to the cameramen. I explain how I didn't know their names, but their suits suggested the shelled creatures. The comparison doesn't seem to bother them. Even without the camera shells, they strongly resemble each other. Same sandy hair, red beards, and blue eyes. The one with close-bitten nails introduces himself as Castor and the other, who's his brother, as Pollux. I wait for Pollux to say hello, but he just nods. At first I think he's shy or a man of few words. But something tugs on me—the position of his lips, the extra effort he takes to swallow—and I know before Castor tells me. Pollux is an Avox. They have cut out his tongue and he will never speak again. And I no longer have to wonder what made him risk everything to help bring down the Capitol.

As the room fills, I brace myself for a less congenial reception. But the only people who register any kind of negativity are Haymitch, who's always out of sorts, and a sour-faced Fulvia Cardew. Boggs wears a flesh-colored plastic mask from his upper lip to his brow—I was right about the broken nose—so his expression's hard to read. Coin and Gale are in the midst of some exchange that seems positively chummy.

When Gale slides into the seat next to my wheelchair, I say, "Making new friends?"

His eyes flicker to the president and back. "Well, one of us has to be accessible." He touches my temple gently. "How do you feel?"

They must have served stewed garlic and squash for the breakfast vegetable. The more people who gather, the stronger the fumes are. My stomach turns and the lights suddenly seem too bright. "Kind of rocky," I say. "How are you?"

"Fine. They dug out a couple of pieces of shrapnel. No big deal," he says.

Coin calls the meeting to order. "Our Airtime Assault has officially launched. For any of you who missed yesterday's twenty-hundred broadcast of our first propo—or the seventeen reruns Beetee has managed to air since—we will begin by replaying it." Replaying it? So they not only got usable footage, they've already slapped together a propo and aired it repeatedly. My palms grow moist in anticipation of seeing myself on television. What if I'm still awful? What if I'm as stiff and pointless as I was in the studio and they've just given up on getting anything better? Individual screens slide up from the table, the lights dim slightly, and a hush falls over the room.

At first, my screen is black. Then a tiny spark flickers in the center. It blossoms, spreads, silently eating up the black-ness until the entire frame is ablaze with a fire so real and intense, I imagine I feel the heat emanating from it. The image of my mockingjay pin emerges, glowing red-gold. The deep, resonant voice that haunts my dreams begins to speak. Claudius Templesmith, the official announcer of the Hunger Games, says, "Katniss Everdeen, the girl who was on fire, burns on."

Suddenly, there I am, replacing the mockingjay, stand-ing before the real flames and smoke of District 8. *"I want to tell the rebels that I am alive. That I'm right here in District Eight, where the Capitol has just bombed a hos-pital full of unarmed men, women, and children. There will be no survivors."* Cut to the hospital collapsing in on itself, the desperation of the onlookers as I continue in voice-over. *"I want to tell people that if you think for one second the Capitol will treat us fairly if there's a cease-fire, you're deluding yourself. Because you know who they are and what they do."* Back to me now, my hands lifting up to indicate the outrage around me. *"This is what they do! And we must fight back!"* Now comes a truly fantastic montage of the battle. The initial bombs falling, us running, being blown to the ground—a close-up of my wound, which looks good and bloody—scaling the roof, diving into the nests, and then some amazing shots of the rebels, Gale, and mostly me, me, me knocking those planes out of the sky. Smash-cut back to me moving in on the camera. *"President Snow says he's sending us a message? Well, I have one for him. You can torture us and bomb us and burn our districts to the ground, but do you see that?"* We're with the camera, tracking to the planes burning on the roof of the warehouse. Tight on the Capitol seal on a wing, which melts back into the image of my face, shouting at the president. *"Fire is catching! And if we burn, you burn with us!"* Flames engulf the screen again. Superimposed on them in black, solid letters are the words:

IF WE BURN

YOU BURN WITH US

The words catch fire and the whole screen burns to blackness.

There's a moment of silent relish, then applause followed by demands to see it again. Coin indulgently hits the REPLAY button, and this time, since I know what will happen, I try to pretend that I'm watching this on my television at home in the Seam. An anti-Capitol statement. There's never been anything like it on television. Not in my lifetime, anyway.

By the time the screen burns to black a second time, I need to know more. "Did it play all over Panem? Did they see it in the Capitol?"

"Not in the Capitol," says Plutarch. "We couldn't override their system, although Beetee's working on it. But in all the districts. We even got it on in Two, which may be more valuable than the Capitol at this point in the game."

"Is Claudius Templesmith with us?" I ask.

This gives Plutarch a good laugh. "Only his voice. But that's ours for the taking. We didn't even have to do any special editing. He said that actual line in your first Games." He slaps his hand on the table. "What say we give another round of applause to Cressida, her amazing team, and, of course, our on-camera talent!"

I clap, too, until I realize I'm the on-camera talent and maybe it's obnoxious that I'm applauding for myself, but no one's paying attention. I can't help noticing the strain on Fulvia's face, though. I think how hard this must be for her, watching Haymitch's idea succeed under Cressida's direction, when Fulvia's studio approach was such a flop.

Coin seems to have reached the end of her tolerance for self-congratulation. "Yes, well deserved. The result is more than we had hoped for. But I do have to question the wide margin of risk that you were willing to operate within. I know the raid was unforeseen. However, given the circumstances, I think we should discuss the decision to send Katniss into actual combat."

The decision? To send me into combat? Then she doesn't know that I flagrantly disregarded orders, ripped out my earpiece, and gave my bodyguards the slip? What else have they kept from her?

"It was a tough call," says Plutarch, furrowing his brow. "But the general consensus was that we weren't going to get anything worth using if we locked her in a bunker somewhere every time a gun went off."

"And you're all right with that?" asks the president.

Gale has to kick me under the table before I realize that she's talking to me. "Oh! Yeah, I'm completely all right with that. It felt good. Doing something for a change."

"Well, let's be just a little more judicious with her exposure. Especially now that the Capitol knows what she can do," says Coin. There's a rumble of assent from around the table.

No one has ratted out Gale and me. Not Plutarch, whose authority we ignored. Not Boggs with his broken nose. Not the insects we led into fire. Not Haymitch — no, wait a minute. Haymitch is giving me a deadly smile and saying sweetly, "Yeah, we wouldn't want to lose our little Mockingjay when she's finally begun to sing." I make a note to myself not to end up alone in a room with him, because he's clearly having vengeful thoughts over that stupid earpiece.

"So, what else do you have planned?" asks the president.

Plutarch nods to Cressida, who consults a clipboard. "We have some terrific footage of Katniss at the hospital in Eight. There should be another propo in that with the theme 'Because you know who they are and what they do.' We'll focus on Katniss interacting with the patients, particularly the children, the bombing of the hospital, and the wreckage. Messalla's cutting that together. We're also thinking about a Mockingjay piece. Highlight some of Katniss's best moments intercut with scenes of rebel uprisings and war footage. We call that one 'Fire is catching.' And then Fulvia came up with a really brilliant idea."

Fulvia's mouthful-of-sour-grapes expression is startled right off her face, but she recovers. "Well, I don't know how brilliant it is, but I was thinking we could do a series of propos called *We Remember*. In each one, we would feature one of the dead tributes. Little Rue from Eleven or old Mags from Four. The idea being that we could target each district with a very personal piece."

"A tribute to your tributes, as it were," says Plutarch.

"That *is* brilliant, Fulvia," I say sincerely. "It's the perfect way to remind people why they're fighting."

"I think it could work," she says. "I thought we might use Finnick to intro and narrate the spots. If there was interest in them."

"Frankly, I don't see how we could have too many *We Remember* propos," says Coin. "Can you start producing them today?"

"Of course," says Fulvia, obviously mollified by the response to her idea.

Cressida has smoothed everything over in the creative department with her gesture. Praised Fulvia for what is, in fact, a really good idea, and cleared the way to continue her own on-air depiction of the Mockingjay. What's interesting is that Plutarch seems to have no need to share in the credit. All he wants is for the Airtime Assault to work. I remember that Plutarch is a Head Gamemaker, not a member of the crew. Not a piece in the Games. Therefore, his worth is not defined by a single element, but by the overall success of the production. If we win the war, that's when Plutarch will take his bow. And expect his reward.

The president sends everyone off to get to work, so Gale wheels me back to the hospital. We laugh a little about the cover-up. Gale says no one wanted to look bad by admitting they couldn't control us. I'm kinder, saying they probably didn't want to jeopardize the chance of taking us out again now that they've gotten some decent footage. Both things are probably true. Gale has to go meet Beetee down in Special Weaponry, so I doze off.

It seems like I've only shut my eyes for a few minutes, but when I open them, I flinch at the sight of Haymitch sitting a couple of feet from my bed. Waiting. Possibly for several hours if the clock is right. I think about hollering for a witness, but I'm going to have to face him sooner or later.

Haymitch leans forward and dangles something on a thin white wire in front of my nose. It's hard to focus on, but I'm pretty sure what it is. He drops it to the sheets. "That is your earpiece. I will give you exactly one more chance to wear it. If you remove it from your ear again, I'll have you fitted with this." He holds up some sort of metal headgear that I instantly name *the head shackle*. "It's an alternative audio unit that locks around your skull and under your chin until it's opened with a key. And I'll have the only key. If for some reason you're clever enough to disable it"—Haymitch dumps the head shackle on the bed and whips out a tiny silver chip—"I'll authorize them to surgically implant this transmitter into your ear so that I may speak to you twenty-four hours a day."

Haymitch in my head full-time. Horrifying. "I'll keep the earpiece in," I mutter.

"Excuse me?" he says.

"I'll keep the earpiece in!" I say, loud enough to wake up half the hospital.

"You sure? Because I'm equally happy with any of the three options," he tells me.

"I'm sure," I say. I scrunch up the earpiece wire protectively in my fist and fling the head shackle back in his face with my free hand, but he catches it easily. Probably was expecting me to throw it. "Anything else?"

Haymitch rises to go. "While I was waiting . . . I ate your lunch."

My eyes take in the empty stew bowl and tray on my bed table. "I'm going to report you," I mumble into my pillow.

"You do that, sweetheart." He goes out, safe in the knowledge that I'm not the reporting kind.

I want to go back to sleep, but I'm restless. Images from yesterday begin to flood into the present. The bombing, the fiery plane crashes, the faces of the wounded who no longer exist. I imagine death from all sides. The last moment before seeing a shell hit the ground, feeling the wing blown from my plane and the dizzying nosedive into oblivion, the warehouse roof falling down at me while I'm pinned helplessly to my cot. Things I saw, in person or on the tape.

Things I caused with a pull of my bowstring. Things I will never be able to erase from my memory.

At dinner, Finnick brings his tray to my bed so we can watch the newest propo together on television. He was assigned quarters on my old floor, but he has so many mental relapses, he still basically lives in the hospital. The rebels air the "Because you know who they are and what they do" propo that Messalla edited. The footage is intercut with short studio clips of Gale, Boggs, and Cressida describing the incident. It's hard to watch my reception in the hospital in 8 since I know what's coming. When the bombs rain down on the roof, I bury my face in my pillow, looking up again at a brief clip of me at the end, after all the victims are dead.

At least Finnick doesn't applaud or act all happy when it's done. He just says, "People should know that happened. And now they do."

"Let's turn it off, Finnick, before they run it again," I urge him. But as Finnick's hand moves toward the remote control, I cry, "Wait!" The Capitol is introducing a special segment and something about it looks familiar. Yes, it's Caesar Flickerman. And I can guess who his guest will be.

Peeta's physical transformation shocks me. The healthy, clear-eyed boy I saw a few days ago has lost at least fifteen pounds and developed a nervous tremor in his hands. They've still got him groomed. But underneath the paint that cannot cover the bags under his eyes, and the fine clothes that cannot conceal the pain he feels when he moves, is a person badly damaged.

My mind reels, trying to make sense of it. I just saw him! Four—no, five—I think it was five days ago. How has he deteriorated so rapidly? What could they possibly have done to him in such a short time? Then it hits me. I replay in my mind as much as I can of his first interview with Caesar, searching for anything that would place it in time. There is nothing. They could have taped that interview a day or two after I blew up the arena, then done whatever they wanted to do to him ever since. "Oh, Peeta . . ." I whisper.

Caesar and Peeta have a few empty exchanges before Caesar asks him about rumors that I'm taping propos for the districts. "They're using her, obviously," says Peeta. "To whip up the rebels. I doubt she even really knows what's going on in the war. What's at stake."

"Is there anything you'd like to tell her?" asks Caesar.

"There is," says Peeta. He looks directly into the camera, right into my eyes. "Don't be a fool, Katniss. Think for yourself. They've turned you into a weapon that could be instrumental in the destruction of humanity. If you've got any real influence, use it to put the brakes on this thing. Use it to stop the war before it's too late. Ask yourself, do you really trust the people you're working with? Do you really know what's going on? And if you don't . . . find out."

Black screen. Seal of Panem. Show over.

Finnick presses the button on the remote that kills the power. In a minute, people will be here to do damage control on Peeta's condition and the words that came out of his mouth. I will need to repudiate them. But the truth is, I don't trust the rebels or Plutarch or Coin. I'm not confident that they tell me the truth. I won't be able to conceal this. Footsteps are approaching.

Finnick grips me hard by the arms. "We didn't see it."

"What?" I ask.

"We didn't see Peeta. Only the propo on Eight. Then we turned the set off because the images upset you. Got it?" he asks. I nod. "Finish your dinner." I pull myself together enough so that when Plutarch and Fulvia enter, I have a mouthful of bread and cabbage. Finnick is talking about how well Gale came across on camera. We congratulate them on the propo. Make it clear it was so powerful, we tuned out right afterward. They look relieved. They believe us.

No one mentions Peeta.

9

I stop trying to sleep after my first few attempts are interrupted by unspeakable nightmares. After that, I just lie still and do fake breathing whenever someone checks on me. In the morning, I'm released from the hospital and instructed to take it easy. Cressida asks me to record a few lines for a new Mockingjay propo. At lunch, I keep waiting for people to bring up Peeta's appearance, but no one does. Someone must have seen it besides Finnick and me.

I have training, but Gale's scheduled to work with Beetee on weapons or something, so I get permission to take Finnick to the woods. We wander around awhile and then ditch our communicators under a bush. When we're a safe distance away, we sit and discuss Peeta's broadcast.

"I haven't heard one word about it. No one's told you anything?" Finnick says. I shake my head. He pauses before he asks, "Not even Gale?" I'm clinging to a shred of hope that Gale honestly knows nothing about Peeta's message. But I have a bad feeling he does. "Maybe he's trying to find a time to tell you privately."

"Maybe," I say.

We stay silent so long that a buck wanders into range. I take it down with an arrow. Finnick hauls it back to the fence.

For dinner, there's minced venison in the stew. Gale walks me back to Compartment E after we eat. When I ask him what's been going on, again there's no mention of Peeta. As soon as my mother and sister are asleep, I slip the pearl from the drawer and spend a second sleepless night clutching it in my hand, replaying Peeta's words in my head. *"Ask yourself, do you really trust the people you're working with? Do you really know what's going on? And if you don't . . . find out."* Find out. What? From who? And how can Peeta know anything except what the Capitol tells him? It's just a Capitol propo. More noise. But if Plutarch thinks it's just the Capitol line, why didn't he tell me about it? Why hasn't anyone let me or Finnick know?

Under this debate lies the real source of my distress: Peeta. What have they done to him? And what are they doing to him right now? Clearly, Snow did not buy the story that Peeta and I knew nothing about the rebellion. And his suspicions have been reinforced, now that I have come out as the Mockingjay. Peeta can only guess about the rebel tactics or make up things to tell his torturers. Lies, once discovered, would be severely punished. How abandoned by me he must feel. In his first interview, he tried to protect me from the Capitol and rebels alike, and not only have I failed to protect him, I've brought down more horrors upon him.

Come morning, I stick my forearm in the wall and stare groggily at the day's schedule. Immediately after breakfast, I am slated for Production. In the dining hall, as I down my hot grain and milk and mushy beets, I spot a communicuff on Gale's wrist. "When did you get that back, Soldier Hawthorne?" I ask.

"Yesterday. They thought if I'm going to be in the field with you, it could be a backup system of communication," says Gale.

No one has ever offered me a communicuff. I wonder, if I asked for one, would I get it? "Well, I guess one of us has to be accessible," I say with an edge to my voice.

"What's that mean?" he says.

"Nothing. Just repeating what you said," I tell him. "And I totally agree that the accessible one should be you. I just hope I still have access to you as well."

Our eyes lock, and I realize how furious I am with Gale. That I don't believe for a second that he didn't see Peeta's propo. That I feel completely betrayed that he didn't tell me about it. We know each other too well for him not to read my mood and guess what has caused it.

"Katniss—" he begins. Already the admission of guilt is in his tone.

I grab my tray, cross to the deposit area, and slam the dishes onto the rack. By the time I'm in the hallway, he's caught up with me.

"Why didn't you say something?" he asks, taking my arm.

"Why didn't *I*?" I jerk my arm free. "Why didn't *you*, Gale? And I did, by the way, when I asked you last night about what had been going on!"

"I'm sorry. All right? I didn't know what to do. I wanted to tell you, but everyone was afraid that seeing Peeta's propo would make you sick," he says.

"They were right. It did. But not quite as sick as you lying to me for Coin." At that moment, his communicuff starts beeping. "There she is. Better run. You have things to tell her."

For a moment, real hurt registers on his face. Then cold anger replaces it. He turns on his heel and goes. Maybe I have been too spiteful, not given him enough time to explain. Maybe everyone is just trying to protect me by lying to me. I don't care. I'm sick of people lying to me for my own good. Because really it's mostly for their own good. Lie to Katniss about the rebellion so she doesn't do anything crazy. Send her into the arena without a clue so we can fish her out. Don't tell her about Peeta's propo because it might make her sick, and it's hard enough to get a decent performance out of her as it is.

I do feel sick. Heartsick. And too tired for a day of production. But I'm already at Remake, so I go in. Today, I discover, we will be returning to District 12. Cressida wants to do unscripted interviews with Gale and me throwing light on our demolished city.

"If you're both up for that," says Cressida, looking closely at my face.

"Count me in," I say. I stand, uncommunicative and stiff, a mannequin, as my prep team dresses me, does my hair, and dabs makeup on my face. Not enough to show, only enough to take the edge off the circles under my sleepless eyes.

Boggs escorts me down to the Hangar, but we don't talk beyond a preliminary greeting. I'm grateful to be spared another exchange about my disobedience in 8, especially since his mask looks so uncomfortable.

At the last moment, I remember to send a message to my mother about my leaving 13, and stress that it won't be dangerous. We board a hovercraft for the short ride to 12 and I'm directed to a seat at a table where Plutarch, Gale, and Cressida are poring over a map. Plutarch's brimming with satisfaction as he shows me the before/after effects of the first couple of propos. The rebels, who were barely maintaining a foothold in several districts, have rallied. They have actually taken 3 and 11 — the latter so crucial since it's Panem's main food supplier — and have made inroads in several other districts as well.

"Hopeful. Very hopeful indeed," says Plutarch. "Fulvia's going to have the first round of *We Remember* spots ready tonight, so we can target the individual districts with their dead. Finnick's absolutely marvelous."

"It's painful to watch, actually," says Cressida. "He knew so many of them personally."

"That's what makes it so effective," says Plutarch. "Straight from the heart. You're all doing beautifully. Coin could not be more pleased."

Gale didn't tell them, then. About my pretending not to see Peeta and my anger at their cover-up. But I guess it's too little, too late, because I still can't let it go. It doesn't matter. He's not speaking to me, either.

It's not until we land in the Meadow that I realize Haymitch isn't among our company. When I ask Plutarch about his absence, he just shakes his head and says, "He couldn't face it."

"Haymitch? Not able to face something? Wanted a day off, more likely," I say.

"I think his actual words were 'I couldn't face it without a bottle,'" says Plutarch.

I roll my eyes, long out of patience with my mentor, his weakness for drink, and what he can or can't confront. But about five minutes after my return to 12, I'm wishing I had a bottle myself. I thought I'd come to terms with 12's demise—heard of it, seen it from the air, and wandered through its ashes. So why does everything bring on a fresh pang of grief? Was I simply too out of it before to fully register the loss of my world? Or is it the look on Gale's face as he takes in the destruction on foot that makes the atrocity feel brand-new?

Cressida directs the team to start with me at my old house. I ask her what she wants me to do. "Whatever you feel like," she says. Standing back in my kitchen, I don't feel like doing anything. In fact, I find myself focusing up at the sky—the only roof left—because too many memories are drowning me. After a while, Cressida says, "That's fine, Katniss. Let's move on."

Gale doesn't get off so easily at his old address. Cressida films him in silence for a few minutes, but just as he pulls the one remnant of his previous life from the ashes—a twisted metal poker—she starts to question him about his family, his job, life in the Seam. She makes him go back to the night of the firebombing and reenact it, starting at his house, working his way down across the Meadow and through the woods to the lake. I straggle behind the film crew and the bodyguards, feeling their presence to be a violation of my beloved woods. This is a private place, a sanctuary, already corrupted by the Capitol's evil. Even after we've left behind the charred stumps near the fence, we're still tripping over decomposing bodies. Do we have to record it for everyone to see?

By the time we reach the lake, Gale seems to have lost his ability to speak. Everyone's dripping in sweat — especially Castor and Pollux in their insect shells — and Cressida calls for a break. I scoop up handfuls of water from the lake, wishing I could dive in and surface alone and naked and unobserved. I wander around the perimeter for a while. When I come back around to the little concrete house beside the lake, I pause in the doorway and see Gale propping the crooked poker he salvaged against the wall by the hearth. For a moment I have an image of a lone stranger, sometime far in the future, wandering lost in the wilderness and coming upon this small place of refuge, with the pile of split logs, the hearth, the poker. Wondering how it came to be. Gale turns and meets my eyes and I know he's thinking about our last meeting here. When we fought over whether or not to run away. If we had, would District 12 still be there? I think it would. But the Capitol would still be in control of Panem as well.

Cheese sandwiches are passed around and we eat them in the shade of the trees. I intentionally sit at the far edge of the group, next to Pollux, so I don't have to talk. No one's talking much, really. In the relative quiet, the birds take back the woods. I nudge Pollux with my elbow and point out a small black bird with a crown. It hops to a new branch, momentarily opening its wings, showing off its white patches. Pollux gestures to my pin and raises his eyebrows questioningly. I nod, confirming it's a mockingjay. I hold up one finger to say *Wait, I'll show you*, and whistle a birdcall. The mockingjay cocks its head and whistles the call right back at me. Then, to my surprise, Pollux whistles a few notes of his own. The bird answers him immediately. Pollux's face breaks into an expression of delight and he has a series of melodic exchanges with the mockingjay. My guess is it's the first conversation he's had in years. Music draws mockingjays like blossoms do bees, and in a short while he's got half a dozen of them perched in the branches over our heads. He taps me on the arm and uses a twig to write a word in the dirt. *SING?*

Usually, I'd decline, but it's kind of impossible to say no to Pollux, given the circumstances. Besides, the mockingjays' song voices are different from their whistles, and I'd like him to hear them. So, before I actually think about what I'm doing, I sing Rue's four notes, the ones she used to signal the end of the workday in 11. The notes that ended up as the background music to her murder. The birds don't know that. They pick up the simple phrase and bounce it back and forth between them in sweet harmony. Just as they did in the Hunger Games before the muttations broke through the trees, chased us onto the Cornucopia, and slowly gnawed Cato to a bloody pulp —

"Want to hear them do a real song?" I burst out. Anything to stop those memories. I'm on my feet, moving back into the trees, resting my hand on the rough trunk of a maple where the birds perch. I have not sung "The Hanging Tree" out loud for ten years, because it's forbidden, but I remember every word. I begin softly, sweetly, as my father did.

> *"Are you, are you*
> *Coming to the tree*
> *Where they strung up a man they say murdered three.*
> *Strange things did happen here*
> *No stranger would it be*
> *If we met up at midnight in the hanging tree."*

The mockingjays begin to alter their songs as they become aware of my new offering.

> *"Are you, are you*
> *Coming to the tree*
> *Where the dead man called out for his love to flee.*
> *Strange things did happen here*
> *No stranger would it be*
> *If we met up at midnight in the hanging tree."*

I have the birds' attention now. In one more verse, surely they will have captured the melody, as it's simple and repeats four times with little variation.

"Are you, are you
Coming to the tree
Where I told you to run, so we'd both be free.
Strange things did happen here
No stranger would it be
If we met up at midnight in the hanging tree."

A hush in the trees. Just the rustle of leaves in the breeze. But no birds, mockingjay or other. Peeta's right. They do fall silent when I sing. Just as they did for my father.

"Are you, are you
Coming to the tree
Wear a necklace of rope, side by side with me.
Strange things did happen here
No stranger would it be
If we met up at midnight in the hanging tree."

The birds are waiting for me to continue. But that's it. Last verse. In the stillness I remember the scene. I was home from a day in the woods with my father. Sitting on the floor with Prim, who was just a toddler, singing "The Hanging Tree." Making us necklaces out of scraps of old rope like it said in the song, not knowing the real meaning of the words. The tune was simple and easy to harmonize to, though, and back then I could memorize almost anything set to music after a round or two. Suddenly, my mother snatched the rope necklaces away and was yelling at my father. I started to cry because my mother never yelled, and then Prim was wailing and I ran outside to hide. As I had exactly one hiding spot — in the Meadow under a honeysuckle bush — my father found me immediately. He calmed me down and told me everything was fine, only we'd better not sing that song anymore. My mother just wanted me to forget it. So, of course, every word was immediately, irrevocably branded into my brain.

We didn't sing it anymore, my father and I, or even speak of it. After he died, it used to come back to me a lot. Being older, I began to understand the lyrics. At the beginning, it sounds like a guy is trying to get his girlfriend to secretly meet up with him at midnight. But it's an odd place for a tryst, a hanging tree, where a man was hung for murder. The murderer's lover must have had something to do with the killing, or maybe they were just going to punish her anyway, because his corpse called out for her to flee. That's weird obviously, the talking-corpse bit, but it's not until the third verse that "The Hanging Tree" begins to get unnerving. You realize the singer of the song is the dead murderer. He's still in the hanging tree. And even though he told his lover to flee, he keeps asking if she's coming to meet him. The phrase *Where I told you to run, so we'd both be free* is the most troubling because at first you think he's talking about when he told her to flee, presumably to safety. But then you wonder if he meant for her to run to him. To death. In the final stanza, it's clear that that's what he's waiting for. His lover, with her rope necklace, hanging dead next to him in the tree.

I used to think the murderer was the creepiest guy imaginable. Now, with a couple of trips to the Hunger Games under my belt, I decide not to judge him without knowing more details. Maybe his lover was already sentenced to death and he was trying to make it easier. To let her know he'd be waiting. Or maybe he thought the place he was leaving her was really worse than death. Didn't I want to kill Peeta with that syringe to save him from the Capitol? Was that really my only option? Probably not, but I couldn't think of another at the time.

I guess my mother thought the whole thing was too twisted for a seven-year-old, though. Especially one who made her own rope necklaces. It wasn't like hanging was something that only happened in a story. Plenty of people were executed that way in 12. You can bet she didn't want me singing it in front of my music class. She probably wouldn't like me doing it here for Pollux even, but at least I'm not — wait, no, I'm wrong. As I glance sideways, I see Castor has been taping me. Everyone is watching me intently. And Pollux has tears running down his cheeks because no doubt my freaky song has dredged up some terrible incident in his life. Great. I sigh and lean back against the trunk. That's when the mockingjays begin their rendition of "The Hanging Tree." In their mouths, it's quite beautiful. Conscious of being filmed, I stand quietly until I hear Cressida call, "Cut!"

Plutarch crosses to me, laughing. "Where do you come up with this stuff? No one would believe it if we made it up!" He throws an arm around me and kisses me on the top of my head with a loud smack. "You're golden!"

"I wasn't doing it for the cameras," I say.

"Lucky they were on, then," he says. "Come on, everybody, back to town!"

As we trudge back through the woods, we reach a boulder, and both Gale and I turn our heads in the same direction, like a pair of dogs catching a scent on the wind. Cressida notices and asks what lies that way. We admit, without acknowledging each other, it's our old hunting rendezvous place. She wants to see it, even after we tell her it's nothing really.

Nothing but a place where I was happy, I think.

Our rock ledge overlooking the valley. Perhaps a little less green than usual, but the blackberry bushes hang heavy with fruit. Here began countless days of hunting and snaring, fishing and gathering, roaming together through the woods, unloading our thoughts while we filled our game bags. This was the doorway to both sustenance and sanity. And we were each other's key.

There's no District 12 to escape from now, no Peacekeepers to trick, no hungry mouths to feed. The Capitol took away all of that, and I'm on the verge of losing Gale as well. The glue of mutual need that bonded us so tightly together for all those years is melting away. Dark patches, not light, show in the spaces between us. How can it be that today, in the face of 12's horrible demise, we are too angry to even speak to each other?

Gale as good as lied to me. That was unacceptable, even if he was concerned about my well-being. His apology seemed genuine, though. And I threw it back in his face with an insult to make sure it stung. What is happening to us? Why are we always at odds now? It's all a muddle, but I somehow feel that if I went back to the root of our troubles, my actions would be at the heart of it. Do I really want to drive him away?

My fingers encircle a blackberry and pluck it from its stem. I roll it gently between my thumb and forefinger. Suddenly, I turn to him and toss it in his direction. "And may the odds—" I say. I throw it high so he has plenty of time to decide whether to knock it aside or accept it.

Gale's eyes train on me, not the berry, but at the last moment, he opens his mouth and catches it. He chews, swallows, and there's a long pause before he says "—be *ever* in your favor." But he does say it.

Cressida has us sit in the nook in the rocks, where it's impossible not to be touching, and coaxes us into talking about hunting. What drove us out into the woods, how we met, favorite moments. We thaw, begin to laugh a little, as we relate mishaps with bees and wild dogs and skunks. When the conversation turns to how it felt to translate our skill with weapons to the bombing in 8, I stop talking. Gale just says, "Long overdue."

By the time we reach the town square, afternoon's sinking into evening. I take Cressida to the rubble of the bakery and ask her to film something. The only emotion I can muster is exhaustion. "Peeta, this is your home. None of your family has been heard of since the bombing. Twelve is gone. And you're calling for a cease-fire?" I look across the emptiness. "There's no one left to hear you."

As we stand before the lump of metal that was the gallows, Cressida asks if either of us has ever been tortured. In answer, Gale pulls off his shirt and turns his back to the camera. I stare at the lash marks, and again hear the whistling of the whip, see his bloody figure hanging unconscious by his wrists.

"I'm done," I announce. "I'll meet you at the Victor's Village. Something for . . . my mother."

I guess I walked here, but the next thing I'm conscious of is sitting on the floor in front of the kitchen cabinets of our house in the Victor's Village. Meticulously lining ceramic jars and glass bottles into a box. Placing clean cotton bandages between them to prevent breaking. Wrapping bunches of dried flowers.

Suddenly, I remember the rose on my dresser. Was it real? If so, is it still up there? I have to resist the temptation to check. If it's there, it will only frighten me all over again. I hurry with my packing.

When the cabinets are empty, I rise to find that Gale has materialized in my kitchen. It's disturbing how soundlessly he can appear. He's leaning on the table, his fingers spread wide against the wood grain. I set the box between us. "Remember?" he asks. "This is where you kissed me."

So the heavy dose of morphling administered after the whipping wasn't enough to erase that from his consciousness. "I didn't think you'd remember that," I say.

"Have to be dead to forget. Maybe even not then," he tells me. "Maybe I'll be like that man in 'The Hanging Tree.' Still waiting for an answer." Gale, who I have never seen cry, has tears in his eyes. To keep them from spilling over, I reach forward and press my lips against his. We taste of heat, ashes, and misery. It's a surprising flavor for such a gentle kiss. He pulls away first and gives me a wry smile. "I knew you'd kiss me."

"How?" I say. Because I didn't know myself.

"Because I'm in pain," he says. "That's the only way I get your attention." He picks up the box. "Don't worry, Katniss. It'll pass." He leaves before I can answer.

I'm too weary to work through his latest charge. I spend the short ride back to 13 curled up in a seat, trying to ignore Plutarch going on about one of his favorite subjects — weapons mankind no longer has at its disposal. High-flying planes, military satellites, cell disintegrators, drones, biological weapons with expiration dates. Brought down by the destruction of the atmosphere or lack of resources or moral squeamishness. You can hear the regret of a Head Gamemaker who can only dream of such toys, who must make do with hovercraft and land-to-land missiles and plain old guns.

After dropping off my Mockingjay suit, I go straight to bed without eating. Even so, Prim has to shake me to get me up in the morning. After breakfast, I ignore my schedule and take a nap in the supply closet. When I come to, crawling out from between the boxes of chalk and pencils, it's dinnertime again. I get an extra-large portion of pea soup and am headed back to Compartment E when Boggs intercepts me.

"There's a meeting in Command. Disregard your current schedule," he says.

"Done," I say.

"Did you follow it at all today?" he asks in exasperation.

"Who knows? I'm mentally disoriented." I hold up my wrist to show my medical bracelet and realize it's gone. "See? I can't even remember they took my bracelet. Why do they want me in Command? Did I miss something?"

"I think Cressida wanted to show you the Twelve propos. But I guess you'll see them when they air," he says.

"That's what I need a schedule of. When the propos air," I say. He shoots me a look but doesn't comment further.

People have crowded into Command, but they've saved me a seat between Finnick and Plutarch. The screens are already up on the table, showing the regular Capitol feed.

"What's going on? Aren't we seeing the Twelve propos?" I ask.

"Oh, no," says Plutarch. "I mean, possibly. I don't know exactly what footage Beetee plans to use."

"Beetee thinks he's found a way to break into the feed nationwide," says Finnick. "So that our propos will air in the Capitol, too. He's down working on it in Special Defense now. There's live programming tonight. Snow's making an appearance or something. I think it's starting."

The Capitol seal appears, underscored by the anthem. Then I'm staring directly into President Snow's snake eyes as he greets the nation. He seems barricaded behind his podium, but the white rose in his lapel is in full view. The camera pulls back to include Peeta, off to one side in front of a projected map of Panem. He's sitting in an elevated chair, his shoes supported by a metal rung. The foot of his prosthetic leg taps out a strange irregular beat. Beads of sweat have broken through the layer of powder on his upper lip and forehead. But it's the look in his eyes — angry yet unfocused — that frightens me the most.

"He's worse," I whisper. Finnick grasps my hand, to give me an anchor, and I try to hang on.

Peeta begins to speak in a frustrated tone about the need for the cease-fire. He highlights the damage done to key infrastructure in various districts, and as he speaks, parts of the map light up, showing images of the destruction. A broken dam in 7. A derailed train with a pool of toxic waste spilling from the tank cars. A granary collapsing after a fire. All of these he attributes to rebel action.

Bam! Without warning, I'm suddenly on television, standing in the rubble of the bakery.

Plutarch jumps to his feet. "He did it! Beetee broke in!"

The room's buzzing with reaction when Peeta's back, distracted. He has seen me on the monitor. He tries to pick up his speech by moving on to the bombing of a water purification plant, when a clip of Finnick talking about Rue replaces him. And then the whole thing breaks down into a broadcast battle, as the Capitol tech masters try to fend off Beetee's attack. But they are unprepared, and Beetee, apparently anticipating he would not hold on to control, has an arsenal of five- to ten-second clips to work with. We watch the official presentation deteriorate as it's peppered with choice shots from the propos.

Plutarch's in spasms of delight and most everybody is cheering Beetee on, but Finnick remains still and speechless beside me. I meet Haymitch's eyes from across the room and see my own dread mirrored back. The recognition that with every cheer, Peeta slips even farther from our grasp.

The Capitol seal's back up, accompanied by a flat audio tone. This lasts about twenty seconds before Snow and Peeta return. The set is in turmoil. We're hearing frantic exchanges from their booth. Snow plows forward, saying that clearly the rebels are now attempting to disrupt the dissemination of information they find incriminating, but both truth and justice will reign. The full broadcast will resume when security has been reinstated. He asks Peeta if, given tonight's demonstration, he has any parting thoughts for Katniss Everdeen.

At the mention of my name, Peeta's face contorts in effort. "Katniss . . . how do you think this will end? What will be left? No one is safe. Not in the Capitol. Not in the districts. And you . . . in Thirteen . . ." He inhales sharply, as if fighting for air; his eyes look insane. "Dead by morning!"

Off camera, Snow orders, "End it!" Beetee throws the whole thing into chaos by flashing a still shot of me standing in front of the hospital at three-second intervals. But between the images, we are privy to the real-life action being played out on the set. Peeta's attempt to continue speaking. The camera knocked down to record the white tiled floor. The scuffle of boots. The impact of the blow that's inseparable from Peeta's cry of pain.

And his blood as it splatters the tiles.

PART II
"THE ASSAULT"

10

The scream begins in my lower back and works its way up through my body only to jam in my throat. I am Avox mute, choking on my grief. Even if I could release the muscles in my neck, let the sound tear into space, would anyone notice it? The room's in an uproar. Questions and demands ring out as they try to decipher Peeta's words. *"And you . . . in Thirteen . . . dead by morning!"* Yet no one is asking about the messenger whose blood has been replaced by static.

A voice calls the others to attention. "Shut up!" Every pair of eyes falls on Haymitch. "It's not some big mystery! The boy's telling us we're about to be attacked. Here. In Thirteen."

"How would he have that information?"

"Why should we trust him?"

"How do you know?"

Haymitch gives a growl of frustration. "They're beating him bloody while we speak. What more do you need? Katniss, help me out here!"

I have to give myself a shake to free my words. "Haymitch's right. I don't know where Peeta got the information. Or if it's true. But he believes it is. And they're—" I can't say aloud what Snow's doing to him.

"You don't know him," Haymitch says to Coin. "We do. Get your people ready."

The president doesn't seem alarmed, only somewhat perplexed, by this turn in events. She mulls over the words, tapping one finger lightly on the rim of the control board in front of her. When she speaks, she addresses Haymitch in an even voice. "Of course, we have prepared for such a scenario. Although we have decades of support for the assumption that further direct attacks on Thirteen would be counterproductive to the Capitol's cause. Nuclear missiles would release radiation into the atmosphere, with incalculable environmental results. Even routine bombing could badly damage our military compound, which we know they hope to regain. And, of course, they invite a counterstrike. It is conceivable that, given our current alliance with the rebels, those would be viewed as acceptable risks."

"You think so?" says Haymitch. It's a shade too sincere, but the subtleties of irony are often wasted in 13.

"I do. At any rate, we're overdue for a Level Five security drill," says Coin. "Let's proceed with the lockdown." She begins to type rapidly on her keyboard, authorizing her decision. The moment she raises her head, it begins.

There have been two low-level drills since I arrived in 13. I don't remember much about the first. I was in intensive care in the hospital and I think the patients were exempted, as the complications of removing us for a practice drill outweighed the benefits. I was vaguely aware of a mechanical voice instructing people to congregate in yellow zones. During the second, a Level Two drill meant for minor crises—such as a temporary quarantine while citizens were tested for contagion during a flu outbreak—we were supposed to return to our living quarters. I stayed behind a pipe in the laundry room, ignored the pulsating beeps coming over the audio system, and watched a spider construct a web. Neither experience has prepared me for the wordless, eardrum-piercing, fear-inducing sirens that now permeate 13. There would be no disregarding this sound, which seems designed to throw the whole population into a frenzy. But this is 13 and that doesn't happen.

Boggs guides Finnick and me out of Command, along the hall to a doorway, and onto a wide stairway. Streams of people are converging to form a river that flows only downward. No one shrieks or tries to push ahead. Even the children don't resist. We descend, flight after flight, speechless, because no word could be heard above this sound. I look for my mother and Prim, but it's impossible to see anyone but those immediately around me. They're both working in the hospital tonight, though, so there's no way they can miss the drill.

My ears pop and my eyes feel heavy. We are coal-mine deep. The only plus is that the farther we retreat into the earth, the less shrill the sirens become. It's as if they were meant to physically drive us away from the surface, which I suppose they are. Groups of people begin to peel off into marked doorways and still Boggs directs me downward, until finally the stairs end at the edge of an enormous cavern. I start to walk straight in and Boggs stops me, shows me that I must wave my schedule in front of a scanner so that I'm accounted for. No doubt the information's going to some computer somewhere to make sure no one's gone astray.

The place seems unable to decide if it's natural or manmade. Certain areas of the walls are stone, while steel beams and concrete heavily reinforce others. Sleeping bunks are hewn right into the rock walls. There's a kitchen, bathrooms, a first-aid station. This place was designed for an extended stay.

White signs with letters or numbers are placed at intervals around the cavern. As Boggs tells Finnick and me to report to the area that matches our assigned quarters—in my case E for Compartment E—Plutarch strolls up. "Ah, here you are," he says. Recent events have had little effect on Plutarch's mood. He still has a happy glow from Beetee's success on the Airtime Assault. Eyes on the forest, not on the trees. Not on Peeta's punishment or 13's imminent blasting. "Katniss, obviously this is a bad moment for you, what with Peeta's setback, but you need to be aware that others will be watching you."

"What?" I say. I can't believe he actually just downgraded Peeta's dire circumstances to a setback.

"The other people in the bunker, they'll be taking their cue on how to react from you. If you're calm and brave, others will try to be as well. If you panic, it could spread like wildfire," explains Plutarch. I just stare at him. "Fire is catching, so to speak," he continues, as if I'm being slow on the uptake.

"Why don't I just pretend I'm on camera, Plutarch?" I say.

"Yes! Perfect. One is always much braver with an audience," he says. "Look at the courage Peeta just displayed!"

It's all I can do not to slap him.

"I've got to get back to Coin before lockdown. You keep up the good work!" he says, and then heads off.

I cross to the big letter *E* posted on the wall. Our space consists of a twelve-by-twelve-foot square of stone floor delineated by painted lines. Carved into the wall are two bunks — one of us will be sleeping on the floor — and a ground-level cube space for storage. A piece of white paper, coated in clear plastic, reads BUNKER PROTOCOL. I stare fixedly at the little black specks on the sheet. For a while, they're obscured by the residual blood droplets that I can't seem to wipe from my vision. Slowly, the words come into focus. The first section is entitled "On Arrival."

1. Make sure all members of your Compartment are accounted for.

My mother and Prim haven't arrived, but I was one of the first people to reach the bunker. Both of them are probably helping to relocate hospital patients.

2. Go to the Supply Station and secure one pack for each member of your Compartment. Ready your Living Area. Return pack(s).

I scan the cavern until I locate the Supply Station, a deep room set off by a counter. People wait behind it, but there's not a lot of activity there yet. I walk over, give our compartment letter, and request three packs. A man checks a sheet, pulls the specified packs from shelving, and swings them up onto the counter. After sliding one on my back and getting a grip on the other two with my hands, I turn to find a group rapidly forming behind me. "Excuse me," I say as I carry my supplies through the others. Is it a matter of timing? Or is Plutarch right? Are these people modeling their behavior on mine?

Back at our space, I open one of the packs to find a thin mattress, bedding, two sets of gray clothing, a toothbrush, a comb, and a flashlight. On examining the contents of the other packs, I find the only discernible difference is that they contain both gray and white outfits. The latter will be for my mother and Prim, in case they have medical duties. After I make up the beds, store the clothes, and return the backpacks, I've got nothing to do but observe the last rule.

3. Await further instructions.

I sit cross-legged on the floor to await. A steady flow of people begins to fill the room, claiming spaces, collecting supplies. It won't take long until the place is full up. I wonder if my mother and Prim are going to stay the night at wherever the hospital patients have been taken. But, no, I don't think so. They were on the list here. I'm starting to get anxious, when my mother appears. I look behind her into a sea of strangers. "Where's Prim?" I ask.

"Isn't she here?" she replies. "She was supposed to come straight down from the hospital. She left ten minutes before I did. Where is she? Where could she have gone?"

I squeeze my lids shut tight for a moment, to track her as I would prey on a hunt. See her react to the sirens, rush to help the patients, nod as they gesture for her to descend to the bunker, and then hesitate with her on the stairs. Torn for a moment. But why?

My eyes fly open. "The cat! She went back for him!"

"Oh, no," my mother says. We both know I'm right. We're pushing against the incoming tide, trying to get out of the bunker. Up ahead, I can see them preparing to shut the thick metal doors. Slowly rotating the metal wheels on either side inward. Somehow I know that once they have been sealed, nothing in the world will convince the soldiers to open them. Perhaps it will even be beyond their control. I'm indiscriminately shoving people aside as I shout for them to wait. The space between the doors shrinks to a yard, a foot; there are only a few inches left when I jam my hand through the crack.

"Open it! Let me out!" I cry.

Consternation shows on the soldiers' faces as they reverse the wheels a bit. Not enough to let me pass, but enough to avoid crushing my fingers. I take the opportunity to wedge my shoulder into the opening. "Prim!" I holler up the stairs. My mother pleads with the guards as I try to wriggle my way out. "Prim!"

Then I hear it. The faint sound of footsteps on the stairs. "We're coming!" I hear my sister call.

"Hold the door!" That was Gale.

"They're coming!" I tell the guards, and they slide the doors open about a foot. But I don't dare move—afraid they'll lock us all out—until Prim appears, her cheeks flushed with running, hauling Buttercup. I pull her inside and Gale follows, twisting an armload of baggage sideways to get it into the bunker. The doors are closed with a loud and final clank.

"What were you thinking?" I give Prim an angry shake and then hug her, squashing Buttercup between us.

Prim's explanation is already on her lips. "I couldn't leave him behind, Katniss. Not twice. You should have seen him pacing the room and howling. He'd come back to protect us."

"Okay. Okay." I take a few breaths to calm myself, step back, and lift Buttercup by the scruff of the neck. "I should've drowned you when I had the chance." His ears flatten and he raises a paw. I hiss before he gets a chance, which seems to annoy him a little, since he considers hissing his own personal sound of contempt. In retaliation, he gives a helpless kitten mew that brings my sister immediately to his defense.

"Oh, Katniss, don't tease him," she says, folding him back in her arms. "He's already so upset."

The idea that I've wounded the brute's tiny cat feelings just invites further taunting. But Prim's genuinely distressed for him. So instead, I visualize Buttercup's fur lining a pair of gloves, an image that has helped me deal with him over the years. "Okay, sorry. We're under the big *E* on the wall. Better get him settled in before he loses it." Prim hurries off, and I find myself face-to-face with Gale. He's holding the box of medical supplies from our kitchen in 12. Site of our last conversation, kiss, fallout, whatever. My game bag's slung across his shoulder.

"If Peeta's right, these didn't stand a chance," he says.

Peeta. Blood like raindrops on the window. Like wet mud on boots.

"Thanks for . . . everything." I take our stuff. "What were you doing up in our rooms?"

"Just double-checking," he says. "We're in Forty-Seven if you need me."

Practically everyone withdrew to their spaces when the doors shut, so I get to cross to our new home with at least five hundred people watching me. I try to appear extra calm to make up for my frantic crashing through the crowd. Like that's fooling anyone. So much for setting an example. Oh, who cares? They all think I'm nuts anyway. One man, who I think I knocked to the floor, catches my eye and rubs his elbow resentfully. I almost hiss at him, too.

Prim has Buttercup installed on the lower bunk, draped in a blanket so that only his face pokes out. This is how he likes to be when there's thunder, the one thing that actually frightens him. My mother puts her box carefully in the cube. I crouch, my back supported by the wall, to check what Gale managed to rescue in my hunting bag. The plant book, the hunting jacket, my parents' wedding photo, and the personal contents of my drawer. My mockingjay pin now lives with Cinna's outfit, but there's the gold locket and the silver parachute with the spile and Peeta's pearl. I knot the pearl into the corner of the parachute, bury it deep in the recesses of the bag, as if it's Peeta's life and no one can take it away as long as I guard it.

The faint sound of the sirens cuts off sharply. Coin's voice comes over the district audio system, thanking us all for an exemplary evacuation of the upper levels. She stresses that this is not a drill, as Peeta Mellark, the District 12 victor, has possibly made a televised reference to an attack on 13 tonight.

That's when the first bomb hits. There's an initial sense of impact followed by an explosion that resonates in my innermost parts, the lining of my intestines, the marrow of my bones, the roots of my teeth. *We're all going to die,* I think. My eyes turn upward, expecting to see giant cracks race across the ceiling, massive chunks of stone raining down on us, but the bunker itself gives only a slight shudder. The lights go out and I experience the disorientation of total darkness. Speechless human sounds—spontaneous shrieks, ragged breaths, baby whimpers, one musical bit of insane laughter—dance around in the charged air. Then there's a hum of a generator, and a dim wavering glow replaces the stark lighting that is the norm in 13. It's closer to what we had in our homes in 12, when the candles and fire burned low on a winter's night.

I reach for Prim in the twilight, clamp my hand on her leg, and pull myself over to her. Her voice remains steady as she croons to Buttercup. "It's all right, baby, it's all right. We'll be okay down here."

My mother wraps her arms around us. I allow myself to feel young for a moment and rest my head on her shoulder. "That was nothing like the bombs in Eight," I say.

"Probably a bunker missile," says Prim, keeping her voice soothing for the cat's sake. "We learned about them during the orientation for new citizens. They're designed to penetrate deep in the ground before they go off. Because there's no point in bombing Thirteen on the surface anymore."

"Nuclear?" I ask, feeling a chill run through me.

"Not necessarily," says Prim. "Some just have a lot of explosives in them. But . . . it could be either kind, I guess."

The gloom makes it hard to see the heavy metal doors at the end of the bunker. Would they be any protection against a nuclear attack? And even if they were one hundred percent effective at sealing out the radiation, which is really unlikely, would we ever be able to leave this place? The thought of spending whatever remains of my life in this stone vault horrifies me. I want to run madly for the door and demand to be released into whatever lies above. It's pointless. They would never let me out, and I might start some kind of stampede.

"We're so far down, I'm sure we're safe," says my mother wanly. Is she thinking of my father's being blown to nothingness in the mines? "It was a close call, though. Thank goodness Peeta had the wherewithal to warn us."

The wherewithal. A general term that somehow includes everything that was needed for him to sound the alarm. The knowledge, the opportunity, the courage. And something else I can't define. Peeta seemed to have been waging a sort of battle in his mind, fighting to get the message out. Why? The ease with which he manipulates words is his greatest talent. Was his difficulty a result of his torture? Something more? Like madness?

Coin's voice, perhaps a shade grimmer, fills the bunker, the volume level flickering with the lights. "Apparently, Peeta Mellark's information was sound and we owe him a great debt of gratitude. Sensors indicate the first missile was not nuclear, but very powerful. We expect more will follow. For the duration of the attack, citizens are to stay in their assigned areas unless otherwise notified."

A soldier alerts my mother that she's needed in the first-aid station. She's reluctant to leave us, even though she'll only be thirty yards away.

"We'll be fine, really," I tell her. "Do you think anything could get past him?" I point to Buttercup, who gives me such a halfhearted hiss, we all have to laugh a little. Even I feel sorry for him. After my mother goes, I suggest, "Why don't you climb in with him, Prim?"

"I know it's silly . . . but I'm afraid the bunk might collapse on us during the attack," she says.

If the bunks collapse, the whole bunker will have given way and buried us, but I decide this kind of logic won't actually be helpful. Instead, I clean out the storage cube and make Buttercup a bed inside. Then I pull a mattress in front of it for my sister and me to share.

We're given clearance in small groups to use the bathroom and brush our teeth, although showering has been canceled for the day. I curl up with Prim on the mattress, double layering the blankets because the cavern emits a dank chill. Buttercup, miserable even with Prim's constant attention, huddles in the cube and exhales cat breath in my face.

Despite the disagreeable conditions, I'm glad to have time with my sister. My extreme preoccupation since I came here — no, since the first Games, really — has left little attention for her. I haven't been watching over her the way I should, the way I used to. After all, it was Gale who checked our compartment, not me. Something to make up for.

I realize I've never even bothered to ask her about how she's handling the shock of coming here. "So, how are you liking Thirteen, Prim?" I offer.

"Right now?" she asks. We both laugh. "I miss home badly sometimes. But then I remember there's nothing left to miss anymore. I feel safer here. We don't have to worry about you. Well, not the same way." She pauses, and then a shy smile crosses her lips. "I think they're going to train me to be a doctor."

It's the first I've heard of it. "Well, of course, they are. They'd be stupid not to."

"They've been watching me when I help out in the hospital. I'm already taking the medic courses. It's just beginner's stuff. I know a lot of it from home. Still, there's plenty to learn," she tells me.

"That's great," I say. Prim a doctor. She couldn't even dream of it in 12. Something small and quiet, like a match being struck, lights up the gloom inside me. This is the sort of future a rebellion could bring.

"What about you, Katniss? How are you managing?" Her fingertip moves in short, gentle strokes between Buttercup's eyes. "And don't say you're fine."

It's true. Whatever the opposite of fine is, that's what I am. So I go ahead and tell her about Peeta, his deterioration on-screen, and how I think they must be killing him at this very moment. Buttercup has to rely on himself for a while, because now Prim turns her attention to me. Pulling me closer, brushing the hair back behind my ears with her fingers. I've stopped talking because there's really nothing left to say and there's this piercing sort of pain where my heart is. Maybe I'm even having a heart attack, but it doesn't seem worth mentioning.

"Katniss, I don't think President Snow will kill Peeta," she says. Of course, she says this; it's what she thinks will calm me. But her next words come as a surprise. "If he does, he won't have anyone left you want. He won't have any way to hurt you."

Suddenly, I am reminded of another girl, one who had seen all the evil the Capitol had to offer. Johanna Mason, the tribute from District 7, in the last arena. I was trying to prevent her from going into the jungle where the jabberjays mimicked the voices of loved ones being tortured, but she brushed me off, saying, *"They can't hurt me. I'm not like the rest of you. There's no one left I love."*

Then I know Prim is right, that Snow cannot afford to waste Peeta's life, especially now, while the Mockingjay causes so much havoc. He's killed Cinna already. Destroyed my home. My family, Gale, and even Haymitch are out of his reach. Peeta's all he has left.

"So, what do you think they'll do to him?" I ask.

Prim sounds about a thousand years old when she speaks.

"Whatever it takes to break you."

11

What will break me?

This is the question that consumes me over the next three days as we wait to be released from our prison of safety. What will break me into a million pieces so that I am beyond repair, beyond usefulness? I mention it to no one, but it devours my waking hours and weaves itself throughout my nightmares.

Four more bunker missiles fall over this period, all massive, all very damaging, but there's no urgency to the attack. The bombs are spread out over the long hours so that just when you think the raid is over, another blast sends shock waves through your guts. It feels more designed to keep us in lockdown than to decimate 13. Cripple the district, yes. Give the people plenty to do to get the place running again. But destroy it? No. Coin was right on that point. You don't destroy what you want to acquire in the future. I assume what they really want, in the short term, is to stop the Airtime Assaults and keep me off the televisions of Panem.

We receive next to no information about what is happening. Our screens never come on, and we get only brief audio updates from Coin about the nature of the bombs. Certainly, the war is still being waged, but as to its status, we're in the dark.

Inside the bunker, cooperation is the order of the day. We adhere to a strict schedule for meals and bathing, exercise and sleep. Small periods of socialization are granted to alleviate the tedium. Our space becomes very popular because both children and adults have a fascination with Buttercup. He attains celebrity status with his evening game of Crazy Cat. I created this by accident a few years ago, during a winter blackout. You simply wiggle a flashlight beam around on the floor, and Buttercup tries to catch it. I'm petty enough to enjoy it because I think it makes him look stupid. Inexplicably, everyone here thinks he's clever and delightful. I'm even issued a special set of batteries — an enormous waste — to be used for this purpose. The citizens of 13 are truly starved for entertainment.

It's on the third night, during our game, that I answer the question eating away at me. Crazy Cat becomes a metaphor for my situation. I am Buttercup. Peeta, the thing I want so badly to secure, is the light. As long as Buttercup feels he has the chance of catching the elusive light under his paws, he's bristling with aggression. (That's how I've been since I left the arena, with Peeta alive.) When the light goes out completely, Buttercup's temporarily distraught and confused, but he recovers and moves on to other things. (That's what would happen if Peeta died.) But the one thing that sends Buttercup into a tailspin is when I leave the light on but put it hopelessly out of his reach, high on the wall, beyond even his jumping skills. He paces below the wall, wails, and can't be comforted or distracted. He's useless until I shut the light off. (That's what Snow is trying to do to me now, only I don't know what form his game takes.)

Maybe this realization on my part is all Snow needs. Thinking that Peeta was in his possession and being tortured for rebel information was bad. But thinking that he's being tortured specifically to incapacitate me is unendurable. And it's under the weight of this revelation that I truly begin to break.

After Crazy Cat, we're directed to bed. The power's been coming and going; sometimes the lamps burn at full brightness, other times we squint at one another in the brownouts. At bedtime they turn the lamps to near darkness and activate safety lights in each space. Prim, who's decided the walls will hold up, snuggles with Buttercup on the lower bunk. My mother's on the upper. I offer to take a bunk, but they make me keep to the floor mattress since I flail around so much when I'm sleeping.

I'm not flailing now, as my muscles are rigid with the tension of holding myself together. The pain over my heart returns, and from it I imagine tiny fissures spreading out into my body. Through my torso, down my arms and legs, over my face, leaving it crisscrossed with cracks. One good jolt of a bunker missile and I could shatter into strange, razor-sharp shards.

When the restless, wiggling majority has settled into sleep, I carefully extricate myself from my blanket and tiptoe through the cavern until I find Finnick, feeling for some unspecified reason that he will understand. He sits under the safety light in his space, knotting his rope, not even pretending to rest. As I whisper my discovery of Snow's plan to break me, it dawns on me. This strategy is very old news to Finnick. It's what broke him.

"This is what they're doing to you with Annie, isn't it?" I ask.

"Well, they didn't arrest her because they thought she'd be a wealth of rebel information," he says. "They know I'd never have risked telling her anything like that. For her own protection."

"Oh, Finnick. I'm so sorry," I say.

"No, I'm sorry. That I didn't warn you somehow," he tells me.

Suddenly, a memory surfaces. I'm strapped to my bed, mad with rage and grief after the rescue. Finnick is trying to console me about Peeta. *They'll figure out he doesn't know anything pretty fast. And they won't kill him if they think they can use him against you.*

"You did warn me, though. On the hovercraft. Only when you said they'd use Peeta against me, I thought you meant like bait. To lure me into the Capitol somehow," I say.

"I shouldn't have said even that. It was too late for it to be of any help to you. Since I hadn't warned you before the Quarter Quell, I should've shut up about how Snow operates." Finnick yanks on the end of his rope, and an intricate knot becomes a straight line again. "It's just that I didn't understand when I met you. After your first Games, I thought the whole romance was an act on your part. We all expected you'd continue that strategy. But it wasn't until Peeta hit the force field and nearly died that I—" Finnick hesitates.

I think back to the arena. How I sobbed when Finnick revived Peeta. The quizzical look on Finnick's face. The way he excused my behavior, blaming it on my pretend pregnancy. "That you what?"

"That I knew I'd misjudged you. That you do love him. I'm not saying in what way. Maybe you don't know yourself. But anyone paying attention could see how much you care about him," he says gently.

Anyone? On Snow's visit before the Victory Tour, he challenged me to erase any doubts of my love for Peeta. *"Convince* me," Snow said. It seems, under that hot pink sky with Peeta's life in limbo, I finally did. And in doing so, I gave him the weapon he needed to break me.

Finnick and I sit for a long time in silence, watching the knots bloom and vanish, before I can ask, "How do you bear it?"

Finnick looks at me in disbelief. "I don't, Katniss! Obviously, I don't. I drag myself out of nightmares each morning and find there's no relief in waking." Something in my expression stops him. "Better not to give in to it. It takes ten times as long to put yourself back together as it does to fall apart."

Well, he must know. I take a deep breath, forcing myself back into one piece.

"The more you can distract yourself, the better," he says. "First thing tomorrow, we'll get you your own rope. Until then, take mine."

I spend the rest of the night on my mattress obsessively making knots, holding them up for Buttercup's inspection.

If one looks suspicious, he swipes it out of the air and bites it a few times to make sure it's dead. By morning, my fingers are sore, but I'm still holding on.

With twenty-four hours of quiet behind us, Coin finally announces we can leave the bunker. Our old quarters have been destroyed by the bombings. Everyone must follow exact directions to their new compartments. We clean our spaces, as directed, and file obediently toward the door.

Before I'm halfway there, Boggs appears and pulls me from the line. He signals for Gale and Finnick to join us. People move aside to let us by. Some even smile at me since the Crazy Cat game seems to have made me more lovable. Out the door, up the stairs, down the hall to one of those multidirectional elevators, and finally we arrive at Special Defense. Nothing along our route has been damaged, but we are still very deep.

Boggs ushers us into a room virtually identical to Command. Coin, Plutarch, Haymitch, Cressida, and everybody else around the table looks exhausted. Someone has finally broken out the coffee — although I'm sure it's viewed only as an emergency stimulant — and Plutarch has both hands wrapped tightly around his cup as if at any moment it might be taken away.

There's no small talk. "We need all four of you suited up and aboveground," says the president. "You have two hours to get footage showing the damage from the bombing, establish that Thirteen's military unit remains not only functional but dominant, and, most important, that the Mockingjay is still alive. Any questions?"

"Can we have a coffee?" asks Finnick.

Steaming cups are handed out. I stare distastefully at the shiny black liquid, never having been much of a fan of the stuff, but thinking it might help me stay on my feet. Finnick sloshes some cream in my cup and reaches into the sugar bowl. "Want a sugar cube?" he asks in his old seductive voice. That's how we met, with Finnick offering me sugar. Surrounded by horses and chariots, costumed and painted for the crowds, before we were allies. Before I had any idea what made him tick. The memory actually coaxes a smile out of me. "Here, it improves the taste," he says in his real voice, plunking three cubes in my cup.

As I turn to go suit up as the Mockingjay, I catch Gale watching me and Finnick unhappily. What now? Does he actually think something's going on between us? Maybe he saw me go to Finnick's last night. I would've passed the Hawthornes' space to get there. I guess that probably rubbed him the wrong way. Me seeking out Finnick's company instead of his. Well, fine. I've got rope burn on my fingers, I can barely hold my eyes open, and a camera crew's waiting for me to do something brilliant. And Snow's got Peeta. Gale can think whatever he wants.

In my new Remake Room in Special Defense, my prep team slaps me into my Mockingjay suit, arranges my hair, and applies minimal makeup before my coffee's even cooled. In ten minutes, the cast and crew of the next propos are making the circuitous trek to the outside. I slurp my coffee as we travel, finding that the cream and sugar greatly enhance its flavor. As I knock back the dregs that have settled to the bottom of the cup, I feel a slight buzz start to run through my veins.

After climbing a final ladder, Boggs hits a lever that opens a trapdoor. Fresh air rushes in. I take big gulps and for the first time allow myself to feel how much I hated the bunker. We emerge into the woods, and my hands run through the leaves overhead. Some are just starting to turn. "What day is it?" I ask no one in particular. Boggs tells me September begins next week.

September. That means Snow has had Peeta in his clutches for five, maybe six weeks. I examine a leaf on my palm and see I'm shaking. I can't will myself to stop. I blame the coffee and try to focus on slowing my breathing, which is far too rapid for my pace.

Debris begins to litter the forest floor. We come to our first crater, thirty yards wide and I can't tell how deep. Very. Boggs says anyone on the first ten levels would likely have been killed. We skirt the pit and continue on.

"Can you rebuild it?" Gale asks.

"Not anytime soon. That one didn't get much. A few backup generators and a poultry farm," says Boggs. "We'll just seal it off."

The trees disappear as we enter the area inside the fence. The craters are ringed with a mixture of old and new rubble. Before the bombing, very little of the current 13 was aboveground. A few guard stations. The training area. About a foot of the top floor of our building—where

Buttercup's window jutted out—with several feet of steel on top of it. Even that was never meant to withstand more than a superficial attack.

"How much of an edge did the boy's warning give you?" asks Haymitch.

"About ten minutes before our own systems would've detected the missiles," says Boggs.

"But it did help, right?" I ask. I can't bear it if he says no.

"Absolutely," Boggs replies. "Civilian evacuation was completed. Seconds count when you're under attack. Ten minutes meant lives saved."

Prim, I think. *And Gale.* They were in the bunker only a couple of minutes before the first missile hit. Peeta might have saved them. Add their names to the list of things I can never stop owing him for.

Cressida has the idea to film me in front of the ruins of the old Justice Building, which is something of a joke since the Capitol's been using it as a backdrop for fake news broadcasts for years, to show that the district no longer existed. Now, with the recent attack, the Justice Building sits about ten yards away from the edge of a new crater.

As we approach what used to be the grand entrance, Gale points out something and the whole party slows down. I don't know what the problem is at first and then I see the ground strewn with fresh pink and red roses. "Don't touch them!" I yell. "They're for me!"

The sickeningly sweet smell hits my nose, and my heart begins to hammer against my chest. So I didn't imagine it. The rose on my dresser. Before me lies Snow's second delivery.

Long-stemmed pink and red beauties, the very flowers that decorated the set where Peeta and I performed our post-victory interview. Flowers not meant for one, but for a pair of lovers.

I explain to the others as best I can. Upon inspection, they appear to be harmless, if genetically enhanced, flowers. Two dozen roses. Slightly wilted. Most likely dropped after the last bombing. A crew in special suits collects them and carts them away. I feel certain they will find nothing extraordinary in them, though. Snow knows exactly what he's doing to me. It's like having Cinna beaten to a pulp while I watch from my tribute tube. Designed to unhinge me.

Like then, I try to rally and fight back. But as Cressida gets Castor and Pollux in place, I feel my anxiety building. I'm so tired, so wired, and so unable to keep my mind on anything but Peeta since I've seen the roses. The coffee was a huge mistake. What I didn't need was a stimulant. My body visibly shakes and I can't seem to catch my breath. After days in the bunker, I'm squinting no matter what direction I turn, and the light hurts. Even in the cool breeze, sweat trickles down my face.

"So, what exactly do you need from me again?" I ask.

"Just a few quick lines that show you're alive and still fighting," says Cressida.

"Okay." I take my position and then I'm staring into the red light. Staring. Staring. "I'm sorry, I've got nothing."

Cressida walks up to me. "You feeling okay?" I nod. She pulls a small cloth from her pocket and blots my face. "How about we do the old Q-and-A thing?"

"Yeah. That would help, I think." I cross my arms to hide the shaking. Glance at Finnick, who gives me a thumbs-up. But he's looking pretty shaky himself.

Cressida's back in position now. "So, Katniss. You've survived the Capitol bombing of Thirteen. How did it compare with what you experienced on the ground in Eight?"

"We were so far underground this time, there was no real danger. Thirteen's alive and well and so am—" My voice cuts off in a dry, squeaking sound.

"Try the line again," says Cressida. "'Thirteen's alive and well and so am I.'"

I take a breath, trying to force air down into my diaphragm. "Thirteen's alive and so—" No, that's wrong.

I swear I can still smell those roses.

"Katniss, just this one line and you're done today. I promise," says Cressida. "'Thirteen's alive and well and so am I.'"

I swing my arms to loosen myself up. Place my fists on my hips. Then drop them to my sides. Saliva's filling my mouth at a ridiculous rate and I feel vomit at the back of my throat. I swallow hard and open my lips so I can get the stupid line out and go hide in the woods and—that's when I start crying.

It's impossible to be the Mockingjay. Impossible to complete even this one sentence. Because now I know that everything I say will be directly taken out on Peeta. Result in his torture. But not his death, no, nothing so merciful as that. Snow will ensure that his life is much worse than death.

"Cut," I hear Cressida say quietly.

"What's wrong with her?" Plutarch says under his breath.

"She's figured out how Snow's using Peeta," says Finnick.

There's something like a collective sigh of regret from the semicircle of people spread out before me. Because I know this now. Because there will never be a way for me to not know this again. Because, beyond the military disadvantage losing a Mockingjay entails, I am broken.

Several sets of arms would embrace me. But in the end, the only person I truly want to comfort me is Haymitch, because he loves Peeta, too. I reach out for him and say something like his name and he's there, holding me and patting my back. "It's okay. It'll be okay, sweetheart." He sits me on a length of broken marble pillar and keeps an arm around me while I sob.

"I can't do this anymore," I say.

"I know," he says.

"All I can think of is — what he's going to do to Peeta — because I'm the Mockingjay!" I get out.

"I know." Haymitch's arm tightens around me.

"Did you see? How weird he acted? What are they — doing to him?" I'm gasping for air between sobs, but I manage one last phrase. "It's my fault!" And then I cross some line into hysteria and there's a needle in my arm and the world slips away.

It must be strong, whatever they shot into me, because it's a full day before I come to. My sleep wasn't peaceful, though. I have the sense of emerging from a world of dark, haunted places where I traveled alone. Haymitch sits in the chair by my bed, his skin waxen, his eyes bloodshot. I remember about Peeta and start to tremble again.

Haymitch reaches out and squeezes my shoulder. "It's all right. We're going to try to get Peeta out."

"What?" That makes no sense.

"Plutarch's sending in a rescue team. He has people on the inside. He thinks we can get Peeta back alive," he says.

"Why didn't we before?" I say.

"Because it's costly. But everyone agrees this is the thing to do. It's the same choice we made in the arena. To do whatever it takes to keep you going. We can't lose the Mockingjay now. And you can't perform unless you know Snow can't take it out on Peeta." Haymitch offers me a cup. "Here, drink something."

I slowly sit up and take a sip of water. "What do you mean, costly?"

He shrugs. "Covers will be blown. People may die. But keep in mind that they're dying every day. And it's not just Peeta; we're getting Annie out for Finnick, too."

"Where is he?" I ask.

"Behind that screen, sleeping his sedative off. He lost it right after we knocked you out," says Haymitch. I smile a little, feel a bit less weak. "Yeah, it was a really excellent shoot. You two cracked up and Boggs left to arrange the mission to get Peeta. We're officially in reruns."

"Well, if Boggs is leading it, that's a plus," I say.

"Oh, he's on top of it. It was volunteer only, but he pretended not to notice me waving my hand in the air," says Haymitch. "See? He's already demonstrated good judgment."

Something's wrong. Haymitch's trying a little too hard to cheer me up. It's not really his style. "So who else volunteered?"

"I think there were seven altogether," he says evasively.

I get a bad feeling in the pit of my stomach. "Who else, Haymitch?" I insist.

Haymitch finally drops the good-natured act. "You know who else, Katniss. You know who stepped up first."

Of course I do.

Gale.

12

Today I might lose both of them.

I try to imagine a world where both Gale's and Peeta's voices have ceased. Hands stilled. Eyes unblinking. I'm standing over their bodies, having a last look, leaving the room where they lie. But when I open the door to step out into the world, there's only a tremendous void. A pale gray nothingness that is all my future holds.

"Do you want me to have them sedate you until it's over?" asks Haymitch. He's not joking. This is a man who spent his adult life at the bottom of a bottle, trying to anesthetize himself against the Capitol's crimes. The sixteen-year-old boy who won the second Quarter Quell must have had people he loved — family, friends, a sweetheart maybe — that he fought to get back to. Where are they now? How is it that until Peeta and I were thrust upon him, there was no one at all in his life? What did Snow do to them?

"No," I say. "I want to go to the Capitol. I want to be part of the rescue mission."

"They're gone," says Haymitch.

"How long ago did they leave? I could catch up. I could—" What? What could I do?

Haymitch shakes his head. "It'll never happen. You're too valuable and too vulnerable. There was talk of sending you to another district to divert the Capitol's attention while the rescue takes place. But no one felt you could handle it."

"Please, Haymitch!" I'm begging now. "I have to do something. I can't just sit here waiting to hear if they died. There must be something I can do!"

"All right. Let me talk to Plutarch. You stay put." But I can't. Haymitch's footsteps are still echoing in the outer hall when I fumble my way through the slit in the dividing curtain to find Finnick sprawled out on his stomach, his hands twisted in his pillowcase. Although it's cowardly—cruel even—to rouse him from the shadowy, muted drug land to stark reality, I go ahead and do it because I can't stand to face this by myself.

As I explain our situation, his initial agitation mysteriously ebbs. "Don't you see, Katniss, this will decide things. One way or the other. By the end of the day, they'll either be dead or with us. It's . . . it's more than we could hope for!"

Well, that's a sunny view of our situation. And yet there's something calming about the idea that this torment could come to an end.

The curtain yanks back and there's Haymitch. He has a job for us, if we can pull it together. They still need post-bombing footage of 13. "If we can get it in the next few hours, Beetee can air it leading up to the rescue, and maybe keep the Capitol's attention elsewhere."

"Yes, a distraction," says Finnick. "A decoy of sorts."

"What we really need is something so riveting that even President Snow won't be able to tear himself away. Got anything like that?" asks Haymitch.

Having a job that might help the mission snaps me into focus. While I knock down breakfast and get prepped, I try to think of what I might say. President Snow must be wondering how that blood-splattered floor and his roses are affecting me. If he wants me broken, then I will have to be whole. But I don't think I will convince him of anything by shouting a couple of defiant lines at the camera. Besides, that won't buy the rescue team any time. Outbursts are short. It's stories that take time.

I don't know if it will work, but when the television crew's all assembled aboveground, I ask Cressida if she could start out by asking me about Peeta. I take a seat on the fallen marble pillar where I had my breakdown, wait for the red light and Cressida's question.

"How did you meet Peeta?" she asks.

And then I do the thing that Haymitch has wanted since my first interview. I open up. "When I met Peeta, I was eleven years old, and I was almost dead." I talk about that awful day when I tried to sell the baby clothes in the rain, how Peeta's mother chased me from the bakery door, and how he took a beating to bring me the loaves of bread that saved our lives. "We had never even spoken. The first time I ever talked to Peeta was on the train to the Games."

"But he was already in love with you," says Cressida.

"I guess so." I allow myself a small smile.

"How are you doing with the separation?" she asks.

"Not well. I know at any moment Snow could kill him. Especially since he warned Thirteen about the bombing. It's a terrible thing to live with," I say. "But because of what they're putting him through, I don't have any reservations anymore. About doing whatever it takes to destroy the Capitol. I'm finally free." I turn my gaze skyward and watch the flight of a hawk across the sky. "President Snow once admitted to me that the Capitol was fragile. At the time, I didn't know what he meant. It was hard to see clearly because I was so afraid. Now I'm not. The Capitol's fragile because it depends on the districts for everything. Food, energy, even the Peacekeepers that police us. If we declare our freedom, the Capitol collapses. President Snow, thanks to you, I'm officially declaring mine today."

I've been sufficient, if not dazzling. Everyone loves the bread story. But it's my message to President Snow that gets the wheels spinning in Plutarch's brain. He hastily calls Finnick and Haymitch over and they have a brief but intense conversation that I can see Haymitch isn't happy with. Plutarch seems to win — Finnick's pale but nodding his head by the end of it.

As Finnick moves to take my seat before the camera, Haymitch tells him, "You don't have to do this."

"Yes, I do. If it will help her." Finnick balls up his rope in his hand. "I'm ready."

I don't know what to expect. A love story about Annie? An account of the abuses in District 4? But Finnick Odair takes a completely different tack.

"President Snow used to . . . sell me . . . my body, that is," Finnick begins in a flat, removed tone. "I wasn't the only one. If a victor is considered desirable, the president gives them as a reward or allows people to buy them for an exorbitant amount of money. If you refuse, he kills someone you love. So you do it."

That explains it, then. Finnick's parade of lovers in the Capitol. They were never real lovers. Just people like our old Head Peacekeeper, Cray, who bought desperate girls to devour and discard because he could. I want to interrupt the taping and beg Finnick's forgiveness for every false thought I've ever had about him. But we have a job to do, and I sense Finnick's role will be far more effective than mine.

"I wasn't the only one, but I was the most popular," he says. "And perhaps the most defenseless, because the people I loved were so defenseless. To make themselves feel better, my patrons would make presents of money or jewelry, but I found a much more valuable form of payment."

Secrets, I think. That's what Finnick told me his lovers paid him in, only I thought the whole arrangement was by his choice.

"Secrets," he says, echoing my thoughts. "And this is where you're going to want to stay tuned, President Snow, because so very many of them were about you. But let's begin with some of the others."

Finnick begins to weave a tapestry so rich in detail that you can't doubt its authenticity. Tales of strange sexual appetites, betrayals of the heart, bottomless greed, and bloody power plays. Drunken secrets whispered over damp pillowcases in the dead of night. Finnick was someone bought and sold. A district slave. A handsome one, certainly, but in reality, harmless. Who would he tell? And who would believe him if he did? But some secrets are too delicious not to share. I don't know the people Finnick names — all seem to be prominent Capitol citizens — but I know, from listening to the chatter of my prep team, the attention the most mild slip in judgment can draw. If a bad haircut can lead to hours of gossip, what will charges of incest, backstabbing, blackmail, and arson produce? Even as the waves of shock and recrimination roll over the Capitol, the people there will be waiting, as I am now, to hear about the president.

"And now, on to our good President Coriolanus Snow," says Finnick. "Such a young man when he rose to power. Such a clever one to keep it. How, you must ask yourself, did he do it? One word. That's all you really need to know. *Poison.*" Finnick goes back to Snow's political ascension, which I know nothing of, and works his way up to the present, pointing out case after case of the mysterious deaths of Snow's adversaries or, even worse, his allies who had the potential to become threats. People dropping dead at a feast or slowly, inexplicably declining into shadows over a period of months. Blamed on bad shellfish, elusive viruses, or an overlooked weakness in the aorta. Snow drinking from the poisoned cup himself to deflect suspicion. But antidotes don't always work. They say that's why he wears the roses that reek of perfume. They say it's to cover the scent of blood from the mouth sores that will never heal. They say, they say, they say . . . Snow has a list and no one knows who will be next.

Poison. The perfect weapon for a snake.

Since my opinion of the Capitol and its noble president are already so low, I can't say Finnick's allegations shock me. They seem to have far more effect on the displaced Capitol rebels like my crew and Fulvia—even Plutarch occasionally reacts in surprise, maybe wondering how a specific tidbit passed him by. When Finnick finishes, they just keep the cameras rolling until finally he has to be the one to say "Cut."

The crew hurries inside to edit the material, and Plutarch leads Finnick off for a chat, probably to see if he has any more stories. I'm left with Haymitch in the rubble, wondering if Finnick's fate would have one day been mine. Why not? Snow could have gotten a really good price for the girl on fire.

"Is that what happened to you?" I ask Haymitch.

"No. My mother and younger brother. My girl. They were all dead two weeks after I was crowned victor. Because of that stunt I pulled with the force field," he answers. "Snow had no one to use against me."

"I'm surprised he didn't just kill you," I say.

"Oh, no. I was the example. The person to hold up to the young Finnicks and Johannas and Cashmeres. Of what could happen to a victor who caused problems," says Haymitch. "But he knew he had no leverage against me."

"Until Peeta and I came along," I say softly. I don't even get a shrug in return.

With our job done, there's nothing left for Finnick and me to do but wait. We try to fill the dragging minutes in Special Defense. Tie knots. Push our lunch around our bowls. Blow things up on the shooting range. Because of the danger of detection, no communication comes from the rescue team. At 15:00, the designated hour, we stand tense and silent in the back of a room full of screens and computers and watch Beetee and his team try to dominate the airwaves. His usual fidgety distraction is replaced with a determination I have never seen. Most of my interview doesn't make the cut, just enough to show I am alive and still defiant. It is Finnick's salacious and gory account of the Capitol that takes the day. Is Beetee's skill improving? Or are his counterparts in the Capitol a little too fascinated to want to tune Finnick out? For the next sixty minutes, the Capitol feed alternates between the standard afternoon newscast, Finnick, and attempts to black it all out. But the rebel techno team manages to override even the latter and, in a real coup, keeps control for almost the entire attack on Snow.

"Let it go!" says Beetee, throwing up his hands, relinquishing the broadcast back to the Capitol. He mops his face with a cloth. "If they're not out of there by now, they're all dead." He spins in his chair to see Finnick and me reacting to his words. "It was a good plan, though. Did Plutarch show it to you?"

Of course not. Beetee takes us to another room and shows us how the team, with the help of rebel insiders, will attempt—has attempted—to free the victors from an underground prison. It seems to have involved knockout gas distributed by the ventilation system, a power failure, the detonation of a bomb in a government building several miles from the prison, and now the disruption of the broadcast. Beetee's glad we find the plan hard to follow, because then our enemies will, too.

"Like your electricity trap in the arena?" I ask.

"Exactly. And see how well that worked out?" says Beetee.

Well . . . not really, I think.

Finnick and I try to station ourselves in Command, where surely first word of the rescue will come, but we are barred because serious war business is being carried out. We refuse to leave Special Defense and end up waiting in the hummingbird room for news.

Making knots. Making knots. No word. Making knots. Tick-tock. This is a clock. Do not think of Gale. Do not think of Peeta. Making knots. We do not want dinner. Fingers raw and bleeding. Finnick finally gives up and assumes the hunched position he took in the arena when the jabberjays attacked. I perfect my miniature noose. The words of "The Hanging Tree" replay in my head. Gale and Peeta. Peeta and Gale.

"Did you love Annie right away, Finnick?" I ask.

"No." A long time passes before he adds, "She crept up on me."

I search my heart, but at the moment the only person I can feel creeping up on me is Snow.

It must be midnight, it must be tomorrow when Haymitch pushes open the door. "They're back. We're wanted in the hospital." My mouth opens with a flood of questions that he cuts off with "That's all I know."

I want to run, but Finnick's acting so strange, as if he's lost the ability to move, so I take his hand and lead him like a small child. Through Special Defense, into the elevator that goes this way and that, and on to the hospital wing. The place is in an uproar, with doctors shouting orders and the wounded being wheeled through the halls in their beds.

We're sideswiped by a gurney bearing an unconscious, emaciated young woman with a shaved head. Her flesh shows bruises and oozing scabs. Johanna Mason. Who actually knew rebel secrets. At least the one about me. And this is how she has paid for it.

Through a doorway, I catch a glimpse of Gale, stripped to the waist, perspiration streaming down his face as a doctor removes something from under his shoulder blade with a long pair of tweezers. Wounded, but alive. I call his name, start toward him until a nurse pushes me back and shuts me out.

"Finnick!" Something between a shriek and a cry of joy. A lovely if somewhat bedraggled young woman — dark tangled hair, sea green eyes — runs toward us in nothing but a sheet. "Finnick!" And suddenly, it's as if there's no one in the world but these two, crashing through space to reach

each other. They collide, enfold, lose their balance, and slam against a wall, where they stay. Clinging into one being. Indivisible.

A pang of jealousy hits me. Not for either Finnick or Annie but for their certainty. No one seeing them could doubt their love.

Boggs, looking a little worse for wear but uninjured, finds Haymitch and me. "We got them all out. Except Enobaria. But since she's from Two, we doubt she's being held anyway. Peeta's at the end of the hall. The effects of the gas are just wearing off. You should be there when he wakes."

Peeta.

Alive and well—maybe not well but alive and here. Away from Snow. Safe. Here. With me. In a minute I can touch him. See his smile. Hear his laugh.

Haymitch's grinning at me. "Come on, then," he says.

I'm light-headed with giddiness. What will I say? Oh, who cares what I say? Peeta will be ecstatic no matter what I do. He'll probably be kissing me anyway. I wonder if it will feel like those last kisses on the beach in the arena, the ones I haven't dared let myself consider until this moment.

Peeta's awake already, sitting on the side of the bed, looking bewildered as a trio of doctors reassure him, flash lights in his eyes, check his pulse. I'm disappointed that mine was not the first face he saw when he woke, but he sees it now. His features register disbelief and something more intense that I can't quite place. Desire? Desperation? Surely both, for he sweeps the doctors aside, leaps to his feet, and moves toward me. I run to meet him, my arms extended to embrace him. His hands are reaching for me, too, to caress my face, I think.

My lips are just forming his name when his fingers lock around my throat.

13

The cold collar chafes my neck and makes the shivering even harder to control. At least I am no longer in the claustrophobic tube, while the machines click and whir around me, listening to a disembodied voice telling me to hold still while I try to convince myself I can still breathe. Even now, when I've been assured there will be no permanent damage, I hunger for air.

The medical team's main concerns — damage to my spinal cord, airway, veins, and arteries — have been allayed. Bruising, hoarseness, the sore larynx, this strange little cough — not to be worried about. It will all be fine. The Mockingjay will not lose her voice. Where, I want to ask, is the doctor who determines if I am losing my mind? Only I'm not supposed to talk right now. I can't even thank Boggs when he comes to check on me. To look me over and tell me he's seen a lot worse injuries among the soldiers when they teach choke holds in training.

It was Boggs who knocked out Peeta with one blow before any permanent damage could be done. I know Haymitch would have come to my defense if he hadn't been utterly unprepared. To catch both Haymitch and myself off guard is a rare thing. But we have been so consumed with saving Peeta, so tortured by having him in the Capitol's hands, that the elation at having him back blinded us. If I'd had a private reunion with Peeta, he would have killed me. Now that he's deranged.

No, not deranged, I remind myself. *Hijacked.* That's the word I heard pass between Plutarch and Haymitch as I was wheeled past them in the hallway. *Hijacked.* I don't know what it means.

Prim, who appeared moments after the attack and has stayed as close to me as possible ever since, spreads another blanket over me. "I think they'll take the collar off soon, Katniss. You won't be so cold then." My mother, who's been assisting in a complicated surgery, has still not been informed of Peeta's assault. Prim takes one of my hands, which is clutched in a fist, and massages it until it opens and blood begins to flow through my fingers again. She's starting on the second fist when the doctors show up, remove the collar, and give me a shot of something for pain and swelling. I lie, as instructed, with my head still, not aggravating the injuries to my neck.

Plutarch, Haymitch, and Beetee have been waiting in the hall for the doctors to give them clearance to see me. I don't know if they've told Gale, but since he's not here, I assume they haven't. Plutarch ushers the doctors out and tries to order Prim to go as well, but she says, "No. If you force me to leave, I'll go directly to surgery and tell my mother everything that's happened. And I warn you, she doesn't think much of a Gamemaker calling the shots on Katniss's life. Especially when you've taken such poor care of her."

Plutarch looks offended, but Haymitch chuckles. "I'd let it go, Plutarch," he says. Prim stays.

"So, Katniss, Peeta's condition has come as a shock to all of us," says Plutarch. "We couldn't help but notice his deterioration in the last two interviews. Obviously, he'd been abused, and we put his psychological state down to that. Now we believe something more was going on. That the Capitol has been subjecting him to a rather uncommon technique known as hijacking. Beetee?"

"I'm sorry," Beetee says, "but I can't tell you all the specifics of it, Katniss. The Capitol's very secretive about this form of torture, and I believe the results are inconsistent. This we do know. It's a type of fear conditioning. The term *hijack* comes from an old English word that means 'to capture,' or even better, 'seize.' We believe it was chosen because the technique involves the use of tracker jacker venom, and the *jack* suggested *hijack*. You were stung in your first Hunger Games, so unlike most of us, you have firsthand knowledge of the effects of the venom."

Terror. Hallucinations. Nightmarish visions of losing those I love. Because the venom targets the part of the brain that houses fear.

"I'm sure you remember how frightening it was. Did you also suffer mental confusion in the aftermath?" asks Beetee. "A sense of being unable to judge what was true and what was false? Most people who have been stung and lived to tell about it report something of the kind."

Yes. That encounter with Peeta. Even after I was

clearheaded, I wasn't sure if he had saved my life by taking on Cato or if I'd imagined it.

"Recall is made more difficult because memories can be changed." Beetee taps his forehead. "Brought to the forefront of your mind, altered, and saved again in the revised form. Now imagine that I ask you to remember something — either with a verbal suggestion or by making you watch a tape of the event — and while that experience is refreshed, I give you a dose of tracker jacker venom. Not enough to induce a three-day blackout. Just enough to infuse the memory with fear and doubt. And that's what your brain puts in long-term storage."

I start to feel sick. Prim asks the question that's in my mind. "Is that what they've done to Peeta? Taken his memories of Katniss and distorted them so they're scary?"

Beetee nods. "So scary that he'd see her as life-threatening. That he might try to kill her. Yes, that's our current theory."

I cover my face with my arms because this isn't happening. It isn't possible. For someone to make Peeta forget he loves me . . . no one could do that.

"But you can reverse it, right?" asks Prim.

"Um . . . very little data on that," says Plutarch. "None, really. If hijacking rehabilitation has been attempted before, we have no access to those records."

"Well, you're going to try, aren't you?" Prim persists. "You're not just going to lock him up in some padded room and leave him to suffer?"

"Of course, we'll try, Prim," says Beetee. "It's just, we don't know to what degree we'll succeed. If any. My guess is that fearful events are the hardest to root out. They're the ones we naturally remember the best, after all."

"And apart from his memories of Katniss, we don't yet know what else has been tampered with," says Plutarch. "We're putting together a team of mental health and military professionals to come up with a counterattack. I, personally, feel optimistic that he'll make a full recovery."

"Do you?" asks Prim caustically. "And what do *you* think, Haymitch?"

I shift my arms slightly so I can see his expression through the crack. He's exhausted and discouraged as he admits, "I think Peeta might get somewhat better. But . . . I don't think he'll ever be the same." I snap my arms back together, closing the crack, shutting them all out.

"At least he's alive," says Plutarch, as if he's losing patience with the lot of us. "Snow executed Peeta's stylist and his prep team on live television tonight. We've no idea what happened to Effie Trinket. Peeta's damaged, but he's here. With us. And that's a definite improvement over his situation twelve hours ago. Let's keep that in mind, all right?"

Plutarch's attempt to cheer me up — laced with the news of another four, possibly five, murders — somehow backfires. Portia. Peeta's prep team. Effie. The effort to fight back tears makes my throat throb until I'm gasping again. Eventually, they have no choice but to sedate me.

When I wake, I wonder if this will be the only way I sleep now, with drugs shot into my arm. I'm glad I'm not supposed to talk for the next few days, because there's nothing I want to say. Or do. In fact, I'm a model patient, my lethargy taken for restraint, obedience to the doctors' orders. I no longer feel like crying. In fact, I can only manage to hold on to one simple thought: an image of Snow's face accompanied by the whisper in my head. *I will kill you.*

My mother and Prim take turns nursing me, coaxing me to swallow bites of soft food. People come in periodically to give me updates on Peeta's condition. The high levels of tracker jacker venom are working their way out of his body. He's being treated only by strangers, natives of 13 — no one from home or the Capitol has been allowed to see him — to keep any dangerous memories from triggering. A team of specialists works long hours designing a strategy for his recovery.

Gale's not supposed to visit me, as he's confined to bed with some kind of shoulder wound. But on the third night, after I've been medicated and the lights turned down low for bedtime, he slips silently into my room. He doesn't speak, just runs his fingers over the bruises on my neck with a touch as light as moth wings, plants a kiss between my eyes, and disappears.

The next morning, I'm discharged from the hospital with instructions to move quietly and speak only when necessary. I'm not imprinted with a schedule, so I wander around aimlessly until Prim's excused from her hospital duties to take me to our family's latest compartment. 2212. Identical to the last one, but with no window.

Buttercup has now been issued a daily food allowance and a pan of sand that's kept under the bathroom sink. As

Prim tucks me into bed, he hops up on my pillow, vying for her attention. She cradles him but stays focused on me. "Katniss, I know this whole thing with Peeta is terrible for you. But remember, Snow worked on him for weeks, and we've only had him for a few days. There's a chance that the old Peeta, the one who loves you, is still inside. Trying to get back to you. Don't give up on him."

I look at my little sister and think how she has inherited the best qualities our family has to offer: my mother's healing hands, my father's level head, and my fight. There's something else there as well, something entirely her own. An ability to look into the confusing mess of life and see things for what they are. Is it possible she could be right? That Peeta could return to me?

"I have to get back to the hospital," Prim says, placing Buttercup on the bed beside me. "You two keep each other company, okay?"

Buttercup springs off the bed and follows her to the door, complaining loudly when he's left behind. We're about as much company for each other as dirt. After maybe thirty seconds, I know I can't stand being confined in the subterranean cell, and leave Buttercup to his own devices. I get lost several times, but eventually I make my way down to Special Defense. Everyone I pass stares at the bruises, and I can't help feeling self-conscious to the point that I tug my collar up to my ears.

Gale must have been released from the hospital this morning as well, because I find him in one of the research rooms with Beetee. They're immersed, heads bent over a drawing, taking a measurement. Versions of the picture litter the table and floor. Tacked on the corkboard walls and occupying several computer screens are other designs of some sort. In the rough lines of one, I recognize Gale's twitch-up snare. "What are these?" I ask hoarsely, pulling their attention from the sheet.

"Ah, Katniss, you've found us out," says Beetee cheerfully.

"What? Is this a secret?" I know Gale's been down here working with Beetee a lot, but I assumed they were messing around with bows and guns.

"Not really. But I've felt a little guilty about it. Stealing Gale away from you so much," Beetee admits.

Since I've spent most of my time in 13 disoriented, worried, angry, being remade, or hospitalized, I can't say Gale's absences have inconvenienced me. Things haven't been exactly harmonious between us, either. But I let Beetee think he owes me. "I hope you've been putting his time to good use."

"Come and see," he says, waving me over to a computer screen.

This is what they've been doing. Taking the fundamental ideas behind Gale's traps and adapting them into weapons against humans. Bombs mostly. It's less about the mechanics of the traps than the psychology behind them. Booby-trapping an area that provides something essential to survival. A water or food supply. Frightening prey so that a large number flee into a greater destruction. Endangering offspring in order to draw in the actual desired target, the parent.

Luring the victim into what appears to be a safe haven — where death awaits it. At some point, Gale and Beetee left the wilderness behind and focused on more human impulses. Like compassion. A bomb explodes. Time is allowed for people to rush to the aid of the wounded. Then a second, more powerful bomb kills them as well.

"That seems to be crossing some kind of line," I say. "So anything goes?" They both stare at me — Beetee with doubt, Gale with hostility. "I guess there isn't a rule book for what might be unacceptable to do to another human being."

"Sure there is. Beetee and I have been following the same rule book President Snow used when he hijacked Peeta," says Gale.

Cruel, but to the point. I leave without further comment. I feel if I don't get outside immediately, I'll just go ballistic, but I'm still in Special Defense when I'm waylaid by Haymitch. "Come on," he says. "We need you back up at the hospital."

"What for?" I ask.

"They're going to try something on Peeta," he answers. "Send in the most innocuous person from Twelve they can come up with. Find someone Peeta might share childhood memories with, but nothing too close to you. They're screening people now."

I know this will be a difficult task, since anyone Peeta shares childhood memories with would most likely be from town, and almost none of those people escaped the flames. But when we reach the hospital room that has been turned into a work space for Peeta's recovery team, there she sits chatting with Plutarch. Delly Cartwright. As always, she gives me a smile that suggests I'm her best friend in the world. She gives this smile to everyone. "Katniss!" she calls out.

"Hey, Delly," I say. I'd heard she and her younger brother had survived. Her parents, who ran the shoe shop in town, weren't as lucky. She looks older, wearing the drab 13 clothes that flatter no one, with her long yellow hair in a practical braid instead of curls. Delly's a bit thinner than I remember, but she was one of the few kids in District 12 with a couple of pounds to spare. The diet here, the stress, the grief of losing her parents have all, no doubt, contributed. "How are you doing?" I ask.

"Oh, it's been a lot of changes all at once." Her eyes fill with tears. "But everyone's really nice here in Thirteen, don't you think?"

Delly means it. She genuinely likes people. All people, not just a select few she's spent years making up her mind about.

"They've made an effort to make us feel welcome," I say. I think that's a fair statement without going overboard. "Are you the one they've picked to see Peeta?"

"I guess so. Poor Peeta. Poor *you*. I'll never understand the Capitol," she says.

"Better not to, maybe," I tell her.

"Delly's known Peeta for a long time," says Plutarch.

"Oh, yes!" Delly's face brightens. "We played together from when we were little. I used to tell people he was my brother."

"What do you think?" Haymitch asks me. "Anything that might trigger memories of you?"

"We were all in the same class. But we never overlapped much," I say.

"Katniss was always so amazing, I never dreamed she would notice me," says Delly. "The way she could hunt and go in the Hob and everything. Everyone admired her so."

Haymitch and I both have to take a hard look at her face to double-check if she's joking. To hear Delly describe it, I had next to no friends because I intimidated people by being so exceptional. Not true. I had next to no friends because I wasn't friendly. Leave it to Delly to spin me into something wonderful.

"Delly always thinks the best of everyone," I explain. "I don't think Peeta could have bad memories associated with her." Then I remember. "Wait. In the Capitol. When I lied about recognizing the Avox girl. Peeta covered for me and said she looked like Delly."

"I remember," says Haymitch. "But I don't know. It wasn't true. Delly wasn't actually there. I don't think it can compete with years of childhood memories."

"Especially with such a pleasant companion as Delly," says Plutarch. "Let's give it a shot."

Plutarch, Haymitch, and I go to the observation room next to where Peeta's confined. It's crowded with ten members of his recovery team armed with pens and clipboards. The one-way glass and audio setup allow us to watch Peeta secretly. He lies on the bed, his arms strapped down. He doesn't fight the restraints, but his hands fidget continuously. His expression seems more lucid than when he tried to strangle me, but it's still not one that belongs to him.

When the door quietly opens, his eyes widen in alarm, then become confused. Delly crosses the room tentatively, but as she nears him she naturally breaks into a smile. "Peeta? It's Delly. From home."

"Delly?" Some of the clouds seem to clear. "Delly. It's you."

"Yes!" she says with obvious relief. "How do you feel?"

"Awful. Where are we? What's happened?" asks Peeta.

"Here we go," says Haymitch.

"I told her to steer clear of any mention of Katniss or the Capitol," says Plutarch. "Just see how much of home she could conjure up."

"Well . . . we're in District Thirteen. We live here now," says Delly.

"That's what those people have been saying. But it makes no sense. Why aren't we home?" asks Peeta.

Delly bites her lip. "There was . . . an accident. I miss home badly, too. I was only just thinking about those chalk drawings we used to do on the paving stones. Yours were so wonderful. Remember when you made each one a different animal?"

"Yeah. Pigs and cats and things," says Peeta. "You said . . . about an accident?"

I can see the sheen of sweat on Delly's forehead as she tries to work around the question. "It was bad. No one . . . could stay," she says haltingly.

"Hang in there, girl," says Haymitch.

"But I know you're going to like it here, Peeta. The people have been really nice to us. There's always food and clean clothes, and school's much more interesting," says Delly.

"Why hasn't my family come to see me?" Peeta asks.

"They can't." Delly's tearing up again. "A lot of people didn't get out of Twelve. So we'll need to make a new life here. I'm sure they could use a good baker. Do you remember when your father used to let us make dough girls and boys?"

"There was a fire," Peeta says suddenly.

"Yes," she whispers.

"Twelve burned down, didn't it? Because of her," says Peeta angrily. "Because of Katniss!" He begins to pull on the restraints.

"Oh, no, Peeta. It wasn't her fault," says Delly.

"Did she tell you that?" he hisses at her.

"Get her out of there," says Plutarch. The door opens immediately and Delly begins to back toward it slowly.

"She didn't have to. I was—" Delly begins.

"Because she's lying! She's a liar! You can't believe anything she says! She's some kind of mutt the Capitol created to use against the rest of us!" Peeta shouts.

"No, Peeta. She's not a—" Delly tries again.

"Don't trust her, Delly," says Peeta in a frantic voice. "I did, and she tried to kill me. She killed my friends. My family. Don't even go near her! She's a mutt!"

A hand reaches through the doorway, pulls Delly out, and the door swings shut. But Peeta keeps yelling. "A mutt! She's a stinking mutt!"

Not only does he hate me and want to kill me, he no longer believes I'm human. It was less painful being strangled.

Around me the recovery team members scribble like crazy, taking down every word. Haymitch and Plutarch grab my arms and propel me out of the room. They lean me up against a wall in the silent hallway. But I know Peeta continues to scream behind the door and the glass.

Prim was wrong. Peeta is irretrievable. "I can't stay here anymore," I say numbly. "If you want me to be the Mockingjay, you'll have to send me away."

"Where do you want to go?" asks Haymitch.

"The Capitol." It's the only place I can think of where I have a job to do.

"Can't do it," Plutarch says. "Not until all the districts are secure. Good news is, the fighting's almost over in all of them but Two. It's a tough nut to crack, though."

That's right. First the districts. Next the Capitol. And then I hunt down Snow.

"Fine," I say. "Send me to Two."

District 2 is a large district, as one might expect, composed of a series of villages spread across the mountains. Each was originally associated with a mine or quarry, although now, many are devoted to the housing and training of Peacekeepers. None of this would present much of a challenge, since the rebels have 13's airpower on their side, except for one thing: At the center of the district is a virtually impenetrable mountain that houses the heart of the Capitol's military.

We've nicknamed the mountain the Nut since I relayed Plutarch's "tough nut to crack" comment to the weary and discouraged rebel leaders here. The Nut was established directly after the Dark Days, when the Capitol had lost 13 and was desperate for a new underground stronghold. They had some of their military resources situated on the outskirts of the Capitol itself—nuclear missiles, aircraft, troops—but a significant chunk of their power was now under an enemy's control. Of course, there was no way they could hope to replicate 13, which was the work of centuries. However, in the old mines of nearby District 2, they saw opportunity. From the air, the Nut appeared to be just another mountain with a few entrances on its faces. But inside were vast cavernous spaces where slabs of stones had been cut, hauled to the surface, and transported down slippery narrow roads to make distant buildings. There was even a train system to facilitate transporting the miners from the Nut to the very center of the main town in District 2. It ran right to the square that Peeta and I visited during the Victory Tour, standing on the wide marble steps of the Justice Building, trying not to look too closely at Cato's and Clove's grieving families assembled below us.

It was not the most ideal terrain, plagued as it was by mudslides, floods, and avalanches. But the advantages outweighed the concerns. As they'd cut deep into the mountain, the miners had left large pillars and walls of stone to support the infrastructure. The Capitol reinforced these and set about making the mountain their new military base. Filling it with computer banks and meeting rooms, barracks and arsenals. Widening entrances to allow the exit of hovercraft from the hangar, installing missile launchers. But on the whole, leaving the exterior of the mountain largely unchanged. A rough, rocky tangle of trees and wildlife. A natural fortress to protect them from their enemies.

By the other districts' standards, the Capitol babied the inhabitants here. Just by looking at the District 2 rebels, you can tell they were decently fed and cared for in childhood. Some did end up as quarry and mine workers. Others were educated for jobs in the Nut or funneled into the ranks of Peacekeepers. Trained young and hard for combat. The Hunger Games were an opportunity for wealth and a kind of glory not seen elsewhere. Of course, the people of 2 swallowed the Capitol's propaganda more easily than the rest of us. Embraced their ways. But for all that, at the end of the day, they were still slaves. And if that was lost on the citizens who became Peacekeepers or worked in the Nut, it was not lost on the stonecutters who formed the backbone of the resistance here.

Things stand as they did when I arrived two weeks ago. The outer villages are in rebel hands, the town divided, and the Nut is as untouchable as ever. Its few entrances heavily fortified, its heart safely enfolded in the mountain. While every other district has now wrested control from the Capitol, 2 remains in its pocket.

Each day, I do whatever I can to help. Visit the wounded. Tape short propos with my camera crew. I'm not allowed in actual combat, but they invite me to the meetings on the status of the war, which is a lot more than they did in 13. It's much better here. Freer, no schedules on my arm, fewer demands on my time. I live aboveground in the rebel villages or surrounding caves. For safety's sake, I'm relocated often. During the day, I've been given clearance to hunt as long as I take a guard along and don't stray too far. In the thin, cold mountain air, I feel some physical strength returning, my mind clearing away the rest of the fogginess. But with this mental clarity comes an even sharper awareness of what has been done to Peeta.

Snow has stolen him from me, twisted him beyond recognition, and made me a present of him. Boggs, who came to 2 when I did, told me that even with all the plotting, it was a little too easy to rescue Peeta. He believes if 13 hadn't made the effort, Peeta would've been delivered to me anyway.

Dropped off in an actively warring district or perhaps 13 itself. Tied up with ribbons and tagged with my name. Programmed to murder me.

It's only now that he's been corrupted that I can fully appreciate the real Peeta. Even more than I would've if he'd died. The kindness, the steadiness, the warmth that had an unexpected heat behind it. Outside of Prim, my mother, and Gale, how many people in the world love me unconditionally? I think in my case, the answer may now be none. Sometimes when I'm alone, I take the pearl from where it lives in my pocket and try to remember the boy with the bread, the strong arms that warded off nightmares on the train, the kisses in the arena. To make myself put a name to the thing I've lost. But what's the use? It's gone. He's gone. Whatever existed between us is gone. All that's left is my promise to kill Snow. I tell myself this ten times a day.

Back in 13, Peeta's rehabilitation continues. Even though I don't ask, Plutarch gives me cheerful updates on the phone like "Good news, Katniss! I think we've almost got him convinced you're not a mutt!" Or "Today he was allowed to feed himself pudding!"

When Haymitch gets on after, he admits Peeta's no better. The only dubious ray of hope has come from my sister. "Prim came up with the idea of trying to hijack him back," Haymitch tells me. "Bring up the distorted memories of you and then give him a big dose of a calming drug, like morphling. We've only tried it on one memory. The tape of the two of you in the cave, when you told him that story about getting Prim the goat."

"Any improvement?" I ask.

"Well, if extreme confusion is an improvement over extreme terror, then yes," says Haymitch. "But I'm not sure it is. He lost the ability to speak for several hours. Went into some sort of stupor. When he came out, the only thing he asked about was the goat."

"Right," I say.

"How's it out there?" he asks.

"No forward motion," I tell him.

"We're sending out a team to help with the mountain. Beetee and some of the others," he says. "You know, the brains."

When the brains are selected, I'm not surprised to see Gale's name on the list. I thought Beetee would bring him, not for his technological expertise, but in the hopes that he could somehow think of a way to ensnare a mountain. Originally, Gale offered to come with me to 2, but I could see I was tearing him away from his work with Beetee. I told him to sit tight and stay where he was most needed. I didn't tell him his presence would make it even more difficult for me to mourn Peeta.

Gale finds me when they arrive late one afternoon. I'm sitting on a log at the edge of my current village, plucking a goose. A dozen or so of the birds are piled at my feet. Great flocks of them have been migrating through here since I've arrived, and the pickings are easy. Without a word, Gale settles beside me and begins to relieve a bird of its feathers. We're through about half when he says, "Any chance we'll get to eat these?"

"Yeah. Most go to the camp kitchen, but they expect me to give a couple to whoever I'm staying with tonight," I say. "For keeping me."

"Isn't the honor of the thing enough?" he says.

"You'd think," I reply. "But word's gotten out that mockingjays are hazardous to your health."

We pluck in silence for a while longer. Then he says, "I saw Peeta yesterday. Through the glass."

"What'd you think?" I ask.

"Something selfish," says Gale.

"That you don't have to be jealous of him anymore?" My fingers give a yank, and a cloud of feathers floats down around us.

"No. Just the opposite." Gale pulls a feather out of my hair. "I thought . . . I'll never compete with that. No matter how much pain I'm in." He spins the feather between his thumb and forefinger. "I don't stand a chance if he doesn't get better. You'll never be able to let him go. You'll always feel wrong about being with me."

"The way I always felt wrong kissing him because of you," I say.

Gale holds my gaze. "If I thought that was true, I could almost live with the rest of it."

"It is true," I admit. "But so is what you said about Peeta."

Gale makes a sound of exasperation. Nonetheless, after we've dropped off the birds and volunteered to go back to the woods to gather kindling for the evening fire, I find myself wrapped in his arms. His lips brushing the faded bruises on my neck, working their way to my mouth. Despite what I feel for Peeta, this is when I accept deep down that he'll never come back to me. Or I'll never go back to him. I'll stay in 2 until it falls, go to the Capitol and kill Snow, and then die for my trouble. And he'll die insane and hating me. So in the fading light I shut my eyes and kiss Gale to make up for all the kisses I've withheld, and because it doesn't matter anymore, and because I'm so desperately lonely I can't stand it.

Gale's touch and taste and heat remind me that at least my body's still alive, and for the moment it's a welcome feeling. I empty my mind and let the sensations run through my flesh, happy to lose myself. When Gale pulls away slightly, I move forward to close the gap, but I feel his hand under my chin. "Katniss," he says. The instant I open my eyes, the world seems disjointed. This is not our woods or our mountains or our way. My hand automatically goes to the scar on my left temple, which I associate with confusion. "Now kiss me." Bewildered, unblinking, I stand there while he leans in and presses his lips to mine briefly. He examines my face closely. "What's going on in your head?"

"I don't know," I whisper back.

"Then it's like kissing someone who's drunk. It doesn't count," he says with a weak attempt at a laugh. He scoops up a pile of kindling and drops it in my empty arms, returning me to myself.

"How do you know?" I say, mostly to cover my embarrassment. "Have you kissed someone who's drunk?" I guess Gale could've been kissing girls right and left back in 12.

He certainly had enough takers. I never thought about it much before.

He just shakes his head. "No. But it's not hard to imagine."

"So, you never kissed any other girls?" I ask.

"I didn't say that. You know, you were only twelve when we met. And a real pain besides. I did have a life outside of hunting with you," he says, loading up with firewood.

Suddenly, I'm genuinely curious. "Who did you kiss? And where?"

"Too many to remember. Behind the school, on the slag heap, you name it," he says.

I roll my eyes. "So when did I become so special? When they carted me off to the Capitol?"

"No. About six months before that. Right after New Year's. We were in the Hob, eating some slop of Greasy Sae's. And Darius was teasing you about trading a rabbit for one of his kisses. And I realized . . . I minded," he tells me.

I remember that day. Bitter cold and dark by four in the afternoon. We'd been hunting, but a heavy snow had driven us back into town. The Hob was crowded with people looking for refuge from the weather. Greasy Sae's soup, made with stock from the bones of a wild dog we'd shot a week earlier, was below her usual standards. Still, it was hot, and I was starving as I scooped it up, sitting cross-legged on her counter. Darius was leaning on the post of the stall, tickling my cheek with the end of my braid, while I smacked his hand away. He was explaining why one of his kisses merited a rabbit, or possibly two, since everyone knows redheaded men are the most virile. And Greasy Sae and I were laughing because he was so ridiculous and persistent and kept pointing out women around the Hob who he said had paid far more than a rabbit to enjoy his lips. "See? The one in the green muffler? Go ahead and ask her. *If* you need a reference."

A million miles from here, a billion days ago, this happened. "Darius was just joking around," I say.

"Probably. Although you'd be the last to figure out if he wasn't," Gale tells me. "Take Peeta. Take me. Or even Finnick. I was starting to worry he had his eye on you, but he seems back on track now."

"You don't know Finnick if you think he'd love me," I say.

Gale shrugs. "I know he was desperate. That makes people do all kinds of crazy things."

I can't help thinking that's directed at me.

Bright and early the next morning, the brains assemble to take on the problem of the Nut. I'm asked to the meeting, although I don't have much to contribute. I avoid the conference table and perch in the wide windowsill that has a view of the mountain in question. The commander from 2, a middle-aged woman named Lyme, takes us on a virtual tour of the Nut, its interior and fortifications, and recounts the failed attempts to seize it. I've crossed paths with her briefly a couple of times since my arrival, and was dogged by the feeling I'd met her before. She's memorable enough, standing over six feet tall and heavily muscled. But it's only when I see a clip of her in the field, leading a raid on the main entrance of the Nut, that something clicks and I realize

I'm in the presence of another victor. Lyme, the tribute from District 2, who won her Hunger Games over a generation ago. Effie sent us her tape, among others, to prepare for the Quarter Quell. I've probably caught glimpses of her during the Games over the years, but she's kept a low profile. With my newfound knowledge of Haymitch's and Finnick's treatment, all I can think is: What did the Capitol do to her after she won?

When Lyme finishes the presentation, the questions from the brains begin. Hours pass, and lunch comes and goes, as they try to come up with a realistic plan for taking the Nut. But while Beetee thinks he might be able to override certain computer systems, and there's some discussion of putting the handful of internal spies to use, no one has any really innovative thoughts. As the afternoon wears on, talk keeps returning to a strategy that has been tried repeatedly—the storming of the entrances. I can see Lyme's frustration building because so many variations of this plan have already failed, so many of her soldiers have been lost. Finally, she bursts out, "The next person who suggests we take the entrances better have a brilliant way to do it, because you're going to be the one leading that mission!"

Gale, who is too restless to sit at the table for more than a few hours, has been alternating between pacing and sharing my windowsill. Early on, he seemed to accept Lyme's assertion that the entrances couldn't be taken, and dropped out of the conversation entirely. For the last hour or so, he's sat quietly, his brow knitted in concentration, staring at the Nut through the window glass. In the silence that follows

Lyme's ultimatum, he speaks up. "Is it really so necessary that we take the Nut? Or would it be enough to disable it?"

"That would be a step in the right direction," says Beetee. "What do you have in mind?"

"Think of it as a wild dog den," Gale continues. "You're not going to fight your way in. So you have two choices. Trap the dogs inside or flush them out."

"We've tried bombing the entrances," says Lyme. "They're set too far inside the stone for any real damage to be done."

"I wasn't thinking of that," says Gale. "I was thinking of using the mountain." Beetee rises and joins Gale at the window, peering through his ill-fitting glasses. "See? Running down the sides?"

"Avalanche paths," says Beetee under his breath. "It'd be tricky. We'd have to design the detonation sequence with great care, and once it's in motion, we couldn't hope to control it."

"We don't need to control it if we give up the idea that we have to possess the Nut," says Gale. "Only shut it down."

"So you're suggesting we start avalanches and block the entrances?" asks Lyme.

"That's it," says Gale. "Trap the enemy inside, cut off from supplies. Make it impossible for them to send out their hovercraft."

While everyone considers the plan, Boggs flips through a stack of blueprints of the Nut and frowns. "You risk killing everyone inside. Look at the ventilation system. It's rudimentary at best. Nothing like what we have in Thirteen. It depends entirely on pumping in air from the mountainsides. Block those vents and you'll suffocate whoever is trapped."

"They could still escape through the train tunnel to the square," says Beetee.

"Not if we blow it up," says Gale brusquely. His intent, his full intent, becomes clear. Gale has no interest in preserving the lives of those in the Nut. No interest in caging the prey for later use.

This is one of his death traps.

15

The implications of what Gale is suggesting settle quietly around the room. You can see the reaction playing out on people's faces. The expressions range from pleasure to distress, from sorrow to satisfaction.

"The majority of the workers are citizens from Two," says Beetee neutrally.

"So what?" says Gale. "We'll never be able to trust them again."

"They should at least have a chance to surrender," says Lyme.

"Well, that's a luxury we weren't given when they fire-bombed Twelve, but you're all so much cozier with the Capitol here," says Gale. By the look on Lyme's face, I think she might shoot him, or at least take a swing. She'd probably have the upper hand, too, with all her training. But her anger only seems to infuriate him and he yells, "We watched children burn to death and there was nothing we could do!"

I have to close my eyes a minute, as the image rips through me. It has the desired effect. I want everyone in that mountain dead. Am about to say so. But then . . . I'm also a girl from District 12. Not President Snow. I can't help it. I can't condemn someone to the death he's suggesting. "Gale," I say, taking his arm and trying to speak in a reasonable tone. "The Nut's an old mine. It'd be like causing a massive coal mining accident." Surely the words are enough to make anyone from 12 think twice about the plan.

"But not so quick as the one that killed our fathers," he retorts. "Is that everyone's problem? That our enemies might have a few hours to reflect on the fact that they're dying, instead of just being blown to bits?"

Back in the old days, when we were nothing more than a couple of kids hunting outside of 12, Gale said things like this and worse. But then they were just words. Here, put into practice, they become deeds that can never be reversed.

"You don't know how those District Two people ended up in the Nut," I say. "They may have been coerced. They may be held against their will. Some are our own spies. Will you kill them, too?"

"I would sacrifice a few, yes, to take out the rest of them," he replies. "And if I were a spy in there, I'd say, 'Bring on the avalanches!'"

I know he's telling the truth. That Gale would sacrifice his life in this way for the cause — no one doubts it. Perhaps we'd all do the same if we were the spies and given the choice. I guess I would. But it's a coldhearted decision to make for other people and those who love them.

"You said we had two choices," Boggs tells him. "To trap them or to flush them out. I say we try to avalanche the mountain but leave the train tunnel alone. People can escape into the square, where we'll be waiting for them."

"Heavily armed, I hope," says Gale. "You can be sure they'll be."

"Heavily armed. We'll take them prisoner," agrees Boggs.

"Let's bring Thirteen into the loop now," Beetee suggests. "Let President Coin weigh in."

"She'll want to block the tunnel," says Gale with conviction.

"Yes, most likely. But you know, Peeta did have a point in his propos. About the dangers of killing ourselves off. I've been playing with some numbers. Factoring in the casualties and the wounded and . . . I think it's at least worth a conversation," says Beetee.

Only a handful of people are invited to be part of that conversation. Gale and I are released with the rest. I take him hunting so he can blow off some steam, but he's not talking about it. Probably too angry with me for countering him.

The call does happen, a decision is made, and by evening I'm suited up in my Mockingjay outfit, with my bow slung over my shoulder and an earpiece that connects me to Haymitch in 13—just in case a good opportunity for a propo arises. We wait on the roof of the Justice Building with a clear view of our target.

Our hoverplanes are initially ignored by the commanders in the Nut, because in the past they've been little more than flies buzzing around a honeypot. But after two rounds of bombings in the higher elevations of the mountain, the planes have their attention. By the time the Capitol's antiaircraft weapons begin to fire, it's already too late.

Gale's plan exceeds anyone's expectations. Beetee was right about being unable to control the avalanches once they'd been set in motion. The mountainsides are naturally unstable, but weakened by the explosions, they seem almost fluid. Whole sections of the Nut collapse before our eyes, obliterating any sign that human beings have ever set foot on the place. We stand speechless, tiny and insignificant, as waves of stone thunder down the mountain. Burying the entrances under tons of rock. Raising a cloud of dirt and debris that blackens the sky. Turning the Nut into a tomb.

I imagine the hell inside the mountain. Sirens wailing. Lights flickering into darkness. Stone dust choking the air. The shrieks of panicked, trapped beings stumbling madly for a way out, only to find the entrances, the launchpad, the ventilation shafts themselves clogged with earth and rock trying to force its way in. Live wires flung free, fires breaking out, rubble making a familiar path a maze. People slamming, shoving, scrambling like ants as the hill presses in, threatening to crush their fragile shells.

"Katniss?" Haymitch's voice is in my earpiece. I try to answer back and find both of my hands are clamped tightly over my mouth. "Katniss!"

On the day my father died, the sirens went off during my school lunch. No one waited for dismissal, or was expected to. The response to a mine accident was something outside the control of even the Capitol. I ran to Prim's class. I still remember her, tiny at seven, very pale, but sitting straight up with her hands folded on her desk. Waiting for me to collect her as I'd promised I would if the sirens ever sounded. She sprang out of her seat, grabbed my coat sleeve, and we wove through the streams of people pouring out onto the streets to pool at the main entrance of the mine. We found our mother clenching the rope that had been hastily strung to keep the crowd back. In retrospect, I guess I should have known there was a problem right then. Because why were we looking for her, when the reverse should have been true?

The elevators were screeching, burning up and down their cables as they vomited smoke-blackened miners into the light of day. With each group came cries of relief, relatives diving under the rope to lead off their husbands, wives, children, parents, siblings. We stood in the freezing air as the afternoon turned overcast, a light snow dusted the earth. The elevators moved more slowly now and disgorged fewer beings. I knelt on the ground and pressed my hands into the cinders, wanting so badly to pull my father free. If there's a more helpless feeling than trying to reach someone you love who's trapped underground, I don't know it. The wounded. The bodies. The waiting through the night. Blankets put around your shoulders by strangers. A mug of something hot that you don't drink. And then finally, at dawn, the grieved expression on the face of the mine captain that could only mean one thing.

What did we just do?

"Katniss! Are you there?" Haymitch is probably making plans to have me fitted for a head shackle at this very moment.

I drop my hands. "Yes."

"Get inside. Just in case the Capitol tries to retaliate with what's left of its air force," he instructs.

"Yes," I repeat. Everyone on the roof, except for the soldiers manning the machine guns, begin to make their way inside. As I descend the stairs, I can't help brushing my fingers along the unblemished white marble walls. So cold and beautiful. Even in the Capitol, there's nothing to match the magnificence of this old building. But there is no give to the surface—only my flesh yields, my warmth taken. Stone conquers people every time.

I sit at the base of one of the gigantic pillars in the great entrance hall. Through the doors I can see the white expanse of marble that leads to the steps on the square. I remember how sick I was the day Peeta and I accepted congratulations there for winning the Games. Worn down by the Victory Tour, failing in my attempt to calm the districts, facing the memories of Clove and Cato, particularly Cato's gruesome, slow death by mutts.

Boggs crouches down beside me, his skin pale in the shadows. "We didn't bomb the train tunnel, you know. Some of them will probably get out."

"And then we'll shoot them when they show their faces?" I ask.

"Only if we have to," he answers.

"We could send in trains ourselves. Help evacuate the wounded," I say.

"No. It was decided to leave the tunnel in their hands. That way they can use all the tracks to bring people out," says Boggs. "Besides, it will give us time to get the rest of our soldiers to the square."

A few hours ago, the square was a no-man's-land, the front line of the fight between the rebels and the Peacekeepers. When Coin gave approval for Gale's plan, the rebels launched a heated attack and drove the Capitol forces back several blocks so that we would control the train station in the event that the Nut fell. Well, it's fallen. The reality has sunk in. Any survivors will escape to the square. I can hear the gunfire starting again, as the Peacekeepers are no doubt trying to fight their way in to rescue their comrades. Our own soldiers are being brought in to counter this.

"You're cold," says Boggs. "I'll see if I can find a blanket." He goes before I can protest. I don't want a blanket, even if the marble continues to leech my body heat.

"Katniss," says Haymitch in my ear.

"Still here," I answer.

"Interesting turn of events with Peeta this afternoon. Thought you'd want to know," he says. Interesting isn't good. It isn't better. But I don't really have any choice but to listen. "We showed him that clip of you singing 'The Hanging Tree.' It was never aired, so the Capitol couldn't use it when he was being hijacked. He says he recognized the song."

For a moment, my heart skips a beat. Then I realize it's just more tracker jacker serum confusion. "He couldn't, Haymitch. He never heard me sing that song."

"Not you. Your father. He heard him singing it one day when he came to trade at the bakery. Peeta was small, probably six or seven, but he remembered it because he was specially listening to see if the birds stopped singing," says Haymitch. "Guess they did."

Six or seven. That would have been before my mother banned the song. Maybe even right around the time I was learning it. "Was I there, too?"

"Don't think so. No mention of you anyway. But it's the first connection to you that hasn't triggered some mental meltdown," says Haymitch. "It's something, at least, Katniss."

My father. He seems to be everywhere today. Dying in the mine. Singing his way into Peeta's muddled consciousness. Flickering in the look Boggs gives me as he protectively wraps the blanket around my shoulders. I miss him so badly it hurts.

The gunfire's really picking up outside. Gale hurries by with a group of rebels, eagerly headed for the battle. I don't petition to join the fighters, not that they would let me. I have no stomach for it anyway, no heat in my blood. I wish Peeta was here — the old Peeta — because he would be able to articulate why it is so wrong to be exchanging fire when people, any people, are trying to claw their way out of the mountain. Or is my own history making me too sensitive? Aren't we at war? Isn't this just another way to kill our enemies?

Night falls quickly. Huge, bright spotlights are turned on, illuminating the square. Every bulb must be burning at full wattage inside the train station as well. Even from my position across the square, I can see clearly through the plate-glass front of the long, narrow building. It would be impossible to miss the arrival of a train, or even a single person. But hours pass and no one comes. With each minute, it becomes harder to imagine that anyone survived the assault on the Nut.

It's well after midnight when Cressida comes to attach a special microphone to my costume. "What's this for?" I ask.

Haymitch's voice comes on to explain. "I know you're not going to like this, but we need you to make a speech."

"A speech?" I say, immediately feeling queasy.

"I'll feed it to you, line by line," he assures me. "You'll just have to repeat what I say. Look, there's no sign of life from that mountain. We've won, but the fighting's continuing. So we thought if you went out on the steps of the Justice Building and laid it out — told everybody that the Nut's defeated, that the Capitol's presence in District Two is finished — you might be able to get the rest of their forces to surrender."

I peer at the darkness beyond the square. "I can't even see their forces."

"That's what the mike's for," he says. "You'll be broadcast, both your voice through their emergency audio system, and your image wherever people have access to a screen."

I know there are a couple of huge screens here on the square. I saw them on the Victory Tour. It might work, if I were good at this sort of thing. Which I'm not. They tried to feed me lines in those early experiments with the propos, too, and it was a flop.

"You could save a lot of lives, Katniss," Haymitch says finally.

"All right. I'll give it a try," I tell him.

It's strange standing outside at the top of the stairs, fully costumed, brightly lit, but with no visible audience to deliver my speech to. Like I'm doing a show for the moon.

"Let's make this quick," says Haymitch. "You're too exposed."

My television crew, positioned out in the square with special cameras, indicates that they're ready. I tell Haymitch to go ahead, then click on my mike and listen carefully to him dictate the first line of the speech. A huge image of me lights up one of the screens over the square as I begin. "People of District Two, this is Katniss Everdeen speaking to you from the steps of your Justice Building, where—"

The pair of trains comes screeching into the train station side by side. As the doors slide open, people tumble out in a cloud of smoke they've brought from the Nut. They must have had at least an inkling of what would await them at the square, because you can see them trying to act evasively. Most of them flatten on the floor, and a spray of bullets inside the station takes out the lights. They've come armed, as Gale predicted, but they've come wounded as well. The moans can be heard in the otherwise silent night air.

Someone kills the lights on the stairs, leaving me in the protection of shadow. A flame blooms inside the station — one of the trains must actually be on fire — and a thick, black smoke billows against the windows. Left with no choice, the people begin to push out into the square, choking but defiantly waving their guns. My eyes dart around the rooftops that ring the square. Every one of them has been fortified with rebel-manned machine gun nests. Moonlight glints off oiled barrels.

A young man staggers out from the station, one hand pressed against a bloody cloth at his cheek, the other dragging a gun. When he trips and falls to his face, I see the scorch marks down the back of his shirt, the red flesh beneath. And suddenly, he's just another burn victim from a mine accident.

My feet fly down the steps and I take off running for him. "Stop!" I yell at the rebels. "Hold your fire!" The words echo around the square and beyond as the mike amplifies my voice. "Stop!" I'm nearing the young man, reaching down to help him, when he drags himself up to his knees and trains his gun on my head.

I instinctively back up a few steps, raise my bow over my head to show my intention was harmless. Now that he has both hands on his gun, I notice the ragged hole in his cheek where something — falling stone maybe — punctured the flesh. He smells of burning things, hair and meat and fuel. His eyes are crazed with pain and fear.

"Freeze," Haymitch's voice whispers in my ear. I follow his order, realizing that this is what all of District 2, all of Panem maybe, must be seeing at the moment. The Mockingjay at the mercy of a man with nothing to lose.

His garbled speech is barely comprehensible. "Give me one reason I shouldn't shoot you."

The rest of the world recedes. There's only me looking into the wretched eyes of the man from the Nut who asks for one reason. Surely I should be able to come up with thousands. But the words that make it to my lips are "I can't."

Logically, the next thing that should happen is the man pulling the trigger. But he's perplexed, trying to make sense of my words. I experience my own confusion as I realize what I've said is entirely true, and the noble impulse that carried me across the square is replaced by despair. "I can't. That's the problem, isn't it?" I lower my bow. "We blew up your mine. You burned my district to the ground. We've got every reason to kill each other. So do it. Make the Capitol happy. I'm done killing their slaves for them." I drop my bow on the ground and give it a nudge with my boot. It slides across the stone and comes to rest at his knees.

"I'm not their slave," the man mutters.

"I am," I say. "That's why I killed Cato . . . and he killed Thresh . . . and he killed Clove . . . and she tried to kill me. It just goes around and around, and who wins? Not us. Not the districts. Always the Capitol. But I'm tired of being a piece in their Games."

Peeta. On the rooftop the night before our first Hunger Games. He understood it all before we'd even set foot in the arena. I hope he's watching now, that he remembers that night as it happened, and maybe forgives me when I die.

"Keep talking. Tell them about watching the mountain go down," Haymitch insists.

"When I saw that mountain fall tonight, I thought . . . they've done it again. Got me to kill you — the people in the districts. But why did I do it? District Twelve and District Two have no fight except the one the Capitol gave us." The young man blinks at me uncomprehendingly. I sink on my knees before him, my voice low and urgent. "And why are you fighting with the rebels on the rooftops? With Lyme, who was your victor? With people who were your neighbors, maybe even your family?"

"I don't know," says the man. But he doesn't take his gun off me.

I rise and turn slowly in a circle, addressing the machine guns. "And you up there? I come from a mining town. Since when do miners condemn other miners to that kind of death, and then stand by to kill whoever manages to crawl from the rubble?"

"Who is the enemy?" whispers Haymitch.

"These people" — I indicate the wounded bodies on the square — "are not your enemy!" I whip back around to the train station. "The rebels are not your enemy! We all have one enemy, and it's the Capitol! This is our chance to put an end to their power, but we need every district person to do it!"

The cameras are tight on me as I reach out my hands to the man, to the wounded, to the reluctant rebels across Panem. "Please! Join us!"

My words hang in the air. I look to the screen, hoping to see them recording some wave of reconciliation going through the crowd.

Instead I watch myself get shot on television.

"Always."

In the twilight of morphling, Peeta whispers the word and I go searching for him. It's a gauzy, violet-tinted world, with no hard edges, and many places to hide. I push through cloud banks, follow faint tracks, catch the scent of cinnamon, of dill. Once I feel his hand on my cheek and try to trap it, but it dissolves like mist through my fingers.

When I finally begin to surface into the sterile hospital room in 13, I remember. I was under the influence of sleep syrup. My heel had been injured after I'd climbed out on a branch over the electric fence and dropped back into 12. Peeta had put me to bed and I had asked him to stay with me as I was drifting off. He had whispered something I couldn't quite catch. But some part of my brain had trapped his single word of reply and let it swim up through my dreams to taunt me now. *"Always."*

Morphling dulls the extremes of all emotions, so instead of a stab of sorrow, I merely feel emptiness. A hollow of dead brush where flowers used to bloom. Unfortunately, there's not enough of the drug left in my veins for me to ignore the pain in the left side of my body. That's where the bullet hit. My hands fumble over the thick bandages encasing my ribs and I wonder what I'm still doing here.

It wasn't him, the man kneeling before me on the square, the burned one from the Nut. He didn't pull the trigger. It was someone farther back in the crowd. There was less a sense of penetration than the feeling that I'd been struck with a sledgehammer. Everything after the moment of impact is confusion riddled with gunfire. I try to sit up, but the only thing I manage is a moan.

The white curtain that divides my bed from the next patient's whips back, and Johanna Mason stares down at me. At first I feel threatened, because she attacked me in the arena. I have to remind myself that she did it to save my life. It was part of the rebel plot. But still, that doesn't mean she doesn't despise me. Maybe her treatment of me was all an act for the Capitol?

"I'm alive," I say rustily.

"No kidding, brainless." Johanna walks over and plunks down on my bed, sending spikes of pain shooting across my chest. When she grins at my discomfort, I know we're not in for some warm reunion scene. "Still a little sore?" With an expert hand, she quickly detaches the morphling drip from my arm and plugs it into a socket taped into the crook of her own. "They started cutting back my supply a few days ago. Afraid I'm going to turn into one of those freaks from Six. I've had to borrow from you when the coast was clear. Didn't think you'd mind."

Mind? How can I mind when she was almost tortured to death by Snow after the Quarter Quell? I have no right to mind, and she knows it.

Johanna sighs as the morphling enters her bloodstream.

"Maybe they were onto something in Six. Drug yourself out and paint flowers on your body. Not such a bad life. Seemed happier than the rest of us, anyway."

In the weeks since I left 13, she's gained some weight back. A soft down of hair has sprouted on her shaved head, helping to hide some of the scars. But if she's siphoning off my morphling, she's struggling.

"They've got this head doctor who comes around every day. Supposed to be helping me recover. Like some guy who's spent his life in this rabbit warren's going to fix me up. Complete idiot. At least twenty times a session he reminds me that I'm totally safe." I manage a smile. It's a truly stupid thing to say, especially to a victor. As if such a state of being ever existed, anywhere, for anyone. "How about you, Mockingjay? You feel totally safe?"

"Oh, yeah. Right up until I got shot," I say.

"Please. That bullet never even touched you. Cinna saw to that," she says.

I think of the layers of protective armor in my Mockingjay outfit. But the pain came from somewhere. "Broken ribs?"

"Not even. Bruised pretty good. The impact ruptured your spleen. They couldn't repair it." She gives a dismissive wave of her hand. "Don't worry, you don't need one. And if you did, they'd find you one, wouldn't they? It's everybody's job to keep you alive."

"Is that why you hate me?" I ask.

"Partly," she admits. "Jealousy is certainly involved. I also think you're a little hard to swallow. With your tacky romantic drama and your defender-of-the-helpless act. Only it isn't an act, which makes you more unbearable. Please feel free to take this personally."

"You should have been the Mockingjay. No one would've had to feed you lines," I say.

"True. But no one likes me," she tells me.

"They trusted you, though. To get me out," I remind her. "And they're afraid of you."

"Here, maybe. In the Capitol, you're the one they're scared of now." Gale appears in the doorway, and Johanna neatly unhooks herself and reattaches me to the morphling drip. "Your cousin's not afraid of me," she says confidentially. She scoots off my bed and crosses to the door, nudging Gale's leg with her hip as she passes him. "Are you, gorgeous?" We can hear her laughter as she disappears down the hall.

I raise my eyebrows at him as he takes my hand. "Terrified," he mouths. I laugh, but it turns into a wince. "Easy." He strokes my face as the pain ebbs. "You've got to stop running straight into trouble."

"I know. But someone blew up a mountain," I answer.

Instead of pulling back, he leans in closer, searching my face. "You think I'm heartless."

"I know you're not. But I won't tell you it's okay," I say.

Now he draws back, almost impatiently. "Katniss, what difference is there, really, between crushing our enemy in a mine or blowing them out of the sky with one of Beetee's arrows? The result is the same."

"I don't know. We were under attack in Eight, for one thing. The hospital was under attack," I say.

"Yes, and those hoverplanes came from District Two," he says. "So, by taking them out, we prevented further attacks."

"But that kind of thinking . . . you could turn it into an argument for killing anyone at any time. You could justify sending kids into the Hunger Games to prevent the districts from getting out of line," I say.

"I don't buy that," he tells me.

"I do," I reply. "It must be those trips to the arena."

"Fine. We know how to disagree," he says. "We always have. Maybe it's good. Between you and me, we've got District Two now."

"Really?" For a moment a feeling of triumph flares up inside me. Then I think about the people on the square. "Was there fighting after I was shot?"

"Not much. The workers from the Nut turned on the Capitol soldiers. The rebels just sat by and watched," he says. "Actually, the whole country just sat by and watched."

"Well, that's what they do best," I say.

You'd think that losing a major organ would entitle you to lie around a few weeks, but for some reason, my doctors want me up and moving almost immediately. Even with the morphling, the internal pain's severe the first few days, but then it slacks off considerably. The soreness from the bruised ribs, however, promises to hang on for a while. I begin to resent Johanna dipping into my morphling supply, but I still let her take whatever she likes.

Rumors of my death have been running rampant, so they send in the team to film me in my hospital bed.

I show off my stitches and impressive bruising and congratulate the districts on their successful battle for unity. Then I warn the Capitol to expect us soon.

As part of my rehabilitation, I take short walks aboveground each day. One afternoon, Plutarch joins me and gives me an update on our current situation. Now that District 2 has allied with us, the rebels are taking a breather from the war to regroup. Fortifying supply lines, seeing to the wounded, reorganizing their troops. The Capitol, like 13 during the Dark Days, finds itself completely cut off from outside help as it holds the threat of nuclear attack over its enemies. Unlike 13, the Capitol is not in a position to reinvent itself and become self-sufficient.

"Oh, the city might be able to scrape along for a while," says Plutarch. "Certainly, there are emergency supplies stockpiled. But the significant difference between Thirteen and the Capitol are the expectations of the populace. Thirteen was used to hardship, whereas in the Capitol, all they've known is *Panem et Circenses*."

"What's that?" I recognize *Panem*, of course, but the rest is nonsense.

"It's a saying from thousands of years ago, written in a language called Latin about a place called Rome," he explains. "*Panem et Circenses* translates into 'Bread and Circuses.' The writer was saying that in return for full bellies and entertainment, his people had given up their political responsibilities and therefore their power."

I think about the Capitol. The excess of food. And the ultimate entertainment. The Hunger Games. "So that's what the districts are for. To provide the bread and circuses."

"Yes. And as long as that kept rolling in, the Capitol could control its little empire. Right now, it can provide neither, at least at the standard the people are accustomed to," says Plutarch. "We have the food and I'm about to orchestrate an entertainment propo that's sure to be popular. After all, everybody loves a wedding."

I freeze in my tracks, sick at the idea of what he's suggesting. Somehow staging some perverse wedding between Peeta and me. I haven't been able to face that one-way glass since I've been back and, at my own request, only get updates about Peeta's condition from Haymitch. He speaks very little about it. Different techniques are being tried. There will never truly be a way to cure him. And now they want me to marry Peeta for a propo?

Plutarch rushes to reassure me. "Oh, no, Katniss. Not your wedding. Finnick and Annie's. All you need to do is show up and pretend to be happy for them."

"That's one of the few things I won't have to pretend, Plutarch," I tell him.

The next few days bring a flurry of activity as the event is planned. The differences between the Capitol and 13 are thrown into sharp relief by the event. When Coin says "wedding," she means two people signing a piece of paper and being assigned a new compartment. Plutarch means hundreds of people dressed in finery at a three-day celebration. It's amusing to watch them haggle over the details. Plutarch has to fight for every guest, every musical note. After Coin vetoes a dinner, entertainment, and alcohol, Plutarch yells,

"What's the point of the propo if no one's having any fun!"

It's hard to put a Gamemaker on a budget. But even a quiet celebration causes a stir in 13, where they seem to have no holidays at all. When it's announced that children are wanted to sing District 4's wedding song, practically every kid shows up. There's no shortage of volunteers to help make decorations. In the dining hall, people chat excitedly about the event.

Maybe it's more than the festivities. Maybe it's that we are all so starved for something good to happen that we want to be part of it. It would explain why — when Plutarch has a fit over what the bride will wear — I volunteer to take Annie back to my house in 12, where Cinna left a variety of evening clothes in a big storage closet downstairs. All of the wedding gowns he designed for me went back to the Capitol, but there are some dresses I wore on the Victory Tour. I'm a little leery about being with Annie since all I really know about her is that Finnick loves her and everybody thinks she's mad. On the hovercraft ride, I decide she's less mad than unstable. She laughs at odd places in the conversation or drops out of it distractedly. Those green eyes fixate on a point with such intensity that you find yourself trying to make out what she sees in the empty air. Sometimes, for no reason, she presses both her hands over her ears as if to block out a painful sound. All right, she's strange, but if Finnick loves her, that's good enough for me.

I got permission for my prep team to come along, so I'm relieved of having to make any fashion decisions. When I open the closet, we all fall silent because Cinna's presence is so strong in the flow of the fabrics. Then Octavia drops to her knees, rubs the hem of a skirt against her cheek, and bursts into tears. "It's been so long," she gasps, "since I've seen anything pretty."

Despite reservations on Coin's side that it's too extravagant, and on Plutarch's side that it's too drab, the wedding is a smash hit. The three hundred lucky guests culled from 13 and the many refugees wear their everyday clothes, the decorations are made from autumn foliage, the music is provided by a choir of children accompanied by the lone fiddler who made it out of 12 with his instrument. So it's simple, frugal by the Capitol's standards. It doesn't matter because nothing can compete with the beauty of the couple. It isn't about their borrowed finery — Annie wears a green silk dress I wore in 5, Finnick one of Peeta's suits that they altered — although the clothes are striking. Who can look past the radiant faces of two people for whom this day was once a virtual impossibility? Dalton, the cattle guy from 10, conducts the ceremony, since it's similar to the one used in his district. But there are unique touches of District 4. A net woven from long grass that covers the couple during their vows, the touching of each other's lips with salt water, and the ancient wedding song, which likens marriage to a sea voyage.

No, I don't have to pretend to be happy for them.

After the kiss that seals the union, the cheers, and a toast with apple cider, the fiddler strikes up a tune that turns every head from 12. We may have been the smallest, poorest district in Panem, but we know how to dance. Nothing has been officially scheduled at this point, but Plutarch, who's calling the propo from the control room, must have his fingers crossed. Sure enough, Greasy Sae grabs Gale by the hand and pulls him into the center of the floor and faces off with him. People pour in to join them, forming two long lines. And the dancing begins.

I'm standing off to the side, clapping to the rhythm, when a bony hand pinches me above the elbow. Johanna scowls at me. "Are you going to miss the chance to let Snow see you dancing?" She's right. What could spell victory louder than a happy Mockingjay twirling around to music? I find Prim in the crowd. Since winter evenings gave us a lot of time to practice, we're actually pretty good partners. I brush off her concerns about my ribs, and we take our places in the line. It hurts, but the satisfaction of having Snow watch me dance with my little sister reduces other feelings to dust.

Dancing transforms us. We teach the steps to the District 13 guests. Insist on a special number for the bride and groom. Join hands and make a giant, spinning circle where people show off their footwork. Nothing silly, joyful, or fun has happened in so long. This could go on all night if not for the last event planned in Plutarch's propo. One I hadn't heard about, but then it was meant to be a surprise.

Four people wheel out a huge wedding cake from a side room. Most of the guests back up, making way for this rarity, this dazzling creation with blue-green, white-tipped icing waves swimming with fish and sailboats, seals and sea flowers. But I push my way through the crowd to confirm what

I knew at first sight. As surely as the embroidery stitches in Annie's gown were done by Cinna's hand, the frosted flowers on the cake were done by Peeta's.

This may seem like a small thing, but it speaks volumes. Haymitch has been keeping a great deal from me. The boy I last saw, screaming his head off, trying to tear free of his restraints, could never have made this. Never have had the focus, kept his hands steady, designed something so perfect for Finnick and Annie. As if anticipating my reaction, Haymitch is at my side.

"Let's you and me have a talk," he says.

Out in the hall, away from the cameras, I ask, "What's happening to him?"

Haymitch shakes his head. "I don't know. None of us knows. Sometimes he's almost rational, and then, for no reason, he goes off again. Doing the cake was a kind of therapy. He's been working on it for days. Watching him . . . he seemed almost like before."

"So, he's got the run of the place?" I ask. The idea makes me nervous on about five different levels.

"Oh, no. He frosted under heavy guard. He's still under lock and key. But I've talked to him," Haymitch says.

"Face-to-face?" I ask. "And he didn't go nuts?"

"No. Pretty angry with me, but for all the right reasons. Not telling him about the rebel plot and whatnot." Haymitch pauses a moment, as if deciding something. "He says he'd like to see you."

I'm on a frosting sailboat, tossed around by blue-green waves, the deck shifting beneath my feet. My palms press into the wall to steady myself. This wasn't part of the plan. I wrote Peeta off in 2. Then I was to go to the Capitol, kill Snow, and get taken out myself. The gunshot was only a temporary setback. Never was I supposed to hear the words *He says he'd like to see you.* But now that I have, there's no way to refuse.

At midnight, I'm standing outside the door to his cell. Hospital room. We had to wait for Plutarch to finish getting his wedding footage, which, despite the lack of what he calls razzle-dazzle, he's pleased with. "The best thing about the Capitol basically ignoring Twelve all these years is that you people still have a little spontaneity. The audience eats that up. Like when Peeta announced he was in love with you or you did the trick with the berries. Makes for good television."

I wish I could meet with Peeta privately. But the audience of doctors has assembled behind the one-way glass, clipboards ready, pens poised. When Haymitch gives me the okay in my earpiece, I slowly open the door.

Those blue eyes lock on me instantly. He's got three restraints on each arm, and a tube that can dispense a knock-out drug just in case he loses control. He doesn't fight to free himself, though, only observes me with the wary look of someone who still hasn't ruled out that he's in the presence of a mutt. I walk over until I'm standing about a yard from the bed. There's nothing to do with my hands, so I cross my arms protectively over my ribs before I speak. "Hey."

"Hey," he responds. It's like his voice, almost his voice, except there's something new in it. An edge of suspicion and reproach.

"Haymitch said you wanted to talk to me," I say.

"Look at you, for starters." It's like he's waiting for me to transform into a hybrid drooling wolf right before his eyes. He stares so long I find myself casting furtive glances at the one-way glass, hoping for some direction from Haymitch, but my earpiece stays silent. "You're not very big, are you? Or particularly pretty?"

I know he's been through hell and back, and yet somehow the observation rubs me the wrong way. "Well, you've looked better."

Haymitch's advice to back off gets muffled by Peeta's laughter. "And not even remotely nice. To say that to me after all I've been through."

"Yeah. We've all been through a lot. And you're the one who was known for being nice. Not me." I'm doing everything wrong. I don't know why I feel so defensive. He's been tortured! He's been hijacked! What's wrong with me? Suddenly, I think I might start screaming at him—I'm not even sure about what—so I decide to get out of there. "Look, I don't feel so well. Maybe I'll drop by tomorrow."

I've just reached the door when his voice stops me. "Katniss. I remember about the bread."

The bread. Our one moment of real connection before the Hunger Games.

"They showed you the tape of me talking about it," I say.

"No. Is there a tape of you talking about it? Why didn't the Capitol use it against me?" he asks.

"I made it the day you were rescued," I answer. The pain in my chest wraps around my ribs like a vise. The dancing was a mistake. "So what do you remember?"

"You. In the rain," he says softly. "Digging in our trash bins. Burning the bread. My mother hitting me. Taking the bread out for the pig but then giving it to you instead."

"That's it. That's what happened," I say. "The next day, after school, I wanted to thank you. But I didn't know how."

"We were outside at the end of the day. I tried to catch your eye. You looked away. And then . . . for some reason, I think you picked a dandelion." I nod. He does remember. I have never spoken about that moment aloud. "I must have loved you a lot."

"You did." My voice catches and I pretend to cough.

"And did you love me?" he asks.

I keep my eyes on the tiled floor. "Everyone says I did. Everyone says that's why Snow had you tortured. To break me."

"That's not an answer," he tells me. "I don't know what to think when they show me some of the tapes. In that first arena, it looked like you tried to kill me with those tracker jackers."

"I was trying to kill all of you," I say. "You had me treed."

"Later, there's a lot of kissing. Didn't seem very genuine on your part. Did you like kissing me?" he asks.

"Sometimes," I admit. "You know people are watching us now?"

"I know. What about Gale?" he continues.

My anger's returning. I don't care about his recovery—this isn't the business of the people behind the glass. "He's not a bad kisser either," I say shortly.

"And it was okay with both of us? You kissing the other?" he asks.

"No. It wasn't okay with either of you. But I wasn't asking your permission," I tell him.

Peeta laughs again, coldly, dismissively. "Well, you're a piece of work, aren't you?"

Haymitch doesn't protest when I walk out. Down the hall. Through the beehive of compartments. Find a warm pipe to hide behind in a laundry room. It takes a long time before I get to the bottom of why I'm so upset. When I do, it's almost too mortifying to admit. All those months of taking it for granted that Peeta thought I was wonderful are over. Finally, he can see me for who I really am. Violent. Distrustful. Manipulative. Deadly.

And I hate him for it.

17

Blindsided. That's how I feel when Haymitch tells me in the hospital. I fly down the steps to Command, mind racing a mile a minute, and burst right into a war meeting.

"What do you mean, I'm not going to the Capitol? I have to go! I'm the Mockingjay!" I say.

Coin barely looks up from her screen. "And as the Mockingjay, your primary goal of unifying the districts against the Capitol has been achieved. Don't worry—if it goes well, we'll fly you in for the surrender."

The surrender?

"That'll be too late! I'll miss all the fighting. You need me—I'm the best shot you've got!" I shout. I don't usually brag about this, but it's got to be at least close to true. "Gale's going."

"Gale has shown up for training every day unless occupied with other approved duties. We feel confident he can manage himself in the field," says Coin. "How many training sessions do you estimate you've attended?"

None. That's how many. "Well, sometimes I was hunting. And . . . I trained with Beetee down in Special Weaponry."

"It's not the same, Katniss," says Boggs. "We all know you're smart and brave and a good shot. But we need soldiers in the field. You don't know the first thing about executing orders, and you're not exactly at your physical peak."

"That didn't bother you when I was in Eight. Or Two, for that matter," I counter.

"You weren't originally authorized for combat in either case," says Plutarch, shooting me a look that signals I'm about to reveal too much.

No, the bomber battle in 8 and my intervention in 2 were spontaneous, rash, and definitely unauthorized.

"And both resulted in your injury," Boggs reminds me. Suddenly, I see myself through his eyes. A smallish seventeen-year-old girl who can't quite catch her breath since her ribs haven't fully healed. Disheveled. Undisciplined. Recuperating. Not a soldier, but someone who needs to be looked after.

"But I have to go," I say.

"Why?" asks Coin.

I can't very well say it's so I can carry out my own personal vendetta against Snow. Or that the idea of remaining here in 13 with the latest version of Peeta while Gale goes off to fight is unbearable. But I have no shortage of reasons to want to fight in the Capitol. "Because of Twelve. Because they destroyed my district."

The president thinks about this a moment. Considers me. "Well, you have three weeks. It's not long, but you can begin training. If the Assignment Board deems you fit, possibly your case will be reviewed."

That's it. That's the most I can hope for. I guess it's my own fault. I did blow off my schedule every single day unless something suited me. It didn't seem like much of a priority, jogging around a field with a gun with so many other things going on. And now I'm paying for my negligence.

Back in the hospital, I find Johanna in the same circumstance and spitting mad. I tell her about what Coin said. "Maybe you can train, too."

"Fine. I'll train. But I'm going to the stinking Capitol if I have to kill a crew and fly there myself," says Johanna.

"Probably best not to bring that up in training," I say. "But it's nice to know I'll have a ride."

Johanna grins, and I feel a slight but significant shift in our relationship. I don't know that we're actually friends, but possibly the word *allies* would be accurate. That's good. I'm going to need an ally.

The next morning, when we report for training at 7:30, reality slaps me in the face. We've been funneled into a class of relative beginners, fourteen- or fifteen-year-olds, which seems a little insulting until it's obvious that they're in far better condition than we are. Gale and the other people already chosen to go to the Capitol are in a different, accelerated phase of training. After we stretch — which hurts — there's a couple of hours of strengthening exercises — which hurt — and a five-mile run — which kills. Even with Johanna's motivational insults driving me on, I have to drop out after a mile.

"It's my ribs," I explain to the trainer, a no-nonsense middle-aged woman we're supposed to address as Soldier York. "They're still bruised."

"Well, I'll tell you, Soldier Everdeen, those are going to take at least another month to heal up on their own," she says.

I shake my head. "I don't have a month."

She looks me up and down. "The doctors haven't offered you any treatment?"

"Is there a treatment?" I ask. "They said they had to mend naturally."

"That's what they say. But they could speed up the process if I recommend it. I warn you, though, it isn't any fun," she tells me.

"Please. I've got to get to the Capitol," I say.

Soldier York doesn't question this. She scribbles something on a pad and sends me directly back to the hospital. I hesitate. I don't want to miss any more training. "I'll be back for the afternoon session," I promise. She just purses her lips.

Twenty-four needle jabs to my rib cage later, I'm flattened out on my hospital bed, gritting my teeth to keep from begging them to bring back my morphling drip. It's been by my bed so I can take a hit as needed. I haven't used it lately, but I kept it for Johanna's sake. Today they tested my blood to make sure it was clean of the painkiller, as the mixture of the two drugs — the morphling and whatever's set my ribs on fire — has dangerous side effects. They made it clear I would have a difficult couple of days. But I told them to go ahead.

It's a bad night in our room. Sleep's out of the question. I think I can actually smell the ring of flesh around my chest burning, and Johanna's fighting off withdrawal symptoms. Early on, when I apologize about cutting off her morphling supply, she waves it off, saying it had to happen anyway. But by three in the morning, I'm the target of every colorful bit of profanity District 7 has to offer. At dawn, she drags me out of bed, determined to get to training.

"I don't think I can do it," I confess.

"You can do it. We both can. We're victors, remember? We're the ones who can survive anything they throw at us," she snarls at me. She's a sick greenish color, shaking like a leaf. I get dressed.

We must be victors to make it through the morning. I think I'm going to lose Johanna when we realize it's pouring outside. Her face turns ashen and she seems to have ceased breathing.

"It's just water. It won't kill us," I say. She clenches her jaw and stomps out into the mud. Rain drenches us as we work our bodies and then slog around the running course. I bail after a mile again, and I have to resist the temptation to take off my shirt so the cold water can sizzle off my ribs. I force down my field lunch of soggy fish and beet stew. Johanna gets halfway through her bowl before it comes back up. In the afternoon, we learn to assemble our guns. I manage it, but Johanna can't hold her hands steady enough to fit the parts together. When York's back is turned, I help her out. Even though the rain continues, the afternoon's an improvement because we're on the shooting range. At last, something I'm good at. It takes some adjusting from a bow to a gun, but by the end of the day, I've got the best score in my class.

We're just inside the hospital doors when Johanna declares, "This has to stop. Us living in the hospital. Everyone views us as patients."

It's not a problem for me. I can move into our family compartment, but Johanna's never been assigned one. When she tries to get discharged from the hospital, they won't agree to let her live alone, even if she comes in for daily talks with the head doctor. I think they may have put two and two together about the morphling and this only adds to their view that she's unstable. "She won't be alone. I'm going to room with her," I announce. There's some dissent, but Haymitch takes our part, and by bedtime, we have a compartment across from Prim and my mother, who agrees to keep an eye on us.

After I take a shower, and Johanna sort of wipes herself down with a damp cloth, she makes a cursory inspection of the place. When she opens the drawer that holds my few possessions, she shuts it quickly. "Sorry."

I think how there's nothing in Johanna's drawer but her government-issued clothes. That she doesn't have one thing in the world to call her own. "It's okay. You can look at my stuff if you want."

Johanna unlatches my locket, studying the pictures of Gale, Prim, and my mother. She opens the silver parachute and pulls out the spile and slips it onto her pinkie. "Makes me thirsty just looking at it." Then she finds the pearl Peeta gave me. "Is this—?"

"Yeah," I say. "Made it through somehow." I don't want to talk about Peeta. One of the best things about training is, it keeps me from thinking of him.

"Haymitch says he's getting better," she says.

"Maybe. But he's changed," I say.

"So have you. So have I. And Finnick and Haymitch and Beetee. Don't get me started on Annie Cresta. The arena messed us all up pretty good, don't you think? Or do you still feel like the girl who volunteered for your sister?" she asks me.

"No," I answer.

"That's the one thing I think my head doctor might be right about. There's no going back. So we might as well get on with things." She neatly returns my keepsakes to the drawer and climbs into the bed across from me just as the lights go out. "You're not afraid I'll kill you tonight?"

"Like I couldn't take you," I answer. Then we laugh, since both our bodies are so wrecked, it will be a miracle if we can get up the next day. But we do. Each morning, we do. And by the end of the week, my ribs feel almost like new, and Johanna can assemble her rifle without help.

Soldier York gives the pair of us an approving nod as we knock off for the day. "Fine job, Soldiers."

When we move out of hearing, Johanna mutters, "I think winning the Games was easier." But the look on her face says she's pleased.

In fact, we're almost in good spirits when we go to the dining hall, where Gale's waiting to eat with me. Receiving a giant serving of beef stew doesn't hurt my mood either.

"First shipments of food arrived this morning," Greasy Sae tells me. "That's real beef, from District Ten. Not any of your wild dog."

"Don't remember you turning it down," Gale tosses back.

We join a group that includes Delly, Annie, and Finnick. It's something to see Finnick's transformation since his marriage. His earlier incarnations—the decadent Capitol heartthrob I met before the Quell, the enigmatic ally in the arena, the broken young man who tried to help me hold it together—these have been replaced by someone who radiates life. Finnick's real charms of self-effacing humor and an easygoing nature are on display for the first time. He never lets go of Annie's hand. Not when they walk, not when they eat. I doubt he ever plans to. She's lost in some daze of happiness. There are still moments when you can tell something slips in her brain and another world blinds her to us. But a few words from Finnick call her back.

Delly, who I've known since I was little but never gave much thought to, has grown in my estimation. She was told what Peeta said to me that night after the wedding, but she's not a gossip. Haymitch says she's the best defender I have when Peeta goes off on some kind of tear about me. Always taking my side, blaming his negative perceptions on the Capitol's torture. She has more influence on him than any of the others do, because he really does know her. Anyway, even if she's sugarcoating my good points, I appreciate it. Frankly, I could use a little sugarcoating.

I'm starving and the stew is so delicious—beef, potatoes, turnips, and onions in a thick gravy—that I have to force myself to slow down. All around the dining hall, you can feel the rejuvenating effect that a good meal can bring on. The way it can make people kinder, funnier, more optimistic, and remind them it's not a mistake to go on living. It's better than any medicine. So I try to make it last and join in the conversation. Sop up the gravy on my bread and nibble on it as I listen to Finnick telling some ridiculous story about a sea turtle swimming off with his hat. Laugh before I realize he's standing there. Directly across the table, behind the empty seat next to Johanna. Watching me. I choke momentarily as the gravy bread sticks in my throat.

"Peeta!" says Delly. "It's so nice to see you out . . . and about."

Two large guards stand behind him. He holds his tray awkwardly, balanced on his fingertips since his wrists are shackled with a short chain between them.

"What's with the fancy bracelets?" asks Johanna.

"I'm not quite trustworthy yet," says Peeta. "I can't even sit here without your permission." He indicates the guards with his head.

"Sure he can sit here. We're old friends," says Johanna, patting the space beside her. The guards nod and Peeta takes a seat. "Peeta and I had adjoining cells in the Capitol. We're very familiar with each other's screams."

Annie, who's on Johanna's other side, does that thing where she covers her ears and exits reality. Finnick shoots Johanna an angry look as his arm encircles Annie.

"What? My head doctor says I'm not supposed to censor my thoughts. It's part of my therapy," replies Johanna.

The life has gone out of our little party. Finnick murmurs things to Annie until she slowly removes her hands. Then there's a long silence while people pretend to eat.

"Annie," says Delly brightly, "did you know it was Peeta who decorated your wedding cake? Back home, his family ran the bakery and he did all the icing."

Annie cautiously looks across Johanna. "Thank you, Peeta. It was beautiful."

"My pleasure, Annie," says Peeta, and I hear that old note of gentleness in his voice that I thought was gone forever. Not that it's directed at me. But still.

"If we're going to fit in that walk, we better go," Finnick tells her. He arranges both of their trays so he can carry them in one hand while holding tightly to her with the other. "Good seeing you, Peeta."

"You be nice to her, Finnick. Or I might try and take her away from you." It could be a joke, if the tone wasn't so cold. Everything it conveys is wrong. The open distrust of Finnick, the implication that Peeta has his eye on Annie, that Annie could desert Finnick, that I do not even exist.

"Oh, Peeta," says Finnick lightly. "Don't make me sorry I restarted your heart." He leads Annie away after giving me a concerned glance.

When they're gone, Delly says in a reproachful voice, "He did save your life, Peeta. More than once."

"For her." He gives me a brief nod. "For the rebellion. Not for me. I don't owe him anything."

I shouldn't rise to the bait, but I do. "Maybe not. But Mags is dead and you're still here. That should count for something."

"Yeah, a lot of things should count for something that don't seem to, Katniss. I've got some memories I can't make sense of, and I don't think the Capitol touched them. A lot of nights on the train, for instance," he says.

Again the implications. That more happened on the train than did. That what did happen — those nights I only kept my sanity because his arms were around me — no longer matters. Everything a lie, everything a way of misusing him.

Peeta makes a little gesture with his spoon, connecting Gale and me. "So, are you two officially a couple now, or are they still dragging out the star-crossed lover thing?"

"Still dragging," says Johanna.

Spasms cause Peeta's hands to tighten into fists, then splay out in a bizarre fashion. Is it all he can do to keep them from my neck? I can feel the tension in Gale's muscles next to me, fear an altercation. But Gale simply says, "I wouldn't have believed it if I hadn't seen it myself."

"What's that?" asks Peeta.

"You," Gale answers.

"You'll have to be a little more specific," says Peeta. "What about me?"

"That they've replaced you with the evil-mutt version of yourself," says Johanna.

Gale finishes his milk. "You done?" he asks me. I rise and we cross to drop off our trays. At the door, an old man stops me because I'm still clutching the rest of my gravy bread in my hand. Something in my expression, or maybe the fact that I've made no attempt to conceal it, makes him go easy on me. He lets me stuff the bread in my mouth and move on. Gale and I are almost to my compartment when he speaks again. "I didn't expect that."

"I told you he hated me," I say.

"It's the way he hates you. It's so . . . familiar. I used to feel like that," he admits. "When I'd watch you kissing him on the screen. Only I knew I wasn't being entirely fair. He can't see that."

We reach my door. "Maybe he just sees me as I really am. I have to get some sleep."

Gale catches my arm before I can disappear. "So that's what you're thinking now?" I shrug. "Katniss, as your oldest friend, believe me when I say he's not seeing you as you really are." He kisses my cheek and goes.

I sit on my bed, trying to stuff information from my Military Tactics books into my head while memories of my nights with Peeta on the train distract me. After about twenty minutes, Johanna comes in and throws herself across the foot of my bed. "You missed the best part. Delly lost her temper at Peeta over how he treated you. She got very squeaky. It was like someone stabbing a mouse with a fork repeatedly. The whole dining hall was riveted."

"What'd Peeta do?" I ask.

"He started arguing with himself like he was two people. The guards had to take him away. On the good side, no one seemed to notice I finished his stew." Johanna rubs her hand over her protruding belly. I look at the layer of grime under her fingernails. Wonder if the people in 7 ever bathe.

We spend a couple of hours quizzing each other on military terms. I visit my mother and Prim for a while. When I'm back in my compartment, showered, staring into the darkness, I finally ask, "Johanna, could you really hear him screaming?"

"That was part of it," she says. "Like the jabberjays in the arena. Only it was real. And it didn't stop after an hour. Tick, tock."

"Tick, tock," I whisper back.

Roses. Wolf mutts. Tributes. Frosted dolphins. Friends. Mockingjays. Stylists. Me.

Everything screams in my dreams tonight.

18

I throw myself into training with a vengeance. Eat, live, and breathe the workouts, drills, weapons practice, lectures on tactics. A handful of us are moved into an additional class that gives me hope I may be a contender for the actual war. The soldiers simply call it the Block, but the tattoo on my arm lists it as S.S.C., short for Simulated Street Combat. Deep in 13, they've built an artificial Capitol city block. The instructor breaks us into squads of eight and we attempt to carry out missions—gaining a position, destroying a target, searching a home—as if we were really fighting our way through the Capitol. The thing's rigged so that everything that can go wrong for you does. A false step triggers a land mine, a sniper appears on a rooftop, your gun jams, a crying child leads you into an ambush, your squadron leader—who's just a voice on the program—gets hit by a mortar and you have to figure out what to do without orders. Part of you knows it's fake and that they're not going to kill you. If you set off a land mine, you hear the explosion and have to pretend to fall over dead. But in other ways, it feels pretty real in there—the enemy soldiers dressed in Peacekeepers' uniforms, the confusion of a smoke bomb. They even gas us. Johanna and I are the only ones who get our masks on in time. The rest of our squad gets knocked out for ten minutes. And the supposedly harmless gas I took a few lungfuls of gives me a wicked headache for the rest of the day.

Cressida and her crew tape Johanna and me on the firing range. I know Gale and Finnick are being filmed as well. It's part of a new propos series to show the rebels preparing for the Capitol invasion. On the whole, things are going pretty well.

Then Peeta starts showing up for our morning workouts. The manacles are off, but he's still constantly accompanied by a pair of guards. After lunch, I see him across the field, drilling with a group of beginners. I don't know what they're thinking. If a spat with Delly can reduce him to arguing with himself, he's got no business learning how to assemble a gun.

When I confront Plutarch, he assures me that it's all for the camera. They've got footage of Annie getting married and Johanna hitting targets, but all of Panem is wondering about Peeta. They need to see he's fighting for the rebels, not for Snow. And maybe if they could just get a couple of shots of the two of us, not kissing necessarily, just looking happy to be back together—

I walk away from the conversation right then. That is not going to happen.

In my rare moments of downtime, I anxiously watch the preparations for the invasions. See equipment and provisions readied, divisions assembled. You can tell when someone's received orders because they're given a very short haircut, the mark of a person going into battle. There is much talk of the opening offensive, which will be to secure the train tunnels that feed up into the Capitol.

Just a few days before the first troops are to move out, York unexpectedly tells Johanna and me she's recommended us for the exam, and we're to report immediately. There are four parts: an obstacle course that assesses your physical condition, a written tactics exam, a test of weapons proficiency, and a simulated combat situation in the Block. I don't even have time to get nervous for the first three and do well, but there's a backlog at the Block. Some kind of technical bug they're working out. A group of us exchanges information. This much seems true. You go through alone. There's no predicting what situation you'll be thrown into. One boy says, under his breath, that he's heard it's designed to target each individual's weaknesses.

My weaknesses? That's a door I don't even want to open. But I find a quiet spot and try to assess what they might be. The length of the list depresses me. Lack of physical brute force. A bare minimum of training. And somehow my standout status as the Mockingjay doesn't seem to be an advantage in a situation where they're trying to get us to blend into a pack. They could nail me to the wall on any number of things.

Johanna's called three ahead of me, and I give her a nod of encouragement. I wish I had been at the top of the list because now I'm really overthinking the whole thing. By the time my name's called, I don't know what my strategy should be. Fortunately, once I'm in the Block, a certain amount of training does kick in. It's an ambush situation.

Peacekeepers appear almost instantly and I have to make my way to a rendezvous point to meet up with my scattered squad. I slowly navigate the street, taking out Peacekeepers as I go. Two on the rooftop to my left, another in the doorway up ahead. It's challenging, but not as hard as I was expecting. There's a nagging feeling that if it's too simple, I must be missing the point. I'm within a couple of buildings from my goal when things begin to heat up. A half dozen Peacekeepers come charging around the corner. They will outgun me, but I notice something. A drum of gasoline lying carelessly in the gutter. This is it. My test. To perceive that blowing up the drum will be the only way to achieve my mission. Just as I step out to do it, my squadron leader, who's been fairly useless up to this point, quietly orders me to hit the ground. Every instinct I have screams for me to ignore the voice, to pull the trigger, to blow the Peacekeepers sky-high. And suddenly, I realize what the military will think my biggest weakness is. From my first moment in the Games, when I ran for that orange backpack, to the firefight in 8, to my impulsive race across the square in 2. I cannot take orders.

I smack into the ground so hard and fast, I'll be picking gravel out of my chin for a week. Someone else blows the gas tank. The Peacekeepers die. I make my rendezvous point. When I exit the Block on the far side, a soldier congratulates me, stamps my hand with squad number 451, and tells me to report to Command. Almost giddy with success, I run through the halls, skidding around corners, bounding down the steps because the elevator's too slow. I bang into the room before the oddity of the situation dawns on me. I shouldn't be in Command; I should be getting my hair buzzed. The people around the table aren't freshly minted soldiers but the ones calling the shots.

Boggs smiles and shakes his head when he sees me. "Let's see it." Unsure now, I hold out my stamped hand. "You're with me. It's a special unit of sharpshooters. Join your squad." He nods over at a group lining the wall. Gale. Finnick. Five others I don't know. My squad. I'm not only in, I get to work under Boggs. With my friends. I force myself to take calm, soldierly steps to join them, instead of jumping up and down.

We must be important, too, because we're in Command, and it has nothing to do with a certain Mockingjay. Plutarch stands over a wide, flat panel in the center of the table. He's explaining something about the nature of what we will encounter in the Capitol. I'm thinking this is a terrible presentation — because even on tiptoe I can't see what's on the panel — until he hits a button. A holographic image of a block of the Capitol projects into the air.

"This, for example, is the area surrounding one of the Peacekeepers' barracks. Not unimportant, but not the most crucial of targets, and yet look." Plutarch enters some sort of code on a keyboard, and lights begin to flash. They're in an assortment of colors and blink at different speeds. "Each light is called a pod. It represents a different obstacle, the nature of which could be anything from a bomb to a band of mutts. Make no mistake, whatever it contains is designed to either trap or kill you. Some have been in place since the Dark Days, others developed over the years. To be honest, I created a fair number myself. This program, which one of our people absconded with when we left the Capitol, is our most recent information. They don't know we have it. But even so, it's likely that new pods have been activated in the last few months. This is what you will face."

I'm unaware that my feet are moving to the table until I'm inches from the holograph. My hand reaches in and cups a rapidly blinking green light.

Someone joins me, his body tense. Finnick, of course. Because only a victor would see what I see so immediately. The arena. Laced with pods controlled by Gamemakers. Finnick's fingers caress a steady red glow over a doorway. "Ladies and gentlemen . . ."

His voice is quiet, but mine rings through the room. "Let the Seventy-sixth Hunger Games begin!"

I laugh. Quickly. Before anyone has time to register what lies beneath the words I have just uttered. Before eyebrows are raised, objections are uttered, two and two are put together, and the solution is that I should be kept as far away from the Capitol as possible. Because an angry, independently thinking victor with a layer of psychological scar tissue too thick to penetrate is maybe the last person you want on your squad.

"I don't even know why you bothered to put Finnick and me through training, Plutarch," I say.

"Yeah, we're already the two best-equipped soldiers you have," Finnick adds cockily.

"Do not think that fact escapes me," he says with an impatient wave. "Now back in line, Soldiers Odair and Everdeen. I have a presentation to finish."

We retreat to our places, ignoring the questioning looks thrown our way. I adopt an attitude of extreme concentration as Plutarch continues, nodding my head here and there, shifting my position to get a better view, all the while telling myself to hang on until I can get to the woods and scream. Or curse. Or cry. Or maybe all three at once.

If this was a test, Finnick and I both pass it. When Plutarch finishes and the meeting's adjourned, I have a bad moment when I learn there's a special order for me. But it's merely that I skip the military haircut because they would like the Mockingjay to look as much like the girl in the arena as possible at the anticipated surrender. For the cameras, you know. I shrug to communicate that my hair length's a matter of complete indifference to me. They dismiss me without further comment.

Finnick and I gravitate toward each other in the hall-way. "What will I tell Annie?" he says under his breath.

"Nothing," I answer. "That's what my mother and sister will be hearing from me." Bad enough that we know we're heading back into a fully equipped arena. No use dropping it on our loved ones.

"If she sees that holograph —" he begins.

"She won't. It's classified information. It must be," I say. "Anyway, it's not like an actual Games. Any number of people will survive. We're just overreacting because — well, you know why. You still want to go, don't you?"

"Of course. I want to destroy Snow as much as you do," he says.

"It won't be like the others," I say firmly, trying to convince myself as well. Then the real beauty of the situation dawns on me. "This time Snow will be a player, too."

Before we can continue, Haymitch appears. He wasn't at the meeting, isn't thinking of arenas but something else. "Johanna's back in the hospital."

I assumed Johanna was fine, had passed her exam, but simply wasn't assigned to a sharpshooters' unit. She's wicked throwing an ax but about average with a gun. "Is she hurt? What happened?"

"It was while she was on the Block. They try to ferret out a soldier's potential weaknesses. So they flooded the street," says Haymitch.

This doesn't help. Johanna can swim. At least, I seem to remember her swimming around some in the Quarter Quell. Not like Finnick, of course, but none of us are like Finnick. "So?"

"That's how they tortured her in the Capitol. Soaked her and then used electric shocks," says Haymitch. "In the Block she had some kind of flashback. Panicked, didn't know where she was. She's back under sedation." Finnick and I just stand there, as if we've lost the ability to respond. I think of the way Johanna never showers. How she forced herself into the rain like it was acid that day. I had attributed her misery to the morphling withdrawal.

"You two should go see her. You're as close to friends as she's got," says Haymitch.

That makes the whole thing worse. I don't really know what's between Johanna and Finnick. But I hardly know her. No family. No friends. Not so much as a token from 7 to set beside her regulation clothes in her anonymous drawer. Nothing.

"I better go tell Plutarch. He won't be happy," Haymitch continues. "He wants as many victors as possible for the cameras to follow in the Capitol. Thinks it makes for better television."

"Are you and Beetee going?" I ask.

"As many young and attractive victors as possible," Haymitch corrects himself. "So, no. We'll be here."

Finnick goes directly down to see Johanna, but I linger outside a few minutes until Boggs comes out. He's my commander now, so I guess he's the one to ask for any special favors. When I tell him what I want to do, he writes me a pass so that I can go to the woods during Reflection, provided I stay within sight of the guards. I run to my compartment, thinking to use the parachute, but it's so full of ugly memories. Instead, I go across the hall and take one of the white cotton bandages I brought from 12. Square. Sturdy. Just the thing.

In the woods, I find a pine tree and strip handfuls of fragrant needles from the boughs. After making a neat pile in the middle of the bandage, I gather up the sides, give them a twist, and tie them tightly with a length of vine, making an apple-sized bundle.

At the hospital room door, I watch Johanna for a moment, realize that most of her ferocity is in her abrasive attitude. Stripped of that, as she is now, there's only a slight young woman, her wide-set eyes fighting to stay awake against the power of the drugs. Terrified of what sleep will bring. I cross to her and hold out the bundle.

"What's that?" she says hoarsely. Damp edges of her hair form little spikes over her forehead.

"I made it for you. Something to put in your drawer." I place it in her hands. "Smell it."

She lifts the bundle to her nose and takes a tentative sniff. "Smells like home." Tears flood her eyes.

"That's what I was hoping. You being from Seven and all," I say. "Remember when we met? You were a tree. Well, briefly."

Suddenly, she has my wrist in an iron grip. "You have to kill him, Katniss."

"Don't worry." I resist the temptation to wrench my arm free.

"Swear it. On something you care about," she hisses.

"I swear it. On my life." But she doesn't let go of my arm.

"On your family's life," she insists.

"On my family's life," I repeat. I guess my concern for my own survival isn't compelling enough. She lets go and I rub my wrist. "Why do you think I'm going, anyway, brainless?"

That makes her smile a little. "I just needed to hear it." She presses the bundle of pine needles to her nose and closes her eyes.

The remaining days go by in a whirl. After a brief workout each morning, my squad's on the shooting range full-time in training. I practice mostly with a gun, but they reserve an hour a day for specialty weapons, which means I get to use my Mockingjay bow, Gale his heavy militarized one. The trident Beetee designed for Finnick has a lot of special features, but the most remarkable is that he can throw it, press a button on a metal cuff on his wrist, and return it to his hand without chasing it down.

Sometimes we shoot at Peacekeeper dummies to become familiar with the weaknesses in their protective gear. The chinks in the armor, so to speak. If you hit flesh, you're rewarded with a burst of fake blood. Our dummies are soaked in red.

It's reassuring to see just how high the overall level of accuracy is in our group. Along with Finnick and Gale, the squad includes five soldiers from 13. Jackson, a middle-aged woman who's Boggs's second in command, looks kind of sluggish but can hit things the rest of us can't even see without a scope. Farsighted, she says. There's a pair of sisters in their twenties named Leeg—we call them Leeg 1 and Leeg 2 for clarity—who are so similar in uniform, I can't tell them apart until I notice Leeg 1 has weird yellow flecks in her eyes. Two older guys, Mitchell and Homes, never say much but can shoot the dust off your boots at fifty yards. I see other squads that are also quite good, but I don't fully understand our status until the morning Plutarch joins us.

"Squad Four-Five-One, you have been selected for a special mission," he begins. I bite the inside of my lip, hoping against hope that it's to assassinate Snow. "We have numerous sharpshooters, but rather a dearth of camera crews. Therefore, we've handpicked the eight of you to be what we call our 'Star Squad.' You will be the on-screen faces of the invasion."

Disappointment, shock, then anger run through the group. "What you're saying is, we won't be in actual combat," snaps Gale.

"You will be in combat, but perhaps not always on the front line. If one can even isolate a front line in this type of war," says Plutarch.

"None of us wants that." Finnick's remark is followed by a general rumble of assent, but I stay silent. "We're going to fight."

"You're going to be as useful to the war effort as possible," Plutarch says. "And it's been decided that you are of most value on television. Just look at the effect Katniss had running around in that Mockingjay suit. Turned the whole rebellion around. Do you notice how she's the only one not complaining? It's because she understands the power of that screen."

Actually, Katniss isn't complaining because she has no intention of staying with the "Star Squad," but she recognizes the necessity of getting to the Capitol before carrying out any plan. Still, to be too compliant may arouse suspicion as well.

"But it's not all pretend, is it?" I ask. "That'd be a waste of talent."

"Don't worry," Plutarch tells me. "You'll have plenty of real targets to hit. But don't get blown up. I've got enough on my plate without having to replace you. Now get to the Capitol and put on a good show."

The morning we ship out, I say good-bye to my family. I haven't told them how much the Capitol's defenses mirror the weapons in the arena, but my going off to war is awful enough on its own. My mother holds me tightly for a long time. I feel tears on her cheek, something she suppressed when I was slated for the Games. "Don't worry. I'll be perfectly safe. I'm not even a real soldier. Just one of Plutarch's televised puppets," I reassure her.

Prim walks me as far as the hospital doors. "How do you feel?"

"Better, knowing you're somewhere Snow can't reach you," I say.

"Next time we see each other, we'll be free of him," says Prim firmly. Then she throws her arms around my neck. "Be careful."

I consider saying a final good-bye to Peeta, decide it would only be bad for both of us. But I do slip the pearl into the pocket of my uniform. A token of the boy with the bread.

A hovercraft takes us to, of all places, 12, where a makeshift transportation area has been set up outside the fire zone. No luxury trains this time, but a cargo car packed to the limit with soldiers in their dark gray uniforms, sleeping with their heads on their packs. After a couple of days' travel, we disembark inside one of the mountain tunnels leading to the Capitol, and make the rest of the six-hour trek on foot, taking care to step only on a glowing green paint line that marks safe passage to the air above.

We come out in the rebel encampment, a ten-block stretch outside the train station where Peeta and I made our previous arrivals. It's already crawling with soldiers. Squad 451 is assigned a spot to pitch its tents. This area has been secured for over a week. Rebels pushed out the Peacekeepers, losing hundreds of lives in the process. The Capitol forces fell back and have regrouped farther into the city. Between us lie the booby-trapped streets, empty and inviting. Each one will need to be swept of pods before we can advance.

Mitchell asks about hoverplane bombings—we do feel very naked pitched out in the open—but Boggs says it's not an issue. Most of the Capitol's air fleet was destroyed in 2 or during the invasion. If it has any craft left, it's holding on to them. Probably so Snow and his inner circle can make a last-minute escape to some presidential bunker somewhere if needed. Our own hoverplanes were grounded after the Capitol's antiaircraft missiles decimated the first few waves. This war will be battled out on the streets with, hopefully, only superficial damage to the infrastructure and a minimum of human casualties. The rebels want the Capitol, just as the Capitol wanted 13.

After three days, much of Squad 451 risks deserting out of boredom. Cressida and her team take shots of us firing. They tell us we're part of the disinformation team. If the rebels only shoot Plutarch's pods, it will take the Capitol about two minutes to realize we have the holograph. So there's a lot of time spent shattering things that don't matter, to throw them off the scent. Mostly we just add to the piles of rainbow glass that's been blown off the exteriors of the candy-colored buildings. I suspect they are intercutting this footage with the destruction of significant Capitol targets. Once in a while it seems a real sharpshooter's services are needed. Eight hands go up, but Gale, Finnick, and I are never chosen.

"It's your own fault for being so camera-ready," I tell Gale. If looks could kill.

I don't think they quite know what to do with the three of us, particularly me. I have my Mockingjay outfit with me, but I've only been taped in my uniform. Sometimes I use a gun, sometimes they ask me to shoot with my bow and arrows. It's as if they don't want to entirely lose the Mockingjay, but they want to downgrade my role to foot soldier. Since I don't care, it's amusing rather than upsetting to imagine the arguments going on back in 13.

While I outwardly express discontent about our lack of any real participation, I'm busy with my own agenda. Each of us has a paper map of the Capitol. The city forms an almost perfect square. Lines divide the map into smaller squares, with letters along the top and numbers down the side to form a grid. I consume this, noting every intersection and side street, but it's remedial stuff. The commanders here are working off Plutarch's holograph. Each has a hand-held contraption called a Holo that produces images like I saw in Command. They can zoom into any area of the grid and see what pods await them. The Holo's an independent unit, a glorified map really, since it can neither send nor receive signals. But it's far superior to my paper version.

A Holo is activated by a specific commander's voice giving his or her name. Once it's working, it responds to the other voices in the squadron so if, say, Boggs were killed or severely disabled, someone could take over. If anyone in the squad repeats "nightlock" three times in a row, the Holo will explode, blowing everything in a five-yard radius sky-high. This is for security reasons in the event of capture. It's understood that we would all do this without hesitation.

So what I need to do is steal Boggs's activated Holo and clear out before he notices. I think it would be easier to steal his teeth.

On the fourth morning, Soldier Leeg 2 hits a mislabeled pod. It doesn't unleash a swarm of muttation gnats, which the rebels are prepared for, but shoots out a sunburst of metal darts. One finds her brain. She's gone before the medics can reach her. Plutarch promises a speedy replacement.

The following evening, the newest member of our squad arrives. With no manacles. No guards. Strolling out of the train station with his gun swinging from the strap over his shoulder. There's shock, confusion, resistance, but *451* is stamped on the back of Peeta's hand in fresh ink. Boggs relieves him of his weapon and goes to make a call.

"It won't matter," Peeta tells the rest of us. "The president assigned me herself. She decided the propos needed some heating up."

Maybe they do. But if Coin sent Peeta here, she's decided something else as well. That I'm of more use to her dead than alive.

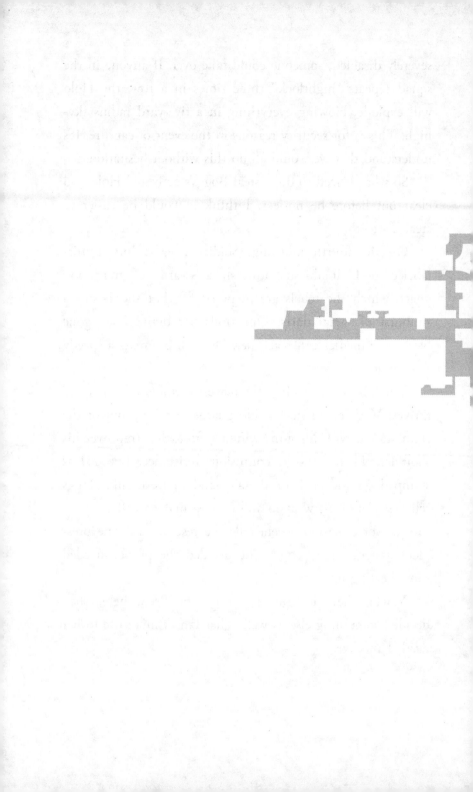

PART III
"THE ASSASSIN"

I've never really seen Boggs angry before. Not when I've disobeyed his orders or puked on him, not even when Gale broke his nose. But he's angry when he returns from his phone call with the president. The first thing he does is instruct Soldier Jackson, his second in command, to set up a two-person, round-the-clock guard on Peeta. Then he takes me on a walk, weaving through the sprawling tent encampment until our squad is far behind us.

"He'll try and kill me anyway," I say. "Especially here. Where there are so many bad memories to set him off."

"I'll keep him contained, Katniss," says Boggs.

"Why does Coin want me dead now?" I ask.

"She denies she does," he answers.

"But we know it's true," I say. "And you must at least have a theory."

Boggs gives me a long, hard look before he answers. "Here's as much as I know. The president doesn't like you. She never did. It was Peeta she wanted rescued from the arena, but no one else agreed. It made matters worse when you forced her to give the other victors immunity. But even that could be overlooked in view of how well you've performed."

"Then what is it?" I insist.

"Sometime in the near future, this war will be resolved. A new leader will be chosen," says Boggs.

I roll my eyes. "Boggs, no one thinks I'm going to be the leader."

"No. They don't," he agrees. "But you'll throw support to someone. Would it be President Coin? Or someone else?"

"I don't know. I've never thought about it," I say.

"If your immediate answer isn't Coin, then you're a threat. You're the face of the rebellion. You may have more influence than any other single person," says Boggs. "Outwardly, the most you've ever done is tolerated her."

"So she'll kill me to shut me up." The minute I say the words, I know they're true.

"She doesn't need you as a rallying point now. As she said, your primary objective, to unite the districts, has succeeded," Boggs reminds me. "These current propos could be done without you. There's only one last thing you could do to add fire to the rebellion."

"Die," I say quietly.

"Yes. Give us a martyr to fight for," says Boggs. "But that's not going to happen under my watch, Soldier Everdeen. I'm planning for you to have a long life."

"Why?" This kind of thinking will only bring him trouble. "You don't owe me anything."

"Because you've earned it," he says. "Now get back to your squad."

I know I should feel appreciative of Boggs sticking his neck out for me, but really I'm just frustrated. I mean, how can I steal his Holo and desert now? Betraying him was complicated enough without this whole new layer of debt. I already owe him for saving my life.

Seeing the cause of my current dilemma calmly pitching his tent back at our site makes me furious. "What time is my watch?" I ask Jackson.

She squints at me in doubt, or maybe she's just trying to get my face in focus. "I didn't put you in the rotation."

"Why not?" I ask.

"I'm not sure you could really shoot Peeta, if it came to it," she says.

I speak up so the whole squad can hear me clearly. "I wouldn't be shooting Peeta. He's gone. Johanna's right. It'd be just like shooting another of the Capitol's mutts." It feels good to say something horrible about him, out loud, in public, after all the humiliation I've felt since his return.

"Well, that sort of comment isn't recommending you either," says Jackson.

"Put her in the rotation," I hear Boggs say behind me.

Jackson shakes her head and makes a note. "Midnight to four. You're on with me."

The dinner whistle sounds, and Gale and I line up at the canteen. "Do you want me to kill him?" he asks bluntly.

"That'll get us both sent back for sure," I say. But even though I'm furious, the brutality of the offer rattles me. "I can deal with him."

"You mean until you take off? You and your paper map and possibly a Holo if you can get your hands on it?" So Gale has not missed my preparations. I hope they haven't been so obvious to the others. None of them know my mind like he does, though. "You're not planning on leaving me behind, are you?" he asks.

Up until this point, I was. But having my hunting partner to watch my back doesn't sound like a bad idea. "As your fellow soldier, I have to strongly recommend you stay with your squad. But I can't stop you from coming, can I?"

He grins. "No. Not unless you want me to alert the rest of the army."

Squad 451 and the television crew collect dinner from the canteen and gather in a tense circle to eat. At first I think that Peeta is the cause of the unease, but by the end of the meal, I realize more than a few unfriendly looks have been directed my way. This is a quick turnaround, since I'm pretty sure when Peeta appeared the whole team was concerned about how dangerous he might be, especially to me. But it's not until I get a phone call through to Haymitch that I understand.

"What are you trying to do? Provoke him into an attack?" he asks me.

"Of course not. I just want him to leave me alone," I say.

"Well, he can't. Not after what the Capitol put him through," says Haymitch. "Look, Coin may have sent him there hoping he'd kill you, but Peeta doesn't know that. He doesn't understand what's happened to him. So you can't blame him —"

"I don't!" I say.

"You do! You're punishing him over and over for things that are out of his control. Now, I'm not saying you shouldn't have a fully loaded weapon next to you round the clock. But I think it's time you flipped this little scenario around in your head. If you'd been taken by the Capitol, and hijacked, and then tried to kill Peeta, is this the way he would be treating you?" demands Haymitch.

I fall silent. It isn't. It isn't how he would be treating me at all. He would be trying to get me back at any cost. Not shutting me out, abandoning me, greeting me with hostility at every turn.

"You and me, we made a deal to try and save him. Remember?" Haymitch says. When I don't respond, he disconnects after a curt "Try and remember."

The autumn day turns from brisk to cold. Most of the squad hunker down in their sleeping bags. Some sleep under the open sky, close to the heater in the center of our camp, while others retreat to their tents. Leeg 1 has finally broken down over her sister's death, and her muffled sobs reach us through the canvas. I huddle in my tent, thinking over Haymitch's words. Realizing with shame that my fixation with assassinating Snow has allowed me to ignore a much more difficult problem. Trying to rescue Peeta from the shadowy world the hijacking has stranded him in. I don't know how to find him, let alone lead him out. I can't even conceive of a plan. It makes the task of crossing a loaded arena, locating Snow, and putting a bullet through his head look like child's play.

At midnight, I crawl out of my tent and position myself on a camp stool near the heater to take my watch with Jackson. Boggs told Peeta to sleep out in full view where the rest of us could keep an eye on him. He isn't sleeping, though. Instead, he sits with his bag pulled up to his chest, clumsily trying to make knots in a short length of rope. I know it well. It's the one Finnick lent me that night in the bunker. Seeing it in his hands, it's like Finnick's echoing what Haymitch just said, that I've cast off Peeta. Now might be a good time to begin to remedy that. If I could think of something to say. But I can't. So I don't. I just let the sounds of soldiers' breathing fill the night.

After about an hour, Peeta speaks up. "These last couple of years must have been exhausting for you. Trying to decide whether to kill me or not. Back and forth. Back and forth."

That seems grossly unfair, and my first impulse is to say something cutting. But I revisit my conversation with Haymitch and try to take the first tentative step in Peeta's direction. "I never wanted to kill you. Except when I thought you were helping the Careers kill me. After that, I always thought of you as . . . an ally." That's a good safe word. Empty of any emotional obligation, but nonthreatening.

"Ally." Peeta says the word slowly, tasting it. "Friend. Lover. Victor. Enemy. Fiancée. Target. Mutt. Neighbor. Hunter. Tribute. Ally. I'll add it to the list of words I use to try to figure you out." He weaves the rope in and out of his fingers. "The problem is, I can't tell what's real anymore, and what's made up."

The cessation of rhythmic breathing suggests that either people have woken or have never really been asleep at all. I suspect the latter.

Finnick's voice rises from a bundle in the shadows. "Then you should ask, Peeta. That's what Annie does."

"Ask who?" Peeta says. "Who can I trust?"

"Well, us for starters. We're your squad," says Jackson.

"You're my guards," he points out.

"That, too," she says. "But you saved a lot of lives in Thirteen. It's not the kind of thing we forget."

In the quiet that follows, I try to imagine not being able to tell illusion from reality. Not knowing if Prim or my mother loved me. If Snow was my enemy. If the person across the heater saved or sacrificed me. With very little effort, my life rapidly morphs into a nightmare. I suddenly want to tell Peeta everything about who he is, and who I am, and how we ended up here. But I don't know how to start. Worthless. I'm worthless.

At a few minutes before four, Peeta turns to me again. "Your favorite color . . . it's green?"

"That's right." Then I think of something to add. "And yours is orange."

"Orange?" He seems unconvinced.

"Not bright orange. But soft. Like the sunset," I say. "At least, that's what you told me once."

"Oh." He closes his eyes briefly, maybe trying to conjure up that sunset, then nods his head. "Thank you."

But more words tumble out. "You're a painter. You're a baker. You like to sleep with the windows open. You never take sugar in your tea. And you always double-knot your shoelaces."

Then I dive into my tent before I do something stupid like cry.

In the morning, Gale, Finnick, and I go out to shoot some glass off the buildings for the camera crew. When we get back to camp, Peeta's sitting in a circle with the soldiers from 13, who are armed but talking openly with him. Jackson has devised a game called "Real or Not Real" to help Peeta. He mentions something he thinks happened, and they tell him if it's true or imagined, usually followed by a brief explanation.

"Most of the people from Twelve were killed in the fire."

"Real. Less than nine hundred of you made it to Thirteen alive."

"The fire was my fault."

"Not real. President Snow destroyed Twelve the way he did Thirteen, to send a message to the rebels."

This seems like a good idea until I realize that I'll be the only one who can confirm or deny most of what weighs on him. Jackson breaks us up into watches. She matches up Finnick, Gale, and me each with a soldier from 13. This way Peeta will always have access to someone who knows him more personally. It's not a steady conversation. Peeta spends a long time considering even small pieces of information, like where people bought their soap back home. Gale fills him in on a lot of stuff about 12; Finnick is the expert on both of Peeta's Games, as he was a mentor in the first and a tribute in the second. But since Peeta's greatest confusion centers around me—and not everything can be explained simply—our exchanges are painful and loaded, even though we touch on only the most superficial of details. The color of my dress in 7. My preference for cheese buns. The name of our math teacher when we were little. Reconstructing his memory of me is excruciating. Perhaps it isn't even possible after what Snow did to him. But it does feel right to help him try.

The next afternoon, we're notified that the whole squad is needed to stage a fairly complicated propo. Peeta's been right about one thing: Coin and Plutarch are unhappy with the quality of footage they're getting from the Star Squad. Very dull. Very uninspiring. The obvious response is that they never let us do anything but playact with our guns. However, this is not about defending ourselves, it's about coming up with a usable product. So today, a special block has been set aside for filming. It even has a couple of active pods on it. One unleashes a spray of gunfire. The other nets the invader and traps them for either interrogation or execution, depending on the captors' preference. But it's still an unimportant residential block with nothing of strategic consequence.

The television crew means to provide a sense of heightened jeopardy by releasing smoke bombs and adding gunfire sound effects. We suit up in heavy protective gear, even the crew, as if we're heading into the heart of battle. Those of us with specialty weapons are allowed to take them along with our guns. Boggs gives Peeta back his gun, too, although he makes sure to tell him in a loud voice that it's only loaded with blanks.

Peeta just shrugs. "I'm not much of a shot anyway." He seems preoccupied with watching Pollux, to the point where it's getting a little worrisome, when he finally puzzles it out and begins to speak with agitation. "You're an Avox, aren't you? I can tell by the way you swallow. There were two Avoxes with me in prison. Darius and Lavinia, but the guards mostly called them the redheads. They'd been our servants in the Training Center, so they arrested them, too. I watched them being tortured to death. She was lucky. They used too much voltage and her heart stopped right off. It took days to finish him off. Beating, cutting off parts. They kept asking him questions, but he couldn't speak, he just made these horrible animal sounds. They didn't want information, you know? They wanted me to see it."

Peeta looks around at our stunned faces, as if waiting for a reply. When none is forthcoming, he asks, "Real or not real?" The lack of response upsets him more. "Real or not real?!" he demands.

"Real," says Boggs. "At least, to the best of my knowledge . . . real."

Peeta sags. "I thought so. There was nothing . . . shiny about it." He wanders away from the group, muttering something about fingers and toes.

I move to Gale, press my forehead into the body armor where his chest should be, feel his arm tighten around me. We finally know the name of the girl who we watched the Capitol abduct from the woods of 12, the fate of the Peacekeeper friend who tried to keep Gale alive. This is no time to call up happy moments of remembrance. They lost their lives because of me. I add them to my personal list of kills that began in the arena and now includes thousands. When I look up, I see it has taken Gale differently. His expression says that there are not enough mountains to crush, enough cities to destroy. It promises death.

With Peeta's grisly account fresh in our minds, we crunch through the streets of broken glass until we reach our target, the block we are to take. It is a real, if small, goal to accomplish. We gather around Boggs to examine the Holo projection of the street. The gunfire pod is positioned about a third of the way down, just above an apartment awning. We should be able to trigger it with bullets. The net pod is at the far end, almost the next corner. This will require someone to set off the body sensor mechanism. Everyone volunteers except Peeta, who doesn't seem to know quite what's going on. I don't get picked. I get sent to Messalla, who dabs some makeup on my face for the anticipated close-ups.

The squad positions itself under Boggs's direction, and then we have to wait for Cressida to get the cameramen in place as well. They're both to our left, with Castor toward the front and Pollux bringing up the rear so they'll be sure not to record each other. Messalla sets off a couple of smoke charges for atmosphere. Since this is both a mission and a shoot, I'm about to ask who's in charge, my commander or my director, when Cressida calls, "Action!"

We slowly proceed down the hazy street, just like one of our exercises in the Block. Everyone has at least one section of windows to blow out, but Gale's assigned the real target. When he hits the pod, we take cover — ducking into doorways or flattening onto the pretty, light orange and pink paving stones — as a hail of bullets sweeps back and forth over our heads. After a while, Boggs orders us forward.

Cressida stops us before we can rise, since she needs some close-up shots. We take turns reenacting our responses.

Falling to the ground, grimacing, diving into alcoves. We know it's supposed to be serious business, but the whole thing feels a little ridiculous. Especially when it turns out that I'm not the worst actor in the squad. Not by a long shot. We're all laughing so hard at Mitchell's attempt to project his idea of desperation, which involves teeth grinding and nostrils flaring, that Boggs has to reprimand us.

"Pull it together, Four-Five-One," he says firmly. But you can see him suppressing a smile as he's double-checking the next pod. Positioning the Holo to find the best light in the smoky air. Still facing us as his left foot steps back onto the orange paving stone. Triggering the bomb that blows off his legs.

20

It's as if in an instant, a painted window shatters, revealing the ugly world behind it. Laughter changes to screams, blood stains pastel stones, real smoke darkens the special effect stuff made for television.

A second explosion seems to split the air and leaves my ears ringing. But I can't make out where it came from.

I reach Boggs first, try to make sense of the torn flesh, missing limbs, to find something to stem the red flow from his body. Homes pushes me aside, wrenching open a first-aid kit. Boggs clutches my wrist. His face, gray with dying and ash, seems to be receding. But his next words are an order. "The Holo."

The Holo. I scramble around, digging through chunks of tile slick with blood, shuddering when I encounter bits of warm flesh. Find it rammed into a stairwell with one of Boggs's boots. Retrieve it, wiping it clean with bare hands as I return it to my commander.

Homes has the stump of Boggs's left thigh cupped by some sort of compression bandage, but it's already soaked through. He's trying to tourniquet the other above the existing knee. The rest of the squad has gathered in a protective formation around the crew and us. Finnick's attempting to revive Messalla, who was thrown into a wall by the explosion.

Jackson's barking into a field communicator, trying unsuccessfully to alert the camp to send medics, but I know it's too late. As a child, watching my mother work, I learned that once a pool of blood has reached a certain size, there's no going back.

I kneel beside Boggs, prepared to repeat the role I played with Rue, with the morphling from 6, giving him someone to hold on to as he's released from life. But Boggs has both hands working the Holo. He's typing in a command, pressing his thumb to the screen for print recognition, speaking a string of letters and numbers in response to a prompt. A green shaft of light bursts out of the Holo and illuminates his face. He says, "Unfit for command. Transfer of prime security clearance to Squad Four-Five-One Soldier Katniss Everdeen." It's all he can do to turn the Holo toward my face. "Say your name."

"Katniss Everdeen," I say into the green shaft. Suddenly, it has me trapped in its light. I can't move or even blink as images flicker rapidly before me. Scanning me? Recording me? Blinding me? It vanishes, and I shake my head to clear it. "What did you do?"

"Prepare to retreat!" Jackson hollers.

Finnick's yelling something back, gesturing to the end of the block where we entered. Black, oily matter spouts like a geyser from the street, billowing between the buildings, creating an impenetrable wall of darkness. It seems to be neither liquid nor gas, mechanical nor natural. Surely it's lethal. There's no heading back the way we came.

Deafening gunfire as Gale and Leeg 1 begin to blast a path across the stones toward the far end of the block. I don't know what they're doing until another bomb, ten yards away, detonates, opening a hole in the street. Then I realize this is a rudimentary attempt at minesweeping. Homes and I latch on to Boggs and begin to drag him after Gale. Agony takes over and he's crying out in pain and I want to stop, to find a better way, but the blackness is rising above the buildings, swelling, rolling at us like a wave.

I'm yanked backward, lose my grip on Boggs, slam into the stones. Peeta looks down at me, gone, mad, flashing back into the land of the hijacked, his gun raised over me, descending to crush my skull. I roll, hear the butt slam into the street, catch the tumble of bodies out of the corner of my eye as Mitchell tackles Peeta and pins him to the ground. But Peeta, always so powerful and now fueled by tracker jacker insanity, gets his feet under Mitchell's belly and launches him farther down the block.

There's a loud snap of a trap as the pod triggers. Four cables, attached to tracks on the buildings, break through the stones, dragging up the net that encases Mitchell. It makes no sense—how instantly bloodied he is—until we see the barbs sticking from the wire that encases him. I know it immediately. It decorated the top of the fence around 12. As I call to him not to move, I gag on the smell of the blackness, thick, tarlike. The wave has crested and begun to fall.

Gale and Leeg 1 shoot through the front door lock of the corner building, then begin to fire at the cables holding Mitchell's net. Others are restraining Peeta now. I lunge back to Boggs, and Homes and I drag him inside the apartment, through someone's pink and white velvet living room, down a hallway hung with family photos, onto the marble floor of a kitchen, where we collapse. Castor and Pollux carry in a writhing Peeta between them. Somehow Jackson gets cuffs on him, but it only makes him wilder and they're forced to lock him in a closet.

In the living room, the front door slams, people shout. Then footsteps pound down the hall as the black wave roars past the building. From the kitchen, we can hear the windows groan, shatter. The noxious tar smell permeates the air. Finnick carries in Messalla. Leeg 1 and Cressida stumble into the room after them, coughing.

"Gale!" I shriek.

He's there, slamming the kitchen door shut behind him, choking out one word. "Fumes!" Castor and Pollux grab towels, aprons to stuff in the cracks as Gale retches into a bright yellow sink.

"Mitchell?" asks Homes. Leeg 1 just shakes her head.

Boggs forces the Holo into my hand. His lips are moving, but I can't make out what he's saying. I lean my ear down to his mouth to catch his harsh whisper. "Don't trust them. Don't go back. Kill Peeta. Do what you came to do."

I draw back so I can see his face. "What? Boggs? Boggs?" His eyes are still open, but dead. Pressed in my hand, glued to it by his blood, is the Holo.

Peeta's feet slamming into the closet door break up the ragged breathing of the others. But even as we listen, his energy seems to ebb. The kicks diminish to an irregular drumming. Then nothing. I wonder if he, too, is dead.

"He's gone?" Finnick asks, looking down at Boggs. I nod. "We need to get out of here. Now. We just set off a streetful of pods. You can bet they've got us on surveillance tapes."

"Count on it," says Castor. "All the streets are covered by surveillance cameras. I bet they set off the black wave manually when they saw us taping the propo."

"Our radio communicators went dead almost immediately. Probably an electromagnetic pulse device. But I'll get us back to camp. Give me the Holo." Jackson reaches for the unit, but I clutch it to my chest.

"No. Boggs gave it to me," I say.

"Don't be ridiculous," she snaps. Of course, she thinks it's hers. She's second in command.

"It's true," says Homes. "He transferred the prime security clearance to her while he was dying. I saw it."

"Why would he do that?" demands Jackson.

Why indeed? My head's reeling from the ghastly events of the last five minutes—Boggs mutilated, dying, dead, Peeta's homicidal rage, Mitchell bloody and netted and swallowed by that foul black wave. I turn to Boggs, very badly needing him alive. Suddenly sure that he, and maybe he alone, is completely on my side. I think of his last orders. . . .

"Don't trust them. Don't go back. Kill Peeta. Do what you came to do."

What did he mean? Don't trust who? The rebels? Coin? The people looking at me right now? I won't go back, but he must know I can't just fire a bullet through Peeta's head. Can I? Should I? Did Boggs guess that what I really came to do is desert and kill Snow on my own?

I can't work all of this out now, so I just decide to carry out the first two orders: to not trust anyone and to move deeper into the Capitol. But how can I justify this? Make them let me keep the Holo?

"Because I'm on a special mission for President Coin. I think Boggs was the only one who knew about it."

This in no way convinces Jackson. "To do what?"

Why not tell them the truth? It's as plausible as anything I'll come up with. But it must seem like a real mission, not revenge. "To assassinate President Snow before the loss of life from this war makes our population unsustainable."

"I don't believe you," says Jackson. "As your current commander, I order you to transfer the prime security clearance over to me."

"No," I say. "That would be in direct violation of President Coin's orders."

Guns are pointed. Half the squad at Jackson, half at me. Someone's about to die, when Cressida speaks up. "It's true. That's why we're here. Plutarch wants it televised. He thinks if we can film the Mockingjay assassinating Snow, it will end the war."

This gives even Jackson pause. Then she gestures with her gun toward the closet. "And why is he here?"

There she has me. I can think of no sane reason that Coin would send an unstable boy, programmed to kill me, along on such a key assignment. It really weakens my story. Cressida comes to my aid again. "Because the two post-Games interviews with Caesar Flickerman were shot in President Snow's personal quarters. Plutarch thinks Peeta may be of some use as a guide in a location we have little knowledge of."

I want to ask Cressida why she's lying for me, why she's fighting for us to go on with my self-appointed mission. Now's not the time.

"We have to go!" says Gale. "I'm following Katniss. If you don't want to, head back to camp. But let's move!"

Homes unlocks the closet and heaves an unconscious Peeta over his shoulder. "Ready."

"Boggs?" says Leeg 1.

"We can't take him. He'd understand," says Finnick. He frees Boggs's gun from his shoulder and slings the strap over his own. "Lead on, Soldier Everdeen."

I don't know how to lead on. I look at the Holo for direction. It's still activated, but it might as well be dead for all the good that does me. There's no time for fiddling around with the buttons, trying to figure out how to work it. "I don't know how to use this. Boggs said you would help me," I tell Jackson. "He said I could count on you."

Jackson scowls, snatches the Holo from me, and taps in a command. An intersection comes up. "If we go out the kitchen door, there's a small courtyard, then the back side of another corner apartment unit. We're looking at an over-view of the four streets that meet at the intersection."

I try to get my bearings as I stare at the cross section of the map blinking with pods in every direction. And those are only the pods Plutarch knows about. The Holo didn't indicate that the block we just left was mined, had the black geyser, or that the net was made from barbed wire. Besides that, there may be Peacekeepers to deal with, now that they know our position. I bite the inside of my lip, feeling every-one's eyes on me. "Put on your masks. We're going out the way we came in."

Instant objections. I raise my voice over them. "If the wave was that powerful, then it may have triggered and absorbed other pods in our path."

People stop to consider this. Pollux makes a few quick signs to his brother. "It may have disabled the cameras as well," Castor translates. "Coated the lenses."

Gale props one of his boots on the counter and examines the splatter of black on the toe. Scrapes it with a kitchen knife from a block on the counter. "It's not corrosive. I think it was meant to either suffocate or poison us."

"Probably our best shot," says Leeg 1.

Masks go on. Finnick adjusts Peeta's mask over his life-less face. Cressida and Leeg 1 prop up a woozy Messalla between them.

I'm waiting for someone to take the point position when I remember that's my job now. I push on the kitchen door and meet with no resistance. A half-inch layer of the black goo has spread from the living room about three-quarters of the way down the hall. When I gingerly test it with the toe of my boot, I find it has the consistency of a gel. I lift my foot and after stretching slightly, it springs back into place. I take three steps into the gel and look back. No footprints. It's the first good thing that's happened today. The gel becomes slightly thicker as I cross the living room. I ease open the front door, expecting gallons of the stuff to pour in, but it holds its form.

The pink and orange block seems to have been dipped in glossy black paint and set out to dry. Paving stones, buildings, even the rooftops are coated in the gel. A large teardrop hangs above the street. Two shapes project from it. A gun barrel and a human hand. Mitchell. I wait on the sidewalk, staring up at him until the entire group has joined me.

"If anyone needs to go back, for whatever reason, now is the time," I say. "No questions asked, no hard feelings." No one seems inclined to retreat. So I start moving into the Capitol, knowing we don't have much time. The gel's deeper here, four to six inches, and makes a sucking sound each time you pick up your foot, but it still covers our tracks.

The wave must have been enormous, with tremendous power behind it, as it's affected several blocks that lie ahead. And though I tread with care, I think my instinct was right about its triggering other pods. One block is sprinkled with the golden bodies of tracker jackers. They must have been set free only to succumb to the fumes. A little farther along, an entire apartment building has collapsed and lies in a mound under the gel. I sprint across the intersections, holding up a hand for the others to wait while I look for trouble, but the wave seems to have dismantled the pods far better than any squad of rebels could.

On the fifth block, I can tell that we've reached the point where the wave began to peter out. The gel's only an inch deep, and I can see baby blue rooftops peeking out across the next intersection. The afternoon light has faded, and we badly need to get under cover and form a plan. I choose an apartment two-thirds of the way down the block. Homes jimmies the lock, and I order the others inside. I stay on the street for just a minute, watching the last of our footprints fade away, then close the door behind me.

Flashlights built into our guns illuminate a large living room with mirrored walls that throw our faces back at us at every turn. Gale checks the windows, which show no damage, and removes his mask. "It's all right. You can smell it, but it's not too strong."

The apartment seems to be laid out exactly like the first one we took refuge in. The gel blacks out any natural daylight in the front, but some light still slips through the shutters in the kitchen. Along the hallway are two bedrooms with baths. A spiral staircase in the living room leads up to an open space that composes much of the second floor. There are no windows upstairs, but the lights have been left on, probably by someone hastily evacuating. A huge television screen, blank but glowing softly, occupies one wall. Plush chairs and sofas are strewn around the room. This is where we congregate, slump into upholstery, try to catch our breath.

Jackson has her gun trained on Peeta even though he's still cuffed and unconscious, draped across a deep-blue sofa where Homes deposited him. What on earth am I going to do with him? With the crew? With everybody, frankly, besides Gale and Finnick? Because I'd rather track down Snow with those two than without them. But I can't lead ten people through the Capitol on a pretend mission, even if I could read the Holo. Should I, could I have sent them back when I had a chance? Or was it too dangerous? Both to them personally and to my mission? Maybe I shouldn't have listened to Boggs, because he might have been in some delusional death state. Maybe I should just come clean, but then Jackson would take over and we'd end up back at camp. Where I'd have Coin to answer to.

Just as the complexity of the mess I've dragged everybody into begins to overload my brain, a distant chain of explosions sends a tremor through the room.

"It wasn't close," Jackson assures us. "A good four or five blocks away."

"Where we left Boggs," says Leeg 1.

Although no one has made a move toward it, the television flares to life, emitting a high-pitched beeping sound, bringing half our party to its feet.

"It's all right!" calls Cressida. "It's just an emergency broadcast. Every Capitol television is automatically activated for it."

There we are on-screen, just after the bomb took out Boggs. A voice-over tells the audience what they are viewing as we try to regroup, react to the black gel shooting from the street, lose control of the situation. We watch the chaos that follows until the wave blots out the cameras. The last thing we see is Gale, alone on the street, trying to shoot through the cables that hold Mitchell aloft.

The reporter identifies Gale, Finnick, Boggs, Peeta, Cressida, and me by name.

"There's no aerial footage. Boggs must have been right about their hovercraft capacity," says Castor. I didn't notice this, but I guess it's the kind of thing a cameraman picks up on.

Coverage continues from the courtyard behind the apartment where we took shelter. Peacekeepers line the roof across from our former hideout. Shells are launched into the row of apartments, setting off the chain of explosions we heard, and the building collapses into rubble and dust.

Now we cut to a live feed. A reporter stands on the roof with the Peacekeepers. Behind her, the apartment block burns. Firefighters try to control the blaze with water hoses. We are pronounced dead.

"Finally, a bit of luck," says Homes.

I guess he's right. Certainly it's better than having the Capitol in pursuit of us. But I just keep imagining how this will be playing back in 13. Where my mother and Prim, Hazelle and the kids, Annie, Haymitch, and a whole lot of people from 13 think that they have just seen us die.

"My father. He just lost my sister and now . . ." says Leeg 1.

We watch as they play the footage over and over. Revel in their victory, especially over me. Break away to do a montage of the Mockingjay's rise to rebel power—I think they've had this part prepared for a while, because it seems pretty polished—and then go live so a couple of reporters can discuss my well-deserved violent end. Later, they promise, Snow will make an official statement. The screen fades back to a glow.

The rebels made no attempt to break in during the broadcast, which leads me to believe they think it's true. If that's so, we really are on our own.

"So, now that we're dead, what's our next move?" asks Gale.

"Isn't it obvious?" No one even knew Peeta had regained consciousness. I don't know how long he's been watching, but by the look of misery on his face, long enough to see what happened on the street. How he went mad, tried to bash my head in, and hurled Mitchell into the pod. He painfully pushes himself up to a sitting position and directs his words to Gale.

"Our next move . . . is to kill me."

21

That makes two requests for Peeta's death in less than an hour.

"Don't be ridiculous," says Jackson.

"I just murdered a member of our squad!" shouts Peeta.

"You pushed him off you. You couldn't have known he would trigger the net at that exact spot," says Finnick, trying to calm him.

"Who cares? He's dead, isn't he?" Tears begin to run down Peeta's face. "I didn't know. I've never seen myself like that before. Katniss is right. I'm the monster. I'm the mutt. I'm the one Snow has turned into a weapon!"

"It's not your fault, Peeta," says Finnick.

"You can't take me with you. It's only a matter of time before I kill someone else." Peeta looks around at our conflicted faces. "Maybe you think it's kinder to just dump me somewhere. Let me take my chances. But that's the same thing as handing me over to the Capitol. Do you think you'd be doing me a favor by sending me back to Snow?"

Peeta. Back in Snow's hands. Tortured and tormented until no bits of his former self will ever emerge again.

For some reason, the last stanza to "The Hanging Tree" starts running through my head. The one where the man wants his lover dead rather than have her face the evil that awaits her in the world.

> Are you, are you
> Coming to the tree
> Wear a necklace of rope, side by side with me.
> Strange things did happen here
> No stranger would it be
> If we met up at midnight in the hanging tree.

"I'll kill you before that happens," says Gale. "I promise."

Peeta hesitates, as if considering the reliability of this offer, and then shakes his head. "It's no good. What if you're not there to do it? I want one of those poison pills like the rest of you have."

Nightlock. There's one pill back at camp, in its special slot on the sleeve of my Mockingjay suit. But there's another in the breast pocket of my uniform. Interesting that they didn't issue one to Peeta. Perhaps Coin thought he might take it before he had the opportunity to kill me. It's unclear if Peeta means he'd finish himself off now, to spare us having to murder him, or only if the Capitol took him prisoner again. In the state he's in, I expect it would be sooner rather than later. It would certainly make things easier on the rest of us. Not to have to shoot him. It would certainly simplify the problem of dealing with his homicidal episodes.

I don't know if it's the pods, or the fear, or watching Boggs die, but I feel the arena all around me. It's as if I've never left, really. Once again I'm battling not only for my own survival but for Peeta's as well. How satisfying, how entertaining it would be for Snow to have me kill him. To have Peeta's death on my conscience for whatever is left of my life.

"It's not about you," I say. "We're on a mission. And you're necessary to it." I look to the rest of the group. "Think we might find some food here?"

Besides the medical kit and cameras, we have nothing but our uniforms and our weapons.

Half of us stay to guard Peeta or keep an eye out for Snow's broadcast, while the others hunt for something to eat. Messalla proves most valuable because he lived in a near replica of this apartment and knows where people would be most likely to stash food. Like how there's a storage space concealed by a mirrored panel in the bedroom, or how easy it is to pop out the ventilation screen in the hallway. So even though the kitchen cupboards are bare, we find over thirty canned goods and several boxes of cookies.

The hoarding disgusts the soldiers raised in 13. "Isn't this illegal?" says Leeg 1.

"On the contrary, in the Capitol you'd be considered stupid not to do it," says Messalla. "Even before the Quarter Quell, people were starting to stock up on scarce supplies."

"While others went without," says Leeg 1.

"Right," says Messalla. "That's how it works here."

"Fortunately, or we wouldn't have dinner," says Gale. "Everybody grab a can."

Some of our company seem reluctant to do this, but it's as good a method as any. I'm really not in the mood to divvy up everything into eleven equal parts, factoring in age, body weight, and physical output. I poke around in the pile, about to settle on some cod chowder, when Peeta holds out a can to me. "Here."

I take it, not knowing what to expect. The label reads LAMB STEW.

I press my lips together at the memories of rain dripping through stones, my inept attempts at flirting, and the aroma of my favorite Capitol dish in the chilly air. So some part of it must still be in his head, too. How happy, how hungry, how close we were when that picnic basket arrived outside our cave. "Thanks." I pop open the top. "It even has dried plums." I bend the lid and use it as a makeshift spoon, scooping a bit into my mouth. Now this place tastes like the arena, too.

We're passing around a box of fancy cream-filled cookies when the beeping starts again. The seal of Panem lights up on the screen and remains there while the anthem plays. And then they begin to show images of the dead, just as they did with the tributes in the arena. They start with the four faces of our TV crew, followed by Boggs, Gale, Finnick, Peeta, and me. Except for Boggs, they don't bother with the soldiers from 13, either because they have no idea who they are or because they know they won't mean anything to the audience. Then the man himself appears, seated at his desk, a flag draped behind him, the fresh white rose gleaming in his lapel. I think he might have recently had more work done, because his lips are puffier than usual. And his prep team really needs to use a lighter hand with his blush.

Snow congratulates the Peacekeepers on a masterful job, honors them for ridding the country of the menace called the Mockingjay. With my death, he predicts a turning of the tide in the war, since the demoralized rebels have no one left to follow. And what was I, really? A poor, unstable girl with a small talent with a bow and arrow. Not a great thinker, not the mastermind of the rebellion, merely a face plucked from the rabble because I had caught the nation's attention with my antics in the Games. But necessary, so very necessary, because the rebels have no real leader among them.

Somewhere in District 13, Beetee hits a switch, because now it's not President Snow but President Coin who's looking at us. She introduces herself to Panem, identifies herself as the head of the rebellion, and then gives my eulogy. Praise for the girl who survived the Seam and the Hunger Games, then turned a country of slaves into an army of freedom fighters. "Dead or alive, Katniss Everdeen will remain the face of this rebellion. If ever you waver in your resolve, think of the Mockingjay, and in her you will find the strength you need to rid Panem of its oppressors."

"I had no idea how much I meant to her," I say, which brings a laugh from Gale and questioning looks from the others.

Up comes a heavily doctored photo of me looking beautiful and fierce with a bunch of flames flickering behind me. No words. No slogan. My face is all they need now.

Beetee gives the reins back to a very controlled Snow. I have the feeling the president thought the emergency channel was impenetrable, and someone will end up dead tonight because it was breached. "Tomorrow morning, when we pull Katniss Everdeen's body from the ashes, we will see exactly who the Mockingjay is. A dead girl who could save no one, not even herself." Seal, anthem, and out.

"Except that you won't find her," says Finnick to the empty screen, voicing what we're all probably thinking. The grace period will be brief. Once they dig through those ashes and come up missing eleven bodies, they'll know we escaped.

"We can get a head start on them at least," I say. Suddenly, I'm so tired. All I want is to lie down on a nearby green plush sofa and go to sleep. To cocoon myself in a comforter made of rabbit fur and goose down. Instead, I pull out the Holo and insist that Jackson talk me through the most basic commands — which are really about entering the coordinates of the nearest map grid intersection — so that I can at least begin to operate the thing myself. As the Holo projects our surroundings, I feel my heart sink even further. We must be moving closer to crucial targets, because the number of pods has noticeably increased. How can we possibly move forward into this bouquet of blinking lights without detection? We can't. And if we can't, we are trapped like birds in a net. I decide it's best not to adopt some sort of superior attitude when I'm with these people. Especially when my eyes keep drifting to that green sofa. So I say, "Any ideas?"

"Why don't we start by ruling out possibilities," says Finnick. "The street is not a possibility."

"The rooftops are just as bad as the street," says Leeg 1.

"We still might have a chance to withdraw, go back the way we came," says Homes. "But that would mean a failed mission."

A pang of guilt hits me since I've fabricated said mission. "It was never intended for all of us to go forward. You just had the misfortune to be with me."

"Well, that's a moot point. We're with you now," says Jackson. "So, we can't stay put. We can't move up. We can't move laterally. I think that just leaves one option."

"Underground," says Gale.

Underground. Which I hate. Like mines and tunnels and 13. Underground, where I dread dying, which is stupid because even if I die aboveground, the next thing they'll do is bury me underground anyway.

The Holo can show subterranean as well as street-level pods. I see that when we go underground the clean, dependable lines of the street plan are interlaced with a twisting, turning mess of tunnels. The pods look less numerous, though.

Two doors down, a vertical tube connects our row of apartments to the tunnels. To reach the tube apartment, we will need to squeeze through a maintenance shaft that runs the length of the building. We can enter the shaft through the back of a closet space on the upper floor.

"Okay, then. Let's make it look like we've never been here," I say. We erase all signs of our stay. Send the empty cans down a trash chute, pocket the full ones for later, flip sofa cushions smeared with blood, wipe traces of gel from the tiles. There's no fixing the latch on the front door, but we lock a second bolt, which will at least keep the door from swinging open on contact.

Finally, there's only Peeta to contend with. He plants himself on the blue sofa, refusing to budge. "I'm not going. I'll either disclose your position or hurt someone else."

"Snow's people will find you," says Finnick.

"Then leave me a pill. I'll only take it if I have to," says Peeta.

"That's not an option. Come along," says Jackson.

"Or you'll what? Shoot me?" asks Peeta.

"We'll knock you out and drag you with us," says Homes. "Which will both slow us down and endanger us."

"Stop being noble! I don't care if I die!" He turns to me, pleading now. "Katniss, please. Don't you see, I want to be out of this?"

The trouble is, I *do* see. Why can't I just let him go? Slip him a pill, pull the trigger? Is it because I care too much about Peeta or too much about letting Snow win? Have I turned him into a piece in my private Games? That's despicable, but I'm not sure it's beneath me. If it's true, it would be kindest to kill Peeta here and now. But for better or worse, I am not motivated by kindness. "We're wasting time. Are you coming voluntarily or do we knock you out?"

Peeta buries his face in his hands for a few moments, then rises to join us.

"Should we free his hands?" asks Leeg 1.

"No!" Peeta growls at her, drawing his cuffs in close to his body.

"No," I echo. "But I want the key." Jackson passes it over without a word. I slip it into my pants pocket, where it clicks against the pearl.

When Homes pries open the small metal door to the

maintenance shaft, we encounter another problem. There's no way the insect shells will be able to fit through the narrow passage. Castor and Pollux remove them and detach emergency backup cameras. Each is the size of a shoe box and probably works about as well. Messalla can't think of anywhere better to hide the bulky shells, so we end up dumping them in the closet. Leaving such an easy trail to follow frustrates me, but what else can we do?

Even going single file, holding our packs and gear out to the side, it's a tight fit. We sidestep our way past the first apartment, and break into the second. In this apartment, one of the bedrooms has a door marked UTILITY instead of a bathroom. Behind the door is the room with the entrance to the tube.

Messalla frowns at the wide circular cover, for a moment returning to his own fussy world. "It's why no one ever wants the center unit. Workmen coming and going whenever and no second bath. But the rent's considerably cheaper." Then he notices Finnick's amused expression and adds, "Never mind."

The tube cover's simple to unlatch. A wide ladder with rubber treads on the steps allows for a swift, easy descent into the bowels of the city. We gather at the foot of the ladder, waiting for our eyes to adjust to the dim strips of lights, breathing in the mixture of chemicals, mildew, and sewage.

Pollux, pale and sweaty, reaches out and latches on to Castor's wrist. Like he might fall over if there isn't someone to steady him.

"My brother worked down here after he became an Avox," says Castor. Of course. Who else would they get to maintain these dank, evil-smelling passages mined with pods? "Took five years before we were able to buy his way up to ground level. Didn't see the sun once."

Under better conditions, on a day with fewer horrors and more rest, someone would surely know what to say. Instead we all stand there for a long time trying to formulate a response.

Finally, Peeta turns to Pollux. "Well, then you just became our most valuable asset." Castor laughs and Pollux manages a smile.

We're halfway down the first tunnel when I realize what was so remarkable about the exchange. Peeta sounded like his old self, the one who could always think of the right thing to say when nobody else could. Ironic, encouraging, a little funny, but not at anyone's expense. I glance back at him as he trudges along under his guards, Gale and Jackson, his eyes fixed on the ground, his shoulders hunched forward. So dispirited. But for a moment, he was really here.

Peeta called it right. Pollux turns out to be worth ten Holos. There is a simple network of wide tunnels that directly corresponds to the main street plan above, underlying the major avenues and cross streets. It's called the Transfer, since small trucks use it to deliver goods around the city. During the day, its many pods are deactivated, but at night it's a minefield. However, hundreds of additional passages, utility shafts, train tracks, and drainage tubes form a multilevel maze. Pollux knows details that would lead to disaster for a newcomer, like which offshoots might require gas masks or have live wires or rats the size of beavers. He alerts us to the gush of water that sweeps through the sewers periodically, anticipates the time the Avoxes will be changing shifts, leads us into damp, obscure pipes to dodge the nearly silent passage of cargo trains. Most important, he has knowledge of the cameras. There aren't many down in this gloomy, misty place, except in the Transfer. But we keep well out of their way.

Under Pollux's guidance we make good time — remarkable time, if you compare it to our aboveground travel. After about six hours, fatigue takes over. It's three in the morning, so I figure we still have a few hours before our bodies are discovered missing, they search through the rubble of the whole block of apartments in case we tried to escape through the shafts, and the hunt begins.

When I suggest we rest, no one objects. Pollux finds a small, warm room humming with machines loaded with levers and dials. He holds up his fingers to indicate we must be gone in four hours. Jackson works out a guard schedule, and, since I'm not on the first shift, I wedge myself in the tight space between Gale and Leeg 1 and go right to sleep.

It seems like only minutes later when Jackson shakes me awake, tells me I'm on watch. It's six o'clock, and in one hour we must be on our way. Jackson tells me to eat a can of food and keep an eye on Pollux, who's insisted on being on guard the entire night. "He can't sleep down here." I drag myself into a state of relative alertness, eat a can of potato and bean stew, and sit against the wall facing the door. Pollux seems wide awake. He's probably been reliving those five years of imprisonment all night. I get out the Holo and manage to input our grid coordinates and scan the tunnels. As expected, more pods are registering the closer we move toward the center of the Capitol. For a while, Pollux and I click around on the Holo, seeing what traps lie where. When my head begins to spin, I hand it over to him and lean back against the wall. I look down at the sleeping soldiers, crew, and friends, and I wonder how many of us will ever see the sun again.

When my eyes fall on Peeta, whose head rests right by my feet, I see he's awake. I wish I could read what's going on in his mind, that I could go in and untangle the mess of lies. Then I settle for something I can accomplish.

"Have you eaten?" I ask. A slight shake of his head indicates he hasn't. I open a can of chicken and rice soup and hand it to him, keeping the lid in case he tries to slit his wrists with it or something. He sits up and tilts the can, chugging back the soup without really bothering to chew it. The bottom of the can reflects the lights from the machines, and I remember something that's been itching at the back of my mind since yesterday. "Peeta, when you asked about what happened to Darius and Lavinia, and Boggs told you it was real, you said you thought so. Because there was nothing shiny about it. What did you mean?"

"Oh. I don't know exactly how to explain it," he tells me. "In the beginning, everything was just complete confusion. Now I can sort certain things out. I think there's a pattern emerging. The memories they altered with the tracker jacker venom have this strange quality about them. Like they're too intense or the images aren't stable. You remember what it was like when we were stung?"

"Trees shattered. There were giant colored butterflies. I fell in a pit of orange bubbles." I think about it. "Shiny orange bubbles."

"Right. But nothing about Darius or Lavinia was like that. I don't think they'd given me any venom yet," he says.

"Well, that's good, isn't it?" I ask. "If you can separate the two, then you can figure out what's true."

"Yes. And if I could grow wings, I could fly. Only people can't grow wings," he says. "Real or not real?"

"Real," I say. "But people don't need wings to survive."

"Mockingjays do." He finishes the soup and returns the can to me.

In the fluorescent light, the circles under his eyes look like bruises. "There's still time. You should sleep." Unresisting, he lies back down, but just stares at the needle on one of the dials as it twitches from side to side. Slowly, as I would with a wounded animal, my hand stretches out and brushes a wave of hair from his forehead. He freezes at my touch, but doesn't recoil. So I continue to gently smooth back his hair. It's the first time I have voluntarily touched him since the last arena.

"You're still trying to protect me. Real or not real," he whispers.

"Real," I answer. It seems to require more explanation. "Because that's what you and I do. Protect each other." After a minute or so, he drifts off to sleep.

Shortly before seven, Pollux and I move among the others, rousing them. There are the usual yawns and sighs that accompany waking. But my ears are picking up something else, too. Almost like a hissing. Perhaps it's only steam escaping a pipe or the far-off whoosh of one of the trains. . . .

I hush the group to get a better read on it. There's a hissing, yes, but it's not one extended sound. More like multiple exhalations that form words. A single word. Echoing throughout the tunnels. One word. One name. Repeated over and over again.

"Katniss."

The grace period has ended. Perhaps Snow had them digging through the night. As soon as the fire died down, anyway. They found Boggs's remains, briefly felt reassured, and then, as the hours went by without further trophies, began to suspect. At some point, they realized that they had been tricked. And President Snow can't tolerate being made to look like a fool. It doesn't matter whether they tracked us to the second apartment or assumed we went directly underground. They know we are down here now and they've unleashed something, a pack of mutts probably, bent on finding me.

"Katniss." I jump at the proximity of the sound. Look frantically for its source, bow loaded, seeking a target to hit. *"Katniss."* Peeta's lips are barely moving, but there's no doubt, the name came out of him. Just when I thought he seemed a little better, when I thought he might be inching his way back to me, here is proof of how deep Snow's poison went. *"Katniss."* Peeta's programmed to respond to the hissing chorus, to join in the hunt. He's beginning to stir. There's no choice. I position my arrow to penetrate his brain. He'll barely feel a thing. Suddenly, he's sitting up, eyes wide in alarm, short of breath. "Katniss!" He whips

his head toward me but doesn't seem to notice my bow, the waiting arrow. "Katniss! Get out of here!"

I hesitate. His voice is alarmed, but not insane. "Why? What's making that sound?"

"I don't know. Only that it has to kill you," says Peeta. "Run! Get out! Go!"

After my own moment of confusion, I conclude I do not have to shoot him. Relax my bowstring. Take in the anxious faces around me. "Whatever it is, it's after me. It might be a good time to split up."

"But we're your guard," says Jackson.

"And your crew," adds Cressida.

"I'm not leaving you," Gale says.

I look at the crew, armed with nothing but cameras and clipboards. And there's Finnick with two guns and a trident. I suggest that he give one of his guns to Castor. Eject the blank cartridge from Peeta's, load it with a real one, and arm Pollux. Since Gale and I have our bows, we hand our guns over to Messalla and Cressida. There's no time to show them anything but how to point and pull the trigger, but in close quarters, that might be enough. It's better than being defenseless. Now the only one without a weapon is Peeta, but anyone whispering my name with a bunch of mutts doesn't need one anyway.

We leave the room free of everything but our scent. There's no way to erase that at the moment. I'm guessing that's how the hissing things are tracking us, because we haven't left much of a physical trail. The mutts' noses will be abnormally keen, but possibly the time we spent slogging through water in drainpipes will help throw them.

Outside the hum of the room, the hissing becomes more distinct. But it's also possible to get a better sense of the mutts' location. They're behind us, still a fair distance. Snow probably had them released underground near the place where he found Boggs's body. Theoretically, we should have a good lead on them, although they're certain to be much faster than we are. My mind wanders to the wolflike creatures in the first arena, the monkeys in the Quarter Quell, the monstrosities I've witnessed on television over the years, and I wonder what form these mutts will take. Whatever Snow thinks will scare me the most.

Pollux and I have worked out a plan for the next leg of our journey, and since it heads away from the hissing, I see no reason to alter it. If we move swiftly, maybe we can reach Snow's mansion before the mutts reach us. But there's a sloppiness that comes with speed: the poorly placed boot that results in a splash, the accidental clang of a gun against a pipe, even my own commands, issued too loudly for discretion.

We've covered about three more blocks via an overflow pipe and a section of neglected train track when the screams begin. Thick, guttural. Bouncing off the tunnel walls.

"Avoxes," says Peeta immediately. "That's what Darius sounded like when they tortured him."

"The mutts must have found them," says Cressida.

"So they're not just after Katniss," says Leeg 1.

"They'll probably kill anyone. It's just that they won't stop until they get to her," says Gale. After his hours studying with Beetee, he is most likely right.

And here I am again. With people dying because of me. Friends, allies, complete strangers, losing their lives for the Mockingjay. "Let me go on alone. Lead them off. I'll transfer the Holo to Jackson. The rest of you can finish the mission."

"No one's going to agree to that!" says Jackson in exasperation.

"We're wasting time!" says Finnick.

"Listen," Peeta whispers.

The screams have stopped, and in their absence my name has rebounded, startling in its proximity. It's below as well as behind us now. *"Katniss."*

I nudge Pollux on the shoulder and we start to run. Trouble is, we had planned to descend to a lower level, but that's out now. When we come to the steps leading down, Pollux and I are scanning for a possible alternative on the Holo when I start gagging.

"Masks on!" orders Jackson.

There's no need for masks. Everyone is breathing the same air. I'm the only one losing my stew because I'm the only one reacting to the odor. Drifting up from the stairwell. Cutting through the sewage. Roses. I begin to tremble.

I swerve away from the smell and stumble right out onto the Transfer. Smooth, pastel-colored tiled streets, just like the ones above, but bordered by white brick walls instead of homes. A roadway where delivery vehicles can drive with ease, without the congestion of the Capitol. Empty now, of everything but us. I swing up my bow and blow up the first pod with an explosive arrow, which kills the nest of flesh-eating rats inside. Then I sprint for the next intersection, where I know one false step will cause the ground beneath our feet to disintegrate, feeding us into something labeled MEAT GRINDER. I shout a warning to the others to stay with me. I plan for us to skirt around the corner and then detonate the Meat Grinder, but another unmarked pod lies in wait.

It happens silently. I would miss it entirely if Finnick didn't pull me to a stop. "Katniss!"

I whip back around, arrow poised for flight, but what can be done? Two of Gale's arrows already lie useless beside the wide shaft of golden light that radiates from ceiling to floor. Inside, Messalla is as still as a statue, poised up on the ball of one foot, head tilted back, held captive by the beam. I can't tell if he's yelling, although his mouth is stretched wide. We watch, utterly helpless, as the flesh melts off his body like candle wax.

"Can't help him!" Peeta starts shoving people forward. "Can't!" Amazingly, he's the only one still functional enough to get us moving. I don't know why he's in control, when he should be flipping out and bashing my brains in, but that could happen any second. At the pressure of his hand against my shoulder, I turn away from the grisly thing that was Messalla; I make my feet go forward, fast, so fast that I can barely skid to a stop before the next intersection.

A spray of gunfire brings down a shower of plaster. I jerk my head from side to side, looking for the pod, before I turn and see the squad of Peacekeepers pounding down the Transfer toward us. With the Meat Grinder pod blocking our way, there's nothing to do but fire back. They outnumber us two to one, but we've still got six original members of the Star Squad, who aren't trying to run and shoot at the same time.

Fish in a barrel, I think, as blossoms of red stain their white uniforms. Three-quarters of them are down and dead when more begin to pour in from the side of the tunnel, the same one I flung myself through to get away from the smell, from the —

Those aren't Peacekeepers.

They are white, four-limbed, about the size of a full-grown human, but that's where the comparisons stop. Naked, with long reptilian tails, arched backs, and heads that jut forward. They swarm over the Peacekeepers, living and dead, clamp on to their necks with their mouths and rip off the helmeted heads. Apparently, having a Capitol pedigree is as useless here as it was in 13. It seems to take only seconds before the Peacekeepers are decapitated. The mutts fall to their bellies and skitter toward us on all fours.

"This way!" I shout, hugging the wall and making a sharp right turn to avoid the pod. When everyone's joined me, I fire into the intersection, and the Meat Grinder activates. Huge mechanical teeth burst through the street and chew the tile to dust. That should make it impossible for the mutts to follow us, but I don't know. The wolf and monkey mutts I've encountered could leap unbelievably far.

The hissing burns my ears, and the reek of roses makes the walls spin.

I grab Pollux's arm. "Forget the mission. What's the quickest way aboveground?"

There's no time for checking the Holo. We follow Pollux for about ten yards along the Transfer and go through a doorway. I'm aware of tile changing to concrete, of crawling through a tight, stinking pipe onto a ledge about a foot wide. We're in the main sewer. A yard below, a poisonous brew of human waste, garbage, and chemical runoff bubbles by us. Parts of the surface are on fire, others emit evil-looking clouds of vapor. One look tells you that if you fall in, you're never coming out. Moving as quickly as we dare on the slippery ledge, we make our way to a narrow bridge and cross it. In an alcove at the far side, Pollux smacks a ladder with his hand and points up the shaft. This is it. Our way out.

A quick glance at our party tells me something's off. "Wait! Where are Jackson and Leeg One?"

"They stayed at the Grinder to hold the mutts back," says Homes.

"What?" I'm lunging back for the bridge, willing to leave no one to those monsters, when he yanks me back.

"Don't waste their lives, Katniss. It's too late for them. Look!" Homes nods to the pipe, where the mutts are slithering onto the ledge.

"Stand back!" Gale shouts. With his explosive-tipped arrows, he rips the far side of the bridge from its foundation.

The rest sinks into the bubbles, just as the mutts reach it.

For the first time, I get a good look at them. A mix of human and lizard and who knows what else. White, tight reptilian skin smeared with gore, clawed hands and feet, their faces a mess of conflicting features. Hissing, shrieking my name now, as their bodies contort in rage. Lashing out with tails and claws, taking huge chunks of one another or their own bodies with wide, lathered mouths, driven mad by their need to destroy me. My scent must be as evocative to them as theirs is to me. More so, because despite its toxicity, the mutts begin to throw themselves into the foul sewer.

Along our bank, everyone opens fire. I choose my arrows without discretion, sending arrowheads, fire, explosives into the mutts' bodies. They're mortal, but only just. No natural thing could keep coming with two dozen bullets in it. Yes, we can eventually kill them, only there are so many, an endless supply pouring from the pipe, not even hesitating to take to the sewage.

But it's not their numbers that make my hands shake so.

No mutt is good. All are meant to damage you. Some take your life, like the monkeys. Others your reason, like the tracker jackers. However, the true atrocities, the most frightening, incorporate a perverse psychological twist designed to terrify the victim. The sight of the wolf mutts with the dead tributes' eyes. The sound of the jabberjays replicating Prim's tortured screams. The smell of Snow's roses mixed with the victims' blood. Carried across the sewer. Cutting through even this foulness. Making my heart run wild, my skin turn to ice, my lungs unable to suck air. It's as if Snow's breathing right in my face, telling me it's time to die.

The others are shouting at me, but I can't seem to respond. Strong arms lift me as I blast the head off a mutt whose claws have just grazed my ankle. I'm slammed into the ladder. Hands shoved against the rungs. Ordered to climb. My wooden, puppet limbs obey. Movement slowly brings me back to my senses. I detect one person above me. Pollux. Peeta and Cressida are below. We reach a platform. Switch to a second ladder. Rungs slick with sweat and mildew. At the next platform, my head has cleared and the reality of what's happened hits me. I begin frantically pulling people up off the ladder. Peeta. Cressida. That's it.

What have I done? What have I abandoned the others to? I'm scrambling back down the ladder when one of my boots kicks someone.

"Climb!" Gale barks at me. I'm back up, hauling him in, peering into the gloom for more. "No." Gale turns my face to him and shakes his head. Uniform shredded. Gaping wound in the side of his neck.

There's a human cry from below. "Someone's still alive," I plead.

"No, Katniss. They're not coming," says Gale. "Only the mutts are."

Unable to accept it, I shine the light from Cressida's gun down the shaft. Far below, I can just make out Finnick, struggling to hang on as three mutts tear at him. As one yanks back his head to take the death bite, something bizarre happens. It's as if I'm Finnick, watching images of my life flash by. The mast of a boat, a silver parachute, Mags laughing, a pink sky, Beetee's trident, Annie in her wedding dress, waves breaking over rocks. Then it's over.

I slide the Holo from my belt and choke out "nightlock, nightlock, nightlock." Release it. Hunch against the wall with the others as the explosion rocks the platform and bits of mutt and human flesh shoot out of the pipe and shower us.

There's a clank as Pollux slams a cover over the pipe and locks it in place. Pollux, Gale, Cressida, Peeta, and me. We're all that's left. Later, the human feelings will come. Now I'm conscious only of an animal need to keep the remnants of our band alive. "We can't stop here."

Someone comes up with a bandage. We tie it around Gale's neck. Get him to his feet. Only one figure stays huddled against the wall. "Peeta," I say. There's no response. Has he blacked out? I crouch in front of him, pulling his cuffed hands from his face. "Peeta?" His eyes are like black pools, the pupils dilated so that the blue irises have all but vanished. The muscles in his wrists are hard as metal.

"Leave me," he whispers. "I can't hang on."

"Yes. You can!" I tell him.

Peeta shakes his head. "I'm losing it. I'll go mad. Like them."

Like the mutts. Like a rabid beast bent on ripping my throat out. And here, finally here in this place, in these circumstances, I will really have to kill him. And Snow will win. Hot, bitter hatred courses through me. Snow has won too much already today.

It's a long shot, it's suicide maybe, but I do the only thing I can think of. I lean in and kiss Peeta full on the mouth. His whole body starts shuddering, but I keep my lips pressed to his until I have to come up for air. My hands slide up his wrists to clasp his. "Don't let him take you from me."

Peeta's panting hard as he fights the nightmares raging in his head. "No. I don't want to . . ."

I clench his hands to the point of pain. "Stay with me."

His pupils contract to pinpoints, dilate again rapidly, and then return to something resembling normalcy. "Always," he murmurs.

I help Peeta up and address Pollux. "How far to the street?" He indicates it's just above us. I climb the last ladder and push open the lid to someone's utility room. I'm rising to my feet when a woman throws open the door. She wears a bright turquoise silk robe embroidered with exotic birds. Her magenta hair's fluffed up like a cloud and decorated with gilded butterflies. Grease from the half-eaten sausage she's holding smears her lipstick. The expression on her face says she recognizes me. She opens her mouth to call for help.

Without hesitation, I shoot her through the heart.

23

Who the woman was calling to remains a mystery, because after searching the apartment, we find she was alone. Perhaps her cry was meant for a nearby neighbor, or was simply an expression of fear. At any rate, there's no one else to hear her.

This apartment would be a classy place to hole up in for a while, but that's a luxury we can't afford. "How long do you think we have before they figure out some of us could've survived?" I ask.

"I think they could be here anytime," Gale answers. "They knew we were heading for the streets. Probably the explosion will throw them for a few minutes, then they'll start looking for our exit point."

I go to a window that overlooks the street, and when I peek through the blinds, I'm not faced with Peacekeepers but with a bundled crowd of people going about their business. During our underground journey, we have left the evacuated zones far behind and surfaced in a busy section of the Capitol. This crowd offers our only chance of escape. I don't have a Holo, but I have Cressida. She joins me at the window, confirms she knows our location, and gives me the good news that we aren't many blocks from the president's mansion.

One glance at my companions tells me this is no time for a stealth attack on Snow. Gale's still losing blood from the neck wound, which we haven't even cleaned. Peeta's sitting on a velvet sofa with his teeth clamped down on a pillow, either fighting off madness or containing a scream. Pollux weeps against the mantel of an ornate fireplace. Cressida stands determinedly at my side, but she's so pale her lips are bloodless. I'm running on hate. When the energy for that ebbs, I'll be worthless.

"Let's check her closets," I say.

In one bedroom we find hundreds of the woman's outfits, coats, pairs of shoes, a rainbow of wigs, enough makeup to paint a house. In a bedroom across the hall, there's a similar selection for men. Perhaps they belong to her husband. Perhaps to a lover who had the good luck to be out this morning.

I call the others to dress. At the sight of Peeta's bloody wrists, I dig in my pocket for the handcuff key, but he jerks away from me.

"No," he says. "Don't. They help hold me together."

"You might need your hands," says Gale.

"When I feel myself slipping, I dig my wrists into them, and the pain helps me focus," says Peeta. I let them be.

Fortunately, it's cold out, so we can conceal most of our uniforms and weapons under flowing coats and cloaks. We hang our boots around our necks by their laces and hide them, pull on silly shoes to replace them. The real challenge, of course, is our faces. Cressida and Pollux run the risk of being recognized by acquaintances, Gale could be familiar from the propos and news, and Peeta and I are known by every citizen of Panem. We hastily help one another apply thick layers of makeup, pull on wigs and sunglasses. Cressida wraps scarves over Peeta's and my mouths and noses.

I can feel the clock ticking away, but stop for just a few moments to stuff pockets with food and first-aid supplies. "Stay together," I say at the front door. Then we march right into the street. Snow flurries have begun to fall. Agitated people swirl around us, speaking of rebels and hunger and me in their affected Capitol accents. We cross the street, pass a few more apartments. Just as we turn the corner, three dozen Peacekeepers sweep past us. We hop out of their way, as the real citizens do, wait until the crowd returns to its normal flow, and keep moving. "Cressida," I whisper. "Can you think of anywhere?"

"I'm trying," she says.

We cover another block, and the sirens begin. Through an apartment window, I see an emergency report and pictures of our faces flashing. They haven't identified who in our party died yet, because I see Castor and Finnick among the photos. Soon every passerby will be as dangerous as a Peacekeeper. "Cressida?"

"There's one place. It's not ideal. But we can try it," she says. We follow her a few more blocks and turn through a gate into what looks like a private residence. It's some kind of shortcut, though, because after walking through a manicured garden, we come out of another gate onto a small back street that connects two main avenues. There are a few poky stores—one that buys used goods, another that sells fake jewelry. Only a couple of people are around, and they pay no attention to us. Cressida begins to babble in a high-pitched voice about fur undergarments, how essential they are during the cold months. "Wait until you see the prices! Believe me, it's half what you pay on the avenues!"

We stop before a grimy storefront filled with mannequins in furry underwear. The place doesn't even look open, but Cressida pushes through the front door, setting off a dissonant chiming. Inside the dim, narrow shop lined with racks of merchandise, the smell of pelts fills my nose. Business must be slow, since we're the only customers. Cressida heads straight for a hunched figure sitting in the back. I follow, trailing my fingers through the soft garments as we go.

Behind a counter sits the strangest person I've ever seen. She's an extreme example of surgical enhancement gone wrong, for surely not even in the Capitol could they find this face attractive. The skin has been pulled back tightly and tattooed with black and gold stripes. The nose has been flattened until it barely exists. I've seen cat whiskers on people in the Capitol before, but none so long. The result is a grotesque, semi-feline mask, which now squints at us distrustfully.

Cressida takes off her wig, revealing her vines. "Tigris," she says. "We need help."

Tigris. Deep in my brain, the name rings a bell. She was a fixture—a younger, less disturbing version of herself—in the earliest Hunger Games I can remember. A stylist,

I think. I don't remember for which district. Not 12. Then she must have had one operation too many and crossed the line into repellence.

So this is where stylists go when they've outlived their use. To sad theme underwear shops where they wait for death. Out of the public eye.

I stare at her face, wondering if her parents actually named her Tigris, inspiring her mutilation, or if she chose the style and changed her name to match her stripes.

"Plutarch said you could be trusted," adds Cressida.

Great, she's one of Plutarch's people. So if her first move isn't to turn us in to the Capitol, it will be to notify Plutarch, and by extension Coin, of our whereabouts. No, Tigris's shop is not ideal, but it's all we have at the moment. If she'll even help us. She's peering between an old television on her counter and us, as if trying to place us. To help her, I pull down my scarf, remove my wig, and step closer so that the light of the screen falls on my face.

Tigris gives a low growl, not unlike one Buttercup might greet me with. She slinks down off her stool and disappears behind a rack of fur-lined leggings. There's a sound of sliding, and then her hand emerges and waves us forward. Cressida looks at me, as if to ask *Are you sure?* But what choice do we have? Returning to the streets under these conditions guarantees our capture or death. I push around the furs and find Tigris has slid back a panel at the base of the wall. Behind it seems to be the top of a steep stone stairway. She gestures for me to enter.

Everything about the situation screams *trap*. I have a moment of panic and find myself turning to Tigris, searching those tawny eyes. Why is she doing this? She's no Cinna, someone willing to sacrifice herself for others. This woman was the embodiment of Capitol shallowness. She was one of the stars of the Hunger Games until . . . until she wasn't. So is that it, then? Bitterness? Hatred? Revenge? Actually, I'm comforted by the idea. A need for revenge can burn long and hot. Especially if every glance in a mirror reinforces it.

"Did Snow ban you from the Games?" I ask. She just stares back at me. Somewhere her tiger tail flicks with displeasure. "Because I'm going to kill him, you know." Her mouth spreads into what I take for a smile. Reassured that this isn't complete madness, I crawl through the space.

About halfway down the steps, my face runs into a hanging chain and I pull it, illuminating the hideout with a flickering fluorescent bulb. It's a small cellar with no doors or windows. Shallow and wide. Probably just a strip between two real basements. A place whose existence could go unnoticed unless you had a very keen eye for dimensions. It's cold and dank, with piles of pelts that I'm guessing haven't seen the light of day in years. Unless Tigris gives us up, I don't believe anyone will find us here. By the time I reach the concrete floor, my companions are on the steps. The panel slides back in place. I hear the underwear rack being adjusted on squeaky wheels. Tigris padding back to her stool. We have been swallowed up by her store.

Just in time, too, because Gale looks on the verge of collapse. We make a bed of pelts, strip off his layers of weapons, and help him onto his back. At the end of the cellar, there's a faucet about a foot from the floor with a drain under it. I turn the tap and, after much sputtering and a lot of rust, clear water begins to flow. We clean Gale's neck wound and I realize bandages won't be enough. He's going to need a few stitches. There's a needle and sterile thread in the first-aid supplies, but what we lack is a healer. It crosses my mind to enlist Tigris. As a stylist, she must know how to work a needle. But that would leave no one manning the shop, and she's doing enough already. I accept that I'm probably the most qualified for the job, grit my teeth, and put in a row of jagged sutures. It's not pretty but it's functional. I smear it with medicine and wrap it up. Give him some painkillers. "You can rest now. It's safe here," I tell him. He goes out like a light.

While Cressida and Pollux make fur nests for each of us, I attend to Peeta's wrists. Gently rinsing away the blood, putting on an antiseptic, and bandaging them beneath the cuffs. "You've got to keep them clean, otherwise the infection could spread and—"

"I know what blood poisoning is, Katniss," says Peeta. "Even if my mother isn't a healer."

I'm jolted back in time, to another wound, another set of bandages. "You said that same thing to me in the first Hunger Games. Real or not real?"

"Real," he says. "And you risked your life getting the medicine that saved me?"

"Real." I shrug. "You were the reason I was alive to do it."

"Was I?" The comment throws him into confusion. Some shiny memory must be fighting for his attention, because his body tenses and his newly bandaged wrists strain against the metal cuffs. Then all the energy saps from his body. "I'm so tired, Katniss."

"Go to sleep," I say. He won't until I've rearranged his handcuffs and shackled him to one of the stair supports. It can't be comfortable, lying there with his arms above his head. But in a few minutes, he drifts off, too.

Cressida and Pollux have made beds for us, arranged our food and medical supplies, and now ask what I want to do about setting up a guard. I look at Gale's pallor, Peeta's restraints. Pollux hasn't slept for days, and Cressida and I only napped for a few hours. If a troop of Peacekeepers were to come through that door, we'd be trapped like rats. We are completely at the mercy of a decrepit tiger-woman with what I can only hope is an all-consuming passion for Snow's death.

"I don't honestly think there's any point in setting up a guard. Let's just try to get some sleep," I say. They nod numbly, and we all burrow into our pelts. The fire inside me has flickered out, and with it my strength. I surrender to the soft, musty fur and oblivion.

I have only one dream I remember. A long and wearying thing in which I'm trying to get to District 12. The home I'm seeking is intact, the people alive. Effie Trinket, conspicuous in a bright pink wig and tailored outfit, travels with me. I keep trying to ditch her in places, but she inexplicably reappears at my side, insisting that as my escort she's responsible for my staying on schedule. Only the schedule is constantly shifting, derailed by our lack of a stamp from an official or delayed when Effie breaks one of her high heels. We camp for days on a bench in a gray station in District 7, awaiting a train that never comes. When I wake, somehow I feel even more drained by this than my usual nighttime forays into blood and terror.

Cressida, the only person awake, tells me it's late afternoon. I eat a can of beef stew and wash it down with a lot of water. Then I lean against the cellar wall, retracing the events of the last day. Moving death by death. Counting them up on my fingers. One, two — Mitchell and Boggs lost on the block. Three — Messalla melted by the pod. Four, five — Leeg 1 and Jackson sacrificing themselves at the Meat Grinder. Six, seven, eight — Castor, Homes, and Finnick being decapitated by the rose-scented lizard mutts. Eight dead in twenty-four hours. I know it happened, and yet it doesn't seem real. Surely, Castor is asleep under that pile of furs, Finnick will come bounding down the steps in a minute, Boggs will tell me his plan for our escape.

To believe them dead is to accept I killed them. Okay, maybe not Mitchell and Boggs — they died on an actual assignment. But the others lost their lives defending me on a mission I fabricated. My plot to assassinate Snow seems so stupid now. So stupid as I sit shivering here in this cellar, tallying up our losses, fingering the tassels on the silver knee-high boots I stole from the woman's home. Oh, yeah — I forgot about that. I killed her, too. I'm taking out unarmed citizens now.

I think it's time I give myself up.

When everyone finally awakens, I confess. How I lied about the mission, how I jeopardized everyone in pursuit of revenge. There's a long silence after I finish. Then Gale says, "Katniss, we all knew you were lying about Coin sending you to assassinate Snow."

"You knew, maybe. The soldiers from Thirteen didn't," I reply.

"Do you really think Jackson believed you had orders from Coin?" Cressida asks. "Of course she didn't. But she trusted Boggs, and he'd clearly wanted you to go on."

"I never even told Boggs what I planned to do," I say.

"You told everyone in Command!" Gale says. "It was one of your conditions for being the Mockingjay. *I kill Snow.*'"

Those seem like two disconnected things. Negotiating with Coin for the privilege of executing Snow after the war and this unauthorized flight through the Capitol. "But not like this," I say. "It's been a complete disaster."

"I think it would be considered a highly successful mission," says Gale. "We've infiltrated the enemy camp, showing that the Capitol's defenses can be breached. We've managed to get footage of ourselves all over the Capitol's news. We've thrown the whole city into chaos trying to find us."

"Trust me, Plutarch's thrilled," Cressida adds.

"That's because Plutarch doesn't care who dies," I say. "Not as long as his Games are a success."

Cressida and Gale go round and round trying to convince me. Pollux nods at their words to back them up. Only Peeta doesn't offer an opinion.

"What do you think, Peeta?" I finally ask him.

"I think . . . you still have no idea. The effect you can have." He slides his cuffs up the support and pushes himself to a sitting position. "None of the people we lost were idiots. They knew what they were doing. They followed you because they believed you really could kill Snow."

I don't know why his voice reaches me when no one else's can. But if he's right, and I think he is, I owe the others a debt that can only be repaid in one way. I pull my paper map from a pocket in my uniform and spread it out on the floor with new resolve. "Where are we, Cressida?"

Tigris's shop sits about five blocks from the City Circle and Snow's mansion. We're in easy walking distance through a zone in which the pods are deactivated for the residents' safety. We have disguises that, perhaps with some embellishments from Tigris's furry stock, could get us safely there. But then what? The mansion's sure to be heavily guarded, under round-the-clock camera surveillance, and laced with pods that could become live at the flick of a switch.

"What we need is to get him out in the open," Gale says to me. "Then one of us could pick him off."

"Does he ever appear in public anymore?" asks Peeta.

"I don't think so," says Cressida. "At least in all the recent speeches I've seen, he's been in the mansion. Even before the rebels got here. I imagine he became more vigilant after Finnick aired his crimes."

That's right. It's not just the Tigrises of the Capitol who hate Snow now, but a web of people who know what he did to their friends and families. It would have to be something bordering on miraculous to lure him out. Something like . . .

"I bet he'd come out for me," I say. "If I were captured. He'd want that as public as possible. He'd want my execution on his front steps." I let this sink in. "Then Gale could shoot him from the audience."

"No." Peeta shakes his head. "There are too many alternative endings to that plan. Snow might decide to keep you and torture information out of you. Or have you executed publicly without being present. Or kill you inside the mansion and display your body out front."

"Gale?" I say.

"It seems like an extreme solution to jump to immediately," he says. "Maybe if all else fails. Let's keep thinking."

In the quiet that follows, we hear Tigris's soft footfall overhead. It must be closing time. She's locking up, fastening the shutters maybe. A few minutes later, the panel at the top of the stairs slides open.

"Come up," says a gravelly voice. "I have some food for you." It's the first time she's talked since we arrived. Whether it's natural or from years of practice, I don't know, but there's something in her manner of speaking that suggests a cat's purr.

As we climb the stairs, Cressida asks, "Did you contact Plutarch, Tigris?"

"No way to." Tigris shrugs. "He'll figure out you're in a safe house. Don't worry."

Worry? I feel immensely relieved by the news that I won't be given—and have to ignore—direct orders from 13. Or make up some viable defense for the decisions I've made over the last couple of days.

In the shop, the counter holds some stale hunks of bread, a wedge of moldy cheese, and half a bottle of mustard. It reminds me that not everyone in the Capitol has full stomachs these days. I feel obliged to tell Tigris about our remaining food supplies, but she waves my objections away. "I eat next to nothing," she says. "And then, only raw meat." This seems a little too in character, but I don't question it. I just scrape the mold off the cheese and divide up the food among the rest of us.

While we eat, we watch the latest Capitol news coverage. The government has the rebel survivors narrowed down to the five of us. Huge bounties are offered for information leading to our capture. They emphasize how dangerous we are. Show us exchanging gunfire with the Peacekeepers, although not the mutts ripping off their heads. Do a tragic tribute to the woman lying where we left her, with my arrow still in her heart. Someone has redone her makeup for the cameras.

The rebels let the Capitol broadcast run on uninterrupted. "Have the rebels made a statement today?" I ask Tigris. She shakes her head. "I doubt Coin knows what to do with me now that I'm still alive."

Tigris gives a throaty cackle. "No one knows what to do with you, girlie." Then she makes me take a pair of the fur leggings even though I can't pay her for them. It's the kind of gift you have to accept. And anyway, it's cold in that cellar.

Downstairs after supper, we continue to rack our brains for a plan. Nothing good comes up, but we do agree that we can no longer go out as a group of five and that we should try to infiltrate the president's mansion before I turn myself into bait. I consent to that second point to avoid further argument. If I do decide to give myself up, it won't require anyone else's permission or participation.

We change bandages, handcuff Peeta back to his support, and settle down to sleep. A few hours later, I slip back into consciousness and become aware of a quiet conversation. Peeta and Gale. I can't stop myself from eavesdropping.

"Thanks for the water," Peeta says.

"No problem," Gale replies. "I wake up ten times a night anyway."

"To make sure Katniss is still here?" asks Peeta.

"Something like that," Gale admits.

There's a long pause before Peeta speaks again. "That was funny, what Tigris said. About no one knowing what to do with her."

"Well, *we* never have," Gale says.

They both laugh. It's so strange to hear them talking like this. Almost like friends. Which they're not. Never have been. Although they're not exactly enemies.

"She loves you, you know," says Peeta. "She as good as told me after they whipped you."

"Don't believe it," Gale answers. "The way she kissed you in the Quarter Quell . . . well, she never kissed me like that."

"It was just part of the show," Peeta tells him, although there's an edge of doubt in his voice.

"No, you won her over. Gave up everything for her. Maybe that's the only way to convince her you love her." There's a long pause. "I should have volunteered to take your place in the first Games. Protected her then."

"You couldn't," says Peeta. "She'd never have forgiven you. You had to take care of her family. They matter more to her than her life."

"Well, it won't be an issue much longer. I think it's unlikely all three of us will be alive at the end of the war. And if we are, I guess it's Katniss's problem. Who to choose." Gale yawns. "We should get some sleep."

"Yeah." I hear Peeta's handcuffs slide down the support as he settles in. "I wonder how she'll make up her mind."

"Oh, that I do know." I can just catch Gale's last words through the layer of fur. "Katniss will pick whoever she thinks she can't survive without."

A chill runs through me. Am I really that cold and calculating? Gale didn't say, "Katniss will pick whoever it will break her heart to give up," or even "whoever she can't live without." Those would have implied I was motivated by a kind of passion. But my best friend predicts I will choose the person who I think I "can't survive without." There's not the least indication that love, or desire, or even compatibility will sway me. I'll just conduct an unfeeling assessment of what my potential mates can offer me. As if in the end, it will be the question of whether a baker or a hunter will extend my longevity the most. It's a horrible thing for Gale to say, for Peeta not to refute. Especially when every emotion I have has been taken and exploited by the Capitol or the rebels. At the moment, the choice would be simple. I can survive just fine without either of them.

In the morning, I have no time or energy to nurse wounded feelings. During a predawn breakfast of liver pâté and fig cookies, we gather around Tigris's television for one of Beetee's break-ins. There's been a new development in the war. Apparently inspired by the black wave, some enterprising rebel commander came up with the idea of confiscating people's abandoned automobiles and sending them unmanned down the streets. The cars don't trigger every pod, but they certainly get the majority. At around four in the morning, the rebels began carving three separate paths — simply referred to as the A, B, and C lines — to the Capitol's heart. As a result, they've secured block after block with very few casualties.

"This can't last," says Gale. "In fact I'm surprised they've kept it going so long. The Capitol will adjust by deactivating specific pods and then manually triggering them when their targets come in range." Almost within minutes of his prediction, we see this very thing happen on-screen. A squad sends a car down a block, setting off four pods. All seems well. Three scouts follow and make it safely to the end of the street. But when a group of twenty rebel soldiers follow them, they're blown to bits by a row of potted rosebushes in front of a flower shop.

"I bet it's killing Plutarch not to be in the control room on this one," says Peeta.

Beetee gives the broadcast back to the Capitol, where a grim-faced reporter announces the blocks that civilians are to evacuate. Between her update and the previous story, I am able to mark my paper map to show the relative positions of the opposing armies.

I hear scuffling out on the street, move to the windows, and peek out a crack in the shutters. In the early morning light, I see a bizarre spectacle. Refugees from the now occupied blocks are streaming toward the Capitol's center. The most panicked are wearing nothing but nightgowns and slippers, while the more prepared are heavily bundled in layers of clothes. They carry everything from lapdogs to jewelry boxes to potted plants. One man in a fluffy robe holds only an overripe banana. Confused, sleepy children stumble along after their parents, most either too stunned or too baffled to cry. Bits of them flash by my line of vision. A pair of wide brown eyes. An arm clutching a favorite doll. A pair of bare feet, bluish in the cold, catching on the uneven paving stones of the alley. Seeing them reminds me of the children of 12 who died fleeing the firebombs. I leave the window.

Tigris offers to be our spy for the day since she's the only one of us without a bounty on her head. After securing us downstairs, she goes out into the Capitol to pick up any helpful information.

Down in the cellar I pace back and forth, driving the others crazy. Something tells me that not taking advantage of the flood of refugees is a mistake. What better cover could we have? On the other hand, every displaced person milling about on the streets means another pair of eyes looking for the five rebels on the loose. Then again, what do we gain by staying here? All we're really doing is depleting our small cache of food and waiting for . . . what? The rebels to take the Capitol? It could be weeks before that happens, and I'm not so sure what I'd do if they did. Not run out and greet them. Coin would have me whisked back to 13 before I could say "nightlock, nightlock, nightlock." I did not come all this way, and lose all those people, to turn myself over to that woman. *I kill Snow.* Besides, there would be an awful lot of things I couldn't easily explain about the last few days. Several of which, if they came to light, would probably blow my deal for the victors' immunity right out of the water. And forget about me, I've got a feeling some of the others are going to need it. Like Peeta. Who, no matter how you spin it, can be seen on tape tossing Mitchell into that net pod. I can imagine what Coin's war tribunal will do with that.

By late afternoon, we're beginning to get uneasy about Tigris's long absence. Talk turns to the possibilities that she has been apprehended and arrested, turned us in voluntarily, or simply been injured in the wave of refugees. But around six o'clock we hear her return. There's some shuffling around upstairs, then she opens the panel. The wonderful smell of frying meat fills the air. Tigris has prepared us a hash of chopped ham and potatoes. It's the first hot food we've had in days, and as I wait for her to fill my plate, I'm in danger of actually drooling.

As I chew, I try to pay attention to Tigris telling us how she acquired it, but the main thing I absorb is that fur underwear is a valuable trading item at the moment. Especially for people who left their homes underdressed. Many are still out on the street, trying to find shelter for the night. Those who live in the choice apartments of the inner city have not flung open their doors to house the displaced. On the contrary, most of them bolted their locks, drew their shutters, and pretended to be out. Now the City Circle's packed with refugees, and the Peacekeepers are going door to door, breaking into places if they have to, to assign houseguests.

On the television, we watch a terse Head Peacekeeper lay out specific rules regarding how many people per square foot each resident will be expected to take in. He reminds the citizens of the Capitol that temperatures will drop well below freezing tonight and warns them that their president expects them to be not only willing but enthusiastic hosts in this time of crisis. Then they show some very staged-looking shots of concerned citizens welcoming grateful refugees into their homes. The Head Peacekeeper says the president himself has ordered part of his mansion readied to receive citizens tomorrow. He adds that shopkeepers should also be prepared to lend their floor space if requested.

"Tigris, that could be you," says Peeta. I realize he's right. That even this narrow hallway of a shop could be appropriated as the numbers swell. Then we'll be truly trapped in the cellar, in constant danger of discovery. How many days do we have? One? Maybe two?

The Head Peacekeeper comes back with more instructions for the population. It seems that this evening there was an unfortunate incident where a crowd beat to death a young man who resembled Peeta. Henceforth, all rebel sightings are to be reported immediately to authorities, who will deal with the identification and arrest of the suspect. They show a photo of the victim. Apart from some obviously bleached curls, he looks about as much like Peeta as I do.

"People have gone wild," Cressida murmurs.

We watch a brief rebel update in which we learn that several more blocks have been taken today. I make note of the intersections on my map and study it. "Line C is only four blocks from here," I announce. Somehow that fills me with more anxiety than the idea of Peacekeepers looking for housing. I become very helpful. "Let me wash the dishes."

"I'll give you a hand." Gale collects the plates.

I feel Peeta's eyes follow us out of the room. In the cramped kitchen at the back of Tigris's shop, I fill the sink with hot water and suds. "Do you think it's true?" I ask. "That Snow will let refugees into the mansion?"

"I think he has to now, at least for the cameras," says Gale.

"I'm leaving in the morning," I say.

"I'm going with you," Gale says. "What should we do with the others?"

"Pollux and Cressida could be useful. They're good guides," I say. Pollux and Cressida aren't actually the problem. "But Peeta's too . . ."

"Unpredictable," finishes Gale. "Do you think he'd still let us leave him behind?"

"We can make the argument that he'll endanger us," I say. "He might stay here, if we're convincing."

Peeta's fairly rational about our suggestion. He readily agrees that his company could put the other four of us at risk. I'm thinking this may all work out, that he can just sit out the war in Tigris's cellar, when he announces he's going out on his own.

"To do what?" asks Cressida.

"I'm not sure exactly. The one thing that I might still be useful at is causing a diversion. You saw what happened to that man who looked like me," he says.

"What if you . . . lose control?" I say.

"You mean . . . go mutt? Well, if I feel that coming on, I'll try to get back here," he assures me.

"And if Snow gets you again?" asks Gale. "You don't even have a gun."

"I'll just have to take my chances," says Peeta. "Like the rest of you." The two exchange a long look, and then Gale reaches into his breast pocket. He places his nightlock tablet in Peeta's hand. Peeta lets it lie on his open palm, neither rejecting nor accepting it. "What about you?"

"Don't worry. Beetee showed me how to detonate my explosive arrows by hand. If that fails, I've got my knife. And I'll have Katniss," says Gale with a smile. "She won't give them the satisfaction of taking me alive."

The thought of Peacekeepers dragging Gale away starts the tune playing in my head again. . . .

Are you, are you
Coming to the tree

"Take it, Peeta," I say in a strained voice. I reach out and close his fingers over the pill. "No one will be there to help you."

We spend a fitful night, woken by one another's nightmares, minds buzzing with the next day's plans. I'm relieved when five o'clock rolls around and we can begin whatever this day holds for us. We eat a mishmash of our remaining food—canned peaches, crackers, and snails—leaving one can of salmon for Tigris as meager thanks for all she's done. The gesture seems to touch her in some way. Her face contorts in an odd expression and she flies into action. She spends the next hour remaking the five of us. She redresses us so regular clothes hide our uniforms before we even don our coats and cloaks. Covers our military boots with some sort of furry slippers. Secures our wigs with pins. Cleans off the garish remains of the paint we so hastily applied to our faces and makes us up again. Drapes our outerwear to conceal our weapons. Then gives us handbags and bundles of knickknacks to carry. In the end, we look exactly like the refugees fleeing the rebels.

"Never underestimate the power of a brilliant stylist," says Peeta. It's hard to tell, but I think Tigris might actually blush under her stripes.

There are no helpful updates on the television, but the alley seems as thick with refugees as the previous morning. Our plan is to slip into the crowd in three groups. First Cressida and Pollux, who will act as guides while keeping a safe lead on us. Then Gale and myself, who intend to position ourselves among the refugees assigned to the mansion today. Then Peeta, who will trail behind us, ready to create a disturbance as needed.

Tigris watches through the shutters for the right moment, unbolts the door, and nods to Cressida and Pollux. "Take care," Cressida says, and they are gone.

We'll be following in a minute. I get out the key, unlock Peeta's cuffs, and stuff them in my pocket. He rubs his wrists. Flexes them. I feel a kind of desperation rising up in me. It's like I'm back in the Quarter Quell, with Beetee giving Johanna and me that coil of wire.

"Listen," I say. "Don't do anything foolish."

"No. It's last-resort stuff. Completely," he says.

I wrap my arms around his neck, feel his arms hesitate before they embrace me. Not as steady as they once were, but still warm and strong. A thousand moments surge through me. All the times these arms were my only refuge from the world. Perhaps not fully appreciated then, but so sweet in my memory, and now gone forever. "All right, then." I release him.

"It's time," says Tigris. I kiss her cheek, fasten my red hooded cloak, pull my scarf up over my nose, and follow Gale out into the frigid air.

Sharp, icy snowflakes bite my exposed skin. The rising sun's trying to break through the gloom without much success. There's enough light to see the bundled forms closest to you and little more. Perfect conditions, really, except that I can't locate Cressida and Pollux. Gale and I drop our heads and shuffle along with the refugees. I can hear what I missed peeking through the shutters yesterday. Crying, moaning, labored breathing. And, not too far away, gunfire.

"Where are we going, Uncle?" a shivering little boy asks a man weighed down with a small safe.

"To the president's mansion. They'll assign us a new place to live," puffs the man.

We turn off the alley and spill out onto one of the main avenues. "Stay to the right!" a voice orders, and I see the Peacekeepers interspersed throughout the crowd, directing the flow of human traffic. Scared faces peer out of the plate-glass windows of the shops, which are already becoming overrun with refugees. At this rate, Tigris may have new houseguests by lunch. It was good for everybody that we got out when we did.

It's brighter now, even with the snow picking up. I catch sight of Cressida and Pollux about thirty yards ahead of us, plodding along with the crowd. I crane my head around to see if I can locate Peeta. I can't, but I've caught the eye of an inquisitive-looking little girl in a lemon yellow coat. I nudge Gale and slow my pace ever so slightly, to allow a wall of people to form between us.

"We might need to split up," I say under my breath. "There's a girl—"

Gunfire rips through the crowd, and several people near me slump to the ground. Screams pierce the air as a second round mows down another group behind us. Gale and I drop to the street, scuttle the ten yards to the shops, and take cover behind a display of spike-heeled boots outside a shoe seller's.

A row of feathery footwear blocks Gale's view. "Who is it? Can you see?" he asks me. What I can see, between alternating pairs of lavender and mint green leather boots, is a street full of bodies. The little girl who was watching me kneels beside a motionless woman, screeching and trying to rouse her. Another wave of bullets slices across the chest of her yellow coat, staining it with red, knocking the girl onto her back. For a moment, looking at her tiny crumpled form, I lose my ability to form words. Gale prods me with his elbow. "Katniss?"

"They're shooting from the roof above us," I tell Gale. I watch a few more rounds, see the white uniforms dropping into the snowy streets. "Trying to take out the Peacekeepers, but they're not exactly crack shots. It must be the rebels." I don't feel a rush of joy, although theoretically my allies have broken through. I am transfixed by that lemon yellow coat.

"If we start shooting, that's it," Gale says. "The whole world will know it's us."

It's true. We're armed only with our fabulous bows. To release an arrow would be like announcing to both sides that we're here.

"No," I say forcefully. "We've got to get to Snow."

"Then we better start moving before the whole block goes up," says Gale. Hugging the wall, we continue along the street. Only the wall is mostly shopwindows. A pattern of sweaty palms and gaping faces presses against the glass. I yank my scarf up higher over my cheekbones as we dart between outdoor displays. Behind a rack of framed photos of Snow, we encounter a wounded Peacekeeper propped against a strip of brick wall. He asks us for help. Gale knees him in the side of the head and takes his gun. At the intersection, he shoots a second Peacekeeper and we both have firearms.

"So who are we supposed to be now?" I ask.

"Desperate citizens of the Capitol," says Gale. "The Peacekeepers will think we're on their side, and hopefully the rebels have more interesting targets."

I'm mulling over the wisdom of this latest role as we sprint across the intersection, but by the time we reach the next block, it no longer matters who we are. Who anyone is. Because no one is looking at faces. The rebels are here, all right. Pouring onto the avenue, taking cover in doorways, behind vehicles, guns blazing, hoarse voices shouting commands as they prepare to meet an army of Peacekeepers marching toward us. Caught in the cross fire are the refugees, unarmed, disoriented, many wounded.

A pod's activated ahead of us, releasing a gush of steam that parboils everyone in its path, leaving the victims intestine-pink and very dead. After that, what little sense of order there was unravels. As the remaining curlicues of steam intertwine with the snow, visibility extends just to the end of my barrel. Peacekeeper, rebel, citizen, who knows? Everything that moves is a target. People shoot reflexively, and I'm no exception. Heart pounding, adrenaline burning through me, everyone is my enemy. Except Gale. My hunting partner, the one person who has my back. There's nothing to do but move forward, killing whoever comes into our path. Screaming people, bleeding people, dead people everywhere. As we reach the next corner, the entire block ahead of us lights up with a rich purple glow. We backpedal, hunker down in a stairwell, and squint into the light. Something's happening to those illuminated by it. They're assaulted by . . . what? A sound? A wave? A laser? Weapons fall from their hands, fingers clutch their faces, as blood sprays from all visible orifices — eyes, noses, mouths, ears. In less than a minute, everyone's dead and the glow vanishes. I grit my teeth and run, leaping over the bodies, feet slipping in the gore. The wind whips the snow into blinding swirls but doesn't block out the sound of another wave of boots headed our way.

"Get down!" I hiss at Gale. We drop where we are. My face lands in a still-warm pool of someone's blood, but I play dead, remain motionless as the boots march over us. Some avoid the bodies. Others grind into my hand, my back, kick my head in passing. As the boots recede, I open my eyes and nod to Gale.

On the next block, we encounter more terrified refugees, but few soldiers. Just when it seems we might have caught a break, there's a cracking sound, like an egg hitting the side of a bowl but magnified a thousand times. We stop, look around for the pod. There's nothing. Then I feel the tips of my boots beginning to tilt ever so slightly. "Run!" I cry to Gale. There's no time to explain, but in a few seconds the nature of the pod becomes clear to everyone. A seam has opened up down the center of the block. The two sides of the tiled street are folding down like flaps, slowly emptying the people into whatever lies beneath.

I'm torn between making a beeline for the next intersection and trying to get to the doors that line the street and break my way into a building. As a result, I end up moving at a slight diagonal. As the flap continues to drop, I find my feet scrambling, harder and harder, to find purchase on the slippery tiles. It's like running along the side of an icy hill that gets steeper at every step. Both of my destinations — the intersection and the buildings — are a few feet away when I feel the flap going. There's nothing to do but use my last seconds of connection to the tiles to push off for the intersection. As my hands latch on to the side, I realize the flaps have swung straight down. My feet dangle in the air, no foothold anywhere. From fifty feet below, a vile stench hits my nose, like rotted corpses in the summer heat. Black forms crawl around in the shadows, silencing whoever survives the fall.

A strangled cry comes from my throat. No one is coming to help me. I'm losing my grip on the icy ledge, when I see I'm only about six feet from the corner of the pod. I inch my hands along the ledge, trying to block out the terrifying sounds from below. When my hands straddle the corner, I swing my right boot up over the side. It catches on something and I painstakingly drag myself up to street level. Panting, trembling, I crawl out and wrap my arm around a lamppost for an anchor, although the ground's perfectly flat.

"Gale?" I call into the abyss, heedless of being recognized. "Gale?"

"Over here!" I look in bewilderment to my left. The flap held up everything to the very base of the buildings. A dozen or so people made it that far and now hang from whatever provides a handhold. Doorknobs, knockers, mail slots. Three doors down from me, Gale clings to the decorative iron grating around an apartment door. He could easily get inside if it was open. But despite repeated kicks to the door, no one comes to his aid.

"Cover yourself!" I lift my gun. He turns away and I drill the lock until the door flies inward. Gale swings into the doorway, landing in a heap on the floor. For a moment, I experience the elation of his rescue. Then the white-gloved hands clamp down on him.

Gale meets my eyes, mouths something at me I can't make out. I don't know what to do. I can't leave him, but

I can't reach him either. His lips move again. I shake my head to indicate my confusion. At any minute, they'll realize who they've captured. The Peacekeepers are hauling him inside now. "Go!" I hear him yell.

I turn and run away from the pod. All alone now. Gale a prisoner. Cressida and Pollux could be dead ten times over. And Peeta? I haven't laid eyes on him since we left Tigris's. I hold on to the idea that he may have gone back. Felt an attack coming and retreated to the cellar while he still had control. Realized there was no need for a diversion when the Capitol has provided so many. No need to be bait and have to take the nightlock—the nightlock! Gale doesn't have any. And as for all that talk of detonating his arrows by hand, he'll never get the chance. The first thing the Peacekeepers will do is to strip him of his weapons.

I fall into a doorway, tears stinging my eyes. *Shoot me.* That's what he was mouthing. I was supposed to shoot him! That was my job. That was our unspoken promise, all of us, to one another. And I didn't do it and now the Capitol will kill him or torture him or hijack him or—the cracks begin opening inside me, threatening to break me into pieces. I have only one hope. That the Capitol falls, lays down its arms, and gives up its prisoners before they hurt Gale. But I can't see that happening while Snow's alive.

A pair of Peacekeepers runs by, barely glancing at the whimpering Capitol girl huddled in a doorway. I choke down my tears, wipe the existing ones off my face before they can freeze, and pull myself back together. Okay, I'm still an anonymous refugee. Or did the Peacekeepers who caught Gale get a glimpse of me as I fled? I remove my cloak and turn it inside out, letting the black lining show instead of the red exterior. Arrange the hood so it conceals my face. Grasping my gun close to my chest, I survey the block. There's only a handful of dazed-looking stragglers. I trail close behind a pair of old men who take no notice of me. No one will expect me to be with old men. When we reach the end of the next intersection, they stop and I almost bump into them. It's the City Circle. Across the wide expanse ringed by grand buildings sits the president's mansion.

The Circle's full of people milling around, wailing, or just sitting and letting the snow pile up around them. I fit right in. I begin to weave my way across to the mansion, tripping over abandoned treasures and snow-frosted limbs. About halfway there, I become aware of the concrete barricade. It's about four feet high and extends in a large rectangle in front of the mansion. You would think it would be empty, but it's packed with refugees. Maybe this is the group that's been chosen to be sheltered at the mansion? But as I draw closer, I notice something else. Everyone inside the barricade is a child. Toddlers to teenagers. Scared and frostbitten. Huddled in groups or rocking numbly on the ground. They aren't being led into the mansion. They're penned in, guarded on all sides by Peacekeepers. I know immediately it's not for their protection. If the Capitol wanted to safeguard them, they'd be down in a bunker somewhere. This is for Snow's protection. The children form his human shield.

There's a commotion and the crowd surges to the left. I'm caught up by larger bodies, borne sideways, carried off course. I hear shouts of "The rebels! The rebels!" and know they must've broken through. The momentum slams me into a flagpole and I cling to it. Using the rope that hangs from the top, I pull myself up out of the crush of bodies. Yes, I can see the rebel army pouring into the Circle, driving the refugees back onto the avenues. I scan the area for the pods that will surely be detonating. But that doesn't happen. This is what happens:

A hovercraft marked with the Capitol's seal materializes directly over the barricaded children. Scores of silver parachutes rain down on them. Even in this chaos, the children know what silver parachutes contain. Food. Medicine. Gifts. They eagerly scoop them up, frozen fingers struggling with the strings. The hovercraft vanishes, five seconds pass, and then about twenty parachutes simultaneously explode.

A wail rises from the crowd. The snow's red and littered with undersized body parts. Many of the children die immediately, but others lie in agony on the ground. Some stagger around mutely, staring at the remaining silver parachutes in their hands, as if they still might have something precious inside. I can tell the Peacekeepers didn't know this was coming by the way they are yanking away the barricades, making a path to the children. Another flock of white uniforms sweeps into the opening. But these aren't Peacekeepers. They're medics. Rebel medics. I'd know the uniforms anywhere. They swarm in among the children, wielding medical kits.

First I get a glimpse of the blond braid down her back. Then, as she yanks off her coat to cover a wailing child, I notice the duck tail formed by her untucked shirt. I have the same reaction I did the day Effie Trinket called her name at the reaping. At least, I must go limp, because I find myself at the base of the flagpole, unable to account for the last few seconds. Then I am pushing through the crowd, just as I did before. Trying to shout her name above the roar. I'm almost there, almost to the barricade, when I think she hears me. Because for just a moment, she catches sight of me, her lips form my name.

And that's when the rest of the parachutes go off.

Real or not real? I am on fire. The balls of flame that erupted from the parachutes shot over the barricades, through the snowy air, and landed in the crowd. I was just turning away when one caught me, ran its tongue up the back of my body, and transformed me into something new. A creature as unquenchable as the sun.

A fire mutt knows only a single sensation: agony. No sight, no sound, no feeling except the unrelenting burning of flesh. Perhaps there are periods of unconsciousness, but what can it matter if I can't find refuge in them? I am Cinna's bird, ignited, flying frantically to escape something inescapable. The feathers of flame that grow from my body. Beating my wings only fans the blaze. I consume myself, but to no end.

Finally, my wings begin to falter, I lose height, and gravity pulls me into a foamy sea the color of Finnick's eyes. I float on my back, which continues to burn beneath the water, but the agony quiets to pain. When I am adrift and unable to navigate, that's when they come. The dead.

The ones I loved fly as birds in the open sky above me. Soaring, weaving, calling to me to join them. I want so badly to follow them, but the seawater saturates my wings, making it impossible to lift them. The ones I hated have taken to the water, horrible scaled things that tear my salty flesh with needle teeth. Biting again and again. Dragging me beneath the surface.

The small white bird tinged in pink dives down, buries her claws in my chest, and tries to keep me afloat. *"No, Katniss! No! You can't go!"*

But the ones I hated are winning, and if she clings to me, she'll be lost as well. *"Prim, let go!"* And finally she does.

Deep in the water, I'm deserted by all. There's only the sound of my breathing, the enormous effort it takes to draw the water in, push it out of my lungs. I want to stop, I try to hold my breath, but the sea forces its way in and out against my will. *"Let me die. Let me follow the others,"* I beg whatever holds me here. There's no response.

Trapped for days, years, centuries maybe. Dead, but not allowed to die. Alive, but as good as dead. So alone that anyone, anything no matter how loathsome would be welcome. But when I finally have a visitor, it's sweet. Morphling. Coursing through my veins, easing the pain, lightening my body so that it rises back toward the air and rests again on the foam.

Foam. I really am floating on foam. I can feel it beneath the tips of my fingers, cradling parts of my naked body. There's much pain but there's also something like reality. The sandpaper of my throat. The smell of burn medicine from the first arena. The sound of my mother's voice. These things frighten me, and I try to return to the deep to make sense of them. But there's no going back. Gradually, I'm forced to accept who I am. A badly burned girl with no wings. With no fire. And no sister.

In the dazzling white Capitol hospital, the doctors work their magic on me. Draping my rawness in new sheets of skin. Coaxing the cells into thinking they are my own. Manipulating my body parts, bending and stretching the limbs to assure a good fit. I hear over and over again how lucky I am. My eyes were spared. Most of my face was spared. My lungs are responding to treatment. I will be as good as new.

When my tender skin has toughened enough to withstand the pressure of sheets, more visitors arrive. The morphling opens the door to the dead and alive alike. Haymitch, yellow and unsmiling. Cinna, stitching a new wedding dress. Delly, prattling on about the niceness of people. My father sings all four stanzas of "The Hanging Tree" and reminds me that my mother—who sleeps in a chair between shifts—isn't to know about it.

One day I awake to expectations and know I will not be allowed to live in my dreamland. I must take food by mouth. Move my own muscles. Make my way to the bathroom. A brief appearance by President Coin clinches it.

"Don't worry," she says. "I've saved him for you."

The doctors' puzzlement grows over why I'm unable to speak. Many tests are done, and while there's damage to my vocal cords, it doesn't account for it. Finally, Dr. Aurelius, a head doctor, comes up with the theory that I've become a mental, rather than physical, Avox. That my silence has been brought on by emotional trauma. Although he's presented with a hundred proposed remedies, he tells them to leave me alone. So I don't ask about anyone or anything, but people bring me a steady stream of information. On the war: The Capitol fell the day the parachutes went off, President Coin leads Panem now, and troops have been sent out to put down the small remaining pockets of Capitol resistance. On President Snow: He's being held prisoner, awaiting trial and most certain execution. On my assassination team: Cressida and Pollux have been sent out into the districts to cover the wreckage of the war. Gale, who took two bullets in an escape attempt, is mopping up Peacekeepers in 2. Peeta's still in the burn unit. He made it to the City Circle after all. On my family: My mother buries her grief in her work.

Having no work, grief buries me. All that keeps me going is Coin's promise. That I can kill Snow. And when that's done, nothing will be left.

Eventually, I'm released from the hospital and given a room in the president's mansion to share with my mother. She's almost never there, taking her meals and sleeping at work. It falls to Haymitch to check on me, make sure I'm eating and using my medicines. It's not an easy job. I take to my old habits from District 13. Wandering unauthorized through the mansion. Into bedrooms and offices, ballrooms and baths. Seeking strange little hiding spaces. A closet of furs. A cabinet in the library. A long-forgotten bathtub in a room of discarded furniture. My places are dim and quiet and impossible to find. I curl up, make myself smaller, try to disappear entirely. Wrapped in silence, I slide my bracelet that reads MENTALLY DISORIENTED around and around my wrist.

My name is Katniss Everdeen. I am seventeen years old. My home is District 12. There is no District 12. I am the Mockingjay. I brought down the Capitol. President Snow hates me. He killed my sister. Now I will kill him. And then the Hunger Games will be over. . . .

Periodically, I find myself back in my room, unsure whether I was driven by a need for morphling or if Haymitch ferreted me out. I eat the food, take the medicine, and am required to bathe. It's not the water I mind, but the mirror that reflects my naked fire-mutt body. The skin grafts still retain a newborn-baby pinkness. The skin deemed damaged but salvageable looks red, hot, and melted in places. Patches of my former self gleam white and pale. I'm like a bizarre patchwork quilt of skin. Parts of my hair were singed off completely; the rest has been chopped off at odd lengths. Katniss Everdeen, the girl who was on fire. I wouldn't much care except the sight of my body brings back the memory of the pain. And why I was in pain. And what happened just before the pain started. And how I watched my little sister become a human torch.

Closing my eyes doesn't help. Fire burns brighter in the darkness.

Dr. Aurelius shows up sometimes. I like him because he doesn't say stupid things like how I'm totally safe, or that he knows I can't see it but I'll be happy again one day, or even that things will be better in Panem now. He just asks if I feel like talking, and when I don't answer, he falls asleep in his chair. In fact, I think his visits are largely motivated by his need for a nap. The arrangement works for both of us.

The time draws near, although I could not give you exact hours and minutes. President Snow has been tried and found guilty, sentenced to execution. Haymitch tells me, I hear talk of it as I drift past the guards in the hallways. My Mockingjay suit arrives in my room. Also my bow, looking no worse for wear, but no sheath of arrows. Either because they were damaged or more likely because I shouldn't have weapons. I vaguely wonder if I should be preparing for the event in some way, but nothing comes to mind.

Late one afternoon, after a long period in a cushioned window seat behind a painted screen, I emerge and turn left instead of right. I find myself in a strange part of the mansion, and immediately lose my bearings. Unlike the area where I'm quartered, there seems to be no one around to ask. I like it, though. Wish I'd found it sooner. It's so quiet, with the thick carpets and heavy tapestries soaking up the sound. Softly lit. Muted colors. Peaceful. Until I smell the roses. I dive behind some curtains, shaking too hard to run, while I await the mutts. Finally, I realize there are no mutts coming. So, what do I smell? Real roses? Could it be that I am near the garden where the evil things grow?

As I creep down the hall, the odor becomes overpowering. Perhaps not as strong as the actual mutts, but purer, because it's not competing with sewage and explosives. I turn a corner and find myself staring at two surprised guards. Not Peacekeepers, of course. There are no more Peacekeepers. But not the trim, gray-uniformed soldiers from 13 either. These two, a man and a woman, wear the tattered, thrown-together clothes of actual rebels. Still bandaged and gaunt, they are now keeping watch over the doorway to the roses. When I move to enter, their guns form an X in front of me.

"You can't go in, miss," says the man.

"Soldier," the woman corrects him. "You can't go in, Soldier Everdeen. President's orders."

I just stand there patiently waiting for them to lower their guns, for them to understand, without my telling them, that behind those doors is something I need. Just a rose. A single bloom. To place in Snow's lapel before I shoot him. My presence seems to worry the guards. They're discussing calling Haymitch, when a woman speaks up behind me. "Let her go in."

I know the voice but can't immediately place it. Not Seam, not 13, definitely not Capitol. I turn my head and find myself face-to-face with Paylor, the commander from 8. She looks even more beat up than she did at the hospital, but who doesn't?

"On my authority," says Paylor. "She has a right to anything behind that door." These are her soldiers, not Coin's. They drop their weapons without question and let me pass.

At the end of a short hallway, I push apart the glass doors and step inside. By now the smell's so strong that it begins to flatten out, as if there's no more my nose can absorb. The damp, mild air feels good on my hot skin. And the roses are glorious. Row after row of sumptuous blooms, in lush pink, sunset orange, and even pale blue. I wander through the aisles of carefully pruned plants, looking but not touching, because I have learned the hard way how deadly these beauties can be. I know when I find it, crowning the top of a slender bush. A magnificent white bud just beginning to open. I pull my left sleeve over my hand so that my skin won't actually have to touch it, take up a pair of pruning shears, and have just positioned them on the stem when he speaks.

"That's a nice one."

My hand jerks, the shears snap shut, severing the stem.

"The colors are lovely, of course, but nothing says perfection like white."

I still can't see him, but his voice seems to rise up from an adjacent bed of red roses. Delicately pinching the stem of the bud through the fabric of my sleeve, I move slowly around the corner and find him sitting on a stool against the wall. He's as well groomed and finely dressed as ever, but weighted down with manacles, ankle shackles, tracking devices. In the bright light, his skin's a pale, sickly green. He holds a white handkerchief spotted with fresh blood. Even in his deteriorated state, his snake eyes shine bright and cold. "I was hoping you'd find your way to my quarters."

His quarters. I have trespassed into his home, the way he slithered into mine last year, hissing threats with his bloody, rosy breath. This greenhouse is one of his rooms, perhaps his favorite; perhaps in better times he tended the plants himself. But now it's part of his prison. That's why the guards halted me. And that's why Paylor let me in.

I'd supposed he would be secured in the deepest dungeon that the Capitol had to offer, not cradled in the lap of luxury. Yet Coin left him here. To set a precedent, I guess. So that if in the future she ever fell from grace, it would be understood that presidents — even the most despicable — get special treatment. Who knows, after all, when her own power might fade?

"There are so many things we should discuss, but I have a feeling your visit will be brief. So, first things first." He begins to cough, and when he removes the handkerchief from his mouth, it's redder. "I wanted to tell you how very sorry I am about your sister."

Even in my deadened, drugged condition, this sends a stab of pain through me. Reminding me that there are no limits to his cruelty. And how he will go to his grave trying to destroy me.

"So wasteful, so unnecessary. Anyone could see the game was over by that point. In fact, I was just about to issue an official surrender when they released those parachutes." His eyes are glued on me, unblinking, so as not to miss a second of my reaction. But what he's said makes no sense. When *they* released the parachutes? "Well, you really didn't think I gave the order, did you? Forget the obvious fact that if I'd had a working hovercraft at my disposal, I'd have been using it to make an escape. But that aside, what purpose could it have served? We both know I'm not above killing children, but I'm not wasteful. I take life for very specific reasons. And there was no reason for me to destroy a pen full of Capitol children. None at all."

I wonder if the next fit of coughing is staged so that I can have time to absorb his words. He's lying. Of course, he's lying. But there's something struggling to free itself from the lie as well.

"However, I must concede it was a masterful move on Coin's part. The idea that I was bombing our own helpless children instantly snapped whatever frail allegiance my people still felt to me. There was no real resistance after that. Did you know it aired live? You can see Plutarch's hand there. And in the parachutes. Well, it's that sort of thinking that you look for in a Head Gamemaker, isn't it?" Snow dabs the corners of his mouth. "I'm sure he wasn't gunning for your sister, but these things happen."

I'm not with Snow now. I'm in Special Weaponry back in 13 with Gale and Beetee. Looking at the designs based on Gale's traps. That played on human sympathies. The first bomb killed the victims. The second, the rescuers. Remembering Gale's words.

"Beetee and I have been following the same rule book President Snow used when he hijacked Peeta."

"My failure," says Snow, "was being so slow to grasp Coin's plan. To let the Capitol and districts destroy one another, and then step in to take power with Thirteen barely scratched. Make no mistake, she was intending to take my place right from the beginning. I shouldn't be surprised. After all, it was Thirteen that started the rebellion that led to the Dark Days, and then abandoned the rest of the districts when the tide turned against it. But I wasn't watching Coin. I was watching you, Mockingjay. And you were watching me. I'm afraid we have both been played for fools."

I refuse for this to be true. Some things even I can't survive. I utter my first words since my sister's death. "I don't believe you."

Snow shakes his head in mock disappointment. "Oh, my dear Miss Everdeen. I thought we had agreed not to lie to each other."

Out in the hall, I find Paylor standing in exactly the same spot. "Did you find what you were looking for?" she asks.

I hold up the white bud in answer and then stumble past her. I must have made it back to my room, because the next thing I know, I'm filling a glass with water from the bathroom faucet and sticking the rose in it. I sink to my knees on the cold tile and squint at the flower, as the whiteness seems hard to focus on in the stark fluorescent light. My finger catches the inside of my bracelet, twisting it like a tourniquet, hurting my wrist. I'm hoping the pain will help me hang on to reality the way it did for Peeta. I must hang on. I must know the truth about what has happened.

There are two possibilities, although the details associated with them may vary. First, as I've believed, that the Capitol sent in that hovercraft, dropped the parachutes, and sacrificed its children's lives, knowing the recently arrived rebels would go to their aid. There's evidence to support this. The Capitol's seal on the hovercraft, the lack of any attempt to blow the enemy out of the sky, and their long history of using children as pawns in their battle against the districts. Then there's Snow's account. That a Capitol hovercraft manned by rebels bombed the children to bring a speedy end to the war. But if this was the case, why didn't the Capitol fire on the enemy? Did the element of surprise throw them? Had they no defenses left? Children are precious to 13, or so it has always seemed. Well, not me, maybe. Once I had outlived my usefulness, I was expendable. Although I think it's been a long time since I've been considered a child in this war. And why would they do it knowing their own medics would likely respond and be taken out by the second blast? They wouldn't. They couldn't. Snow's lying. Manipulating me as he always has. Hoping to turn me against the rebels and possibly destroy them. Yes. Of course.

Then what's nagging at me? Those double-exploding bombs, for one. It's not that the Capitol couldn't have the same weapon, it's just that I'm sure the rebels did. Gale and Beetee's brainchild. Then there's the fact that Snow made no escape attempt, when I know him to be the consummate survivor. It seems hard to believe he didn't have a retreat somewhere, some bunker stocked with provisions where he could live out the rest of his snaky little life. And finally, there's his assessment of Coin. What's irrefutable is that she's done exactly what he said. Let the Capitol and the districts run one another into the ground and then sauntered in to take power. Even if that was her plan, it doesn't mean she dropped those parachutes. Victory was already in her grasp. Everything was in her grasp.

Except me.

I recall Boggs's response when I admitted I hadn't put much thought into Snow's successor. *"If your immediate answer isn't Coin, then you're a threat. You're the face of the rebellion. You may have more influence than any other single person. Outwardly, the most you've ever done is tolerated her."*

Suddenly, I'm thinking of Prim, who was not yet fourteen, not yet old enough to be granted the title of soldier, but somehow working on the front lines. How did such a thing happen? That my sister would have wanted to be there, I have no doubt. That she would be more capable than many older than she is a given. But for all that, someone very high up would have had to approve putting a thirteen-year-old in combat. Did Coin do it, hoping that losing Prim would push me completely over the edge? Or, at least, firmly on her side? I wouldn't even have had to witness it in person. Numerous cameras would be covering the City Circle. Capturing the moment forever.

No, now I am going crazy, slipping into some state of paranoia. Too many people would know of the mission. Word would get out. Or would it? Who would have to know besides Coin, Plutarch, and a small, loyal or easily disposable crew?

I badly need help working this out, only everyone I trust is dead. Cinna. Boggs. Finnick. Prim. There's Peeta, but he couldn't do any more than speculate, and who knows what state his mind's in, anyway. And that leaves only Gale. He's far away, but even if he were beside me, could I confide in him? What could I say, how could I phrase it, without implying that it was his bomb that killed Prim? The impossibility of that idea, more than any, is why Snow must be lying.

Ultimately, there's only one person to turn to who might know what happened and might still be on my side. To broach the subject at all will be a risk. But while I think Haymitch might gamble with my life in the arena, I don't think he'd rat me out to Coin. Whatever problems we may have with each other, we prefer resolving our differences one-on-one.

I scramble off the tiles, out the door, and across the hall to his room. When there's no response to my knock, I push inside. Ugh. It's amazing how quickly he can defile a space. Half-eaten plates of food, shattered liquor bottles, and pieces of broken furniture from a drunken rampage scatter his quarters. He lies, unkempt and unwashed, in a tangle of sheets on the bed, passed out.

"Haymitch," I say, shaking his leg. Of course, that's insufficient. But I give it a few more tries before I dump the pitcher of water in his face. He comes to with a gasp, slashing blindly with his knife. Apparently, the end of Snow's reign didn't equal the end of his terror.

"Oh. You," he says. I can tell by his voice that he's still loaded.

"Haymitch," I begin.

"Listen to that. The Mockingjay found her voice." He laughs. "Well, Plutarch's going to be happy." He takes a swig from a bottle. "Why am I soaking wet?" I lamely drop the pitcher behind me into a pile of dirty clothes.

"I need your help," I say.

Haymitch belches, filling the air with white liquor fumes. "What is it, sweetheart? More boy trouble?" I don't know why, but this hurts me in a way Haymitch rarely can. It must show on my face, because even in his drunken state, he tries to take it back. "Okay, not funny." I'm already at the door. "Not funny! Come back!" By the thud of his body hitting the floor, I assume he tried to follow me, but there's no point.

I zigzag through the mansion and disappear into a wardrobe full of silken things. I yank them from hangers until I have a pile and then burrow into it. In the lining of my pocket, I find a stray morphling tablet and swallow it dry, heading off my rising hysteria. It's not enough to right things, though. I hear Haymitch calling me in the distance, but he won't find me in his condition. Especially not in this new spot. Swathed in silk, I feel like a caterpillar in a cocoon awaiting metamorphosis. I always supposed that to be a peaceful condition. At first it is. But as I journey into night, I feel more and more trapped, suffocated by the slippery bindings, unable to emerge until I have transformed into something of beauty. I squirm, trying to shed my ruined body and unlock the secret to growing flawless wings. Despite enormous effort, I remain a hideous creature, fired into my current form by the blast from the bombs.

The encounter with Snow opens the door to my old repertoire of nightmares. It's like being stung by tracker jackers again. A wave of horrifying images with a brief respite I confuse with waking—only to find another wave knocking me back. When the guards finally locate me, I'm sitting on the floor of the wardrobe, tangled in silk, screaming my head off. I fight them at first, until they convince me they're trying to help, peel away the choking garments, and escort me back to my room. On the way, we pass a window and I see a gray, snowy dawn spreading across the Capitol.

A very hungover Haymitch waits with a handful of pills and a tray of food that neither of us has the stomach for. He makes a feeble attempt to get me to talk again but, seeing it's pointless, sends me to a bath someone has drawn. The tub's deep, with three steps to the bottom. I ease down into the warm water and sit, up to my neck in suds, hoping the medicines kick in soon. My eyes focus on the rose that has spread its petals overnight, filling the steamy air with its strong perfume. I rise and reach for a towel to smother it, when there's a tentative knock and the bathroom door opens, revealing three familiar faces. They try to smile at me, but even Venia can't conceal her shock at my ravaged mutt body. "Surprise!" Octavia squeaks, and then bursts into tears. I'm puzzling over their reappearance when I realize that this must be it, the day of the execution. They've come to prep me for the cameras. Remake me to Beauty Base Zero. No wonder Octavia's crying. It's an impossible task.

They can barely touch my patchwork of skin for fear of hurting me, so I rinse and dry off myself. I tell them I hardly notice the pain anymore, but Flavius still winces as he drapes a robe around me. In the bedroom, I find another surprise. Sitting upright in a chair. Polished from her metallic gold wig to her patent leather high heels, gripping a clipboard. Remarkably unchanged except for the vacant look in her eyes.

"Effie," I say.

"Hello, Katniss." She stands and kisses me on the cheek as if nothing has occurred since our last meeting, the night before the Quarter Quell. "Well, it looks like we've got another big, big, big day ahead of us. So why don't you start your prep and I'll just pop over and check on the arrangements."

"Okay," I say to her back.

"They say Plutarch and Haymitch had a hard time keeping her alive," comments Venia under her breath. "She was imprisoned after your escape, so that helps."

It's quite a stretch. Effie Trinket, rebel. But I don't want Coin killing her, so I make a mental note to present her that way if asked. "I guess it's good Plutarch kidnapped you three after all."

"We're the only prep team still alive. And all the stylists from the Quarter Quell are dead," says Venia. She doesn't say who specifically killed them. I'm beginning to wonder if it matters. She gingerly takes one of my scarred hands and holds it out for inspection. "Now, what do you think for the nails? Red or maybe a jet black?"

Flavius performs some beauty miracle on my hair, managing to even out the front while getting some of the longer locks to hide the bald spots in the back. My face, since it was spared from the flames, presents no more than the usual challenges. Once I'm in Cinna's Mockingjay suit, the only scars visible are on my neck, forearms, and hands. Octavia secures my Mockingjay pin over my heart and we step back to look in the mirror. I can't believe how normal they've made me look on the outside when inwardly I'm such a wasteland.

There's a tap at the door and Gale steps in. "Can I have a minute?" he asks. In the mirror, I watch my prep team. Unsure of where to go, they bump into one another a few times and then closet themselves in the bathroom. Gale comes up behind me and we examine each other's reflection. I'm searching for something to hang on to, some sign of the girl and boy who met by chance in the woods five years ago and became inseparable. I'm wondering what would have happened to them if the Hunger Games had not reaped the girl. If she would have fallen in love with the boy, married him even. And sometime in the future, when the brothers and sisters had been raised up, escaped with him into the woods and left 12 behind forever. Would they have been happy, out in the wild, or would the dark, twisted sadness between them have grown up even without the Capitol's help?

"I brought you this." Gale holds up a sheath. When I take it, I notice it holds a single, ordinary arrow. "It's supposed to be symbolic. You firing the last shot of the war."

"What if I miss?" I say. "Does Coin retrieve it and bring it back to me? Or just shoot Snow through the head herself?"

"You won't miss." Gale adjusts the sheath on my shoulder.

We stand there, face-to-face, not meeting each other's eyes. "You didn't come see me in the hospital." He doesn't answer, so finally I just say it. "Was it your bomb?"

"I don't know. Neither does Beetee," he says. "Does it matter? You'll always be thinking about it."

He waits for me to deny it; I want to deny it, but it's true. Even now I can see the flash that ignites her, feel the heat of the flames. And I will never be able to separate that moment from Gale. My silence is my answer.

"That was the one thing I had going for me. Taking care of your family," he says. "Shoot straight, okay?" He touches my cheek and leaves. I want to call him back and tell him that I was wrong. That I'll figure out a way to make peace with this. To remember the circumstances under which he created the bomb. Take into account my own inexcusable crimes. Dig up the truth about who dropped the parachutes. Prove it wasn't the rebels. Forgive him. But since I can't, I'll just have to deal with the pain.

Effie comes in to usher me to some kind of meeting. I collect my bow and at the last minute remember the rose, glistening in its glass of water. When I open the door to the bathroom, I find my prep team sitting in a row on the edge of the tub, hunched and defeated. I remember I'm not the only one whose world has been stripped away. "Come on," I tell them. "We've got an audience waiting."

I'm expecting a production meeting in which Plutarch instructs me where to stand and gives me my cue for shooting Snow. Instead, I find myself sent into a room where six people sit around a table. Peeta, Johanna, Beetee, Haymitch, Annie, and Enobaria. They all wear the gray rebel uniforms from 13. No one looks particularly well. "What's this?" I say.

"We're not sure," Haymitch answers. "It appears to be a gathering of the remaining victors."

"We're all that's left?" I ask.

"The price of celebrity," says Beetee. "We were targeted from both sides. The Capitol killed the victors they suspected of being rebels. The rebels killed those thought to be allied with the Capitol."

Johanna scowls at Enobaria. "So what's she doing here?"

"*She* is protected under what we call the Mockingjay Deal," says Coin as she enters behind me. "Wherein Katniss Everdeen agreed to support the rebels in exchange for captured victors' immunity. Katniss has upheld her side of the bargain, and so shall we."

Enobaria smiles at Johanna. "Don't look so smug," says Johanna. "We'll kill you anyway."

"Sit down, please, Katniss," says Coin, closing the door. I take a seat between Annie and Beetee, carefully placing Snow's rose on the table. As usual, Coin gets right to the point. "I've asked you here to settle a debate. Today we will execute Snow. In the previous weeks, hundreds of his accomplices in the oppression of Panem have been tried and now await their own deaths. However, the suffering in the districts has been so extreme that these measures appear insufficient to the victims. In fact, many are calling for a complete annihilation of those who held Capitol citizenship. However, in the interest of maintaining a sustainable population, we cannot afford this."

Through the water in the glass, I see a distorted image of one of Peeta's hands. The burn marks. We are both fire mutts now. My eyes travel up to where the flames licked across his forehead, singeing away his brows but just missing his eyes. Those same blue eyes that used to meet mine and then flit away at school. Just as they do now.

"So, an alternative has been placed on the table. Since my colleagues and I can come to no consensus, it has been agreed that we will let the victors decide. A majority of four will approve the plan. No one may abstain from the vote," says Coin. "What has been proposed is that in lieu of eliminating the entire Capitol population, we have a final, symbolic Hunger Games, using the children directly related to those who held the most power."

All seven of us turn to her. "What?" says Johanna.

"We hold another Hunger Games using Capitol children," says Coin.

"Are you joking?" asks Peeta.

"No. I should also tell you that if we do hold the Games, it will be known it was done with your approval, although the individual breakdown of your votes will be kept secret for your own security," Coin tells us.

"Was this Plutarch's idea?" asks Haymitch.

"It was mine," says Coin. "It seemed to balance the need for vengeance with the least loss of life. You may cast your votes."

"No!" bursts out Peeta. "I vote no, of course! We can't have another Hunger Games!"

"Why not?" Johanna retorts. "It seems very fair to me. Snow even has a granddaughter. I vote yes."

"So do I," says Enobaria, almost indifferently. "Let them have a taste of their own medicine."

"This is why we rebelled! Remember?" Peeta looks at the rest of us. "Annie?"

"I vote no with Peeta," she says. "So would Finnick if he were here."

"But he isn't, because Snow's mutts killed him," Johanna reminds her.

"No," says Beetee. "It would set a bad precedent. We have to stop viewing one another as enemies. At this point, unity is essential for our survival. No."

"We're down to Katniss and Haymitch," says Coin.

Was it like this then? Seventy-five years or so ago? Did a group of people sit around and cast their votes on initiating the Hunger Games? Was there dissent? Did someone make a case for mercy that was beaten down by the calls for the deaths of the districts' children? The scent of Snow's rose curls up into my nose, down into my throat, squeezing it tight with despair. All those people I loved, dead, and we are discussing the next Hunger Games in an attempt to avoid wasting life. Nothing has changed. Nothing will ever change now.

I weigh my options carefully, think everything through. Keeping my eyes on the rose, I say, "I vote yes . . . for Prim."

"Haymitch, it's up to you," says Coin.

A furious Peeta hammers Haymitch with the atrocity he could become party to, but I can feel Haymitch watching me. This is the moment, then. When we find out exactly just how alike we are, and how much he truly understands me.

"I'm with the Mockingjay," he says.

"Excellent. That carries the vote," says Coin. "Now we really must take our places for the execution."

As she passes me, I hold up the glass with the rose. "Can you see that Snow's wearing this? Just over his heart?"

Coin smiles. "Of course. And I'll make sure he knows about the Games."

"Thank you," I say.

People sweep into the room, surround me. The last touch of powder, the instructions from Plutarch as I'm guided to the front doors of the mansion. The City Circle runs over, spills people down the side streets. The others take their places outside. Guards. Officials. Rebel leaders. Victors. I hear the cheers that indicate Coin has appeared on the balcony. Then Effie taps my shoulder, and I step out into the cold winter sunlight. Walk to my position, accompanied by the deafening roar of the crowd. As directed, I turn so they see me in profile, and wait. When they march Snow out the door, the audience goes insane. They secure his hands behind a post, which is unnecessary. He's not going anywhere. There's nowhere to go. This is not the roomy stage before the Training Center but the narrow terrace in front of the president's mansion. No wonder no one bothered to have me practice. He's ten yards away.

I feel the bow purring in my hand. Reach back and grasp the arrow. Position it, aim at the rose, but watch his face. He coughs and a bloody dribble runs down his chin. His tongue flicks over his puffy lips. I search his eyes for the slightest sign of anything, fear, remorse, anger. But there's only the same look of amusement that ended our last conversation. It's as if he's speaking the words again. *"Oh, my dear Miss Everdeen. I thought we had agreed not to lie to each other."*

He's right. We did.

The point of my arrow shifts upward. I release the string. And President Coin collapses over the side of the balcony and plunges to the ground. Dead.

27

In the stunned reaction that follows, I'm aware of one sound. Snow's laughter. An awful gurgling cackle accompanied by an eruption of foamy blood when the coughing begins. I see him bend forward, spewing out his life, until the guards block him from my sight.

As the gray uniforms begin to converge on me, I think of what my brief future as the assassin of Panem's new president holds. The interrogation, probable torture, certain public execution. Having, yet again, to say my final goodbyes to the handful of people who still maintain a hold on my heart. The prospect of facing my mother, who will now be entirely alone in the world, decides it.

"Good night," I whisper to the bow in my hand and feel it go still. I raise my left arm and twist my neck down to rip off the pill on my sleeve. Instead my teeth sink into flesh. I yank my head back in confusion to find myself looking into Peeta's eyes, only now they hold my gaze. Blood runs from the teeth marks on the hand he clamped over my nightlock. "Let me go!" I snarl at him, trying to wrest my arm from his grasp.

"I can't," he says. As they pull me away from him, I feel the pocket ripped from my sleeve, see the deep violet pill fall to the ground, watch Cinna's last gift get crunched under a guard's boot. I transform into a wild animal, kicking, clawing, biting, doing whatever I can to free myself from this web of hands as the crowd pushes in. The guards lift me up above the fray, where I continue to thrash as I'm conveyed over the crush of people. I start screaming for Gale. I can't find him in the throng, but he will know what I want. A good clean shot to end it all. Only there's no arrow, no bullet. Is it possible he can't see me? No. Above us, on the giant screens placed around the City Circle, everyone can watch the whole thing being played out. He sees, he knows, but he doesn't follow through. Just as I didn't when he was captured. Sorry excuses for hunters and friends. Both of us.

I'm on my own.

In the mansion, they handcuff and blindfold me. I'm half dragged, half carried down long passages, up and down elevators, and deposited on a carpeted floor. The cuffs are removed and a door slams closed behind me. When I push the blindfold up, I find I'm in my old room at the Training Center. The one where I lived during those last precious days before my first Hunger Games and the Quarter Quell. The bed's stripped to the mattress, the closet gapes open, showing the emptiness inside, but I'd know this room anywhere.

It's a struggle to get to my feet and peel off my Mockingjay suit. I'm badly bruised and might have a broken finger or two, but it's my skin that's paid most dearly for my struggle with the guards. The new pink stuff has shredded like tissue paper and blood seeps through the laboratory-grown cells. No medics show up, though, and as I'm too far gone to care, I crawl up onto the mattress, expecting to bleed to death.

No such luck. By evening, the blood clots, leaving me stiff and sore and sticky but alive. I limp into the shower and program in the gentlest cycle I can remember, free of any soaps and hair products, and squat under the warm spray, elbows on my knees, head in my hands.

My name is Katniss Everdeen. Why am I not dead? I should be dead. It would be best for everyone if I were dead. . . .

When I step out on the mat, the hot air bakes my damaged skin dry. There's nothing clean to put on. Not even a towel to wrap around me. Back in the room, I find the Mockingjay suit has disappeared. In its place is a paper robe. A meal has been sent up from the mysterious kitchen with a container of my medications for dessert. I go ahead and eat the food, take the pills, rub the salve on my skin. I need to focus now on the manner of my suicide.

I curl back up on the bloodstained mattress, not cold but feeling so naked with just the paper to cover my tender flesh. Jumping to my death's not an option — the window glass must be a foot thick. I can make an excellent noose, but there's nothing to hang myself from. It's possible I could hoard my pills and then knock myself off with a lethal dose, except that I'm sure I'm being watched round the clock. For all I know, I'm on live television at this very moment while commentators try to analyze what could possibly have motivated me to kill Coin. The surveillance makes almost any suicide attempt impossible. Taking my life is the Capitol's privilege. Again.

What I can do is give up. I resolve to lie on the bed without eating, drinking, or taking my medications. I could do it, too. Just die. If it weren't for the morphling with-drawal. Not bit by bit like in the hospital in 13, but cold turkey. I must have been on a fairly large dose because when the craving for it hits, accompanied by tremors, and shoot-ing pains, and unbearable cold, my resolve's crushed like an eggshell. I'm on my knees, raking the carpet with my finger-nails to find those precious pills I flung away in a stronger moment. I revise my suicide plan to slow death by morph-ling. I will become a yellow-skinned bag of bones, with enormous eyes. I'm a couple of days into the plan, making good progress, when something unexpected happens.

I begin to sing. At the window, in the shower, in my sleep. Hour after hour of ballads, love songs, mountain airs. All the songs my father taught me before he died, for certainly there has been very little music in my life since. What's amazing is how clearly I remember them. The tunes, the lyrics. My voice, at first rough and breaking on the high notes, warms up into something splendid. A voice that would make the mockingjays fall silent and then tumble over themselves to join in. Days pass, weeks. I watch the snows fall on the ledge outside my window. And in all that time, mine is the only voice I hear.

What are they doing, anyway? What's the holdup out there? How difficult can it be to arrange the execution of one murderous girl? I continue with my own annihilation. My body's thinner than it's ever been and my battle against hunger is so fierce that sometimes the animal part of me gives in to the temptation of buttered bread or roasted meat. But still, I'm winning. For a few days I feel quite unwell and think I may finally be traveling out of this life, when I realize my morphling tablets are shrinking. They are trying to slowly wean me off the stuff. But why? Surely a drugged Mockingjay will be easier to dispose of in front of a crowd. And then a terrible thought hits me: What if they're not going to kill me? What if they have more plans for me? A new way to remake, train, and use me?

I won't do it. If I can't kill myself in this room, I will take the first opportunity outside of it to finish the job. They can fatten me up. They can give me a full body polish, dress me up, and make me beautiful again. They can design dream weapons that come to life in my hands, but they will never again brainwash me into the necessity of using them. I no longer feel any allegiance to these monsters called human beings, despise being one myself. I think that Peeta was onto something about us destroying one another and letting some decent species take over. Because something is significantly wrong with a creature that sacrifices its children's lives to settle its differences. You can spin it any way you like. Snow thought the Hunger Games were an efficient means of control. Coin thought the parachutes would expedite the war. But in the end, who does it benefit? No one. The truth is, it benefits no one to live in a world where these things happen.

After two days of my lying on my mattress with no attempt to eat, drink, or even take a morphling tablet, the door to my room opens. Someone crosses around the bed into my field of vision. Haymitch. "Your trial's over," he says. "Come on. We're going home."

Home? What's he talking about? My home's gone. And even if it were possible to go to this imaginary place, I am too weak to move. Strangers appear. Rehydrate and feed me. Bathe and clothe me. One lifts me like a rag doll and carries me up to the roof, onto a hovercraft, and fastens me into a seat. Haymitch and Plutarch sit across from me. In a few moments, we're airborne.

I've never seen Plutarch in such a good mood. He's positively glowing. "You must have a million questions!" When I don't respond, he answers them anyway.

After I shot Coin, there was pandemonium. When the ruckus died down, they discovered Snow's body, still tethered to the post. Opinions differ on whether he choked to death while laughing or was crushed by the crowd. No one really cares. An emergency election was thrown together and Paylor was voted in as president. Plutarch was appointed secretary of communications, which means he sets the programming for the airwaves. The first big televised event was my trial, in which he was also a star witness. In my defense, of course. Although most of the credit for my exoneration must be given to Dr. Aurelius, who apparently earned his naps by presenting me as a hopeless, shell-shocked lunatic. One condition for my release is that I'll continue under his care, although it will have to be by phone because he'd never live in a forsaken place like 12, and I'm confined there until further notice. The truth is, no one quite knows what to do with me now that the war's over, although if another one should spring up, Plutarch's sure they could find a role for me. Then Plutarch has a good laugh. It never seems to bother him when no one else appreciates his jokes.

"Are you preparing for another war, Plutarch?" I ask.

"Oh, not now. Now we're in that sweet period where everyone agrees that our recent horrors should never be repeated," he says. "But collective thinking is usually short-lived. We're fickle, stupid beings with poor memories and a great gift for self-destruction. Although who knows? Maybe this will be it, Katniss."

"What?" I ask.

"The time it sticks. Maybe we are witnessing the evolution of the human race. Think about that." And then he asks me if I'd like to perform on a new singing program he's launching in a few weeks. Something upbeat would be good. He'll send the crew to my house.

We land briefly in District 3 to drop off Plutarch. He's meeting with Beetee to update the technology on the broadcast system. His parting words to me are "Don't be a stranger."

When we're back among the clouds, I look at Haymitch. "So why are you going back to Twelve?"

"They can't seem to find a place for me in the Capitol either," he says.

At first, I don't question this. But doubts begin to creep in. Haymitch hasn't assassinated anyone. He could go anywhere. If he's coming back to 12, it's because he's been ordered to. "You have to look after me, don't you? As my mentor?" He shrugs. Then I realize what it means. "My mother's not coming back."

"No," he says. He pulls an envelope from his jacket pocket and hands it to me. I examine the delicate, perfectly formed writing. "She's helping to start up a hospital in District Four. She wants you to call as soon as we get in." My finger traces the graceful swoop of the letters. "You know why she can't come back." Yes, I know why. Because between my father and Prim and the ashes, the place is too painful to bear. But apparently not for me. "Do you want to know who else won't be there?"

"No," I say. "I want to be surprised."

Like a good mentor, Haymitch makes me eat a sandwich and then pretends he believes I'm asleep for the rest of the trip. He busies himself going through every compartment on the hovercraft, finding the liquor, and stowing it in his bag. It's night when we land on the green of the Victor's Village. Half of the houses have lights in the windows, including Haymitch's and mine. Not Peeta's. Someone has built a fire in my kitchen. I sit in the rocker before it, clutching my mother's letter.

"Well, see you tomorrow," says Haymitch.

As the clinking of his bag of liquor bottles fades away, I whisper, "I doubt it."

I am unable to move from the chair. The rest of the house looms cold and empty and dark. I pull an old shawl over my body and watch the flames. I guess I sleep, because the next thing I know, it's morning and Greasy Sae's banging around at the stove. She makes me eggs and toast and sits there until I've eaten it all. We don't talk much. Her little granddaughter, the one who lives in her own world, takes a bright blue ball of yarn from my mother's knitting basket. Greasy Sae tells her to put it back, but I say she can have it. No one in this house can knit anymore. After breakfast, Greasy Sae does the dishes and leaves, but she comes back up at dinnertime to make me eat again. I don't know if she's just being neighborly or if she's on the government's payroll, but she shows up twice every day. She cooks, I consume. I try to figure out my next move. There's no obstacle now to taking my life. But I seem to be waiting for something.

Sometimes the phone rings and rings and rings, but I don't pick it up. Haymitch never visits. Maybe he changed his mind and left, although I suspect he's just drunk. No one comes but Greasy Sae and her granddaughter. After months of solitary confinement, they seem like a crowd.

"Spring's in the air today. You ought to get out," she says. "Go hunting."

I haven't left the house. I haven't even left the kitchen except to go to the small bathroom a few steps off of it. I'm in the same clothes I left the Capitol in. What I do is sit by the fire. Stare at the unopened letters piling up on the mantel. "I don't have a bow."

"Check down the hall," she says.

After she leaves, I consider a trip down the hall. Rule it out. But after several hours, I go anyway, walking in silent sock feet, so as not to awaken the ghosts. In the study, where I had my tea with President Snow, I find a box with my father's hunting jacket, our plant book, my parents' wedding photo, the spile Haymitch sent in, and the locket Peeta gave me in the clock arena. The two bows and a sheath of arrows Gale rescued on the night of the firebombing lie on the desk. I put on the hunting jacket and leave the rest of the stuff untouched. I fall asleep on the sofa in the formal living room. A terrible nightmare follows, where I'm lying at the bottom of a deep grave, and every dead person I know by name comes by and throws a shovel full of ashes on me. It's quite a long dream, considering the list of people, and the deeper I'm buried, the harder it is to breathe. I try to call out, begging them to stop, but the ashes fill my mouth and nose and I can't make any sound. Still the shovel scrapes on and on and on. . . .

I wake with a start. Pale morning light comes around the edges of the shutters. The scraping of the shovel continues. Still half in the nightmare, I run down the hall, out the front door, and around the side of the house, because now I'm pretty sure I can scream at the dead. When I see him, I pull up short. His face is flushed from digging up the ground under the windows. In a wheelbarrow are five scraggly bushes.

"You're back," I say.

"Dr. Aurelius wouldn't let me leave the Capitol until yesterday," Peeta says. "By the way, he said to tell you he can't keep pretending he's treating you forever. You have to pick up the phone."

He looks well. Thin and covered with burn scars like me, but his eyes have lost that clouded, tortured look. He's frowning slightly, though, as he takes me in. I make a half-hearted effort to push my hair out of my eyes and realize it's matted into clumps. I feel defensive. "What are you doing?"

"I went to the woods this morning and dug these up. For her," he says. "I thought we could plant them along the side of the house."

I look at the bushes, the clods of dirt hanging from their roots, and catch my breath as the word *rose* registers. I'm about to yell vicious things at Peeta when the full name comes to me. Not plain rose but evening primrose. The flower my sister was named for. I give Peeta a nod of assent and hurry back into the house, locking the door behind me. But the evil thing is inside, not out. Trembling with weakness and anxiety, I run up the stairs. My foot catches on the last step and I crash onto the floor. I force myself to rise and enter my room. The smell's very faint but still laces the air. It's there. The white rose among the dried flowers in the vase. Shriveled and fragile, but holding on to that unnatural perfection cultivated in Snow's greenhouse. I grab the vase, stumble down to the kitchen, and throw its contents into the embers. As the flowers flare up, a burst of blue flame envelops the rose and devours it. Fire beats roses again. I smash the vase on the floor for good measure.

Back upstairs, I throw open the bedroom windows to clear out the rest of Snow's stench. But it still lingers, on my clothes and in my pores. I strip, and flakes of skin the size of playing cards cling to the garments. Avoiding the mirror, I step into the shower and scrub the roses from my hair, my body, my mouth. Bright pink and tingling, I find something clean to wear. It takes half an hour to comb out my hair. Greasy Sae unlocks the front door. While she makes breakfast, I feed the clothes I had shed to the fire. At her suggestion, I pare off my nails with a knife.

Over the eggs, I ask her, "Where did Gale go?"

"District Two. Got some fancy job there. I see him now and again on the television," she says.

I dig around inside myself, trying to register anger, hatred, longing. I find only relief.

"I'm going hunting today," I say.

"Well, I wouldn't mind some fresh game at that," she answers.

I arm myself with a bow and arrows and head out, intending to exit 12 through the Meadow. Near the square are teams of masked and gloved people with horse-drawn carts. Sifting through what lay under the snow this winter. Gathering remains. A cart's parked in front of the mayor's house. I recognize Thom, Gale's old crewmate, pausing a moment to wipe the sweat from his face with a rag. I remember seeing him in 13, but he must have come back. His greeting gives me the courage to ask, "Did they find anyone in there?"

"Whole family. And the two people who worked for them," Thom tells me.

Madge. Quiet and kind and brave. The girl who gave me the pin that gave me a name. I swallow hard. Wonder if she'll be joining the cast of my nightmares tonight. Shoveling the ashes into my mouth. "I thought maybe, since he was the mayor . . ."

"I don't think being the mayor of Twelve put the odds in his favor," says Thom.

I nod and keep moving, careful not to look in the back of the cart. All through the town and the Seam, it's the same. The reaping of the dead. As I near the ruins of my old house, the road becomes thick with carts. The Meadow's gone, or at least dramatically altered. A deep pit has been dug, and they're lining it with bones, a mass grave for my people. I skirt around the hole and enter the woods at my usual place. It doesn't matter, though. The fence isn't charged anymore and has been propped up with long branches to keep out the predators. But old habits die hard. I think about going to the lake, but I'm so weak that I barely make it to my meeting place with Gale. I sit on the rock where Cressida filmed us, but it's too wide without his body beside me. Several times I close my eyes and count to ten, thinking that when I open them, he will have materialized without a sound as he so often did. I have to remind myself that Gale's in 2 with a fancy job, probably kissing another pair of lips.

It is the old Katniss's favorite kind of day. Early spring. The woods awakening after the long winter. But the spurt of energy that began with the primroses fades away. By the time I make it back to the fence, I'm so sick and dizzy, Thom has to give me a ride home in the dead people's cart. Help me to the sofa in the living room, where I watch the dust motes spin in the thin shafts of afternoon light.

My head snaps around at the hiss, but it takes awhile to believe he's real. How could he have gotten here? I take in the claw marks from some wild animal, the back paw he holds slightly above the ground, the prominent bones in his face.

He's come on foot, then, all the way from 13. Maybe they kicked him out or maybe he just couldn't stand it there without her, so he came looking.

"It was the waste of a trip. She's not here," I tell him. Buttercup hisses again. "She's not here. You can hiss all you like. You won't find Prim." At her name, he perks up. Raises his flattened ears. Begins to meow hopefully. "Get out!" He dodges the pillow I throw at him. "Go away! There's nothing left for you here!" I start to shake, furious with him. "She's not coming back! She's never ever coming back here again!" I grab another pillow and get to my feet to improve my aim. Out of nowhere, the tears begin to pour down my cheeks. "She's dead." I clutch my middle to dull the pain. Sink down on my heels, rocking the pillow, crying. "She's dead, you stupid cat. She's dead." A new sound, part crying, part singing, comes out of my body, giving voice to my despair. Buttercup begins to wail as well. No matter what I do, he won't go. He circles me, just out of reach, as wave after wave of sobs racks my body, until eventually I fall unconscious. But he must understand. He must know that the unthinkable has happened and to survive will require previously unthinkable acts. Because hours later, when I come to in my bed, he's there in the moonlight. Crouched beside me, yellow eyes alert, guarding me from the night.

In the morning, he sits stoically as I clean the cuts, but digging the thorn from his paw brings on a round of those kitten mews. We both end up crying again, only this time we comfort each other. On the strength of this, I open the letter Haymitch gave me from my mother, dial the phone number, and weep with her as well. Peeta, bearing a warm loaf of bread, shows up with Greasy Sae. She makes us breakfast and I feed all my bacon to Buttercup.

Slowly, with many lost days, I come back to life. I try to follow Dr. Aurelius's advice, just going through the motions, amazed when one finally has meaning again. I tell him my idea about the book, and a large box of parchment sheets arrives on the next train from the Capitol.

I got the idea from our family's plant book. The place where we recorded those things you cannot trust to memory. The page begins with the person's picture. A photo if we can find it. If not, a sketch or painting by Peeta. Then, in my most careful handwriting, come all the details it would be a crime to forget. Lady licking Prim's cheek. My father's laugh. Peeta's father with the cookies. The color of Finnick's eyes. What Cinna could do with a length of silk. Boggs reprogramming the Holo. Rue poised on her toes, arms slightly extended, like a bird about to take flight. On and on. We seal the pages with salt water and promises to live well to make their deaths count. Haymitch finally joins us, contributing twenty-three years of tributes he was forced to mentor. Additions become smaller. An old memory that surfaces. A late primrose preserved between the pages. Strange bits of happiness, like the photo of Finnick and Annie's newborn son.

We learn to keep busy again. Peeta bakes. I hunt. Haymitch drinks until the liquor runs out, and then raises geese until the next train arrives. Fortunately, the geese can take pretty good care of themselves. We're not alone. A few hundred others return because, whatever has happened, this is our home. With the mines closed, they plow the ashes into the earth and plant food. Machines from the Capitol break ground for a new factory where we will make medicines. Although no one seeds it, the Meadow turns green again.

Peeta and I grow back together. There are still moments when he clutches the back of a chair and hangs on until the flashbacks are over. I wake screaming from nightmares of mutts and lost children. But his arms are there to comfort me. And eventually his lips. On the night I feel that thing again, the hunger that overtook me on the beach, I know this would have happened anyway. That what I need to survive is not Gale's fire, kindled with rage and hatred. I have plenty of fire myself. What I need is the dandelion in the spring. The bright yellow that means rebirth instead of destruction. The promise that life can go on, no matter how bad our losses. That it can be good again. And only Peeta can give me that.

So after, when he whispers, "You love me. Real or not real?"

I tell him, "Real."

EPILOGUE

They play in the Meadow. The dancing girl with the dark hair and blue eyes. The boy with blond curls and gray eyes, struggling to keep up with her on his chubby toddler legs. It took five, ten, fifteen years for me to agree. But Peeta wanted them so badly. When I first felt her stirring inside of me, I was consumed with a terror that felt as old as life itself. Only the joy of holding her in my arms could tame it. Carrying him was a little easier, but not much.

The questions are just beginning. The arenas have been completely destroyed, the memorials built, there are no more Hunger Games. But they teach about them at school, and the girl knows we played a role in them. The boy will know in a few years. How can I tell them about that world without frightening them to death? My children, who take the words of the song for granted:

Deep in the meadow, under the willow
A bed of grass, a soft green pillow
Lay down your head, and close your sleepy eyes
And when again they open, the sun will rise.

Here it's safe, here it's warm
Here the daisies guard you from every harm

Here your dreams are sweet and tomorrow brings
them true
Here is the place where I love you.

My children, who don't know they play on a graveyard.

Peeta says it will be okay. We have each other. And the book. We can make them understand in a way that will make them braver. But one day I'll have to explain about my nightmares. Why they came. Why they won't ever really go away.

I'll tell them how I survive it. I'll tell them that on bad mornings, it feels impossible to take pleasure in anything because I'm afraid it could be taken away. That's when I make a list in my head of every act of goodness I've seen someone do. It's like a game. Repetitive. Even a little tedious after more than twenty years.

But there are much worse games to play.

THE END

acknowledgments

I would like to pay tribute to the following people who gave their time, talent, and support to The Hunger Games.

First off, I must thank my extraordinary triumvirate of editors. Kate Egan, whose insight, humor, and intelligence have guided me through eight novels; Jen Rees, whose clear vision catches the things the rest of us miss; and David Levithan, who moves so effortlessly through his multiple roles of Note Giver, Title Master, and Editorial Director.

Through rough drafts, food poisoning, every up and down, you are there with me, Rosemary Stimola, equal parts gifted creative advisor and professional guardian, my literary agent and my friend. And Jason Dravis, my longtime entertainment agent, I feel so lucky to have you watching over me as we head for the screen.

Thanks to designer Elizabeth B. Parisi and artist Tim O'Brien for the beautiful book jackets that so successfully captured both the mockingjays and people's attention.

All hail the incredible team at Scholastic for getting The Hunger Games out into the world: Sheila Marie Everett, Tracy van Straaten, Rachel Coun, Leslie Garych, Adrienne Vrettos, Nick Martin, Jacky Harper, Lizette Serrano, Kathleen Donohoe, John Mason, Stephanie Nooney, Karyn Browne, Joy Simpkins, Jess White, Dick Robinson, Ellie Berger, Suzanne Murphy, Andrea Davis Pinkney, the entire Scholastic sales force, and the many others who have devoted so much energy, smarts, and savvy to this series.

To the five writer-friends I rely on most heavily, Richard Register, Mary Beth Bass, Christopher Santos, Peter Bakalian, and James Proimos, much gratitude for your advice, perspective, and laughter.

Special love to my late father, Michael Collins, who laid the groundwork for this series with his deep commitment to educating his children on war and peace, and my mother, Jane Collins, who introduced me to the Greeks, sci-fi, and fashion (although that last one didn't stick); my sisters, Kathy and Joanie; my brother, Drew; my in-laws, Dixie and Charles Pryor; and the many members of my extended family whose enthusiasm and support have kept me going.

And finally, I turn to my husband, Cap Pryor, who read *The Hunger Games* in its earliest draft, insisted on answers to questions I hadn't even imagined, and remained my sounding board through the entire series. Thanks to him and my wonderful kids, Charlie and Isabel, for their daily love, their patience, and the joy they bring me.